Death in the East

ALSO BY ABIR MUKHERJEE

A Necessary Evil

Smoke and Ashes

A Novel

WITHDRAWN

ABIR MUKHERJEE

PEGASUS CRIME

NEW YORK LONDON

DEATH IN THE EAST

Pegasus Crime is an imprint of
Pegasus Books, Ltd.
148 West 37th Street, 13th Floor
New York, NY 10018

First Pegasus Books hardcover edition May 2020

ISBN: 978-1-64313-468-0

10 9 8 7 6 5 4 3 2 1

Printed in the United States of America
Distributed by Simon & Schuster

For Milan and Aran,
my wonderful boys

There's an east wind coming, Watson ... such a wind as never blew on England yet ... But it's God's own wind none the less, and a cleaner, better, stronger land will lie in the sunshine when the storm has cleared.
Arthur Conan Doyle, *His Last Bow*

PROLOGUE

February 1922

Jatinga, Assam

The birds were killing themselves.

Not a few, but thousands.

'They're starlings,' said the woman. 'Suicide birds.'

A long-dead schoolmaster's question echoed inside my skull.

'You, Wyndham. The collective noun for a flock of starlings is ...?'

My ignorance, met by the crack of ruler upon desk.

'*Murmuration*, boy! A flock of starlings is called a murmuration! Now don't forget.'

Murmuration.

It suggested the clandestine. Something whispered. Something hidden.

Maybe it had to do with the way they flew, vast flocks pirouetting through the clouds as though of one mind, receiving instructions from one voice.

And tonight, in the void of a new moon, did that voice tell them to plummet earthward through mountain mists and to break themselves on the floor of this valley in the middle of nowhere? I leaned on the veranda's wooden balustrade and watched.

In the valley below, the flames from a hundred torches illuminated a scene from Dante as half-naked tribesmen shrieked and ran and set about the fallen creatures with clubs and sticks.

'Why do they do it?' I asked.

The woman turned to me, her expression suddenly sombre.

'Fear,' she said. 'The same reason men the world over attack anything they don't understand.'

'I meant the birds. Why do they come here to die?'

She smiled. 'Everyone has to die somewhere. And personally, Captain, I can't think of a better place. Can you?' She looked down at the tribesmen. 'Of course the locals say the valley is cursed. That the birds become possessed by evil spirits.'

'And you?' I asked. 'What do you believe?'

'Me?'

She feigned surprise, a pretence for my benefit, then moved closer. When she spoke, her voice was a whisper. 'If you decide to stay in our little outpost for any length of time, Captain, you may find a fair few of our number who are possessed of a certain malevolence. Who's to say there isn't evil at work here?'

The cries from the valley floor started to ebb and the air began to still, no longer roiled by the constant swoop and smack of birds crashing to their deaths.

Behind us a door opened. Yellow light spilled onto the velvet blackness of the veranda. A starched servant in white tunic and stiff-fanned turban made the call to dinner, then stood aside as the sahibs and mems of the Jatinga Club downed drinks and processed inside.

Emily Carter took a final sip from her flute. 'Brace yourself, Captain,' she said. 'This is where the fun starts.'

She handed the empty glass to the servant and disappeared inside, though not before kicking a bloodstained bird off the balcony and away into the darkness below.

ONE

Two weeks earlier

I'd left Calcutta with a grim resolve, a suitcase-full of *kerdū* gourd, and, in case of emergencies, a bullet-sized ball of opium resin hidden between the folds of my clothes. My destination was an ashram in the Cachar hills, a forgotten backwater in a far-flung corner of the distant province of Assam, three days' travel and a million miles from the sophistication, such as it was, of Calcutta. It had come, if not highly recommended, then at least loudly lauded, by my physician, Dr Chatterjee, a quack who specialised in Ayurvedic potions and whom I'd have dismissed as a charlatan had it not been for the fact that his remedies seemed to work. In hallowed tones, he'd explained that the place was run by a holy man called Devraha Swami, a 250-year-old sage who could cure most anything from acid reflux to yellow fever with nothing but a few herbs and a lot of prayer. It wasn't much to pin one's hopes on, but in my present situation I had little option. And as they say, a drowning man will clutch at a straw ... or a herb.

The *kerdū* gourd had been Chatterjee's suggestion too: smashed, mashed and mixed with a few other elements, it formed a pulp that when imbibed tasted like boot polish, but offered temporary respite from the opium pangs. I'd packed enough to last me the three-day journey – with some to spare, because when it came to rail transport, or anything else for that matter in India, nothing ever ran to schedule.

I'd arrived in the country almost four years earlier, sauntered off the boat at Kidderpore docks and straight into the first of a thousand opium dens. If that's an exaggeration, it's only slight, and I'd certainly found my first fix within a week of arrival.

I hadn't come here an addict – an *opium fiend* – as the priests and the pedants called it. My use had been medicinal: a means of staunching nightmares and stimulating sleep. Addiction had come later, gradually, *perniciously*, and my realisation of the fact more slowly still.

I'd tried to wean myself off it. Who wouldn't? After all, a policeman with an opium habit is like a long-distance runner with his laces tied together. You might manage to stay on your feet for a while, but sooner or later, you're going to end up falling on your face.

And people notice when you fall.

Unfortunately for me, the people who'd noticed first had been the all-seeing men and women of Section H, the intelligence arm of the military, responsible for the political stability of the Raj. They tended to interpret their brief in the widest possible terms, which meant they spied on anyone and everyone, and that included me and my nocturnal pilgrimages to the wrong sort of temples.

For now they'd kept the information to themselves, less as a kindness and more as leverage to force me to dance to their tune. Either way, there was no guarantee they wouldn't change their minds and report it to my superiors, and the threat was there like a knife to my throat.

Not being overly keen on such blades, I'd decided to do something about it, hence my sojourn, first by rail and then road to the ashram of Devraha Swami.

*

The journey had started smoothly enough. I'd caught the Darjeeling Mail from Sealdah station to Santahar Junction in the north of Bengal, hoping to make the connection to Guwahati, the capital of Assam. But the connection failed to turn up, due, apparently, to a flash strike by the 'no-good-bloody-awful' native railway workers further up the line.

Faced with such adversity, I did what any self-respecting Englishman would do. I paid a railway urchin a few annas to direct me to the nearest alcoholic drink and climbed inside.

I spent the best part of a day cooling my heels and propping up the bar in a flyblown joint called Duncan's Hotel where the beer was wet but the company sadly lacking. It's no fun drinking alone, not much anyway, and when it came to comrades in ale, or comrades of any sort for that matter, I really only had one: my friend and junior officer, Sergeant Surrender-not Banerjee. He'd saved my life once but I didn't hold that against him. Of course Surrender-not wasn't his real name. Indians didn't go in for stiff-upper-lip Victorian nomenclature, not when it came to naming their children at least. His real name was Surendranath, which was difficult to pronounce, and so everyone called him Surrender-not. Everyone British at any rate.

Surrender-not, however, was on his way to Dacca, Bengal's second city, situated in the arse end of the province and separated from Calcutta by two hundred miles and half the Ganges delta. He was off to his aunt's house, to seek refuge from the torrid independence fever that had infected Calcutta's native populace and divided families down the middle, setting brother against brother, father against son.

Half a day in and I was already missing him, mainly, I realised, because over the last six months we'd spent hardly any time just sitting and having a drink like we used to do in the days when I'd first arrived, when Calcutta was new and shining and the opium was my servant and not my master. I sat at the bar in Duncan's Hotel and raised a glass to him in tribute, which was ironic, given his tolerance for alcohol was on a par with that of the average English schoolgirl.

At dusk, the urchin returned with news of the arrival of the Assam Mail and I followed him back out the door, still none the wiser as to who Duncan was, or had been, or what terrible madness had possessed him to put up his hotel here in the middle of nowhere.

Any relief I derived from finally being aboard the Assam Mail evaporated upon the realisation that I could probably have walked to Guwahati faster than the little narrow-gauge train was trundling. Nevertheless, as the geriatric locomotive groped its way ponderously through the darkness, I attempted the impossible and tried to make myself comfortable on the stiff wooden benches of the second-class carriage that would be my home for the night.

A red sun was rising by the time the train pulled into its platform in the Assamese capital, light enough for me to watch my connecting train to Lumding puff merrily out of the station. Another man might have waited for the next train, but that man probably didn't have a couple of *kerdū* gourds rotting in his suitcase. Instead I waylaid a lorry driver and paid him to ferry me hell for leather to the next station up the line, arriving there just as the platform guard was about to blow his whistle.

Lumding arrived nine hours later, by which time I and my stock of *kerdū* gourd were close to exhaustion. I fell off the train and into the fragrant, multicoloured mayhem of Indian provincial life, with its traders and travellers, its station hawkers, crying out their wares with the urgency of Seventh-Day Adventists proclaiming the second coming, and its market-bound smallholders doubled over like beasts of burden with their produce, their livelihoods, weighing on their narrow backs. There were even a few red-cheeked, baby-faced colonial officials, each freshly minted and making his solitary way upcountry, to some remote outpost to take up his station as the only white authority within a fifty-mile radius.

And it was on the platform that it happened. That thunderclap of shock. The electric bolt of fear. For a heartbeat, no more than an instant, I saw a ghost: a dead man; a man I'd last seen almost twenty years before. His eyes bored into me from across the concourse, older, time-ravaged, but with the same cold, unwavering stare. Time plays tricks on the memory, but it's hard to forget the face of a man who's tried to kill you.

Cold sweat trickled down my collar. I told myself I was mistaken: deceived by the light, a casualty of exhaustion, a victim of the O – willing to accept anything except the evidence before me. Maybe that's why I just stood there dumbstruck.

A second later he was gone, just one more eddy in a sea of bodies. I came to my senses in a panic and, head pounding, grabbed my suitcase and gave chase, shoving my way through the crowd and still not fully trusting of either eyes or memory. I pushed aside protesting bodies and caught a glimpse of a linen-suited back making for the exit before losing him once more in the throng.

I ran on, now breathless and sweat-soaked, and emerged onto the station steps just in time to see him disappear into a large, black motor car that had been waiting with its engine idling. I watched as a porter loaded his valise and a white-clad chauffeur revved the engine. As it moved off, I caught one last silhouetted glimpse of the man in the back. I told myself it was impossible. Here, now, in this remotest of corners, could it really be that I was staring at a man who'd got away with murder, a man who'd also tried to kill me? He'd come pretty close too.

I shivered and looked on helplessly as the car sped off. The aching in my head and bones grew stronger and I doubled over in pain. I told myself it was nonsense: an aberration, a paranoid delusion, a hallucination – call it what you will – and that the figure had been someone else, just another trader or tax inspector or tea planter going about his business. After all, I'd had opium-induced hallucinations before, though nothing like this. Never anything so tangible. So vivid. What's more, they'd always occurred when I'd been under the influence and in the seclusion of some opium den; never as now, knee-deep in a sea of people. And while the thought that after all these years I should suddenly hallucinate about a long-dead murderer was perplexing, what really terrified me was the fear that I might be descending into madness.

TWO

February 1905

Whitechapel, east London

It was her screams that first drew our attention. Piercing cries that sliced through the pelting rain and echoed off the weeping, crumbling walls.

'Come on, Wyndham. Keep up!'

The voice was deep and harsh as a strop, and I did my best to comply. The narrow lanes of Whitechapel, never pleasant, were now a slick, sodden maze of backstreets and blind alleys. Ahead of me, Sergeant Whitelaw raised his whistle to his lips and blew.

We sprinted along Black Eagle Street, past the towering, razor-tipped wall of the Truman brewery, through a mud bog of a tenement yard, and on to Grey Eagle Street.

Two figures stood out, silhouetted in the arc of a distant street lamp and locked in combat. Beside them, a woman, judging by the length of her hair and her screams, seemed to have been knocked to the ground.

Candlelight blossomed in upstairs windows. Whitelaw blew his whistle again – a mistake, as all it did was alert the two combatants to our presence at a distance still too far to intervene. Sure enough, the men stopped, stared, and after a moment's pause, high-tailed it up the street.

We gave chase, at least we did until we reached the woman, who paid us little heed and kept on screaming. Her left cheek was starting to swell and blood mingled with the rivulets of rainwater trickling down the side of her face. Suddenly, my stomach churned. I knew her.

'Bessie?' I whispered.

'Get after them, Wyndham!' shouted Whitelaw. 'I'll see to the girl.'

I did as ordered. Without a second thought. Even though I knew her better than I knew almost any other woman in London. She was twenty years old, not yet six months married, and her name was Bessie Drummond.

To me though, she'd always be Bessie May.

Looking back, things might have been different if I'd stayed with her, but Whitelaw was a sergeant and I was a constable, on the force a mere nine months, and orders were orders.

I left him there, kneeling beside Bessie, while I chased after the two figures, already little more than shadows in the dark. A hundred yards on, they split, one cutting left into Pearl Street, the other sprinting straight ahead. I followed the latter. He seemed closer and, more importantly, weaker, possibly injured, running with one hand clasping the other.

Behind me Whitelaw blew his whistle again, summoning more officers to the scene. I just hoped it was to help catch the two fugitives rather than because Bessie's injuries required serious attention.

The man ahead disappeared into the gloom, then reappeared in the halo of a street lamp, darting across the junction with Quaker Street. I afforded myself a smile. Another hundred yards on, I knew, came a dead end, a wall, and a forty-foot drop onto railway sidings.

I slowed down. A cornered man is a dangerous man, and I wanted to be ready, should he try to double back or fancy his chances with his fists. The street descended once more into darkness but I could still hear him running. Thin soles slapping on wet cobblestones. Then, suddenly, he stopped.

'Give it up!' I called. 'There's nowhere to go.'

I walked forward, senses heightened, until finally I saw him. A thin man in a cloth cap, holding his right arm with his left. God knows how he'd managed, but he'd heaved himself up and onto the wall separating the street from the drop to the railway tracks.

He turned round and peered down into the void. I cursed, and once more broke into a run, hoping to stop him before he did something foolish.

'Don't try it! You'll break your neck!'

He hesitated. I was only yards away now. He glanced over his shoulder, smiled at me, then swivelled round once more and in an almost balletic movement, jumped.

I heard the thump of him hitting the ground and for a moment I stood there, frozen. Then gathering my wits, I sprinted over to the wall and pulled myself up. Peering down, I steeled myself against the sight of his broken body on the tracks. Instead, I saw half a dozen freight bogies parked directly below, and the man clambering down the side of one and running off up the tracks to Shoreditch.

I jumped down, landing heavily on the curved roof of the freight car. The rain had left it slick and the soles of my boots offered as much grip as a greased pig on a frozen lake. Before I knew it, I was on my arse, scrabbling for a handhold and hurtling off the top of the wagon. As I reached the edge, I grabbed at the metal guttering that ran along the car's length. Momentum carried me over and I cursed as a streak of pain speared up my right arm. But my grip held. I cursed again, this time in relief, then let go and dropped onto the wet earth. Stumbling backwards, I tripped on a rail, then fell onto the tracks behind.

A whistle screamed, far louder than Whitelaw's. I looked up, and in a matter of seconds, aged ten years as a juggernaut of a locomotive rumbled angrily towards me.

With the fear of God suddenly and violently instilled into every fibre of my being, I pulled myself up and rolled off the tracks with an alacrity that would have impressed the wing-heeled god, Mercury. The thing hurtled past moments later, and I lay there, face down, my heart hammering against my ribs.

I turned and sat up. A wave of nausea swelled in my stomach. I scanned the vista, searching frantically for sight of my quarry. Then in the distance came the crunch of footsteps sprinting on gravel. I struggled to my feet and ran after them: along the track towards Shoreditch station, past the rain-lashed hulks of freight trains idling in their sidings. The station stood out in the darkness, lit up like a Christmas tree. A few late-night travellers stood sheltering under a rusting Victorian awning, looking out onto the tracks in hope of a train which, like the man I was chasing, was nowhere to be seen. I ran on, further down the tracks, before turning the corner into the Shoreditch goods depot and straight into a chapter from the book of Exodus. A gang of men, their heads bowed, were busy unloading hessian sacks from a goods wagon. A line of them, like Israelites in bondage in the land of Egypt, stood soaking silently in the rain, each man awaiting his turn for two others to hoist a pregnant sack onto his shoulders. Then, swaying under his burden, he walked slowly off towards a nearby warehouse, making way for the next in line.

I ran up to the foreman.

'Did you see anyone pass here?'

He struggled to hear me over the noise of the yard.

Up close, he looked older than I'd expected, grizzled, in his fifties. But work like this aged a man, and it was possible he was a decade or more younger.

I repeated the question.

He shook his head. 'Who'd be mad enough to be out on a night like this?'

I scoured the compound but there was no sign of the fugitive. Desperately I sprinted back out to the tracks and peered into the black. In the distance a figure was climbing onto the platform at Shoreditch.

I started running, but it was already too late. The distance was too great, and once out of the station, he would disappear into the warren of streets and I would never see him again. Nevertheless I ran, reaching the platform just as the Liverpool Street train pulled up. I scanned the tired faces of the few passengers, but there was no sign of him.

Forlornly, I walked out of the station, stood under the awning as the rain pelted down. Bruised and sodden, I contemplated what I'd have to say to Sergeant Whitelaw. Across the road, the lights burned in a public house and served only to compound my misery. I began the long walk back towards Grey Eagle Street, past a group of destitute wretches taking shelter under the railway arches.

THREE

February 1922

Assam

The last leg of the journey, from the town of Lumding to the ashram, would need to wait until the morning. For the present, I was in no real state to travel anywhere. Instead I checked into the nearest hotel and paid for a meal, preferably without spice, to be brought to my room.

I'd begun to shiver by the time a young girl in pigtails and bare feet came to deliver it. I tipped her a few annas, and then a few more, and handed her my last *kerdū* gourd, asking her to get it mashed and to bring back a glass of the pulp as soon as possible.

After a glacial fifteen minutes, she returned, and I drank half of the pulp, saving the rest for the morning. My appetite somewhat revived, I felt able to face the food, opening the package to discover rice, dal and some curried mutton. I ate slowly, then placed the detritus outside my door and collapsed into bed.

The next morning, having finished the rest of the pulp, I set about searching for a vehicle to take me the last seventy miles to the ashram. It was located near an outpost called Jatinga, so small that it didn't appear on my map, but which, Dr Chatterjee had assured me, most definitely did exist. An hour later, with the help of a local shipping agent, I managed to negotiate passage on a logging truck heading south to Silchar. The driver, a bearded, dust-blown Sikh with a row of beads round his grey neck and a picture of his sainted guru in his cab, spoke no English but was happy enough to accept a donation and drop me off en route.

Six hours later, and with precious few words uttered in the interim, he deposited me at the top of a hillside, beside a walled compound at the end of a dirt track. If this truly was the ashram of Devraha Swami, my goal for the last three days and nights, there was precious little to see: just a pair of iron gates set in a high stone wall and, somewhere beyond, the summit of a dome peeking over the top. There was the view down the mountain though: the light was fading and the valley below was shrouded in the bluish mist of an alpine evening. Not that I was in much of a position to appreciate it, seeing as I was out of *kerdū*. The landscape could have come straight out of a Claude Monet canvas and I wouldn't have given it a second look. Opium, alas, has a way of reordering one's priorities.

At a push, the gates shrieked open in complaint and, with a breath, I girded my loins and nervously entered a courtyard at the end of which stood a squat, ochre building. To one side a group of saffron-clad, shaven-headed monks stood talking.

One of them, a short man with Nepalese features, walked over. I felt my chest tighten and a mild panic come over me. My words failed.

'May I help you?'

He couldn't have been more than twenty-five.

My tongue cleft to the top of my palate. 'Wyndham,' I stammered. 'My name is Wyndham ... I ...'

The monk smiled. 'You are expected. Please do come with me.'

I followed him in silence, through the courtyard, up a set of stone steps and into a candlelit corridor. Somewhere nearby a bell began to toll. The monk stopped outside a door, and taking a wick, lit it from the flame of the nearest candle.

'Please come.'

The dim glow of the flame illuminated a small, windowless room that smelled of the ages and cast shadows over a wooden table and two chairs. The monk held the wick to a candle in a holder on the far wall, and then to another on the wall to its left.

He gestured to one of the chairs. 'Please,' he said. 'Take few minutes' rest. I will inform Brother Shankar of your arrival.'

Before I had a chance to ask questions, he'd turned and left, closing the door soundlessly behind him. So once more I did as asked, dropping my valise onto the floor and flopping down onto one of the chairs for a 'few minutes' rest'.

The room was empty save for the table and chairs, the walls bare, except for a calendar hanging on a nail on the one facing me, one of those religious calendars so popular among the Hindus: a picture of a divinity – in this case the goddess Kali, above the individual months of the year, which could be ripped off, one by one. That was my first surprise. For some reason I'd expected this to be a Buddhist monastery, but the calendar was clearly Hindu, and also out of date.

No one, it seemed, was too concerned that it still read June 1920. Maybe the passage of time mattered less here. Or maybe they just liked the picture.

I stared at the portrait of Kali, the goddess of destruction, standing upon the prone body of her consort, Lord Shiva, a sword held aloft in one hand and a severed head in another. The blood-red tongue distended over jet-black skin. The garland of skulls and the kilt fashioned from severed limbs.

I'd grown used to her depiction. In Bengal, she was ubiquitous, and along with Durga, the mother goddess, her countenance graced almost every street in the native parts of Calcutta. Indeed, some said the city even took its name from her – Calcutta, the city of Kali – but there was no proof of that. Nevertheless, sitting in that small room, I felt something I hadn't before. Maybe it was the effects of opium withdrawal, or maybe it was the first time that I'd really spent time looking at her, but there was something in those wide bloodshot eyes – an expression of wild ecstasy – that caused a shiver to run down my spine.

The door creaked open and in stepped another saffron-robed monk, this one a full head taller than the first one, who stood a few paces behind him. He was different in other ways too, older, chubbier and whiter. He acknowledged my surprise with a smile, the crow's feet around his eyes creasing behind round, steel-rimmed spectacles.

'Captain Wyndham,' he said, pressing his palms together in *pranam*, 'it's a pleasure to meet you. I'm Brother Shankar. I can't imagine you expected to find someone like me here.'

That much was true.

'I can't imagine many people expect to find an Englishman dressed as a Hindu monk out here in the middle of nowhere,' I said. 'Or, for that matter, anywhere. Especially one with a Home Counties accent.'

He let out a laugh that echoed off the walls. 'I'm not sure that my accent makes much of a difference, Captain.'

He was right of course. There was no logical reason why a Hindu monk who spoke like he hailed from Sandhurst should be any more surprising than one who sounded like he was from Swansea, or Sunderland, but to me it seemed subtly worse. After all, Celts and Northerners could be peculiar, but one expected better of a man who spoke the King's English.

As an opium fiend, though, I realised I was hardly in a position to judge him. Yet when it came down to it, I wondered if, in at least some politer Surrey circles, the tag *opium fiend* might in fact be preferable to *Hindu convert*.

'I suppose not,' I said.

The Nepalese-looking monk who'd led me in handed him a sheet of paper, which the Englishman scanned over the top of his spectacles.

'So,' he said, reading from the sheet, 'I understand you're here upon the recommendation of your physician, Dr Chatterjee.'

'I wouldn't go as far as to call him my physician, exactly.'

Brother Shankar looked up. 'Yes, well, let's not get into technicalities. Suffice it to say, this Dr Chatterjee –' he waved the sheet at me – 'is the party who suggested you come to us to deal with your addiction to …' he scanned the paper once more, like an exotically attired civil servant.

'Opium,' I said.

'Yes, of course. Opium.'

A few minutes later, I found myself accompanying him, further into the compound. We walked out into a larger courtyard bordered by a number of single-storey stone buildings on one side, and on the other by what I assumed was a temple of sorts, and from which emanated a rhythmic chanting.

'Evening prayers,' said the monk.

I was still coming to terms with it all. This place was alien to me. It was still India, but different from *my* India, the India of the plains and the jungle and cities that I'd begrudgingly learned not to hate over the last four years. This was a Hindu ashram, but unlike the clanging chaos of the Calcutta temples. And this was a Hindu monk, who was also an Englishman.

'How did you end up with a name like Shankar?' I asked.

'You mean, how does an Englishman find himself living as a monk in the middle of Assam? That's a long story, Captain, and one that can wait for now. As for the name, Devraha Swami chose it for me. Before that I was called Stephen.'

'Like the apostle,' I said.

The comment seemed to take him by surprise.

'Well, yes,' he said affably, 'I suppose so.'

'The Church's first martyr. Stoned to death, wasn't he?'

'Maybe that's why I prefer Shankar,' he smiled. 'It means *the one who brings joy.*'

He led the way onwards towards one of four wooden buildings which looked a lot like barracks huts.

'You'll be staying in the European men's dormitory.'

'You mean there are more Europeans here?'

It hadn't occurred to me that there might be any other non-Indians here seeking a cure.

'Oh yes,' he replied nonchalantly. 'We have six others at the moment: two more Englishmen, though one is leaving us tomorrow, an American, a German and couple of Frenchmen ... actually one of them is Belgian. Then there are the Asiatics: the Chinese of course, the Burmese, and a smattering of Nepalese. They share dormitories with the Indians. We've a few women here too, but you won't see them. They're in a separate section of the ashram.'

'Your very own League of Nations,' I said. 'Maybe when we're all cured you could host the Post-Opium Olympics.'

'Not all of our guests are opium addicts,' he said. 'Some are here because of addiction to alcohol, or heroin, or a number of other substances. Opium addicts though make up the largest group, and,' he sighed, 'I must say, tend to have the toughest time of it. You've some painful nights in store, I'm afraid.'

'I thought you were supposed to be the harbinger of joy?'

'Don't worry,' he said. 'There'll be joy enough thereafter. Now let's get you settled in.'

The dormitory was little more than a wooden box lit by a couple of hurricane lamps, with twelve beds, six along either side of a central passage, each separated from the next by three feet and a small, rough-hewn, wooden cabinet. It was also empty.

'The others are undergoing cleansing,' said Brother Shankar, displaying a disconcerting ability to read my thoughts. 'Unfortunately you've arrived a little late to start your treatment tonight.'

Some of the beds were unmade, their sheets askew, knotted and trailing onto the floor. I guessed that stood to reason. This wasn't an army barracks and men going cold turkey generally had more pressing concerns than the neatness of their beds.

Brother Shankar led me to a cot at the far end with fresh, folded sheets.

'Make yourself at home, Captain.' He pointed to the cabinet beside the bed. 'You'll find a set of clothes in there. Should you wish to wash, there's a shower block just behind the dormitory. As for the latrines, they're beside the shower block, and they're Eastern-style so you'll have to squat.'

He uttered the last comment without a hint of disparagement, which, in my experience, was a rare thing for an Englishman discussing Indian toilets.

'The others should be back soon,' he continued, 'after which there's dinner in the dining hall, for those who are up to it. I'd offer to come and fetch you, but I'm sure your bunk-mates will show you the way. Now if you'll excuse me ...'

With a nod he turned and walked back out into the dusk, leaving me standing in the empty dorm. Wearily, I dropped my bag to the floor, flopped down on the bed's thin mattress and placed my hands over my face.

The room settled into a silence, perforated only by the distant sound of chanting. I lay there for several minutes, listening to the rhythmic cantillation, my head emptying of thoughts, until a drum sounded, wrenching me from my reverie. Remembering that Brother Shankar – Stephen – had instructed me to change into the vestments provided, I rose to my feet, opened the bedside cabinet and took out the contents: a pair of worn brown sandals, a coarse grey cotton shirt with two buttons and a pair of loose drawstring trousers. It was the uniform of a convict. Or a penitent.

Beneath the clothes was a thin Indian towel known as a *gamcha*. At least that's what it was called in Calcutta. I'd no idea what they called it here. Whatever its name, the item was comprehensively useless: as suited to the task of mopping up moisture as a sou'wester; yet they were cheap and therefore ubiquitous. Stripping down to my shorts, I picked it up and headed for the showers.

The block was cold and missing a roof, its walls the greenish-grey of old concrete ingrained with algae, and its floor slick with moss. Against the far wall stood several stalls, and above each stall, a bucket from which hung a rope. In the half-light, the room felt treacherous: one false step could lead to a slip, a fall and a crack of the skull. Placing the towel and my clothes on a dry ledge, I picked up the small, hard shard of cracked soap that sat there and stepped carefully into the nearest stall. I braced myself and pulled the rope. With an ancient creak, the bucket turned on a hinge and a deluge of ice-cold water fell over my head. I gasped, steeling myself against it, then quickly began lathering my body. As my teeth chattered, I heard the sounds of trickling water as the bucket began to refill. I waited a few seconds, took a deep breath, then pulled the chain again. The shock wasn't so bad the second time. Rinsing soap-scum from my body, I reached for the *gamcha* and began the Sisyphean task of towelling myself down.

With the *gamcha* tied around my waist, I made it back to the dormitory in time to see the door open and my dorm-mates stumble in. They seemed a motley collection. What little conversation there was between them ceased at the sight of me standing there, naked from the waist up and dripping like a haddock caught in the rain. I gave them a cursory nod and dripped more water onto the stone floor. The man first through the door – a short dark-haired chap, not much more than a boy – gave me a pained half-smile of acknowledgement before collapsing onto his cot.

None seemed much in the mood for conversation. The last to enter, a middle-aged man with a thick, reddish, bespectacled face and greying hair, walked over and sat down on the bunk across from mine. Around his neck hung a thin chain and a small golden Star of David.

'You should put on some clothes, friend.' His accent was unmistakably German. He nodded towards the cabinet beside my bed. 'You don't want to catch a cold. Trust me, the last thing you need is to be heaving your guts out all week while also coughing up your lungs.' He let out a gruff laugh and proffered a hand. 'Adler. Jacob Adler.'

'Wyndham,' I said, shaking his hand, 'Sam Wyndham.' I took his advice, leaned over and retrieved the monastic vestments and began putting them on.

'English.' He nodded matter-of-factly. 'You are in good company.' He gestured to the bunks nearest the door. 'Cooper and Green, they also are English. But your first name, this is short for Samuel, no? You are Jewish?'

I shook my head. 'I'm not anything,' I said as I buttoned the rough shirt, 'at least not anything that a rabbi or a vicar might recognise as one of his flock.' I slipped my feet into the sandals and sat down on the edge of my cot. 'I fear whatever deity might be up there, he's long since washed his hands of me.'

Adler nodded sagely. 'And yet here you are, in a monastery, looking for help from men of God to rid you of your affliction.'

'Believe me,' I said, 'I'd much rather be seeking a cure in an Alpine health spa run by Viennese psychoanalysts, but I can't afford the cost of the voyage let alone their hourly rate, so I'm stuck with Assam, Hindu monks and a week's worth of vomiting.'

The Jew laughed.

'And you?' I continued. 'What's your excuse for coming here? I'd have thought Austria was closer to home for you than Assam.'

'You're correct about that,' he said, 'if not about the efficacy of Viennese men of science. I am here because the monastery of Devraha Swami was recommended by an old friend who was once treated here.'

'What's your poison?' I asked.

His brow creased. 'Poison?'

'Your affliction of choice. Opium? Heroin? You don't strike me as an alcoholic.'

His face lightened.

'Ah, I take your meaning. My "poison", I'm afraid, is internal,' he said, pressing the fingers of one hand to his chest. 'I have a tumour which my doctor tells me is cancerous.'

'And is the treatment doing any good?'

He gave a world-weary shrug. 'Eh, who knows? They give me the herbal tonic. I drink the herbal tonic. They give me *more* tonic. I drink more tonic. And then I go to the latrines and I spritz the whole lot down the drain.'

'You're not on the vomiting regime?'

'If I am,' he chuckled, 'it isn't working.'

Adler lay back on his cot. 'Now, Mr Wyndham, with your permission, I might take a rest before dinner. The exertions leave me weak.'

'Of course,' I said, and turned to survey the other inmates. None of them had taken much of an interest in me, or, it seemed, in anything else. They lay silently on their bunks, exhaustion etched on their faces, reminding me of a group of sailors I'd once seen pulled from the North Sea after their ship had been torpedoed from under them. Suddenly, a shiver passed through me. A black wave of fear of what lay ahead.

I distracted myself by focusing on the others and trying to deduce who was who. I was a detective, after all, and deduction was something I was supposed to be good at. So far I knew that Adler was German, and that the two nearest the door were Englishmen. Brother Shankar had mentioned that the others were French, Belgian and American.

From Adler I'd learned that the two Englishmen were called Cooper and Green, though I didn't know which was which. The one nearest the door was a tall, pale, skeletal man with fair hair and a nose that might have fallen off the face of Julius Caesar. The other was shorter and darker, with the tanned, leathery skin that spoke of a lifetime spent exiled in the tropics. If I had to choose, I'd have guessed Cooper to be the walking cadaver and Green as the one with the face like a saddle.

I moved on to the three foreigners in the remaining bunks: an American, a Frenchman and a Belgian. That sounded like the start of a promising joke, but none of them looked like they might find it funny. In the absence of gen on any of them, I decided to fall back on the natural intuition of the Englishman in regard to foreigners. Or to put it another way, I'd rely on deep prejudices, honed over generations.

The bed next to Green was occupied by the young boy who'd been first through the door and who seemed to have passed into some sort of stupor as soon as his head hit the thin pillow of wadded cotton on his cot. I decided that he must be the Belgian, equating his shortness of stature with the smallness of the country.

The man across the aisle from him was cut from a different cloth, or by the look of him, dynamited out of a quarry. He was well over six foot and sported a shock of flame-red hair that put me in mind of that legendary Irish giant, Finn MacCool, who, in true Celtic fashion, and with his Caledonian counterpart, Benandonner, decided to build a bridge between their countries, just so that they could have a fight. This, I determined, must be the American, probably a descendant of Scotch or Irish immigrants, or both.

That left the man in the bed opposite Adler. He looked in worse shape than all the others. Beads of sweat glistened on his pale brow and his body shivered uncontrollably as it cried out for whatever drug of which it had suddenly been robbed. The flesh on his arms was yellow and dimpled, and every so often, he let out what sounded like a muffled plea. I should have felt some sympathy for him, but I felt nothing. Instead, all I could do was consider myself in his position. The man was about my height, and build, with the same dirty blond hair. It was as though I was looking at a vision of myself twenty-four or forty-eight hours hence. Or maybe less. Maybe two. Maybe three.

The fact is, opium robs you of empathy, and most other noble emotions besides. The only thing that matters is getting the next hit of O, and the visceral suffering of others becomes nothing more than a curiosity, playing out in front of you like a film in a picture house. I *should* have felt sympathy. Instead I listened to his moans to see if I could tell if they were in French.

FOUR

The gong for dinner had sounded an hour later. Now I was seated, along with Adler and three of the others, at one of a dozen wooden benches in the monastery's mess hall, staring at a bowl of coarse brown rice and a thin yellowish soup of lentils. The food was bland, lacking both taste and smell, which was miraculous given this was India, but maybe it was purposely this way. After all, the last thing a recovering addict needed after an evening's vomiting was his senses assailed by a curry.

Across from me sat the man mountain I'd correctly guessed was the American. His name was Fitzgerald and he hailed from the city of New York. It occurred to me that if more of his fellow citizens were built like him, it could explain the city's need for so many skyscrapers. Beside him sat the diminutive young man I'd deduced was Belgian. It turned out he was actually French, and named Lavalle, but the barrier of language and possibly a natural desire to keep his circumstances to himself meant he did little in the way of talking.

To my left sat the German, Adler, and to my right, the pale Englishman I'd determined, rightly as it turned out, to be Cooper. Green and the other member of our dormitory, a man named Le Corbeau who *was* the Belgian, both seemed caught in the throes of withdrawal and hadn't the strength or the stomach for food.

Around us, and after allowing for an appropriate *cordon sanitaire* of a few spaces, sat Indians and assorted orientals, all in groups of their own kinsmen.

There must have been thirty or so people in the dining hall: all men and all eating the same food served by a group of monks who wandered from table to table dolling out the rice and dal from large metal pots. The hum of conversation around us was muted, at least by Indian standards, with tired faces concentrating on their plates and once more reinforcing the feeling that I'd stumbled into some labour camp.

Our group was little different, though out of the five of us, surprisingly, it was the Englishman, Cooper, who was the most talkative. Maybe it was our shared nationality that prompted his repartee. More likely was the fact that he'd almost completed his regimen and, now clean, was leaving us the next day.

'Back to Bombay,' he said, swallowing a mouthful of rice, 'and not a day too soon. It'll still be the best part of a week before I get there, of course.' He scraped his spoon along his metal plate and shovelled another load into his mouth. He seemed to be particularly hungry, which made me think that maybe he'd been starved close to death before his arrival here, or that his cure had led him to lose half his body weight. Either way, he was making up for it now.

'How long have you been here?' I asked.

'Three weeks I think, though at times it's felt longer. Like eternity in purgatory.'

That brought a derogatory chuckle from the American, Fitzgerald.

'Don't worry, Wyndham,' he said. 'The cure takes less than half that time. A week to ten days normally. Any longer than that and it's liable to kill you.'

'The rest of the time,' interjected Cooper, 'is recuperation. You can either stay here or with some friendly soul in Jatinga. The monks like farming you out so that the beds are freed up, but they keep you close by so that they can keep an eye on you.'

'They're keen to ensure there's no backsliding,' added Fitzgerald. 'That we truly are clean. Of course, Adler here's a special case. He's been here longer than any of us.'

I turned to the German.

'How long *have* you been here?'

Adler ruminated, then swallowed. 'Who knows? One loses track of time.'

The conversation jerked and stuttered, with no one, save for Cooper, much in the mood for it. For minutes it died completely, then spluttered back to life, sparked by a stray question or comment. Then there would be a burst of chatter: opinions given in staccato before all too quickly the silence descended once more.

It seemed impolite to ask what vices the others were in for, and honestly it didn't matter. Other than Adler, it was clear we were all addicts of one sort or another, and, as in wartime, that spawned the natural camaraderie of disparate men whom fate had thrown together in difficult circumstances. Indeed the notion of a group of international strangers, all huddled up together in a monastery in the middle of nowhere, might have even struck some as being rather poetic. But only if you overlooked the vomiting, of course.

A Hindu might have told you that our fates had been written long ago: in the stars the moment each of us was born; that we had always been destined to meet here and now in the hills of Assam; that we'd been predestined to become addicts, to fall to the lowest ebb, and to wind up here.

But that was nonsense.

They say the human mind seeks to make sense out of chaos. How much easier it was to simply ascribe these things to the fates or the gods than to face the truth: that the universe was a callous, capricious place, where bad things happened to good people because there was no good reason why they shouldn't.

One by one my comrades finished and headed back towards the dormitory. Soon, only Cooper and I remained. Having undergone the cure, he was now effusive, and buoyed by the prospect of leaving in the morning, was more than happy to hang around the refectory. I was in no hurry to get back either. I knew from bitter experience that the night ahead would be long and arduous, and I was quite prepared to delay matters for as long as possible. For me, opium and nightfall were inextricably intertwined. Night was when I smoked – and when I didn't, it was at night that the cravings were at their worst. Already my hands were shaking and my skin beginning to burn. And as the night went on, things would only get worse. To date, I'd experienced the agony of withdrawal in the seclusion of my own rooms, or, on one occasion, locked in a cell under a military base – which was just as solitary. If my anguish had had one saving grace, it was that my pain had been private, my screams secret and unwitnessed. Tonight, though, my cries would be all too public, and that unnerved me, both as a policeman and as an Englishman.

I could have done with a cigarette, but I'd assumed, wrongly as it happened, that it was banned at the monastery. To take my mind off things, I struck up conversation once more.

'Tell me about the cure.'

Cooper's demeanour changed. He shook his head and looked away. 'It's hell. Or as close to it as you're likely to find in this life. But seven days in hell is better than a lifetime enslaved to opium. Think of it as penance: the price to be paid for the sin of addiction and the misdeeds you've done in furtherance of it.'

I thought of the lies I'd told because of the O; the friends I'd lost and the woman I'd hurt. Given the context, seven days in hell seemed a good deal.

'When was your last hit?' he asked.

'Four days ago.'

He turned and stared. 'You're doing pretty well to have survived this long. At my worst, I couldn't get through twenty-four hours without a pipe.'

'I've been surviving on *kerdū* pulp. But I've run out now.'

'*Kerdū* pulp?'

'A gourd,' I said, 'recommended by a quack I found back in Calcutta. It quells the cravings. At least temporarily.'

'The monks have something similar. A sort of herbal tea that helps take the edge off.' He pointed to a large steel pot at the far end of the room where a couple of the native inmates were ladling a liquid into enamel mugs. 'They keep a constant supply brewing. I suggest you have a few cupfuls now, and don't be afraid to come back during the night if the need takes you.'

It seemed like good advice, and I was close to uttering a heart-felt hallelujah. Instead I rose from my place, and without seeming to rush, walked over to the cauldron simmering in the corner. A few orientals congregated around it watched me approach, then moved off to a safe distance. Two others, Indians who were waiting their turn to fill their mugs, stepped back to let me partake first. Even here among drug addicts, it seemed the racial pyramid of empire still held firm.

From a table, I picked up a chipped blue enamel cup, and with the ladle that hung from one of the pot's handles, clumsily spooned in a measure of the watery brown liquid. I held the cup to my lips, drank, and immediately felt like retching the whole mouthful out. It tasted like trench water, with a hint of barbed wire to give it a kick as it went down. Nevertheless I steeled myself and knocked back the whole cupful, then refilled and repeated the process.

With the cup filled a third time, I walked back to the bench where Cooper sat waiting.

A wry smile played on his lips. 'So, what do you think?'

'It's not quite a single malt.'

'That much is true.'

'I'm hoping it's an acquired taste.'

'Well, let's hope you won't need to acquire it for too long.'

As I sat back down, Cooper began to set out a typical day's treatment.

'Reveille is at 5 a.m. No need to set an alarm clock, you'll know it's time to rise because they keep banging that bloody great gong in the courtyard. No need to get up either if you can't, or just don't want to. The gong just calls the monks for their morning prayers, though many of us get up anyway and partake of the daily chores. Got to keep the ashram ship-shape.' He smiled sardonically. 'There's more prayers at six, then an hour of physical jerks. The monks call it *joge* – it's mainly exercises in stretching and funny breathing, and again it's optional, but Brother Shankar says it helps relax the body and soul. You will, however, want to be up by eight. That's when breakfast is served.'

'Brother Shankar,' I said. 'What do you make of him?'

Cooper scratched at an earlobe. 'He's an eccentric bird all right. I've never heard of an Englishman converting to the religion of the Hindus before, but ...' he paused, 'after the last month, who am I to judge?'

He continued listing the daily itinerary. Most of the time seemed to alternate between idling away hours in the dormitory – *recuperation* he called it – and the opportunity for meditation or light work for those who felt up to it. Either side of lunch, there was a session in the steam room. 'Mandatory,' he explained. 'Something to do with sweating the poisons out of one's body.'

So far, it sounded more like a holiday than the hell Cooper had attested to, and I told him as much.

He gave a short laugh. 'Wait,' he said. 'I'm coming to that.

'It's around teatime when the fun and games really kick off. That's when we all assemble in the courtyard for *the cure*. Now I can only tell you what others have told me, which is that it's a concoction of certain special herbs and leaves with medicinal properties that grow in the hills around here. They say the recipe was created in the mists of time by Devraha Swami himself, when he was a young initiate. The story goes that as a young itinerant monk he came across a man, feverish from opium withdrawal. The man thought he was about to die, and he asked the monk to pray for his soul.

'They say Devraha Swami did just that: prayed and meditated all night, and that during his prayers, he had a vision. It seems one of the Hindu gods, the god of medicine, or maybe cookery, gave him the recipe for the elixir – if not of life, then of something that could at least restore life to the damned such as us.

'Anyway, by some miracle the poor bastard survived the night. But the next morning he was in a bad way. Devraha Swami left him with some villagers and told him he'd return soon. He went off into the hills and collected the ingredients as the god had instructed, then boiled them up while praying. He then gave the potion to the man to drink.'

'And that cured him?'

'No. It made him vomit up his guts. Did you really think it would be that simple? That night, though, the swami sat beside him and prayed, and once more, the man survived the night. Better still, the pangs had lessened. The next day, the swami repeated the ritual, leaving the man with villagers while he went off to gather the ingredients for his potion. Again the man drank it and again he was sick as a dog, but gradually, over the course of seven nights, he recovered.'

It sounded promising. Stripped of the mumbo jumbo, it appeared the old monk had stumbled upon a herbal remedy which counteracted the withdrawal symptoms and, unlike *kerdū* pulp, banished them once and for all.

'And he wasn't tempted by the O again?'

'Actually he was. A few months later, so the story goes, the poor sap returned. He'd fallen back into his old ways. He beseeched the swami to help him once more. This time, though, the old man refused. Told him to go take a running jump, so to speak.'

'Really?'

'Absolutely. This isn't the Church of England, Wyndham, with its love and forgiveness. This is sensible, hard-nosed Hinduism. You mess up once, they'll help you. You do it again, you're on your own. You don't believe me? Ask our friend Brother Shankar. He'll tell you the same. The cure is a one-time thing. Once you're clean, staying so is up to you. The monastery never takes you in twice.'

I nodded slowly in appreciation. It stood to reason. There were a million opium fiends out there, most of them wishing they were free of the drug. Why should the monastery continue to waste its time on men who lapsed back into sin when there were so many others needing their help? And there was a valuable lesson there too, namely if the universe gave you a chance for redemption, you'd bloody well better take it, because second chances were rare and third chances were non-existent.

It was a lesson I'd already learned the hard way.

FIVE

February 1905

East London

My first view of Bessie had been of her head poking out of the second-storey window of her ramshackle tenement, bold as the bust on the prow of a ship, and aiming curses at the crowd in the street below. She had the dark hair and sharp features of a Boudicca and the tongue of a dock worker, and she couldn't have been much older than twenty.

But when you saw her close-up, it was the eyes you really noticed: deep and brown and quick. You couldn't read them, but one glance from them and you knew, you just knew, this girl was smart, smarter than most men at any rate, and that given half a chance she'd show you just how much smarter. She was pretty too, but the eyes: the spark within them and the window they afforded into the mind beyond, they made her special.

She shared the lodgings at number 42 Fashion Street with a cat, a caged canary and a half-dozen other folk: all of them poor, and most of them behind with the rent.

Bessie, though, was different. She worked as a live-out house-keeper for a man named Caine. He was a businessman, of sorts, involved in the trade of all manner of things to and from the four corners of the empire. He also owned a number of dwellings around Whitechapel, the usual decrepit, tumbledown flophouses, which he rented out by the room and packed to the rafters. Bessie was one of his tenants and she collected the rents from the rest of the house on his behalf, making a bit of extra cash on the side.

The morning I first met her, she was overseeing the eviction of one of them, a chap called O'Keefe, whose rent arrears, in Bessie's view had, like his soul, become irredeemable. And given his tendency to drink through every shilling that came his way, it was hard to disagree with her.

O'Keefe of course didn't quite see it that way. He claimed he was down on his luck, which was true, and had promised to make full restitution by the next Friday, which almost certainly wasn't. Not being a fool, Bessie had thrown him out and he'd taken his complaint to the court of the street, raging at the injustice of it all. Bessie's response had been to throw his belongings out of the window.

I'd waded in to see what all the fuss was about and she'd spotted me, shining in my new uniform. 'Wait there, Constable,' she said, in a tone that left me little choice in the matter. The head disappeared and a minute later, the whole of her came striding out of the front door.

'I want you to pack this useless bastard off on his merry way. 'E's been evicted and now 'e's causin' a scene.'

I couldn't help but feel that at least part of the responsibility for any scene-causing had lain with her propelling his suitcase and half the contents of a wardrobe out of a window two floors up, but it seemed wise to keep my opinions to myself.

In the end, I hadn't had to do much at all. O'Keefe was hardly a stranger to the police. He'd spent more than the occasional night in the cells and had little appetite for another visit. After a few minutes more of muted protest, he'd moved on and the crowd melted away.

For me and Bessie though, things only spiralled from there.

I'd arrived in London a month earlier, wide-eyed and wet behind the ears. To the East End, where I had an uncle who was a magistrate. We'd met but once in my seventeen years, but kin is kin, and he'd obtained for me an opening with the Metropolitan Police.

For a middle-class boy from the middle of nowhere, the East End was an education, and Bessie provided a lot of the lessons. The week after O'Keefe's eviction, I saw her again, this time outside the police station in Leman Street. Maybe it was fate, or maybe she'd been waiting for me. Either way, the next thing I knew, I was buying her a gin in the Ten Bells.

She was a little older than me and troublesomely pretty. Before long, I was calling on her, two or three times a week and, as they say, twice on Sundays.

For the next few months I was happy. God knows what she saw in me. Maybe it was innocence. More likely it was the uniform. My uncle, however, when word reached him, was in no doubt: what she saw was the chance for social improvement. Invoking the name of the Lord, and of my dear departed father, and stressing the shame I was heaping on both, he made it clear that my prospects were dependent upon his patronage, and that those auspices were in turn dependent upon my ending things with Bessie.

Of course I argued my position, raged like any young fool who believes he's in love would, pointed out those of Bessie's virtues which might bolster my case: her honesty, her intelligence (and kept quiet on those other qualities which, in my uncle's eyes, might damn her straight to hell). I offered to introduce her, bring her round for tea so that my uncle might see that she wasn't some scheming Jezebel ... and yet it all counted for naught. My every assertion and contention dashed on the rock of his intransigence, as they were always destined to.

I spent the next week in personal purgatory. Finally I did as he commanded. I told myself I had no choice. The shameful truth – that it was nothing but the betrayal of Bessie, and of my feelings for her – I buried deep down. In the aftermath, my guilt was tempered with a sense of relief. The end of my relationship with Bessie meant the continuation of my prospects. Love sacrificed on the altar of expediency. I expected Bessie would see it as treachery. My uncle saw it as plain common sense.

I ended it. In the kitchen of the house in Fashion Street, on a bright, grim September day. I told her that our relationship was *inappropriate*. She took it without tears or lamentation, without the gnashing of teeth or the smashing of crockery. She had too much self-respect to put on such a show for the neighbours. Instead she reacted with a cold, caustic dignity. And a month later she married Tom Drummond.

There was no sign of Whitelaw, Bessie, or for that matter anyone else in Grey Eagle Street. I took that to be a good sign. Had she been seriously hurt, there would have been people here: a constable at least, and the obligatory gawkers.

I considered what to do next. I should have returned to the station house in Leman Street, but the thought of going there having let both attackers escape didn't exactly fill me with joy. Besides, assuming I was correct and that Bessie hadn't been badly injured, the chances were Whitelaw would have escorted her home, back to 42 Fashion Street.

I made my way there and rapped on the door.

The fall of heavy footsteps emanated from the corridor beyond, then a thin slash of yellow light pierced the darkness.

'Yes?'

The voice was a growl.

'Police,' I said. 'Open up.'

The door opened wider. In front of me stood the considerable frame of Tom Drummond: minor thug, waster and Bessie's husband. Most people around here knew Tom Drummond, the police certainly did. A docker by trade and a drinker by nature, he was the sort of chap who fancied himself as a leader of men, but whose men had had the good sense to desert. Steady work was never easy to come by in Whitechapel, and Drummond, like thousands of others, often found himself scrabbling around in search of piecemeal day jobs. When, more often than not, he didn't find it, he'd make his way to the Bleeding Hart public house on the Bethnal Green Road and drink himself happy on his wife's money.

Drummond's tired shirt was open at the neck, its sleeves rolled up to the elbows. His trousers, patched on one knee and held up by a pair of greying, fraying braces, appeared to have escaped from a suit that should have been put out of its misery several years ago.

'What do you want?'

You could normally smell the alcohol on him from a distance of twenty feet, but tonight it seemed he'd abstained. Maybe he was turning over a new leaf. Or maybe he'd just run out of cash.

'Your wife,' I said. 'Has she been brought back here?'

He gestured behind him with a nod. 'She's upstairs. One of your lot brought her in ten minutes ago. He's up there with her.'

I pushed my way past him into the hallway beyond. The air smelled lived-in, streaked through with the scent of too many human bodies. A door opened down the corridor and an old, creased-faced woman peered out.

'Close the door and mind your own business, you old cow!' roared Drummond. 'It's nothing to do with you. Get back to looking after your old man.'

I caught the look of shock on the woman's desiccated face before it disappeared and the door clicked shut.

'Bloody Yids,' said Drummond by way of explanation, as he led me to the stairs.

Whitelaw was standing in the doorway on the first floor. He turned at the sound of us ascending the stairs, coming out of the room and closing the door. He seemed surprised to see me.

'Wyndham? What are you doing here?'

It wasn't a question that needed an answer, and when none was forthcoming, he turned to Drummond behind me.

'You,' he barked. 'Get downstairs, put the kettle on the stove and make your wife a cuppa.'

Drummond's face flushed. I guessed he wanted to protest, possibly with his fists, but his brain quickly worked out that taking a swing at a copper or two could land him in a cell ... or a hospital. In the end he thought better of it and slunk back down the stairs. Whitelaw turned to me.

'Did you get 'em?'

I shook my head. 'They split up. I chased one onto the railway lines, but he gave me the slip at Shoreditch.'

I expected a dressing-down, but after a moment the irritation on his face cleared to an expression of resigned equanimity.

'I don't suppose it matters,' he sighed. 'Your woman in there isn't saying much of anything.'

'Bessie's not hurt then?'

It was a mistake to use her name, and I realised as soon as I'd said it.

'You know her then?'

'I've seen her around.'

'Anyway, she's fine. A few bruises, but no bones broken. I daresay she's had worse from that husband of hers.'

'She know who attacked her?'

'That's just the thing.' Whitelaw lowered his voice. 'She ain't sayin' a word.' He paused. A thin smile played on his lips. 'But maybe she'll speak to a handsome young copper like you.'

I knocked and entered with Whitelaw a step behind. Shadows danced on the bare walls as the weak light from a solitary candle did battle with the darkness and flickered in the breeze from the door.

In the centre of the room, beneath blankets and on an old brass bed that sagged halfway to the floor, lay Bessie, her hair still damp, and with one arm over her eyes. In a corner, hanging from a stand and covered with a black rag, was the canary's cage, just as I remembered it. I wondered where the cat was, but then cats came and went of their own accord. They knew better than to conform to the ways of men.

I cleared my throat. 'Mrs Drummond,' I said, martialling all the officiousness of my office.

The hand moved to reveal swelling around her cheekbone. She raised her head and looked over. For a second, I feared she was about to use my Christian name. Whitelaw would surely pick up on something like that.

'Yes?'

'I'm Constable Wyndham,' I said, moving into the light so that she might get a better view. 'You might remember I assisted you when you needed rid of a tenant, last year.'

The statement was for Whitelaw's benefit.

She nodded slowly. 'I remember.'

Her voice was hoarse and subdued.

'Do you know who attacked you?'

'I didn't see his face.'

'Then tell us what happened.'

Bessie lay back. Behind me, the floor creaked as Whitelaw shifted his weight.

'I was coming back from work ... on me way home when ... I didn't rightly see what happened. A man came up from behind an' grabbed me round the throat. I tried to scream but he held his hand over me mouth. So I bit him. Then another bloke appeared an' the next thing I know, I'm lyin' on the ground, screamin' bloody murder, an' the two of 'em are fightin'. Then you two fine gentleman show up blowin' yer whistles an' come runnin' to me rescue.'

'The one who attacked you,' said Whitelaw. 'What did he want?'

She gave a short, bitter laugh. 'What they always want, I 'spect.'

'And the man who came to help you?' I asked. 'Did you get a look at him?'

'No,' she said definitively. 'Like I said, I was too busy screamin'.'

'Quite a stroke of luck for you that a good Samaritan just happened to be passing when you needed him?' said Whitelaw.

'More importantly,' I said, 'why did he run off when we got there?'

The candle flickered once more.

'Maybe he didn't want gettin' involved with the police?' she said. 'Maybe he's bin in trouble with you boys before? Can't say as I blame him. I could count on the fingers of one hand the number of honest coppers roun' here … An' still have a coupla fingers left over.'

The last comment seemed to touch a nerve with Whitelaw.

'So a man collars you in the street, and you can't tell us anything about him. Another man just *happens* to come to your rescue and then scarpers and you can't tell us anything about him either?'

'That's right,' she said.

I tried a different approach. 'Do you normally come back from work so late?'

'I work the hours my employer tells me to.'

'And who might your employer be?' asked Whitelaw.

'Jeremiah Caine.'

I felt Whitelaw stiffen at the mention of the name. Caine was a man of some stature in these parts, which is to say he was rich, happy to throw his money around and not particularly scrupulous in whose direction he threw it, just so long as it achieved his ends.

They said he harboured ambitions to become a Member of Parliament. His pockets were certainly deep enough, and, rumour had it, those pockets contained a prize collection of coppers, from common beat constables to detective inspectors.

'I'm his 'ousekeeper.'

'She's his rent collector too,' I added.

'And why shouldn't I be?'

A note of defiance crept into her voice. Or was it wounded pride? If Bessie Drummond had come into this world with the twin misfortunes of her sex and lowly birth, then the gift of intelligence had only made matters worse. Where a man, born into similar circumstances, might find in his intellect an opportunity for advancement or improvement, in a woman it led mostly to suspicion, and sometimes a smack in the mouth.

Beside me, Whitelaw had fallen mute. Mention of Jeremiah Caine seemed to have sucked the wind out of his sails.

'You're *sure* you didn't recognise either of them?' I asked.

Bessie gave me a look of towering indifference – a look to be bestowed on the likes of a street sweeper or a bus conductor – as though the time we'd spent together had never transpired, banished from memory and from the record. It stabbed at my heart, but I could hardly blame her for that.

'It was dark an' it was wet, an' a man had just attacked an' thrown me to the ground,' she said acidly. 'You'll forgive me for not having paid more attention to what either he or the other one looked like.'

'Easy now, dear,' said Whitelaw. 'The constable's only trying to help you.'

Bessie stared at him.

'Of course,' she said. 'I'm sorry if my words were *inappropriate*.'

*

'What did she mean by that?' Whitelaw asked as we descended the stairs.

'She's probably still in shock from the attack.'

Whitelaw shook his head in exasperation.

'Probably.'

Tom Drummond was loitering at the foot of the stairway.

The sergeant stepped towards him. 'You made that cup of tea for her?'

Drummond nodded his head in the direction of the scullery. 'One of the women is makin' it.'

Whitelaw stared at him intently, and the husband appeared to shrink under his scrutiny.

'How long you and her been married?' he asked.

The question seemed to throw Drummond. 'Near as you like five months now. Why?'

'Your wife's just been attacked,' he said. 'She's had a very lucky escape. She could have been dead by now – or worse – but you don't seem too concerned about any of it. Is there something you're not telling us, Tommy boy?'

Sweat glistened on Drummond's upper lip. 'I don't know what you're getting at.'

'I'm asking if you have any idea why someone would attack your wife. You haven't been upsetting anyone, have you? Someone likely to take it out on Bessie?'

Drummond looked at his feet, then shook his head. 'You don't know what you're saying, copper. You think I know who beat up my Bessie?'

From behind him, a girl appeared carrying a tray with a pot of tea, cups and small jugs of milk and sugar. Even in the darkness of the passageway, there was something striking about her: a vitality at odds with the decrepit surroundings. Her brown hair was swept back and fell over the shoulders of a plain white blouse, buttoned to the neck. She was attractive, in a dark, foreign sort of way, and if I had to guess, I'd have said she was about nineteen.

'Excuse me,' she said, and Drummond moved aside, eyeing her as she passed up the stairs.

Whitelaw gave a growl of a laugh. 'What I'm saying, Tommy, is that if someone attacked my wife, I'd want to find out who did it and maybe smash their teeth in. I certainly wouldn't be standing in my hallway watching a Jewess take her up a cup of tea. What I'd be doing is searching the streets, making sure the bastard never tried anything like that again.'

For a moment the words seemed to form in Drummond's mouth, but he seemed to think better of it.

'You want to say something?' urged Whitelaw, but Drummond refused to take the bait.

'As I said, I ain't got a clue who attacked her.'

Whitelaw and I stepped back out into the rain. I looked over my shoulder to see Tom Drummond watching like a wolf in the doorway. We walked in silence. Both of us knew our odds of catching whoever had attacked Bessie Drummond had disappeared the moment I'd lost my man at Shoreditch. Indeed, if anyone was likely to find out who'd attacked her, it was probably Tom Drummond. He had connections we didn't have. Rumour had it he did the odd job now and again for the Spiller brothers, two very large, very persuasive Yorkshire lads, who'd found God's own country to be too small and had relocated to London's East End. If you believed the stories (and why wouldn't you?) they had their fingers in pretty much every illicit activity that centred on the docks: from prostitution to protection rackets, by way of a nice line in smuggling everything from bootleg booze to drugs. If it passed through the docks, the chances were the Spillers took a cut.

What was beyond doubt was the network they controlled throughout Whitechapel, Bethnal Green, Limehouse, Poplar and all the way down to the far side of the Isle of Dogs. If Tom Drummond really wanted to find out who'd attacked his wife, and assuming he was in their good books, all he had to do was to ask Martin and Wesley Spiller to put the word out. Of course Whitelaw knew that too, and as we trudged back to the station house in Leman Street, I got the feeling that his final remarks to Drummond had been to encourage the man to do exactly that.

SIX

February 1922

Assam

I filled my cup once more from the cauldron of herbal tea, then followed Cooper back to our dormitory.

A single hurricane lamp hung limply from a rusty hook on the ceiling, bathing the room in its dim glow. The lamp shuddered as I closed the door behind me. There was no electricity in the monastery. Indeed, there was precious little of the stuff anywhere in the country east of Calcutta.

Most of the occupied beds were now shrouded under the fine mesh of mosquito nets, their occupants ensconced like moths in their cocoons. The exception was the Belgian, Le Corbeau, who lay there thrashing from side to side, his face, hair, chest and clothes all doused in sweat. I doubted he was in any state to stand let alone hoist a mosquito net.

'Don't worry about him.'

I turned to see Adler, inside his gauze sarcophagus, his back propped up against the wall and a book in his hands.

'He's going to be like this all night. A mosquito won't even be able to land on him, let alone suck him dry. Besides, you put a net over the bed and in his state he's liable to get caught in it when he tries to get up. He'd probably trip and break his neck.'

Le Corbeau let out a scream and flung his hands over his ears.

'He's almost a week in but it always seems to hit the young ones hardest.'

I made my way to my own bed.

The old man sat up, untucked one side of the net from under his mattress and lifted it so that he had a clear view of me.

'How are you feeling?'

'Not too bad.'

It was a lie, but a healthy one. The pint of herbal tea I'd just drunk hadn't done much to reduce my cravings, and the truth was I felt as though I'd been stepped on by a bull elephant, but it was important to keep a stiff upper lip about these things.

He nodded. 'I hope you continue to hold up. To be on the safe side though, I'd suggest you too dispense with your mosquito net tonight.'

It seemed like good advice, if only because in my current state, I doubted I had the wherewithal to hoist the damn thing.

Adler returned to his book, and I made my way out the back of the dormitory to the washroom under the stars where I splashed cold water from a bucket onto my face. I looked up to see the tapestry of the night sky and searched among the constellations for that one special point of light, the talisman that was Venus, brightest of all. Napoleon, on the eve of battle, had taken it to be a portent of victory, and I too, while in the trenches, had on more than one occasion turned my head skyward in search of it. Tonight, once again, I looked for it, scouring every inch of sky, but found nothing, and its absence felt like abandonment.

The hut was dark by the time I returned, bathed only in the pale blue light which fell through two small windows. As for the hurricane lamp, the smell told me that its weak flame was put out not by human hand but by having exhausted its supply of paraffin. Slipping off my sandals, I lay down on the mattress as the wooden cot creaked in complaint. I pulled my blanket tightly around my shoulders as the chills started and my teeth began to chatter.

Across the aisle, I heard Adler snore. Beside him, Le Corbeau was grappling with his sheets and groaning like a man fighting a fever. Of the others, I couldn't see much but the odds were that they, like me, were awake, each battling their individual demons.

I waited in anticipation of the torture to come. The agony, the fear, the half-formed pleas to God for relief or even just a quick death ... I'd been here before of course. Twice before to be exact. Twice I'd tried to kick the habit, and twice I'd failed, crawling wretchedly back into the all-forgiving embrace of the O. There is nothing like opium withdrawal to make you realise your own weakness. The pain, both physical and mental, is absolute.

It would be worse here, in front of other men, even if they were going through their own hell. I wished my limbs could be bound to stop me from thrashing and my mouth stuffed with cotton to stifle my screams. But screams and thrashing, however undignified, were only the tip. Withdrawal brought with it nausea and vomiting, and uncontrollable excretions of a sort that made death seem preferable to shaming oneself in such a fashion.

Under my breath, I began to recite the Lord's Prayer, over and over again like a mantra, not through any religious conviction, but because the rhythmic repetition helped to stem the growing panic within. And with this home-made hypnosis, I settled in for what would be one of the longest nights of my life.

Next came the sneezing, then the opium cold: the rhinorrhoea, the goosebumps on the flesh, and the uncontrollable shivering. My head pounded in time with my pulse, every heartbeat spearing a shaft of white pain through my temples and my convulsing, sweat-soaked torso.

It could have been five hours or fifty minutes, but at some point I cracked. Pain coursing through every sinew, I fell from the bunk onto the cold cement floor, then dragged myself to my feet and out to the latrines. Leaning over the porcelain-clad hole in the ground, I vomited bile as black as the sky above.

The events of the rest of the night are little more than a tableau of scenes from a moving picture. I must have hallucinated: I was in the courtyard, surrounded by shadows, then back on the concourse at Lumding station, running, fighting my way through the bodies, not in pursuit of the faceless man, but sprinting for my life, pursued by an unseen presence. Running till the crowd became too thick, enveloping, suffocating. The sky went black, I saw a crow, falling to earth and lying on wet ground with its neck broken, and I heard the laughter of a dead man. I clutched at my ears, screwed my eyes shut, called out to heaven. It must have worked because I opened my eyes to the sight of an angel, all golden hair and beatific face. She ministered to me, led me back to the dormitory. Then next thing I recall is Adler's face. I remember shouting something at him. I remember him dragging me out into the courtyard, fetching me a cup from the cauldron of herbal tea.

Convulsing with pain, I knocked it from his hands, cursing and hurling obscenities at him. I must have been screaming my head off for one of the Indian monks came running over. He shoved something between my teeth and the two of them forced me to swallow. And that's all I remember.

The gong sounded at 5 a.m. and I opened my eyes to daylight. The cold, grey dawn of the hill country seeped through the dormitory windows. The pain in my head and limbs had receded somewhat, as it always did with the passing of night. Opium fever, like all fevers, is worse at night, preying on our fears in the darkness.

Around me, my room-mates were rising. For a moment, I lay there, wondering what they'd made of my antics. Slowly I sat up.

Across the aisle, Adler was already on his feet, fiddling with his mosquito net. He looked over and smiled.

'So, you survived the night?'

'Possibly.'

He unhooked the net from above his bed and began to fold it.

'Are you well enough to get up?'

'Only if it's for breakfast.'

He shook his head. 'That's not for another few hours yet, but if you can, you should get up all the same.'

I did as he advised. The others in the dorm were also up, all except the Belgian, Le Corbeau, who lay with the sheet over his head like a shroud as though he were already dead. Cooper in particular looked full of the joys of spring. He walked over to my bunk.

'Still with us then, old man? That was quite some aria you treated us to last night.'

His tone wasn't malicious, and he must have sensed my embarrassment.

'Don't worry,' he continued. 'Every one of us in here has given our own rendition of that particular song. Yours was, if anything, one of the milder efforts. Shame on you.'

He proffered a hand and helped me up from the cot and patted me on the shoulder.

I slipped on the pair of ashram-issued sandals and then examined the state of my ashram-issued shirt. Other than a few dried stains, there was surprisingly little to point to the fun and games of the night before.

'Come on,' he said. 'Welcome to your first full day of the cure.'

SEVEN

February 1905

East London

The first we knew about it was the roar of the crowd heaving at the entrance to the house. Less than forty-eight hours after the incident in Grey Eagle Street, I was shouldering my way through a mob towards Bessie's door. Sergeant Whitelaw was less circumspect, waving his truncheon and clearing his path with a cheery *'out of the bloody way'* and a degree of vigour that suggested more than his usual level of animus. But then, he wasn't keen on people, especially foreigners, and if there was one thing Whitechapel wasn't short of, it was foreigners: Irish, Chinese, Jews, Armenians; Whitelaw cursed them all – but especially the Jews, and especially the denizens of the streets and alleys around Brick Lane.

I caught up with him in the unlit hallway where we'd stood two nights earlier, his face in the half-light, set in the rictus grimace of distaste. Perspiration beaded on his forehead and mutton chops, and the sharp tang of sweat hung over him like an aura.

We'd been on our usual beat: from Shoreditch back towards Leman Street station by way of Brick Lane, killing thirty minutes en route through some of the piss-poorest streets in London. We were ten minutes from home and a cuppa when we heard them: individual shouts coalescing into the massed clamour of a crowd. It was hard to tell what was going on. Brick Lane was always mobbed with men and beasts, which made it difficult to see what was happening on the pavement opposite, let alone a couple of hundred yards up the road. But the noise had us sprinting to the mouth of Fashion Street, and it was there that we saw them, six deep and seventy strong, crushed around a doorway a few blocks down.

Even as we ran, I knew it involved Bessie, and somewhere within, I already feared the worst. Sure enough, it was around the black door of number 42 that the crowd had massed, and for a split second I froze in my tracks, only to be reanimated, snapped back to my senses, by the roar of Whitelaw's voice.

The sergeant leaned against the banister and exhaled. A ragged, wheezing breath. 'These people,' he said, directing his glance at the old woman who now stood, uncomprehending, in front of him. Her small, weathered mouth gaped open in fear, as she pointed to the first floor.

'Up. Up stair.'

Whitelaw shook his head. 'Bloody hell, woman. English! Does anyone here speak English?'

The old woman turned and called out in a confused, faltering voice, 'Rivkah!'

A door opened and a figure appeared: a feminine outline in the dark hallway. As she came down the corridor, I realised it was the same girl who'd made the tea for Bessie two nights ago. Her eyes were red and puffy.

The older woman fired off a panicked sentence in a foreign tongue.

'I speak English,' the girl said.

'Saints be praised,' said Whitelaw. 'And what's your name, love?'

'Rebecca.'

'Well, maybe you can tell us what the devil's going on.'

I steeled myself.

'It's Mrs Drummond,' said Rebecca. 'She's been attacked.'

Before I knew it, I was halfway up the stairs, Whitelaw puffing his way up behind me. The grey day penetrated through a skylight, illuminating the first-floor landing. Two more women, middle-aged and shawl-wrapped like Russian dolls come to life, were standing at the threshold to Bessie and Tom Drummond's room. The door hung limply on its hinges as though forced open by a gale.

I pushed past the women, then stopped dead.

Yellow light fell through thin curtains. The canary clung to the iron bars of its cage, and stared out. In years to come, it would be this scene and this light that would stay in my memory, frozen in amber.

Bessie lay atop the old brass bed, her face hidden beneath a mass of dark curls and her head framed by a halo of crimson blood. Her skin was grey, her body limp. The vital spark that was Bessie Drummond seemed to be seeping away before my eyes.

I was kneeling beside her by the time Whitelaw made it to the doorway.

'God's teeth. Is she ...?'

I took her wrist. It was already displaying that strange, clammy chill which heralded death.

'She's still alive,' I said, then turned. Rebecca stood behind Whitelaw. 'Have you called for a doctor?'

'Yes, sir. Dr Ludlow. His rooms are round the corner. He's been sent for.'

I knew the doctor: a Christian gentleman who ministered to the poor and had a reputation second to none, but I feared that there was little even he could do for Bessie now.

Despite the proximity of his surgery, the crowd had managed to arrive at the front door before the good doctor had. But then bad news had always travelled quickly through the streets of Whitechapel. It had been the same in Jack the Ripper's time. A sinister bush-telepathy faster than telegraph.

'Where's Tom Drummond?' I asked.

'I don't know,' said Rebecca. 'Out looking for work, I expect.'

'Who found her?' asked Whitelaw, now standing beside me, peering over Bessie's prone body.

'I did,' said the girl. 'That's to say, me and Mrs Rosen from downstairs. It's she who's gone to fetch Dr Ludlow.'

Before she could continue, there came the rumble of noise from below. I heard the front door open and the sound of boots on the stairs. Soon the tall, bespectacled frame of Dr Ludlow entered the room, his Gladstone bag in his hand.

'How is she?' he asked, throwing off his overcoat and dropping it to the floor, then coming to kneel beside me.

'She's a pulse,' I said, moving aside, 'but it's faint and her breathing is ...'

Ludlow carried out a cursory examination, then turned towards Whitelaw and me. 'I can't tell where all this blood is coming from. Help me move her onto her side.'

I steeled myself and took hold of her shoulders. Whitelaw held her legs. At Ludlow's instruction, we gently rolled Bessie onto her side, and immediately furnished the doctor with the answer to his question. The back of her head was matted with blood, the skull staved in.

Ludlow's composure faltered.

'We'll need to move her, and quickly.' He turned to me. 'Go out and hail a cab. We need to get her to the London.'

I nodded and headed back towards the door, past an ashen-faced, open-mouthed Whitelaw. Rebecca was standing in the open doorway and I grabbed her arm, taking her with me as I rushed down the stairs. We were almost at the front door before I released my grip.

There was a look of fear in her eyes. 'What are you doing?'

I tried to keep my voice low. 'What happened?'

The girl looked at me. 'I don't know. When Bessie didn't come down for a cup of tea this morning, I went up to fetch her but found the door locked. I could hear noises inside, so I fetched Mrs Rosen and we broke the door down.'

Before I could say anything further, she'd opened the front door and plunged into the crowd, hurrying towards Brick Lane in search of a passing cab.

The street was narrow and always bustling with traffic, yet there was a point, a few yards to the south, where the road widened and where the cabbies rested their horses while waiting for passing trade. Today, however, the spot was empty. The girl tried to hail a couple of passing carriages but neither stopped. She was about to try again when I stepped out into the road, raised my hand and ordered the driver to stop. The power of the police uniform never failed to impress me. The cabbie pulled sharply on his reins, bringing his nag to a halt.

I ordered the passenger, a suited, booted, well-coiffured gent, out. He wasn't best pleased, but one of the dependable features of the British middle class is their unquestioning obeisance of anyone in a uniform.

'So who's going to be paying *my* fare then, son?' grumbled the cabbie as I directed him along Fashion Street towards number 42. 'I picked up that gent in Bethnal Green. Was takin' 'im all the way to Ludgate Circus.'

'I'll pay it,' I said, 'and the fare to the hospital.'

The cabbie smiled at me through a yellow, well-ventilated mouth. 'Very good of you, sir.'

I pulled some coins from my pocket. 'Here,' I said, handing them to him. 'Forget the change.'

That bought me a tip of his head and another yellow smile.

Back in the house, Ludlow and Whitelaw had fashioned the sheet on which Bessie lay into a makeshift stretcher. At the doctor's direction, Whitelaw, the cabbie and I carried her gently down the stairs and out to the hackney carriage. By now, more constables had arrived and were busy corralling the crowd.

'Do you want me to go with her and the doctor?' I asked Whitelaw.

'So you're a medical man, are you, Wyndham?'

'No ...' I stammered. 'I just thought –'

'Leave the thinking to me, son,' he said. 'You stick to what you're good at. Stand here and make sure no one comes in or out.'

EIGHT

February 1922

Assam

'Grab a broom,' said Fitzgerald.

We'd left our dormitory, all seven of us, and joined the straggle of inmates, making for the compound near the main monastery building. There, a rake-thin monk in an orange robe was handing out brooms to the assembled congregation.

'First task, every morning,' continued the American, 'is to sweep the ashram. Everyone gets involved. Everyone able to stand, that is.'

I looked over at Cooper. He was leaving that morning but had still joined the queue for a broom.

'You know, I never in my life picked up one of these before coming here,' said Fitzgerald, brandishing the broom in his large hands like a child with a special toy. He stared at it, fascinated. I might have laughed but I realised that I too hadn't held one in years. Not since arriving in India.

'You spoken much to Brother Shankar?' He pronounced it *Shankaar*, placing emphasis on the second syllable. 'He talks a whole heap about the road to enlightenment. Says that the best place to start is right here, sweeping this floor.' The American stared at the broom once more. 'I reckon the guy might be on to something.'

I quickly began to understand what he meant. There was something soothing in the rhythmic motion of sweeping the dust and the leaves that had fallen overnight into the compound, and soon I found my mind wandering. Once more I recalled the previous night: the angelic vision and Adler's restraining hand as a monk placed something in my mouth. A recollection of the taste and texture of it came back to me. Rough, herbal. Like a spinach leaf, only thicker, waxier. More bitter.

The chores lasted about an hour, and, having returned my broom, I once more followed my dorm-mates, this time into the large, open courtyard dominated by the statue of the goddess Kali, beside which a small fire burned, tended to by an old monk squatting on his haunches.

The inmates gathered in rows, segregated, informally, by race. Unusually, we Westerners gravitated towards the back: our natural sense of privilege for once eclipsed by an aversion to offering invocations to a heathen deity, even while we sought salvation from her monks.

Brother Shankar walked along our row handing out sticks of incense, and, like the others, I took one as he passed. Around us, the monks lined up in their saffron robes, chanting their mantras and offering up prayers to the goddess. Beside me, Adler stood head bowed in reverence. The Frenchman, Lavalle, wore a look of disdain that suggested a degree of distaste for the whole business or a severe case of indigestion.

The air filled with the fragrance of sandalwood and one by one the rows of devotees approached the fire, lit their incense sticks in its sacred flame, then planted them in the soft ground in front of the idol. When it came to our turn, however, no one moved. Instead Brother Shankar returned and took the sticks from us.

'What now?' I whispered to Fitzgerald.

'Joge,' he replied.

I felt a sweat break out on my forehead. Weak from hunger, fatigued from my exertions of the night before and with my muscles still cramping from opium withdrawal, the last thing I needed now was to embark on a session of physical jerks. I was, of course, free to walk away – the exercises weren't compulsory – and yet, because there were natives present, I felt I had no choice but to take part. It was a curious thing. I was an opium fiend, the lowest of the low, and hardly a poster boy for the campaign to defend the prestige of the white man, and yet such was the nature of empire that, even now, part of me believed that I had to maintain a certain standard. As though it was vital to show that an English opium fiend was superior to a native opium fiend. And the worst of it was, I did this not so much for my own sake, but because I felt the natives expected it of me.

As it happened, there was nothing to be scared of. *Joge* turned out to be little more than some stretching and breathing exercises, the most peculiar of which involved pressing down with a finger on one nostril and inhaling deeply through the other while wearing an expression of extreme surprise. As with the rest of the morning's theatrics, I went along with it, mainly because I had nothing to lose.

It must have been close to eight by the time these callisthenics drew to a close. I couldn't be sure because my watch had been confiscated along with my clothes and was now, according to Brother Shankar, stored safely in a strongbox somewhere in the ashram. The exercises were followed by roll call, then a breakfast of more rice, more dal and more herbal tea.

Over breakfast, Adler explained the daily routine of monastic life.

'They like you to get involved,' he said, mopping up the last of his dal, 'preparing the meals, helping in the fields. You could even take part in the prayers, assuming you were that way inclined. But I would suggest that, today at least, you save your strength. Just rest in the dormitory. Take the steam bath, then maybe read a book.'

After breakfast, I joined the others in bidding adieu to Cooper, which proved to be a surprisingly emotional affair, tinged with more tears than an Italian funeral.

'When you suffer alongside a man,' said Adler, 'you build a bond with him. And that bond is all the stronger because no one else quite understands that shared suffering.'

I knew what he meant. I'd spent three years in the trenches after all.

Sweat: tar black, opium-leavened, leached from my pores, and trickled earthward, returning to the Indian dust from whence it came. I lay on my back on a plank bed, a glistening forearm over my eyes.

The air hung like sweet, sweltering fog, singeing the skin and stinging the sinuses, the silence punctuated by the lonely, metronome splash of water condensing on the concrete ceiling and falling to the dirt floor. To one side, a wood-fired stove broiled gently, a thin metal chimney running from it to a hole in the roof. Atop it, a pan filled with water and leaves, blackened and battered with age, sat bubbling. The steam's herbal tang reminded me of a Turkish bath. Missing, though, was the birch branch for self-flagellation. Penitence in the ashram took a different form.

The heat reminded me of Calcutta before the monsoon: that torrid, clinging, sweltering miasma that hung for months like a fever over the city until finally breaking to the blessed, life-affirming rain. I recalled that first Calcutta summer: when a young man's fancy turns to thoughts of shade, and midday pur-dah and the release of late afternoon when the temperature dropped but the humidity remained. I thought of Surrender-not and his walks by the river at sunset to catch the single whisper of wind to be found there. I thought too of Annie Grant, the woman who had been the source of so much, if not happiness, then at least hope in my life since I'd arrived in India. I didn't know whether I loved her. I didn't know if it was even possible for me to love another after the death of my wife, but I did care for her. As for *her* feelings, if she *had* ever loved me, then that love had been tested to, and well past, breaking point. I couldn't blame her for that. I was hardly an easy man to love, even at the best of times, and if there was one thing you could say about the last few years, it was that they'd hardly been the best of times. I usually didn't like thinking about it. After all, to dwell on matters of love, like admitting to a liking of French food, is a rather distasteful and decidedly un-English state of affairs. But here, in the heat and isolation of a steam-powered concrete box, my mind returned to her and what I might do upon my return, to right things with her.

I lay there in little more than a loincloth, basting like a pig in an oven. Yet as experiences in the ashram went, this was one of the most pleasant, and over far too soon.

The door opened and the heat evaporated like a pleasant dream. At the threshold stood a native monk with a *gamcha* folded over his wrist like a waiter at the Ritz.

'Come,' he said. 'Brother Shankar wishes to see you.'

I dried and dressed in my ashram best – shirt and drawstring trousers – then slipped the sandals onto my feet and followed him across the noonday courtyard.

He left me at the door to Shankar's room, with a smile of such serene contentment that, anywhere else, I'd have suspected him of having just smoked a pipe of O himself.

From inside came the inflexion of pleasant conversation and the timbre of a woman's voice. I knocked gently, yet firm enough to silence the discourse within.

It was Shankar who answered.

'Come in.'

I opened the door, entered, and quickly became aware of the weight of two sets of eyes upon me. The small room smelled of expensive perfume. I breathed it in, lapping it up like a starving man.

'There you are, Sam,' beamed the monk, rising from his chair. He walked over and placed a protective hand on each of my shoulders, then turned to show me off to his guest.

'I'd like you to meet a friend of mine. This is Mrs Emily Carter.'

Seated on a chair in front of Shankar's desk was a woman of about thirty. She smiled, white teeth between rouged lips, and I realised I'd seen her before. The blonde angel from the previous night.

'You seem familiar,' I said. 'Last night, did you help me back to my dormitory?'

Emily Carter sat there, a vision in a summer dress, and gave a nod. 'I thought maybe you wouldn't recall.'

'Mrs Carter helps out with some of our female patients at the ashram,' said Shankar. 'She found you wandering in the courtyard. I thought it might be nice for her to meet you under more . . . benign circumstances.'

That was an interesting way of putting it. By *benign*, I took him to mean circumstances where I wasn't raving like a lunatic.

'It's a pleasure to meet you, Mrs Carter,' I said. And it was. A real pleasure. We might all be created in the image of the Divine, but some of us were clearly closer to the original than others. It wasn't just her film actress looks. There was something more, something inextricably linked to the kindness she'd shown me the night before.

'She's also a great benefactor of our work here.'

'She seems very much the good Samaritan,' I said.

Emily Carter waved away the compliment, on her finger a wedding ring the size of the iceberg that sank the *Titanic* catching the light.

'Brother Shankar tells me you're up from Calcutta, Captain Wyndham.'

'That's right,' I said. 'Thought I'd get away for a few weeks. See the sights of Assam.'

Once more, she flashed that heavenly smile. 'I hope you'll get a chance to do just that. Once you've completed your time here.'

My mouth was suddenly as dry as the salt plains of Gujarat. 'I ... I hope so too.'

Before I could make any further scintillating comment, there came a knock. The door opened and the monk who'd led me over appeared once more.

'Mrs Carter,' he said, 'your car has arrived.'

Emily Carter rose from her chair.

Venus ascending.

'If you'll excuse me, Captain. It's a pleasure to make your acquaintance.'

Shankar clasped her hands in his and beamed a smile. 'Thank you, Emily, for everything.'

A moment later she was gone, leaving only the memory of her wrapped in the lingering fragrance of her perfume. I caught Brother Shankar's expression: the distant, faraway look that suggested thoughts not entirely consistent with monastic life. Not that I blamed him. Emily Carter looked like the sort of woman who would unsettle any red-blooded male, monk or otherwise, including old Devraha Swami or the Pope for that matter.

'Interesting lady,' I said.

'Hmm?' Shankar snapped out of his reverie. 'Oh yes, wonderful. Simply wonderful. She's done so much for us since coming to Jatinga. Most English ladies wouldn't be seen dead up here at the ashram. It's not the done thing to keep company with drug addicts or Hindus. Mrs Carter, though,' he marvelled. 'What a lady. She comes up here every few weeks to help out in any way she can.

Mainly with the women patients, naturally, but also in the kitchens at times. She's a real interest in things: from the running of the ashram to the preparation of the herbal cures.'

'Careful,' I said. 'Next thing you know you'll have her converting to Hinduism and I'm not sure her husband would approve.'

Shankar's expression darkened. 'No fear. She's shown no interest in that.'

Through the window behind him, I saw Emily Carter cross the courtyard to where a large black car stood waiting. At her approach, a chauffeur exited the car with alacrity and quickly opened the rear door. She graced him with a smile then she lowered her head and disappeared inside.

The driver closed the door behind her, and made his way to his own seat. The engine growled to life and within seconds the car was heading for the ashram gates, throwing a halo of dust skywards in its wake.

With the memory of Mrs Carter lingering pleasantly in my head, and with time to spare before lunch, I left Brother Shankar and went off in search of the ashram library.

The room was larger than I'd expected, though what expectations I should have of an ashram library are still unclear to me. Three walls were lined from floor to ceiling with shelves of religious texts. There was something for everyone, assuming you liked your literature with a theological bent, from thick, hide-bound, hand-printed tomes with covers decorated with fine filigree detailing, to the flimsy, mass-produced, badly bound paperbacks that every book-wallah in Calcutta's College Street sold by the barrowload for a few annas each.

I wondered why Adler had suggested I come here. It was obvious I was no scholar of Sanskrit, and even if I had been interested in learning the Hindu holy texts, today was hardly the most auspicious occasion on which to start. Then I noticed that a few dusty shelves near the bottom of one wall contained a number of books in English, and to my joy, these weren't even religious tomes. I knelt down, scanned them quickly and smiled. Towards the end of one row was a title I recognised. I wiped the dust from the spine. *The Four Just Men*. It was a detective novel published back in 1905. I knew, because I'd bought it the week it had come out. It had been a bestseller, not because it was any good, but because the author, Edgar Wallace, had left out the last chapter. Instead he'd advertised in the *Daily Mail*, offering £250 for the correct solution to the crime. Of course Wallace, like most writers, overestimated his own intelligence. For a start, the solution wasn't that hard to figure out – as a young beat copper in the East End of London at the time, I'd managed it and duly wrote in to the *Mail*. More importantly, Wallace forgot to state there would be only one winner, so anyone who wrote in with the right answer was entitled to the money. The upshot was that Wallace went bankrupt, and seventeen years on, I was still waiting for my £250.

I picked up the book and walked back to the dormitory, lay on my bunk, and to the hum of prayers and the twitter of birds, I opened the book.

'If you leave the Plaza del Mina, go down the narrow street, where, from ten till four, the big flag of the United States Consulate hangs lazily . . .'

I closed the book and placed it on my chest. It was strange how 1905 kept cropping up. Since arriving in Assam, it seemed as though an unseen presence was directing my thoughts back to that year: the figure at Lumding station; the memories of Bessie Drummond; the compassion shown by the Jew, Adler; and now this book.

1905.

The year I hadn't been strong enough.

I felt I was reading entrails, portents of something ominous.

A religious man might have seen in them the hand of God or gods, and after all, here I was in an ashram dedicated to Kali the Destroyer. Was this all part of some supernatural reckoning? The past, they say, catches up with us all. Maybe it had finally caught up with me.

NINE

February 1905

East London

With Bessie's unconscious body removed from the scene, the crowd, in the way that crowds do, sensed the show was over and began to thin. Those that remained morphed from mob to judge and jury, expounding several theories as to who'd attacked her.

Surely the answer was cut and dried. It had to be Tom Drummond, the waste of space whom Bessie had married in such haste. He'd a temper and a history of sorting out his problems with his fists. But here, in the ragged atmosphere of the East End, nothing was ever that simple.

I waited till the crowd had drifted off, then re-entered the house and climbed the stairs. The door to Bessie's room was ajar, the room itself empty and the bed stripped down to the blood-soaked mattress. These four walls had contained the sum total of her worldly possessions: the canary in its cage; a ramshackle writing desk, chipped and scarred; a shabby chair on which was draped Bessie's red shawl; a knackered wardrobe with its door hanging open and with a suitcase on its roof; and, in the space beneath the bed, a steel trunk of the type favoured by sailors, secured by a sturdy padlock.

I entered and tried to close the broken door behind me, but it swung open once more. I took a closer look at the damage. The lock looked sturdy enough, the bolt still fully extended. But even the best lock is useless when the door frame is rotten. The jamb itself was thin and had come away easily. I doubted it would have taken more than a few hefty shoves to detach it from the frame.

That's when I spotted it, though the truth is I all but tripped over it. On the floor, not far from the door, lay its key. That seemed odd. The only reason I could think of as to why the key should be lying there on the floor was if it had been dislodged from the lock when the door had been forced. And if the door had been locked from the inside, then how could Tom Drummond, or anyone else for that matter, have attacked Bessie and got out of the room? It would imply that her attacker beat her to a pulp then left while she locked the door behind him before collapsing on the bed. That made no sense.

Taking a handkerchief, I carefully picked up the key, wrapped it and placed it in my tunic pocket. I spent the next few minutes scouring the room, looking for whatever weapon had been used to attack her. I found nothing. I was about to look outside the open window when I heard Whitelaw's voice coming from somewhere along the landing. I hurried back out into the hallway in the hope that, with the crowd gone, he might permit me to go to the hospital to check on Bessie.

In a room two doors along, I found Whitelaw standing over an old couple seated on the edge of a bed. Beside them stood Rebecca. Her face was flushed. As for the couple, one was the old lady who'd opened the door to us earlier. The other, I presumed, was her husband. He looked as old as Adam, and as frail, with a face thick and gnarled like tree bark. Thin strands of white, wispy hair strayed from under a small black skullcap. In one shaking hand, he held the crook of a walking stick, and in the other, he held the hand of his wife.

'So they didn't hear anything?' asked Whitelaw.

Rebecca nodded her head. 'That is what I've been trying to tell you.'

'A woman is beaten to a bloody pulp a few feet away and Mr and Mrs Rip Van Winkle didn't hear a peep? They just slept through it, did they?'

The girl sighed. 'Mrs Feldman left the room before seven o'clock this morning. She's been in the kitchen or the yard for most of the morning. Mr Feldman is partially deaf in one ear and quite deaf in the other. A train could have gone through the landing and he wouldn't have heard it.'

I introduced myself with a cough.

'Wyndham?' said Whitelaw. 'I thought I told you to keep watch downstairs.'

'Yes, sir, but there's no one left to keep watch over. I thought I might –'

'Well, seeing as you're here, why don't you see if you can get some sense out of this pair? A woman is attacked down the hall and they don't hear a flippin' thing apparently. If they're to be believed it might as well have happened on the moon.'

Rebecca interceded on the old couple's behalf. 'I've been trying to explain to your colleague that Mr Feldman is almost totally deaf and Mrs Feldman wasn't in the room, but he doesn't seem to understand English.'

Beside me, Whitelaw stiffened, and I quickly suppressed any sign of amusement.

'Have you seen any strangers enter or exit the building today?'

The girl shrugged. 'I don't think so.' Suddenly her expression tightened. 'Wait. There was one man. He came with Tom, Mr Drummond.'

'With?' I asked. 'What time was this?'

'It must have been after eight. The whistle at the docks had gone some time before. Mr Drummond brought him. They came in and sat down in the kitchen. I know because I was in there when they arrived, preparing breakfast.'

'And you say he arrived *with* Drummond?'

She nodded. 'Yes. I didn't see Tom go out, but he normally leaves for St Katharine Docks around six in the morning to join the men looking for day work. If he doesn't find any, he normally comes back here and has breakfast.'

'Does he usually bring others back?'

'This is the first time I've seen him with a guest.'

It was an odd choice of word. Tom Drummond didn't strike me as the sort of man who entertained guests, especially at eight in the morning.

'What did he look like, this *guest*?'

She thought for a moment. 'Medium height, shorter than Mr Drummond. His nose was odd.'

'Odd?'

'Like a shark's fin.'

'Anything else?'

'He had a brown coat. Patched.'

'Like everyone else's around here,' said Whitelaw.

She glared at him. 'The patches were green. Who patches a brown coat with green fabric?'

'Someone who hasn't got any other colour?' I asked.

She seemed to find that amusing. 'In Whitechapel? There are thirty tailors on Brick Lane alone.'

It was a fair point. Around here you couldn't throw a stone without hitting a tailor, and every tailor had a bin full of offcuts, scraps of fabrics in all colours.

'Maybe he's just eccentric?' said Whitelaw.

'Maybe. It simply struck me as unusual.'

From her seat on the bed, the old woman, Mrs Feldman, spoke up nervously: Yiddish words, aimed at Rebecca.

The girl's expression changed, the cockiness suddenly, if temporarily, vanishing.

'What is it?' I asked. 'What did she say?'

'She said there was another visitor this morning ... not a visitor exactly, and not a stranger.'

'Who?'

'The landlord, Mr Caine.'

'What time was this?' asked Whitelaw.

Rebecca consulted the old woman, who now looked like she was rueing having opened her mouth.

'She thinks around half past seven. Before Tom Drummond returned with his friend.'

'And he called on Bessie?'

Another round of question, answer and translation.

'That's right,' said Rebecca. 'He came to see if she was all right ... and to collect the rent, no doubt.'

'You didn't see him?'

'I had errands to run,' she said. 'I was out of the house between seven and eight.'

Mrs Feldman piped up again. Rebecca turned to her.

'She's asking if you have any further need of her or her husband.'

Whitelaw gave a brief, sardonic laugh. 'No, you tell them they're all right, love. Tell them they've been very helpful.'

'In that case, do you think we might leave their room?'

'The noise is bothering Mr Feldman, is it?' he said acerbically.

Rebecca Kravitz seemed unamused.

Old man Feldman flashed us a hollow, toothless grin as we left. I closed their door, then continued with the questions.

'When he came back with his guest, did Drummond go up to see his wife?'

The girl scratched her earlobe. 'I didn't see him, but I expect so.'

'Why?'

'Because that's what he usually does when he can't find work. He comes home and scrounges what he can from Bessie before going off to the pub.'

'Do you know what time they left, Drummond and this man in the brown coat?'

Rebecca shrugged.

'I don't. I was in my room, but I came down to the kitchen around nine. They were gone by then.'

'Did you see Bessie after Drummond left?' I asked.

'You mean before we found her ... in her room?'

I nodded.

She shook her head. 'No. The last time I saw her was at around six o'clock, when I went to the kitchen. She had the kettle on the stove, boiling water for tea.'

'Did anyone else see her this morning?'

She pondered the question. 'I can't be sure. Certainly not the Feldmans, or my parents.'

'Who else lives in the building?'

'There's Mrs Rosen. She's a widow. Rents the room next to ours on the ground floor. She's an apothecary's assistant on the Whitechapel Road. And there's the man who has the attic room, Israel Vogel. I haven't seen him this morning.'

'So for now, as far as we know Drummond was the last person to see his wife before she was attacked?' asked Whitelaw.

'Where's Drummond now?' I asked.

The girl stared back blankly. 'I don't know.'

'I could hazard a guess,' said Whitelaw. 'If, as the girl says, he's gone to a boozer, five'll get you ten he's in the Bleeding Hart, drinking himself silly.'

'We should get down there,' I said, heading for the stairs.

'Not so fast, lad,' said Whitelaw. 'I'll post a constable here. Then we should inform CID. Mark my words, this'll end up a murder case.'

I wasn't about to accept that. 'Surely the doctors will save her.'

Whitelaw's face was suddenly grave. Slowly he shook his head. 'Son,' he said, his voice little more than a whisper, 'the Lord Himself would have a hard time saving her. She's not coming back.'

TEN

February 1922

Assam

It was late afternoon. In India, the time of daily rebirth after the stupefying heat of midday. The time when men and women re-emerged from huts, dogs came out from the shadows, and birds took wing.

I lay on my bunk in the dormitory having woken from another sweat-soaked nightmare: again I was running – a frenzied chase, this time through the alleys of east London, pursued once more by that same unseen menace as in the dream at Lumding station. I tried to keep still as every movement triggered stark needles of pain to shoot through my shivering frame and into my skull.

The door opened. Brother Shankar entered and walked over.

'Are you able to sit?'

I croaked a response, then pulled myself up, resting my back against the wood of the wall.

Brother Shankar smiled, like Francis of Assisi from a Sunday-school storybook, come to life and clad in saffron.

'We should talk about your treatment.'

He sat on the corner of my bed.

'How are you feeling?'

'I've been better. Though I don't actually remember when.'

He listened and nodded, like a doctor administering palliative care.

'Well, the good news is, we'll be commencing your treatment in about an hour.'

'And the bad news? On second thoughts, ignore that. I don't really want to know.'

The monk smiled. 'The cure consists of a broth, brewed and consecrated by Devraha Swami. It's different from the herbal tea you've been having so far, in that you won't be keeping this in your stomach. The key is to drink it down quickly, then vomit it back up.' He pointed to my ashram uniform. 'I suggest you come bare-chested, and it's probably best if you don't eat anything in advance. I've seen men eat a full meal beforehand, and believe me, it's not a pleasant sight when it comes back up.'

An hour later, the gong sounded.

I unwrapped my cocoon of blankets and slowly rose from my bunk. Around me, most of the others did likewise. Only Adler remained in his cot. He put down his book.

'Good luck,' he said. 'The next hour will not be easy, but remember that in the war to rid yourself of your addiction, this is the start of the last battle, and it will be won in ten days.'

The inmates gathered in the compound in front of the idol of the goddess Kali, where roll call had been taken that morning. This time we were divided differently, split between the shirtless and the shirted: those undergoing treatment, and those who had completed their ten days and moved on to recuperation.

The monks then divided those of us without shirts into smaller groups, lining us up in front of long wooden troughs on which sat a row of steel buckets, each filled to the brim with water. Hooked to the side of each was a metal cup.

Brother Shankar walked over.

'This way,' he said, separating me from my dorm-mates and directing me to the first row of troughs close to the idol of the goddess. 'New initiates at the front.'

On either side of the idol stood a monk, each carrying a double-sided Indian drum called a *dhol*. As we took our places, the monks began to beat out a steady rhythm. From the ashram a red-robed figure appeared. Small, fragile as a bird, and flanked by two more monks, he walked slowly out into the courtyard and I surmised that this must be the fabled Devraha Swami. Shaven-headed, his skin looked parchment-thin – almost translucent – and for a moment I wondered if maybe he really was as old as Dr Chatterjee had stated. His face, though, was smooth, and soft-featured, and under the lines of ash on his forehead, his eyes were clear and focused.

He passed along the line, sharing a few words with each initiate until he reached me. Brother Shankar made the introductions. 'Swami-ji,' he said, in tones that another man might have used to address the king, 'we are honoured by your presence.' The old man smiled up at him, then at me, and for a moment I felt strangely at peace, as though all that it would take to cure me of my opium addiction was for this man to lay his hands upon me.

But nothing was ever that simple.

Instead the swami turned to one of the monks behind him and took a large glass bottle, filled with a greenish liquid that looked like river water. Suddenly the drums stopped. There was silence. Utter and disconcerting. Not even the wind blew. The swami pulled the cork out of the bottle. The monk held out a small glass vessel and the swami poured out a measure. Taking the glass, he held it out to me.

'Drink.'

A sea of faces stared at me.

'Bottoms up,' I said, and downed the cocktail.

A sharp, bitter taste spread through my mouth, before the liquid hit the back of my throat like a bullet and buried its way down to my gut.

The drums began to beat again. Faster. Louder.

My head spun.

I felt Brother Shankar beside me. 'Hold your body straight.'

I'd imagined I'd start to vomit the instant the liquid hit my stomach – it was, after all, a vomiting potion – but as the seconds ticked by, nothing happened.

'Here,' said Shankar, taking the metal cup from the bucket and filling it with water. 'Drink. All of it.'

I did as he ordered, gulping down the water till the cup was empty, then handed it back.

'Again,' he said, refilling it. 'Keep drinking until you can't drink any more.'

I stared at him in confusion, and suddenly it was Francis of Assisi who was smiling back.

'Trust me.'

So I drank. I drank until my stomach began to distend and I couldn't face another drop.

By now, Devraha Swami had dispensed his potion to all of the front row. The drums were beating and the onlookers were shouting encouragement. Around me, others were already retching, their bodies doubled over the trough.

I stood there, punch-drunk, a boxer out on his feet and looking to my corner for the towel. I struggled to hear Brother Shankar above the noise.

'Put your fingers down your throat!'

I followed the order without question, and then it began – the first fitful heaves – and suddenly I was gagging: retching, vomiting, expelling great tides of greenish water. On and on it went, a wave of rhythmic, involuntary heaving, as with each ejection I was reduced further to a crumpled, groaning mess, my face streaming with tears and mucus.

At some point the vomiting ceased, replaced by dry heaves. Collapsing to the ground, I wiped a hand across my mouth and tried to catch my breath. As my body convulsed in pain, I looked around. The drums were still beating, the crowd still shouting, but I could hear none of it. Beside and behind me, others continued to retch. St Francis was changing back into Brother Shankar, and suddenly I was struck by a deep clarity: a chain of events that had begun that day in 1918 when I was blown up by a German shell; which had continued with the death of my wife, and my decision to leave England for India and opium; all of it led to and culminated here, in this moment, with me lying collapsed and wretched in the dust of a monastery courtyard under the pitying gaze of the goddess Kali.

ELEVEN

February 1905

East London

Whitelaw was right.

By the time we made it to Leman Street, word had reached that Bessie hadn't survived the journey to the London Hospital.

The news hit me like a howitzer shell and I felt the world spin out of control. I walked back outside, and gripping the iron railing in front of the station house, I fought for a lungful of air.

Bessie Drummond … Bessie May … was dead, and it was as though I'd struck the first blow myself.

I felt hollowed out: an emptiness in my breast; a clawing realisation that, on some level, I still cared for her and that now it was too late and I'd lost her. There could be no amends. If I'd been more of a man, if I'd stayed with her two nights earlier, questioned her more thoroughly, maybe she'd still be alive. Suddenly the guilt, the grief, the bite of self-loathing and the red heat of anger coalesced and I doubled over and heaved into the gutter.

Behind me I heard Whitelaw's voice, then felt his hand on my shoulder.

'You all right, lad?'

I turned to find a look of paternal concern on his face.

I merely nodded, unwilling to speak lest my voice betray me.

'Good,' he said. 'Being a copper ain't for the faint-hearted. You're going to need to toughen up. Still, you're young. You'll learn.'

'What now?' I asked.

'Now? Now it's a murder investigation. Scotland Yard are sending a detective inspector. We'll need to brief him.'

'What do we tell him?'

The question seemed to surprise him.

'We tell him everything we know: that we saw a commotion outside the house, went in to investigate and found a woman with her head staved in. We tell him that the husband was probably the last person to see her alive; that he came home with a mate, went up to their room, probably to scrounge some drinking money; that he left, and an hour later a couple of Jewesses break down the door and find Bessie with her head cracked open like an egg.'

'You think Drummond killed her?'

Whitelaw moved aside to allow a couple of constables to exit the station.

'I don't think he meant to kill her. I think he went up to ask for cash. She refused and Drummond lost his temper, didn't want to lose face in front of his mate, and lashed out and hit her on the head with something heavy. Now she's dead, they'll hang him for sure.'

It all made sense, except for one thing.

'The door,' I said.

'What about it?'

'It was locked from the inside.'

'You're sure?'

I pulled the handkerchief from my pocket and carefully unwrapped the key. 'I found it on the floor at the foot of the bed. I think it was dislodged when the two women broke down the door.'

Whitelaw realised the significance immediately.

'That's not good.'

'What if someone entered the room, attacked Bessie, then locked the door and left through the window?'

With a meaty hand, Whitelaw rubbed the mutton chop on his left cheek. His face didn't seem convinced.

'We should go back there and check the window.'

'Let's not get ahead of ourselves, lad,' he said, raising a palm. 'The room's secured. We should wait for the detective inspector to get here.'

I felt the bile rising. Bessie was dead and Whitelaw was suggesting that we sit around waiting for some bigwig from Scotland Yard to show up while the trail went cold.

I punched the rail, hard and almost oblivious to the pain that ran up my fist. The bar reverberated with a hollow, metallic ring.

'We have to do *something*.'

Whitelaw gave me a weary look that encompassed a lifetime of disappointments.

'What would you suggest, lad?'

'I suggest we find Tom Drummond.'

We headed out and up bustling Commercial Street.

In some ways London was like Calcutta, only less honest. If Calcutta was split between White Town and Black, London was no less bifurcated: between west and east, rich and poor. Here, too, the bare facts were laid out in black and white, or rather in shades of red and blue, by Charles Booth in his map of London's poor. Affluent areas were coloured blue and poorer ones in hues of red, with the most wretched streets painted a deep crimson. There wasn't much blue within a mile of Whitechapel, and the reddest areas were packed to the rafters with foreigners, these days mainly the Jews: a hundred thousand of them escaping the bloody terror of the pogroms that always seemed to be occurring somewhere in the Russias.

Penniless and persecuted, they had come to England, which is to say they'd come to London, and in particular to the East End.

Why Whitechapel? Because this is where they got off the boats, and because no one with any other choice wanted to live there.

It had always been this way. Before the Jews had come the Irish, fleeing famine, and before them the Huguenots, running from religious wars. Always someone escaping something, and coming here with nothing because they had no choice, and because a life of nothing was better than no life at all.

Tom and Bessie Drummond were just about the only native English folk in Fashion Street, and throughout the whole of Whitechapel things were little different. Thousands of immigrants crammed into a space fit for hundreds, often five or six to a room and sleeping in shifts. The Jews even had a saying: '*Sleep quickly. We need the pillows.*'

Whitechapel was a different England, and while it wasn't quite a foreign country, it was still a world away from anywhere else in the land, its incomers viewed with a mix of hostility and fear by more than a few.

'Round 'em up and put 'em on a steamer back to wherever it is they came from,' Sergeant Whitelaw had opined more than once as we'd walked our beat, and whatever my opinions, I couldn't deny the man's consistency. He advocated similar treatment for the Chinese in Limehouse, the Irish in Millwall, and the Catholics in general, though I was never clear on exactly where he expected them to be shipped back to.

Yet he and others seemed to harbour a special distaste for the Jews. It couldn't just be because of their foreign tongue and worship of an alien god – the Chinese, after all, did both too – but Jews committed the additional sin of looking like us. The Chinese looked and acted so differently that they were dismissed as a law unto themselves. Yet a Jew, dressed in a suit and clean shirt, could pass for an Englishman, and maybe that's what people found unforgivable.

As if to emphasise the point, Whitelaw shook his head. 'Listen to that,' he said as we passed a group of men who stood engaged in animated discussion outside a bakery.

'What?'

'You heard anyone speak a single word of English since we left the station?'

'I wasn't listening. I was still thinking about Bessie Drummond.'

'Well, you ain't missed much. You can walk from Bishopsgate to Stepney on a Sunday and I'll wager you'll be lucky to hear a full sentence in English. It's all Hebrew, isn't it?'

'Yiddish.'

'What?'

'Their language. It's called Yiddish.'

'You're an expert on foreign languages as well now?' He paused, then continued. 'Conspiracy, is what it is. The way things are going, you won't be able to recognise this country in fifty years. There's already Jews in Parliament. Next thing you know, we'll have a Jew prime minister.'

'Haven't we already had one?'

'What?'

'Benjamin Disraeli. Wasn't he a Jew?'

He mulled it over for a moment. His response, when it came, was enigmatic.

'Well, there you go, then,' he said. 'See? You can't trust 'em.'

The Bleeding Hart public house was little more than a hundred square feet of long bar and short tables on a sawdust-covered floor, nestled between a grocer's and an ironmonger's on the Bethnal Green Road. Its diminutive size, however, belied its significance to a certain strand of the East End's criminal fraternity, acting, as it did, not only as a watering hole, but also as the centre of operations for the multitude of enterprises controlled or connected to the

Spiller brothers. It was where ne'er-do-wells went to discuss business, plan operations and hire an assortment of talents including lock-pickers, forgers and just plain muscle. As such, the Bleeding Hart was part social club, part business headquarters and part labour exchange. And the Bleeding Hart was famous.

For a while, the good souls of the Salvation Army had mounted a noisy, placard-waving vigil on the pavement outside, urging the sinners within to turn away from the Devil, but in the end, it was the Sally Army stalwarts who'd been forced to change direction. Word had it the Spillers had mounted a protest of their own, at the house of a senior officer of the Salvation Army. Whether it was Martin's threats or Wesley's fists which proved more persuasive wasn't clear, but the message had got through and the preachers and their placards had melted away.

Despite it being a mile or so from Fashion Street, the Bleeding Hart was Tom Drummond's regular, partly because a man of his dubious skills could often find work there, and partly because the Bethnal Green Road and the rail tracks nearby formed an informal border between the 'foreign' areas to the south and the more English streets to the north. In its fifty-two years of operation, I doubted a single non-Englishman had ever been through the doors of the Bleeding Hart other than by mistake or because of a summons from the Spiller brothers, and the reception was unlikely to have been warm either way.

Its exterior was unremarkable. Peeling black paint framed a dun-coloured door and windows opaque with dirt. Above the entrance swung a faded board emblazoned with the picture of the creature that gave the place its name: a white stag with a crown around its neck and an arrow stuck in its side. Blood dripped from the creature's flank, and while the expression on its face wasn't quite one of pain, it did suggest the animal wasn't particularly thrilled by the whole experience of being used for target practice.

Whitelaw pushed open the door and I followed him into the fog beyond. Trade was brisk, despite the early hour. Several bodies propped up the counter, old men with yellowing hair and sallow, capillary-pinched cheeks poring over copies of the *Pink 'Un* or nursing stale beer between cracked fingers, and resembling nothing so much as the jetsam that washed up on the black banks of the Thames at low tide.

To offer some privacy to those who wanted it, a set of booths, separated by wood-and-glass partitions lined one wall. In plush West End boozers, the fashion was for the glass to be frosted and decorated with acid-etched cornucopia. Here in the east, the same effect was achieved with dust and grime and crude drawings made with one finger.

Hunched over the table in one of these was Drummond, the pint glass in his rough, calloused hand empty save for the dregs of foam and discoloured liquid that clung like shipwreck victims to the sides. Across from him sat a thin man with grey skin, receding black hair, and a nose like a parish pickaxe. Neither man looked up as we entered, and neither seemed to be doing much talking. Drummond in particular seemed to stare unfocused at the table in front of him, with, for the longest of seconds, not even the stimulus of Whitelaw calling out his name, eliciting a nod.

Finally he looked over.

Whitelaw removed his helmet. 'Tom,' he said. 'You need to come with us.'

Drummond said nothing. It was his drinking partner who piped up.

'What's this all about?'

The sergeant fixed him with a stare.

'And who might you be, sonny?'

If the look was meant to intimidate, I doubted its efficacy. The man seemed about as cowed as Fred Karno putting on his act at the Hippodrome. A hint of a smirk played at the corners of his mouth.

'Finlay,' he said. 'Archibald Finlay.'

'Well, Mr Finlay, I'll thank you to keep your mouth shut.'

Drummond fiddled nervously with the glass between his fingers, then made to slide out of the booth. Opposite him, Finlay mirrored his actions and tried to rise till Whitelaw put a heavy hand on his shoulder and shoved him back down.

'Maybe, Mr Finlay,' said Whitelaw, 'you should stay here with my colleague while I have a quick word with your friend.'

Tom Drummond rose from his seat and I took his place on the bench opposite Finlay as Sergeant Whitelaw led him back towards the front door. I didn't envy him. Tom Drummond was hardly an angel, but informing him of his wife's murder wasn't something I'd have wanted to do.

I watched them exit and waited for the door to swing shut once more, then turned to Finlay. He was swilling the remnants of his pint around the bottom of his glass.

'So what line of work you in, Mr Finlay?'

'Me?' he said, looking up. 'I'm a handyman, you might say. Odd jobs. A bit of this an' that really. Whatever comes my way.'

'You and Drummond good friends?'

He stopped swilling his drink. 'Good enough.'

'How long you known him?'

Finlay stared upwards as though the answer might be written on the ceiling. 'Six months? Maybe longer.'

'How'd you come to meet him?'

'We were introduced. In here as it happens.'

'By whom?'

Finlay took a sip of his beer. 'A mutual acquaintance. I forget his name.'

'You been to his lodgings?'

For the first time, he eyed me suspiciously.

'What's this about?'

'Just answer the question.'

'Yeah, I been to his gaff. Was there not three hours ago.'

'What were you doing there?'

Finlay shrugged. 'Nothing, really. Bumped into him down the docks this morning. We was both lookin' for work but there was none goin' so we decided we might come 'ere to pass the time, so to speak. We stopped off at Tommy's place while 'e had his breakfast.'

The sound of raised voices filtered in from outside. Through the haze of the windows, I could make out the shapes of Whitelaw and Drummond: the sergeant with his helmet under his arm; and Drummond, larger, taller, facing him. I watched as the bigger man seemed to slump to one side. The door opened once more, and Sergeant Whitelaw stood at the threshold.

'Come on, Wyndham. Time to go.'

I nodded, then turned back to Finlay, and from my breast pocket, extracted my notebook and pencil.

'I'm going to need your address.'

'Why?' he asked.

'Because I so enjoy your sparkling conversation.'

He rattled off a location on Durant Street.

'Right,' I said, rising from the banquette. 'One last thing, Mr Finlay. Don't plan on going anywhere.'

TWELVE

With Drummond between us, Whitelaw and I started out for Leman Street under a sky the colour of cast lead. As the first spots of rain began to fall, we hailed a hackney carriage and began the journey back to the station house. Whitelaw sat beside Drummond, with me across from them. For now, we were treating him as a bereaved husband rather than a suspect in his wife's murder, and given his demeanour, it seemed an apt decision. He sat there as though struck dumb, robbed of the cloak of confident aggression which he usually and so casually wore.

As we drove, a thought occurred to me.

'Do you have your keys?' I asked him.

'What?'

'The keys. To your lodgings?'

I watched the confusion pass across his face.

'Yes.'

'Can I see them, please?'

He fished through the pockets of his coat before drawing out a small bunch of three keys on a ring. One was large and heavy, the other two, smaller, flatter and made of a lighter metal.

'What's each of them for?' I asked.

Drummond picked out the largest. 'This is me front-door key. An' these two are for padlocks.'

'Padlocks on what?'

'One's for the chest what contains me valuables. The other's for me suitcase.'

'And the key to your room?'

Drummond's face reddened. 'Ain't got one.'

'Why not?' asked Whitelaw.

'Bessie never got round to makin' me a copy.'

'What if you were both going out?' I asked.

Drummond shrugged. 'When Bessie went out, she'd lock up and leave it with the Rosen woman downstairs.'

Back at Leman Street, we deposited Drummond into the hands of the desk sergeant while Whitelaw and I sought out our new boss who, we were informed, was waiting for us in the spare office.

Whitelaw knocked on the open door. Across the room, the besuited figure of Detective Inspector Robert Gooch stood staring out of the window amid a fog of blue cigarette smoke. He was something of a celebrity, among both police and public, thanks to his involvement in a case the previous year involving the murder of the maid of a prominent banker in Holland Park. Gooch had a reputation for incorruptibility in pursuit of the truth. He'd been the subject of acres of newsprint and was now known to the masses as Old Upright or simply, Gooch of the Yard.

The first thing that struck me was his height, or rather his lack of it. He couldn't have been more than five feet five inches in his heels, and given that the minimum height requirement for a member of the Metropolitan Police was five feet seven, it raised the question of how he came to be a policeman in the first place.

He turned, and with his cigarette clamped between two fingers, gestured for us to enter. He must have been in his fifties, greying, and with the sort of thick, gentle features one associated more with the local parish priest than a detective. Yet if the rumours were to be believed, the man had steel in his veins.

'You must be Whitelaw,' he said to the sergeant.

'Yes, sir, and this is Constable Wyndham.'

'Sir,' I said, and received a nod of acknowledgement in return.

'I understand that you two gentlemen were first on the scene this morning.'

'Correct, sir,' said Whitelaw, standing to attention as though he'd just joined the army.

'Good,' said Gooch. 'Tell me what I need to know.'

He took a seat behind the desk as Whitelaw recounted the facts: not just the details of this morning's incident, but also the attack on Bessie Drummond two nights earlier, and ending with our return from the Bleeding Hart with Tom Drummond. I, of course, said nothing. It wasn't my place to add to or contradict anything, especially as Whitelaw glossed over the part where I'd failed to apprehend either of the men I'd chased from Grey Eagle Street.

The sergeant brought his account to a close as Gooch stubbed out the butt of his cigarette in a glass ashtray on the desk.

'You think the two events are linked?'

'We can't say either way, sir,' said Whitelaw.

'And you're sure the door was locked from the inside?'

For a moment there was silence. Whitelaw gave a cough. 'I best let Constable Wyndham explain, sir, it being him what found the key.'

Sweat prickled on the back of my neck.

'The women who raised the alarm said the door was locked,' I said. 'They had to break the jamb to enter the room. According to the husband, there was only one key, and I found that on the floor near the door. My guess is, it was in the keyhole on the inside and was knocked out when the women broke the door open.'

The inspector scratched at his temple.

'Where's the husband now?'

'Downstairs, sir. The desk sergeant is organising for him to be accompanied to the London Hospital on Whitechapel Road to carry out the formal identification.'

'And did you find the implement?'

The question threw me.

'Sir?'

'The murder weapon, Constable,' he said irritably. 'The woman died from one or more massive blows to the head, presumably from a large, and now probably bloodstained, implement. Did you find anything that might fit that bill?'

'No, sir,' I said, 'though we didn't –'

'What the constable means to say, sir,' Whitelaw interjected, 'is that our first priority was to tend to the victim, who was still alive when we arrived upon the scene. That took precedence, as it were, over any search for the weapon or weapons used to attack her.'

'You mean you didn't look,' said Gooch. 'Well, that's our starting point, gentlemen. I want a thorough search of the room, the house and its environs conducted before we lose the daylight, and I want the husband brought along too. Bring him straight from the hospital.'

THIRTEEN

February 1922

Assam

The sound of the drums died.

In the periphery of my vision, I saw people begin to disperse. Slowly, and like a newborn foal, I got to my feet. Brother Shankar offered me a steadying hand but I declined, and trembling, with my mouth bone-dry and my throat aflame, made my way back to the dormitory.

I entered to words of congratulation, acknowledging them with barely a nod. Then, exhausted, I fell onto my cot and pulled the blankets close. I shut my eyes and prayed for sleep, but none came. Instead I lay there in the limbo of delirium, in pain and too weak to move.

The hours passed. The gong for dinner sounded. My dorm-mates departed for the mess hall, and I lay where I was. If I'd been able to think, I might have realised that there was something new about my pain; something different from the usual symptoms of withdrawal. I might have taken it as a sign that things were changing, maybe even improving. But lying there, having undergone my first treatment, all that was beyond me, and eventually, I passed out.

I awoke to darkness and in the full grip of a fever, my body drenched in sweat. Trembling, I wrenched myself up, and as I started to shiver, realised I was still without my shirt. I fumbled, looking for it, then gave up and staggered out of the hut, making for the mess hall and the cauldron of herbal tea. Out of the corner of my eye, I caught something, a shadow watching me across the courtyard. I turned, but the figure dissolved into the blackness and for a moment I thought I heard padded footsteps receding into the night. I tried to pull myself together. My body felt hollow, and as I filled a cup and drank it down, it seemed as though the tea was simply soaking through my desiccated shell, straight into my cells.

Two more cupfuls and I headed back to the dorm. Once more, sleep eluded me. My muscles began to cramp. In an effort to quell the pain, I found myself standing, then walking, pacing to and fro, up and down the length of the hut. I must have kept that up for hours, just walking back and forth and muttering all sorts of non-sense to myself, until finally, overcome once more with exhaustion, I fell onto my bed and suddenly I was back in 1905, running through the rain, with Bessie Drummond's voice echoing in my ears, chasing after a man who'd jumped onto the tracks at Shoreditch.

It was Adler who woke me. A gentle shake of my shoulder.

'You survived again, my friend. How do you feel?'

'What time is it?'

'Half past seven. You missed roll call and prayers but I thought it best to wake you for breakfast. You need to keep your strength up.'

'Thank you,' I said, rubbing the sleep from my eyes.

'Besides, we've had other things to deal with.'

'Don't tell me we've run out of herbal tea,' I said, then caught the look on his face.

'The boy, Philippe Le Corbeau. He's disappeared.'

I looked over at the Belgian's bunk which lay empty, save for dishevelled sheets half spilled onto the floor.

'Disappeared?'

'Some men have trouble overcoming their addictions,' said Adler. 'The pain gets too much for them. They try to run, to escape to the nearest town or a village where they might find a dose of heroin or opium or even just a drink.'

'He just walked out?'

'There are no locks on the doors. The monks keep an eye out, but if a man's truly desperate, he'll find a way. Now and again, someone gets out, but there's nowhere to go except Jatinga village, and Le Corbeau's hardly going to get what he wants from the white residents. As for the natives, they know better than to take in a fugitive from the monastery.'

A strange expression, like the first tendrils of winter, descended over his crumpled face.

'What is it?' I asked.

'It's just that we generally find them by first light. They either make their way back or are handed in by the locals.'

'It's still early,' I said. 'Maybe he'll show up.'

'Maybe,' said the Jew.

I found my shirt on the floor beside the bed, put it on and headed for the latrines. When I returned, Adler was waiting. He stowed his mosquito net into his cabinet and walked over.

'One question, Mr Wyndham,' he said. 'Last night, when you were walking all the way to Jerusalem, you called out some names. One, I think, was Jewish. A man called Vogel. He is a friend of yours?'

I stared up at him. *Vogel* – in my mind it was a name inextricably linked with that of Bessie and the man I'd thought I'd seen at Lumding station.

Suddenly, more images of the night flitted across my mind. I remembered Adler once more at my side, trying to feed me herbal tea as I ranted.

'He was just someone I once met in London, a long time ago.'

'Jewish?'

'Yes.'

Adler considered this for a moment, then moved on.

'Well ... are you ready for breakfast?'

'Yes.'

'Then come.'

He turned towards the door, but I stopped him with a hand.

'I wanted to say, *thank you.*'

He looked at me curiously.

'For what?'

'For ...' It was difficult for me to say the words. 'For helping me get through the night.'

He smiled. 'You would have done the same for me.'

I nodded. But if history was anything to go by, that was a lie. And I wondered what he'd say if he knew the truth.

FOURTEEN

February 1905

East London

A solitary constable stood watch outside the entrance to number 42 Fashion Street. Inspector Gooch barely gave the man a glance as he brushed past into the hallway with Whitelaw and me in tow.

The corridor was empty, the remaining residents of the house shrewdly confining themselves to their rooms and out of our path. Even the hum of their conversations, muffled behind thin walls, fell silent, cut short at the sound of our footsteps.

'Which way?' asked Gooch.

'Upstairs,' said Whitelaw.

The door to the Drummonds' room had been crudely fastened by a length of string tied around the doorknob and secured to a nail hammered into what was left of the jamb. Gooch untied it and entered.

The scene looked unchanged from how I'd left it several hours earlier: the brass bed and bloodstained mattress in the middle of the room, with the steel trunk beneath it; the writing desk; the chair with Bessie's shawl draped over the back; and the old wardrobe with its door ajar and the suitcase on its roof.

Gooch did a slow tour of the room, stopping at the desk and opening the small drawer under its top. Nothing among the contents seemed to catch his eye, and pushing it shut, he turned his attention to the bed.

He ran his hand along the metal head rail, then pressed down on the mattress which complained with a metallic creak. Bending down, he pulled the trunk out from under the bed and rattled the padlock. The thing was locked tight.

Gooch straightened then took a step back and examined the scene.

'Where are the bedsheets?'

Whitelaw and I looked at each other.

'We used them to carry the woman down to a hackney carriage,' said Whitelaw. 'I don't recall what happened to them after that. They may have ended up at the hospital, or one of the other tenants might have taken them to be washed, sir.'

Gooch fixed him with a stare. 'Those sheets are evidence from a crime scene, Sergeant. Go and find them. Now!'

The order had been directed at Whitelaw, but as the junior officer, I assumed it was my task to carry it out. I made for the door.

'Not you,' said Gooch. 'I've got some questions for you, Constable.' He turned to Whitelaw. 'You go, Sergeant. Find me those sheets.'

He waited till Whitelaw had left, then walked over to the door and examined the lock and the shattered jamb, running his fingers slowly over the splintered wood.

'You say it was locked from the inside?'

'I think so, sir. I found the key over there on the floor.' I pulled the handkerchief from my pocket, unwrapped the key, and showed it to him. For the first time since I'd met him, a smile appeared on his face.

'You haven't touched this with your bare hands?'

'No, sir.'

Sometimes the fates smile on you. I knew precious little about detective work, but I'd read enough to know that the future of policing lay in scientific method, and that fingerprints were a key part of that future.

'Good lad,' said Gooch, taking the bundle from me. He adjusted the handkerchief so that it covered only the round bow of the key, then inserted it into the lock and turned it. The bolt slid smoothly back with a snap. He turned it once more, returning the bolt to its original position, then jerked the key from side to side in the lock. There was enough give to suggest that the few violent blows needed to force the door from the jamb could have been enough to dislodge it.

On cue, Gooch left the key in the lock, exited the room and closed the door behind him. Then came an almighty crash and the door flew open, the side of it striking the wall. The key fell heavily to the floor, though close to the wall rather than near the door frame where I'd first found it, but that could have been down to the fact that the door had been locked at the time. The key might have been dislodged by one jolt, while the door might have flown open on a subsequent hit. Gooch re-entered and, with my handkerchief, retrieved the key and rewrapped it. 'I take it you can live without the hanky,' he said, placing it in his own pocket.

'So,' he continued, 'if we are to assume that the door was indeed locked from the inside, and with the key still in the lock, and assuming that our attacker isn't a ghost, then the question becomes, how did he get out?'

Both our gazes turned at the same time to the window.

Whitelaw returned with the bloodstained bedsheets, just as I was about to lean out of the window. Behind him stood Tom Drummond, ashen-faced and cap in hand.

The sergeant introduced him to Gooch.

'You have my condolences, Mr Drummond,' said the inspector. 'Rest assured we'll catch whoever did this.'

Drummond didn't look like he was listening.

'As of now,' Gooch continued, 'I'm given to understand that you are the last person known to have seen your wife before she was attacked.'

Drummond's response was subdued. 'If you say so.'

'Tell me, in your own words, what happened this morning.'

The husband recounted a story that chimed with what his mate, Finlay, had told me back at the Bleeding Hart: that he'd risen at 5 a.m. and after Bessie had made him a cup of coffee, he'd left for St Katharine Docks to look for day work. There, he'd met Finlay, and having failed to secure paid employment, they'd decided to try their luck at the Bleeding Hart, stopping off at Fashion Street on the way.

'And why precisely did you do that?' asked Gooch. 'Stop off on the way, that is.'

Drummond blinked. 'To have something to eat.'

'What did you have?'

'What?'

'For breakfast,' said Gooch. 'What did you eat?'

'Bread and cheese,' said Drummond, running a hand through his hair.

'Did you see your wife?'

'No. She was upstairs.'

'So to be clear, you're saying you didn't see her?'

'Not in the scullery, no.'

'Did you go up to the room afterwards?'

Drummond looked from Gooch to Whitelaw, before settling his gaze on me. Something was going on in that skull of his.

'Yes,' he said finally. 'Before leaving, I went up to say goodbye to Bessie.'

'What time was that?'

'Round half past eight.'

'Tell me what happened.'

Drummond hesitated. 'There's little to tell. I went up the stairs. The door was locked. I knocked, told her it was me. She opened it, we spoke for a minute, then I left.'

'What did you speak about, in that minute?'

'I told her I was off to Bethnal Green,' he said, his voice suddenly a whisper, 'an' that hopefully there'd be work to be had there.'

'And what did she say?'

'Not much.'

'That took you a minute?' asked Gooch.

Drummond said nothing.

'What else did you talk about?' the inspector said, this time with menace in his voice.

'I ... I don't remember.'

It wasn't my place, but that didn't stop me.

'Did you ask her for money?'

Both Gooch and Drummond turned towards me. It was Gooch who spoke first.

'Well? Answer the constable's question. Did you ask your wife for money?'

Drummond shifted uncomfortably. 'I might have done ...'

The inspector gave me look of encouragement.

Emboldened, I continued. 'Bessie Drummond, sir. She had a job as a housekeeper and also collected the rent from the other tenants in this building. She probably made more money than Drummond here. At the very least, her wages were regular.'

Bessie was hardly unique in that respect. If all you did was read the papers you might think that the only women who worked in London were schoolmarms, nannies and whores, but here in the east at least, that was laughably false. The truth was that most of the women in Whitechapel worked: as seamstresses, cooks, cleaners and a dozen other trades besides. They had to, just to ensure

there was food on the table when there was no work for their men-
folk at the docks. Indeed, I suspected her income was part of the
reason Drummond had married Bessie in the first place. And yet
for Drummond, like other men in his position, set against the boon
of extra cash from his woman, was the stigma and the sense of
emasculation fostered by such a state of affairs; emasculation that
was often salved only by physical violence – just to remind her who
was boss. Bessie wouldn't have been the first woman in the East
End to suffer the irony of handing over beer money to her husband
only to receive a black eye in return. She wouldn't be the last, either.

Gooch stared at him. 'How much d'you ask for?'

'A few shillings,' said Drummond, twisting his cap tight
between his fingers.

'And did she give it you?'

Drummond nodded.

'Just like that? You ask her for her hard-earned money so that
you can sit in a pub all day, drinking with your mates, and she just
smiles and hands it over?'

'That's what she did,' repeated Drummond. 'She was my wife.
She knew her place.'

'I'm sure she did,' said Gooch, appraising the size of the man in
front of him. 'I'm sure she did. So what then? You took the money
and left?'

'S'right,' said Drummond. 'Went back down, got Finlay, and
left.'

'And that was the last time you saw your wife?'

Drummond swallowed hard. 'S'right.'

'And when you left, did Bessie lock the door behind you?'

'I 'spect so,' said Drummond. 'S'what she usually did ... force of
habit, like.'

'Did you have a key?'

Drummond shook his head. 'She never gave me one.'

'Is there another key to this door other than the one in your wife's possession?'

'If there was, she didn't tell me about it.'

Gooch pondered Drummond's words.

'Well, that leaves us at practically the same point as when you and the sergeant walked in. The only other exit is the window.' He turned to me. 'Constable. Would you be so kind?'

I leaned on the ledge and looked out of the window. Beyond lay an inner courtyard between the rear of the tenements of this side of Fashion Street and those of the buildings opposite. The layout of number 42 was such that while at the front there was a mere drop of one floor to street level, at the rear the drop was more like two storeys, on account of a basement cellar.

There was little to see below. The muddy courtyard contained a ramshackle outbuilding, a line of grey washing and the usual detritus of East End life: a graveyard of rusting prams, broken furniture and mounds of rubbish, all converted into a playground by a tribe of barefoot, half-naked children.

From the window ledge, there was no way down to the ground other than a leap of faith and a drop of almost thirty feet. Too far to jump if you valued your limbs. Leaning further, I scanned the walls on either side: a facade of miserable brick, soot-covered and crumbling in places to reveal yellow sand beneath. Beyond were other window ledges, but all at a distance of ten or more feet – a leap too far for anyone save a suicidal trapeze artist.

On one side, though, ran a drainpipe. Affixed to the rotting wall by ancient brackets, the thing had broken off about a foot below the level of the window, the wall immediately beneath it stained an algal green and damp from the trickle of water that dripped from it into a muddy cesspool below. The pipe was just about within arm's reach. If a man stood on the ledge and had a decent head for heights, it was conceivable he could reach it.

Scaling it downwards was impossible, but there was always up. I craned my neck skyward and followed the pipe's path to the guttering along the roof. It passed within touching distance of a window ledge one floor up.

I pulled myself back in and straightened up.

'There's no way down,' I said, 'but a man in good shape could conceivably have used the drainpipe to reach a window ledge directly above us, or possibly even the roof.'

Gooch turned to Drummond. 'Who has the room upstairs?'

Drummond looked at the floor and slowly shook his head. 'I should have bloody known.'

'Known what?'

'Vogel,' said Drummond. 'The Yid upstairs. He's taken some sort of unhealthy fancy to Bessie. More than once I've caught the bastard staring.'

Gooch looked to Sergeant Whitelaw, then to me. His expression told us everything we needed to know.

A minute later, we were at the top of the stairs outside Vogel's door. Sergeant Whitelaw tried the knob, then rapped loudly on the peeling paint.

'Open up! Police!'

From inside came silence.

Whitelaw knocked again.

He looked to Gooch. 'Should I break it down, sir?'

The inspector thought for a moment.

'Do it.'

Whitelaw braced and made ready to throw himself against the door.

'Wait!' I shouted. 'There might be another way.'

I returned with Tom Drummond to his room downstairs and instructed him to open the wardrobe door.

'Bessie would have had keys to all the other rooms,' I explained, 'on account of her looking after the building on behalf of the landlord.'

From under a pile of clothes, Drummond pulled out a small metal strongbox.

'Is that where she kept the rent money?' I asked.

'That's right,' said Drummond.

He took it over to the writing desk and opened the drawer under the desk top.

'Here it is,' he said, extracting a small key. I took it from him, unlocked the strong box and lifted the lid. As far as money was concerned, the thing was empty, save for a few shillings. I pushed the coins and a small notebook aside, before pulling out a set of keys on a ring.

Closing the box, I passed it back to Drummond, who returned it to the wardrobe, and a moment later we headed back up the stairs to where Gooch and Whitelaw were waiting. I held the ring of keys aloft like a trophy.

Gooch stopped me before I could try one in the lock.

'Perhaps Mr Drummond should try the keys.'

Drummond picked one, then slotted it into the lock and turned.

There was a satisfying click as the bolt yielded, but before Drummond could turn the knob, Whitelaw placed a restraining arm across his chest.

'If you don't mind, Mr Drummond,' he said. 'This is police business now.'

Inspector Gooch went first through the door and into a low-ceilinged room smaller and barer than the Drummonds', with only a bed, a chest of drawers with a suitcase placed under it, a chair and a table, on which sat what looked like a vice and some metal tools.

The first thing that struck me was the smell, a pungent, acrid, suffocating stench that hit you at the back of the throat like neat vodka. My eyes began to sting.

Gooch gave a cough, then took his handkerchief from his pocket and held it to his face. I'd have done the same, only my handkerchief was in his pocket, wrapped round a key.

'Blimey,' said Whitelaw, 'what the hell is that stink?'

'Search me,' said Drummond, holding a hand to his nose.

'It's nitric acid,' said Gooch.

'What's this chap Vogel doing with nitric acid?' asked Whitelaw.

I walked over to the chest and pulled out the topmost of the set of three drawers. It contained little but odds and ends: a few letters marked with what I assumed were Russian postmarks, their contents written in an alien script, two whittling knives, a strop and other flotsam. Closing it, I moved on to the lower two. Though hardly brimming, these contained two shirts, one missing a button and both frayed at the cuffs, a pair of trousers, threadbare at the knees, a thin green cardigan and a few items of underwear. It might not have been much, but it was plenty for a man of Vogel's means.

Gooch, still with his hanky to his face, traversed the room and stood over the table, inspecting the tools. He knelt down and picked what looked like wood shavings from the floor. 'What does the man do for a living?'

'According to Bessie, he makes walking sticks, shafts for umbrellas, that sort of thing,' said Drummond. 'Used to work for another Yid, but got the sack a few weeks ago and decided to go into business for hisself. He even had the gall to ask Bessie for a loan.'

Gooch raised an eyebrow. 'She lent money to people?'

'Sometimes she did. If she knew them well enough and thought she'd get her money back. With interest of course.'

'She lend money to Vogel?'

'No chance,' said Drummond. 'She'd have had to be off her rocker to do that. She told him to sling his hook.'

'You were present when this occurred?' asked Gooch.

Drummond shifted nervously. 'Not as such, but she told me. Said he was standin' outside our door, just waitin' for her. Said he made her nervous.'

'And did *you* do anything about that?'

'Damn right I did,' said Drummond, suddenly on surer ground. 'I came up here and told him to stay the hell away from my wife.'

'Did you hit him?' asked Gooch, but Drummond had no time to reply.

'Inspector,' interjected Whitelaw, kneeling beside the bed, 'you better take a look at this.'

FIFTEEN

February 1922

Assam

Le Corbeau had turned up.

The first I knew about it was Brother Shankar shaking me awake, wrenching me from a rather pleasant delirium where a woman who might have been Emily Carter or Annie Grant was soothing my fevered brow.

He imparted the facts to me in rushed, hushed whispers, and then I was following him, sandal-shod and with drawstring trousers tightened, out of the dormitory door and then the ashram.

We headed down the hillside, along the dirt track that led to Jatinga village, and then cutting onto a minor trail, a path of flattened grass, into the living forest. The air was heavy with the scent of new wood and the drone of insects flitting from chrysanthemum to cobra saffron. We kept walking, through the sun-dappled wood, towards the whistle of onrushing water. Finally, at a clearing, we came to a stream running cold and fast down the hillside. It would have been idyllic, were it not for the body lying face down in the water, its head resting on a rock as though asleep on a pillow.

On the bank nearby stood another saffron-robed monk, his moon face expressionless. Beside him were two natives in shirts and shorts, less sanguine and in animated conversation, and beside them, a European, dressed in a linen suit and a gold silk tie so bright it hurt the eyes, and who didn't seem quite sure how to react.

I pointed to the European, who instinctively ran a nervous hand through his hair. 'Is that the chap who found him?'

Shankar nodded. 'His name's Preston, one of the local engineer-wallahs. He's chiefly concerned with drainage – irrigation and the like.'

'Sounds fascinating.'

Shankar turned to me. 'He's a good man, Captain, and a friend.'

'Of course,' I said.

'He and his men were out surveying the area this morning and came across the body.'

'It's definitely Le Corbeau?'

We moved closer. The body came into focus. Male, European, tall, dirty blond hair. From behind at least, it certainly looked like the Belgian.

'It's him,' said Shankar.

The monk stopped beside Preston and the two men wordlessly shook hands. I, meanwhile, descended the bank and slipped off my sandals. Stepping into stone-cold water, I walked over to the corpse. I turned and called out to the men on the bank.

'He was found like this?'

'That's right,' Preston replied. He pointed to his native helpers. 'My men went to check if he was breathing, but once they realised he wasn't . . . No one's moved him.'

Balancing precariously on a rock, I knelt down beside the body and felt uselessly for a pulse. Suddenly I wished Surrender-not was here. He was a damn clever lad and I could have used his insight into the situation. More importantly, I could have got him to stand in the river and check the body rather than getting my own feet wet. Rank has its privileges after all.

The corpse was cold, chilled by death and the river. I tried to turn him over, but a dead man in waterlogged clothes weighs more than you'd imagine. In the process, I lost my footing, slipped and fell into the stream beside him. Two bodies, side by side. One dead, the other not quite ... not yet. I clambered out as Preston's two native assistants tried to stifle their amusement. I decided to help them with that and ordered them to retrieve Le Corbeau's body and bring it onto the bank.

They hauled the Belgian from the stream and lay him, face up, upon the grass. I took a closer look. There was a wound on his temple. A two-inch gash, crimson and purple, and puckered and grey at the edges.

'He must have got lost,' said Shankar. 'Stumbled off the main track and down here. Then fell into the river, hit his head on the rock and drowned.'

I stared at him, but the monk's face suggested nothing other than sincerity.

'Has this sort of thing happened before?'

'You mean has anyone ever died like this? The answer's *no*. As far as I know, we've never lost anyone before, certainly never a European.'

'And Le Corbeau? Did he ever wander off before?'

The monk nodded. 'The second night after he'd arrived. But we stopped him. That's not particularly uncommon. A lot of people find the first week difficult. Some try to make it to Jatinga in search of a hit, but ...' Shankar looked perplexed.

'But?'

'I know Philippe was having difficulties, but it's rare for someone to try and leave a second time. Especially when they're as far into the treatment as he was.'

I got to my feet and pondered the situation. Le Corbeau, in agony from his withdrawal symptoms, finds a way out of the ashram and heads for Jatinga. In his delirium, he staggers from the main path, into the forest and ends up here, where he slips, falls and hits his head on a rock.

It was possible.

I turned to the engineer, Preston, who was staring down at Le Corbeau's corpse. He looked in his early thirties, medium height, thick brown hair, and a pallid complexion that suggested he was close to throwing up.

'What were you and your men doing up here?'

He looked up. 'What?'

'Don't tell me you just stumbled across him, out here in the middle of nowhere.'

'We were surveying the stream,' he said. 'It flows through marshy ground further down which the owner wants to drain. We were moving uphill, mapping its course, assessing the feasibility of diverting it, and there he was, just lying there.'

Preston turned a pastel shade of green, doubled over and vomited onto the grass.

His explanation sounded plausible enough, and the vomiting certainly added a degree of credibility.

'We need to move the body,' I said. 'Is there a hospital nearby?'

'Nearest one's in Lumding,' said Preston. 'Best part of a day away. But there's Deakin, our local doctor. He has a clinic in Haflong.'

'Do you have transport?'

Preston shook his head. 'No, but I know where we can borrow a car.'

'Fine,' I said. 'Send someone for the doctor and the car.'

Preston's assistants now sat a safe distance away, squatting on their haunches, and watching our conversation. The engineer called over to one, summoning him with a bark in a language I didn't understand. The man rose lethargically and ambled over. Preston barked at him some more and the man nodded, then turned and headed slowly for the path. A final shout from Preston, a verbal kick in the rear, caused him to up his pace, at least until he reached the treeline and disappeared from sight.

*

The next hour passed slowly. More so as my cravings seemed to be returning. My muscles began to cramp and my head felt like someone was smashing rocks against it. I lay down on the grass a respectful distance from Le Corbeau's body, closed my eyes and tried to block out the pain. Shankar and Preston sat close by, talking in hushed tones. It looked as though the monk was offering advice, or ablution, to the engineer.

Finally the stillness was broken, rent asunder by the whine of an engine in low gear. I sat up. The note changed to a growl and grew gradually louder. A car horn blared and a flock of birds exploded from the trees. Suddenly a vehicle burst through the treeline and came to a halt further up the bank. The engine cut out and the silence of the forest descended once more. Preston's assistant appeared, this time accompanied by a rotund gentleman with pink face, silver hair and a three-piece linen suit whose waistcoat buttons seemed to creak under the strain as he walked.

'Dr Deakin,' said Shankar, rising to meet him. He strode over and clasped the doctor's ample right hand between his own. 'I'm sorry to drag you out here without warning.'

The monk led the doctor towards Le Corbeau's body, the top half of which was now respectfully covered with a rough saffron-coloured shawl. I got to my feet and walked over as one of Preston's assistants pulled back the cowl.

Standing above it, the doctor appraised rather than examined the corpse, in the manner that an art critic might a painting, or a butcher a haunch of meat. Maybe he didn't want to get his suit dirty, or maybe the physical act of kneeling and carrying out an examination was too strenuous. Either way, he stared down at the corpse, a look of weary disappointment on his face, as though the boy should have known better than to go getting himself killed in the middle of the night.

'Dr Deakin,' said Shankar, 'may I introduce Captain Wyndham of the Calcutta police?'

The doctor turned and stretched out a hand. 'Captain.'

'Doctor,' I said, taking it.

'Bit far from your usual beat, I'd presume?'

'You could say that.'

'Friend of yours?'

I shook my head. 'I just happened to be in the area.'

Deakin exchanged a glance with Brother Shankar, then noticed Preston.

'Yes, well,' said the doctor, 'where was he found?'

I pointed to the spot in the stream. 'There. Taking a bath with his head on that rock.'

The doctor walked over to the bank, looked down, then wandered back and stared once more at Le Corbeau's battered skull. 'We'll need to get the body back to the clinic.' He turned to Preston. 'Get your men to place him in the back of the car.'

Preston nodded, then gave the order. The two Indians lifted the body, one taking its feet, the other grabbing under its arms, and carried it jerkily towards the vehicle.

'Anything you can tell us now?' I asked.

Deakin snorted, as though the question itself was ridiculous, then pointed to the wound on the corpse's head. 'Looks to me like he slipped, fell and hit his head on that rock. The question is, was the blow enough to kill him or was he just knocked out and then drowned? We'll be able to tell by the amount of water in his lungs. Either way, it's a tragic accident.'

With that, he turned and headed up the slope in the direction of the car. Shankar, Preston and I fell in behind him, following in silence like a funeral cortège.

The driver opened the rear doors and slowly, awkwardly, Le Corbeau's body was interred on the banquette. One of Preston's assistants fumbled with the corpse's feet, pushing them in so that they wouldn't obstruct the door, and it was then that I noticed.

'Wait!' I shouted, as he went to close the rear door.

The man looked over in shock and instinctively stepped back as I ran over. I bent down and began to examine Le Corbeau's trousers, then the back of his calves. I cursed myself for not spotting it sooner. He was wearing monastery-issue grey drawstring trousers identical to mine. I estimated we'd both walked roughly the same route through the forest, we'd both fallen into the river, and we'd both spent the last hour or so lying on the grass. But the back of Le Corbeau's trouser legs were brown and muddied, whereas mine were grey.

Of course, in and of itself, that meant nothing. Le Corbeau might have taken a fall en route, or his trousers might have been muddied at some point earlier. So I examined his ankles and the back of his legs. There wasn't much to see, nothing definitive at least, but there, on the back of the left ankle, just above the heel were a series of scratches. A picture began forming in my mind. Could it be that Le Corbeau had been accosted, hit over the head and then dragged to the stream to make it look like an accident? The scratches and the muddied trouser legs suggested that might be a possibility, but if so, why? Why would anyone kill an unknown Belgian out here in the middle of nowhere? The simplest answer would have been robbery, but Le Corbeau was dressed in the same monastery garb as I was. It would have been obvious he had no money on him. I thought back to the previous night, to my sojourn across the courtyard in the dead of night. The sense I'd had of someone else being there, watching me. Could that have been Le Corbeau? Or could it have been someone lying in wait for him?

I heard Shankar's voice behind me. 'What is it?'

I hesitated. What could I tell him? That the man had mud on his trousers and a scratch on his leg? That I suspected the possibility of foul play?

There was also the larger issue. Could I trust him? I shook my head. This was madness. Opium was known to cause heightened paranoia. The withdrawal symptoms must be clouding my judgement.

'Nothing,' I said.

Only Deakin, the driver and the moon-faced monk continued with Le Corbeau's corpse on to Haflong. I had wanted to accompany the body, but Shankar, seeing the sweat on my face, had decided I wasn't fit for the trip. I was in no state to protest. Instead he promised I'd be the first to hear what the doctor had to report.

I agreed, and with a glance back at the stream, I turned and followed him back up the hill towards the path to the ashram.

SIXTEEN

February 1905

East London

Vogel's bed was low and narrow and propped against one wall opposite the window. Whitelaw was on his knees, peering under it, resurfacing as Gooch and I walked over.

'Give me a hand, Constable.'

We each took one side of the bed frame and together lifted and moved it out from the wall. A thick film of dust lay over the space beneath and covered an assortment of items: a battered suitcase, a stock of half-finished canes with their handles carved but unvarnished, and more wood shavings. There was another object too: a thick, wood-handled hammer, which unlike the other items, was encrusted not with dust, but sticky, crimson blood.

Whitelaw let out a whistle of satisfaction.

'Don't touch it,' said Gooch. He turned to Drummond.

'Do you recognise that object?'

Drummond looked to be in a state of shock. 'It's a hammer.'

'But does it belong to you? Have you seen it before?'

Drummond shook his head. 'Never seen it before in me life.'

Gooch looked to me. 'Constable, get back to the station. I want two men down here to conduct an inch-by-inch search. Make sure they bring evidence bags.'

*

An hour later, with the search of Vogel's attic room under way two floors above, Gooch, Whitelaw and I reconvened in the scullery. The inspector was seated at the pitted wooden table in the centre of the room where, less than nine months earlier, I'd broken up with Bessie.

Drummond, for his part, had been taken back to the station for a formal statement, after which he'd be at liberty to go where he pleased, which would probably be back to the Bleeding Hart, or if that proved too far, one of umpteen other boozers along the way. To be fair to him, the room he'd shared with Bessie was now the scene of a crime and off-limits, at least till we'd finished with it, and I doubted he had anywhere else to go. In such circumstances, I could hardly begrudge him if he decided the best course of action was to climb inside a bottle for as long as was practicable.

Gooch lit a cigarette.

'What do we know about Vogel?'

'Not much, sir,' I said. 'The girl who lives on the ground floor said he was from somewhere in Russia. He's been renting here for about six months, but where he was before that is a mystery. It's possible he was fresh off the boat, or he might have been here some time longer. His English is poor.'

'Not that that's much of a problem in Whitechapel,' said Whitelaw.

'This girl,' said Gooch, exhaling a stream of grey smoke, 'the one who told you about Vogel, where is she?'

'I imagine she's gone to work. She's a seamstress – works for a number of the tailors round here.'

'See if you can find her. I want to learn more about our Mr Vogel. Now what else do we know about him?'

'Just what Drummond told us,' I said, 'about him losing his job and setting up in business making canes and shafts for umbrellas, his fascination with Bessie, and her unwillingness to lend him money.'

Gooch tapped his cigarette and a flurry of ash fell to the floor. 'That's two grounds for murder right there. Now what do we have in terms of potential timeline?'

Whitelaw recounted the probable course of events.

'Sometime after eight o'clock, when Tom Drummond leaves for the second time, Vogel comes down the stairs from his room to the first-floor landing. He knocks on Bessie's door with the intention of either threatening her for money or … something worse. She refuses to give him whatever he wants, and in a fit of anger, he attacks her with the hammer. He then locks the door from the inside and flees, out of the window and up the drainpipe to his own room, where he hides the weapon under his bed.'

'You're forgetting one thing, Sergeant,' said Gooch. 'Assuming it was Vogel's hammer, he would have had to have brought it with him, either to simply threaten her with, or because he knew he was going to attack her – which would suggest a degree of premeditation.' He took another pull of his cigarette and exhaled. 'He'll hang for this.'

I ran through the theory in my head.

'I have a question, sir.'

'Yes?'

'The strongbox in which she kept the rent she collected,' I said. 'It was still in her room. That's where we retrieved the key for Vogel's door earlier. There were a few shillings left in it.'

Gooch stared. 'What's your point, Constable?'

'I'm wondering why a man who was desperate enough to murder a woman for money would then leave without bothering to find the strongbox. Maybe his motive wasn't money.'

'Or maybe he panicked,' said Whitelaw.

'It's possible,' I said, 'but if it was premeditated and he'd brought the hammer, why would he panic? And if he had the forethought to lock the door with himself inside and then escape out of the window, wouldn't he have spared a few minutes to search for what he'd come for?'

Gooch folded his arms across his chest. 'Well, there's one way to find out what his motives were,' he said. 'We'll just have to bloody well find him.'

SEVENTEEN

The light was fading by the time Gooch and Whitelaw left Fashion Street. They were headed back to the station, Gooch to supervise the cataloguing of evidence gleaned from the scene and Whitelaw to coordinate the search for Vogel.

As for me, I'd been tasked with speaking to the residents of the house and finding out what else I could about our fugitive. But the Feldmans, who occupied the room beside Bessie's, and the Kravitzes – Rebecca's parents – had added little. Her father, Carl Kravitz, who'd left for work at six and returned at 4 p.m., had only ever passed Vogel a handful of times in the hallway, and his wife seemed to have spent a lot of her time ensuring their daughter had nothing to do with him. Only Mrs Rosen, on the ground floor, appeared willing to talk about Vogel, though what she added, through polyglot sentences in cracked English and Yiddish, quickly degenerated into reminiscences of shtetls and synagogues and life in the Pale of Settlement.

Still, from her I learned that Vogel hailed from Warsaw, then still part of the Russian Empire. At the age of eighteen, to avoid conscription into the tsar's army, he'd fled, smuggled first into Germany, which treated its Jews better than the Russians, but still hardly well, and thence to England.

It seemed the only one who'd spoken regularly to him was Rebecca. Her mother informed me that Rebecca was employed by a tailor on Brick Lane called Shmuel Eckstein. She usually worked a twelve-hour shift and wasn't expected home before seven or eight at the earliest. Today, of course, with everything that had happened, she hadn't left till the afternoon and it was anyone's guess when she'd be back.

After a word with the constable stationed at the front door, I adjusted my collar against the cold and headed out towards Brick Lane. There was a raw, biting chill in the air, an east wind that felt like it blew straight in from the Urals and froze you to the marrow.

The streets rang to the sound of carts on the cobblestones. Beside stalls, men gathered around braziers, their heads bent against the cold, warming their hands while waiting for passing trade.

A lamp shone out between two bare and headless mannequins in the front window of Eckstein's shop. A bell rang as I pushed open the door and entered a room not much warmer than the street outside. Behind a wood-and-glass counter stood a man of about fifty in a thin cardigan, with round, steel-rimmed spectacles and a skullcap on his head. He looked nervous, but so did most of the men in Whitechapel when confronted by an officer in uniform.

'May I help you?' he said, his voice heavily accented.

A row of shelves covered the length of the wall behind him, each further split into a lattice of squares by wooden dividers, so that the whole wall looked like a series of giant pigeonholes, with each square containing a different bolt of cloth.

'Mr Eckstein?' I asked.

'Yes,' he said cautiously.

'I'm looking for Rebecca Kravitz.'

The wariness intensified. I suspected Rebecca hadn't mentioned the reason for her tardiness this morning. A murder, even one she had nothing to do with, tended to spell trouble, especially for people already used to it. Suddenly I regretted barging in. If Eckstein thought Rebecca was somehow in trouble with the police, he might think it safer to simply sack her than take the risk that she might bring down the evil eye of the authorities upon him and his business. But there was little I could do about it now.

'She's not in any trouble,' I clarified. 'I simply need to speak to her.'

He nodded slowly. 'Excuse me, please. You wait here. I fetch her.'

Eckstein headed for a door which I assumed led to the rear of the shop and to stairs down to the basement where his seamstresses probably worked. Silence descended. I walked over to the counter and examined a couple of bolts of grey cloth which had been left out. The material was cheap and coarse, but that's what sold in this part of town.

I heard footsteps on wooden stairs. The door opened and in stepped Eckstein with Rebecca a few paces behind. The girl walked over while the tailor lurked in the doorway.

'How can I help you, Constable?'

Her voice was polite but her expression suggested my presence here was about as welcome as a poke in the eye.

'I need to ask you a few more questions.'

'I am at work. I don't have time to talk now. Besides, I've already told you everything.'

I looked to Eckstein, who seemed little more than a smudge among the shadows. 'Your assistance would be invaluable to us,' I said. 'And I'm sure the Metropolitan Police will be most grateful to your employer for allowing you some time to aid us.'

Eckstein looked confused.

'Maybe you should translate that for him,' I said.

The girl did just that, and soon the old tailor was nodding profusely. He gave me an ingratiating smile.

'Please, go. Talk. Rivkah is good girl.'

'It seems Mr Eckstein is keen for you to help me,' I said. 'Have you got a coat? It's cold outside.'

Fifteen minutes later, we were seated in the bay window of a tea room on Hanbury Street. Rebecca had wanted to speak in the street, but the cold and the promise of a hot cuppa helped change her mind.

The tea was Russian, served sweet and black from a silver-coloured samovar. The waitress poured out two glasses and placed them on the table in front of us, then set the pot down beside a small bowl of jam.

Rebecca watched the steam rise from her cup.

'Tell me about Israel Vogel,' I said.

She looked up, surprise playing on her face. 'Why do you want to know about *him*?'

'Because those are my orders.'

'He moved in about six months ago,' she said with a shrug. 'I think he'd arrived here from Warsaw a while before that.' Her expression changed to one of irritation. 'Why not just ask *him* your questions?'

'He seems to have disappeared,' I said. 'We think he might be responsible for Bessie's death.'

She shook her head. 'That's absurd.'

'Is it? We've been told Vogel was obsessed with Bessie.'

The girl bridled. 'Who told you that?'

'Tom Drummond.'

'Well, there you are,' she said, as though I'd made her argument for her. 'You shouldn't believe anything he tells you.'

'He also said Vogel asked her for money and that she refused him.'

She looked like she was about to say something, then bit her lip. A spark of anger played in her eyes.

'It's true,' she said finally. 'Bessie did lend money to people, either to pay the rent, or to help with business, but she was shrewd about who she lent to. I can understand it if she'd decided not to loan money to Israel. But then, if he needed cash, he wouldn't have gone to her anyway.'

'Why not?' I asked.

'Because he could have simply gone to the Board.'

'The Board?'

'The Board of Guardians of the Jewish Poor,' she said. 'They give loans, free of interest, to Jewish immigrants looking to set up in business. So you see he had no need of Bessie's money.'

'Maybe he'd already tried them?' I said. 'Maybe they turned him down?'

'You could always ask them. Their offices are round the corner.'

I took a sip of tea and made a mental note. When they opened tomorrow, I'd pay a visit to the Board of Guardians of the Jewish Poor and check whether they'd been approached for a loan by Israel Vogel.

'Either way,' I said, 'that still leaves the matter of Vogel's interest in Bessie. Was he keen on her? Did Bessie ever mention his attentions?'

She gave me a sour glance, then clasped her hands tightly together.

'I don't know why you would think that.'

I feigned surprise. 'Really? Weren't you and Bessie close? She never mentioned any untoward advances from Vogel? Her husband seems sure of it.'

'I've already told you, you should take what Tom Drummond says with a large dose of salt. Maybe you should pay closer attention to him.'

'Why?'

'Their marriage was hardly a bed of roses. He spent most of his time drinking and gambling away her money. He'd come home from the pub or the horses and take out his bad luck on her with his fists.'

She had a point. Tom Drummond had a temper and past form. He'd been my first suspect too, only he had an alibi, and *he* hadn't done a runner. And then of course, there was the hammer.

'We think we've found the weapon used to attack Bessie,' I said softly. 'It was under Vogel's bed.'

'No!' she said, shaking her head vigorously. 'That can't be. Israel would never harm Bessie!' A tear ran down her cheek.

'Why?' I asked. 'Why wouldn't he harm her?' And then a thought struck me.

'Is it possible your judgement of him is clouded?'

Her eyes widened. 'You think I'm ... in love with him?'

'Are you?'

'No!'

'Then why?' I asked again, this time with urgency. 'Why wouldn't he harm her? Were he and Bessie ...?'

I didn't finish the sentence. I couldn't bring myself to utter the final word.

She looked up, sensing my unease. 'Were they *lovers*, you mean?' Suddenly she seemed to relish my discomfort. 'You find it distasteful that an Englishwoman should find solace in the arms of a Jew?'

'It's not that,' I stammered, and my denial even had the benefit of being partly true.

She lifted the glass between slender thumb and forefinger and took a sip.

'I remember you,' she said suddenly, almost in accusation. 'It must be almost a year ago now, just after we moved into the house. Didn't *you* used to call round for Bessie? Is that why you find it difficult to accept the idea that Bessie may have liked him?'

I felt my ears burn. I didn't remember ever seeing this girl when I'd called round for Bessie, but that didn't mean she hadn't been there. Tenants came and went and the faces changed and blended into one. It had been a strange time, especially towards the end. I wondered if Mrs Rosen or the Feldmans also remembered me. As for Vogel, I didn't know why I found it so hard to stomach the possibility that Bessie might have been involved with him, but in truth, it didn't matter.

'What I find difficult to accept is the fact that she's been murdered,' I said, 'and the evidence points to her killer being Israel Vogel. So if Bessie truly was your friend, maybe you should offer me some cooperation.'

She pulled a handkerchief from the sleeve of her blouse and dabbed at her cheeks. I felt a rush of guilt. The truth was, this girl was a far better friend to Bessie than I'd ever been and I'd no right to accuse her of being otherwise.

I mumbled an apology, then tried a more conciliatory approach.

'Let's assume you're right, and Vogel is innocent. Who else might have reason to kill Bessie?'

'I don't know,' she said, 'but ...'

'But what?'

'The last few weeks, she seemed different. As though she had some secret but couldn't share it. I asked her if she was in the family way, but she laughed. She said chance would be a fine thing. Then, after she was attacked in the street two nights ago, there was another change. Yesterday she seemed positively terrified. She was too scared to leave the house. She even refused to go into work, which was unlike her. In the past, she'd gone in even when she had the flu and a high temperature. I thought she was in shock.'

'You think the attack on her in Grey Eagle Street was more than just a random assault?'

'I don't know, but I had the impression yesterday that Bessie certainly thought so.'

'Did you see Vogel that night?'

The girl thought back. 'He came in late, about an hour after your sergeant had brought Bessie home. He was soaked to the skin. I remember thinking, what sort of an umbrella maker goes out in such weather without an umbrella?'

'Describe him for me.'

'Medium height. Slim. Dark hair.'

That could have described half the men in Whitechapel ... including the Chinese.

'When you saw him that night did it look like he'd injured his right arm?'

She looked at me in alarm. 'Why do you ask that?'

'Please,' I said. 'It's important.'

Her forehead creased as she tried to recall. 'I ... I can't be sure. You can't think Vogel attacked Bessie in the street? That's ridiculous! It doesn't make any sense. If Vogel had attacked Bessie the other night, she'd have recognised him. And she'd have told me. As I said, she was in fear of her life the next day.' She shook her head. 'No, it couldn't have been him.'

'Either way,' I said, 'it still leaves us with the question of where he is now.'

'If he *has* gone into hiding, you could try the soup kitchen, or the Jewish Temporary Shelter, though he'd be brave to go there.'

'Why?'

'Because it's on Leman Street, down the road from your police station.'

'Has he any friends he might stay with, people who'll put him up?'

She gave a thin smile. 'These are law-abiding people, Constable. And they talk – it's a tight-knit community after all. Nevertheless, they look out for each other. If he's being sheltered by friends, I'd suggest you speak to the elders of the community, the rabbis in the *shuls* or the leaders in the *chevrot*. They might be able to put pressure on people to give him up. If he really is involved though, he's more likely to try his luck with the anarchists or one of the other radical groups. The *chaverim* are always looking for new recruits. If he's gone to them, chances are you'll never find him.'

EIGHTEEN

February 1922

Assam

Le Corbeau's post-mortem report had come back ... or rather it hadn't. Instead it had gone to the district superintendent of police, whoever that was, in a place called Silchar, wherever that was. Still the gist of it had filtered through to the ashram, and during one of my more lucid moments, Brother Shankar had sat me down and given me the summary.

'Philippe's lungs were empty,' he said, his hands steepled in front of his face like an Oxford don as he sat opposite. 'Dr Deakin says he died instantly on hitting that rock. He wouldn't have suffered.'

I nodded back numbly.

Shankar stared at me as though able to read my soul.

'You are troubled by that?'

'No.' I shrugged. 'If that's how he went, then at least it was painless. It's just ...'

'What?'

'I'm wondering just how hard he would have needed to fall onto that rock for it to have killed him outright. I'd have thought the chances of a blow that severe were, I don't know, a thousand to one? Surely the more likely scenario would have been for the blow to knock him out and into the water, leading to death by drowning.'

The monk's expression changed. 'What are you saying?'

'I ...' I hesitated, scratched the back of my skull. Could I even trust this man? If Le Corbeau had been murdered, then how could I be sure Shankar wasn't in on it? After all, I only had his word that the boy had actually gone missing from the ashram in the first place. For all I knew, he might have been murdered here, maybe in this very room, and then dragged out to the stream.

'Sam?'

'I ...'

I tried to get a grip of myself. Told myself to stop being ridiculous. If Shankar *was* involved in whatever had befallen Le Corbeau, why would he have taken me down to see the body? He would only do that if he thought that I, as a policeman, might be able to shed some light on the circumstances. I decided to trust him.

'It sounds ridiculous but maybe Le Corbeau died in a different fashion. Maybe he was hit on the head by someone. Maybe he was killed and then dragged to the river to make it look like an accident?'

The monk looked horrified. 'But why would anyone want to kill him?'

'Did he have any connections to the area?' I asked.

Shankar shook his head. 'He came to us directly from Antwerp. His family there have been contacted. As far as I'm aware, he knew no one here outside the ashram.'

'Maybe a robbery gone wrong?'

'I can't believe that. He was dressed as you are. All the local tribespeople know that none of the initiates or other people under the ashram's care carry money. I can't see how this is anything but a very tragic accident.'

He was right, of course, at least in the sense that there was no rational reason why anyone around Jatinga would want to kill Le Corbeau. But sometimes people were killed for irrational reasons or no reason at all. I'd come across men murdered for simply looking the wrong way at a chap in the pub; for being in the wrong place at the wrong time; for having the wrong religion, the wrong accent or the wrong bloody surname; or because they were born in a year that made them the correct age to be conscripted and sent to wholesale slaughter. It might have been hard for a man like Shankar to fathom, but in my world, people died for irrational reasons all the time. Death was indiscriminate, as random as a lottery. And when your number came up, you'd no option but to shuffle off this mortal coil to whatever, if anything, came next.

I'd left him shortly afterwards, headed back to the dormitory and tried to put Le Corbeau out of my mind. Adler was lying on his bunk, his head buried in a Hebrew book, reading it from back to front.

On seeing me, he closed it, placed it on the cabinet beside him and sat up.

'Wyndham, my friend. Something is troubling you?'

'Le Corbeau,' I said. 'The doctor's report confirms his death as an accident ...'

'But you don't believe it?'

'I've no reason not to ... except a feeling in my gut.'

The Jew pondered, working his jaw in a circular motion while he ruminated.

'Maybe Philippe's passing, the randomness of it, reminds you of your own transience, your helplessness in the face of death.'

'What?'

'Come now, Captain. Is it really so great a stretch? Philippe shared your height, your build, even your hair colour. Could it be that you see yourself in him? And if he, a young man, could be taken in so senseless a fashion, then why not you?'

Something in his words hit home. Not the metaphysical mush about my own mortality, but the real, physical similarity between

Le Corbeau and me. Shankar had said it was rare for a man to leave the monastery as far into the treatment as Le Corbeau was. And Adler had said that men were more prone to run off and try to find a hit of their poison during their first few days here. Could it be that someone had mistaken Le Corbeau for me?

I all but collapsed backwards onto my cot and feared for my sanity. There was something about this place, a malevolence that crackled in the air. Since stepping off the train in Lumding, reality had begun to spin out of control: the nightly hallucinations of the apparition at the station, the memories of Bessie Drummond, and now the death of Le Corbeau. I couldn't help but feel they were all connected in some way, and yet, that was ridiculous.

I felt suddenly cold, chilled to the marrow. I closed my eyes and held the pillow over my face as a new and uncontrollable wave of shivering descended.

NINETEEN

February 1905

East London

There was no doubt about it. Vogel was on the run.

It was 8 a.m. and Gooch, Whitelaw and I were gathered around the chalk board in the cramped, airless room which Gooch had commandeered as his base of operations.

The inspector wiped his spectacles with the corner of his waistcoat.

'So, what do we know?'

'So far, sir,' said Whitelaw, with the air of a man confident of his facts, 'we've two confirmed sightings of Vogel yesterday morning, but none after midday. At around 10 a.m. he met with his old employer, a Mr Herzl. According to Herzl, our man Vogel was looking to supply him with finished canes. Nothing was agreed, but Herzl told him to come back with a sample. Then, about an hour later, he was seen by the assistant at an ironmonger's, where he purchased a shilling's worth of nitric acid.'

'How much is that?'

'A few ounces,' said the sergeant. 'The assistant says Vogel brought his own bottle, which he filled.'

'What did he want with such a small amount of acid?' asked Gooch. 'It's not enough to dispose of any evidence.'

'It's used in the varnishing process,' said Whitelaw, 'for the canes and umbrella stalks he was working on.'

'Doesn't that seem odd?' I asked. 'He kills a woman at around 9 a.m., and an hour later he's negotiating a sale and buying nitric acid for his business?'

Whitelaw puffed out his cheeks. 'Maybe he didn't expect Bessie's body to be discovered as quickly as it was. Maybe he was hoping to use the ironmonger as an alibi?'

That made no sense to me.

'What about his room?' I said. 'He left his clothes and his suitcase and legged it. Why would he plan a meticulous alibi, but then flee with only the clothes on his back?'

'Maybe,' said Whitelaw, 'he went to the ironmonger's to establish his alibi but on seeing the crowd outside the door on his return, he panicked and made a run for it?'

Gooch wasn't interested in our theories. 'Did you enquire about Vogel's demeanour?' he asked the sergeant. 'Did he seem agitated at all?'

'Not so the assistant could tell.'

From his suit pocket, Gooch took out a box of matches and a packet of Navy Cut, extracted a cigarette and stuck it in the corner of his mouth. 'There's always another possibility,' he said, striking a match. He held the flame close. 'Our man Vogel may have had a pang of remorse. Maybe he bought the acid to kill himself?'

Whitelaw blinked. 'You think he might already be lying dead somewhere?'

'It's possible,' the inspector replied, 'though we can't put any store by it. Not yet. For now, we need to institute a manhunt: find out who his friends are, check out the dosshouses.' He gestured to Whitelaw with a nod of the head. 'I want you to take charge of that. He may also try to do a runner if he's able. We need to make sure he doesn't leave town. His description needs to be circulated and watch put on the stations and the ports. I'll get on to Scotland Yard about that.'

'Where's he likely to head?' asked Whitelaw. 'I doubt he's ever set foot anywhere outside the East End.'

'There are immigrant Jews in Manchester and Birmingham,' said Gooch. 'He may have friends there, or he may try and pass himself off as a new arrival, straight off the boat. As for the ports, he might try his luck and find passage on a boat bound for New York.' He blew a stream of cigarette smoke skyward. 'Seems all the Jews want to go to America.

'As for you, Wyndham, I want you to find out what you can about his financial circumstances. Had he borrowed money from anyone else? Was he behind on his rent? Then I want you to go and speak to Bessie Drummond's employer. See what he knows of the fate of his housekeeper. More importantly, find out what you can about his visit to the house that morning. Find out what she did for him. Did she collect the rent at other properties or just number 42 Fashion Street?'

He pointed to the door.

'Well? What are you waiting for? Make haste, gentlemen. We've a killer to find.'

The Board of Guardians of the Jewish Poor occupied a shabby brick building on Middlesex Street. Outside, a few bearded men stood leaning against the wall, guillotining their conversation as I walked past.

I asked the old man at the front desk the way to the loans office and was directed to an ill-lit stairwell and advised to make my way to the second floor. No other directions were needed, as a queue of bodies snaked from the stairs and along a corridor towards the light of an open door. Once more the general chatter faltered and died as I walked past.

A knot of men at the entrance to the loans office parted to let me through. Beyond was a room overflowing with paperwork, in the midst of which sat three large desks, one to either side of the door and the third placed between it and the window so that the three clerks who sat behind them all looked inwards at whoever entered.

Around them, every available inch of wall was taken up by shelves containing a mountain of brown and grey files, some bulging with papers, others sheet-thin, and each sealed with a knot of brown string. The clerks on either side wore the look of harassed bank tellers. Each was dressed in striped shirt, tie, waistcoat, spectacles and skullcap. The younger looked to be pushing seventy, and the elder, like he should be pushing up the daisies. On their desks were more files and loose papers, and facing each, a chair occupied by men who, I assumed, were there to seek financial assistance, but from their demeanour seemed more like supplicants at the court of a king than applicants for a loan.

It was the third clerk, the one at the desk directly in front, who creaked slowly up from his chair and addressed me.

'Can I help you, Constable?' His English was heavily accented, like Eckstein's and a thin halo of grey hair framed a bald dome of a head, topped once more by a skullcap. I guessed he was the senior man in the room. There was no applicant before him and, instead of files, his desk was dominated by a large, gilt-edged ledger, open to a column-filled page somewhere near the middle. From his tired expression and frayed attire, though, it was clear that he was merely the first among equals, still just a functionary rather than plenipotentiary.

'I need some information on a man who may have taken a loan from you.'

The man scratched his neck. 'We don't normally give out details of our borrowers. You'd need to speak to Mr Sebag.'

'Where can I find him?'

He smiled. 'This way please.'

I followed him out and back down the corridor. He stopped outside a door, knocked, then opened it a crack and stuck his head round.

'Mr Sebag? There's a constable here to see you.'

There was a muffled response, before the old man opened the door and bade me enter. The room was identical in dimensions to the one we'd just left, except this one had a sole desk and a sole occupant, a grey-haired chap in a dark suit with a salt-and-pepper beard and half-moon spectacles. Unlike the others, he wore no skullcap. He stood up and directed me to a chair.

'How can I be of assistance, Constable?' he said, dismissing the old man with a nod.

The door closed behind me and Sebag returned to his seat, removed his spectacles and placed them on top of a sheaf of papers on his desk.

'Constable Wyndham,' I said, 'from Leman Street station. I'm here in connection with a murder inquiry.'

His face took on that look of horror peculiar to bankers whenever they encounter something that may be bad for business.

'Murder?'

'Of a local woman. We suspect a man called Israel Vogel may be responsible.'

Sebag stroked his beard. 'I don't believe there's anyone by that name employed here.'

'You misunderstand, sir,' I said. 'We believe that Vogel arrived in the country from Russia about six months ago and took up lodgings in Fashion Street. He was initially employed by a man named Herzl, making canes and umbrellas, but recently he'd gone into business for himself.'

'And you think he might have taken a loan from us?'

'Precisely.'

'That would make sense.' He picked up his spectacles and placed them on his face. 'We have a policy whereby we only provide loans to those who have been here for six months or more. We can certainly check our records.'

He walked over to the door and opened it.

'Mr Shofer –' he raised his voice so that it would be heard down the corridor – 'can you come back in, please?'

He returned to his desk and sat down.

'Would you care for some tea?'

The door opened just as I politely declined, and the old clerk entered.

'Ah, Mr Shofer, bring me the new loans ledger for ...' He turned to me. 'When did you say he started his business?'

'Probably in the last month.'

Sebag turned back to the clerk. 'The ledgers for the last two months please, Mr Shofer.'

The old man nodded and left the room.

'This may take a few minutes,' he said apologetically, then continued, almost as if to avert an uncomfortable silence. 'The unfortunate lady, the victim,' he said. 'Was she Jewish?'

'No,' I said. 'English.'

'You mean she was a Christian,' he corrected.

'Pardon me?'

'It's possible to be both Jewish and English, Constable. I am myself.'

'Of course,' I said hastily. 'I meant no ... It's just that in this part of town, most Jews are foreigners.'

'That much is true,' he said with a smile, 'and the irony is, a lot of *them* would also question whether it's possible to be both Jewish and English.'

He sensed my confusion.

'Our Eastern brothers,' he explained, 'can be quite fervent in their maintenance of religious practices. If you asked half of the men in the queue outside, they'd probably tell you with disdain just how lax we British Jews have become in terms of observing our religion. It doesn't stop them taking our funds though.'

There was a knock at the door. The clerk, Shofer, entered carrying a large black ledger and deposited it on Sebag's desk with a solid thump, then left.

'The name was Vogel, you say?'

'That's right. Israel Vogel.'

Sebag adjusted his spectacles before opening the ledger and flicking through a number of pages. His brow furrowed. 'Vogel ... Vogel ... Vogel ...' He turned the page. 'Ah, here we are: Vogel, Israel.' He smiled, his face flush with the joy of administrative success. 'You're quite right, he did take out a loan. Just over three weeks ago.'

'Can you tell me how much?'

'Three pounds ... not in cash but in kind.'

'In kind?'

'That's right. We only lend cash as a last resort. We prefer to lend in assets which we can reclaim if the repayments aren't met. A tailor might come to us and we might purchase for him a sewing machine, that sort of thing. In Vogel's case, we purchased a series of wood-working tools, including a vice, a saw, a wooden mallet and a set of chisels.'

'What about a hammer?'

Sebag scanned the notes on the page. 'Not according to the inventory.'

That didn't mean the hammer wasn't Vogel's. He may have purchased it separately.

'What about repayments on the loan?' I asked.

'He was to repay us out of his income at the rate of one shilling and sixpence per week.'

'And is he keeping up with his repayments?'

Sebag pored over the ledger once more, running a finger over a column of figures.

'He has so far. His last repayment was on Thursday.'

'What happens if he's late?'

Sebag rubbed his chin. 'That would depend on the circumstances. If he informed us of the reasons, we could try and work out a revised repayment schedule. If he simply absconded, we'd take things up with whoever has agreed to stand as his character witness when the loan was granted. It's not a guarantor per se, generally just a reputable member of the community who can vouch for the man.'

'And who was that in Vogel's case?'

Sebag consulted the ledger, then lifted a hand to his mouth in consternation. 'I say, that *is* odd.'

'What?'

'It seems that in Vogel's case, the character witness was a woman, and a Gentile at that. A Mrs Elizabeth Drummond.'

TWENTY

February 1922

Assam

'How do you feel?'

Brother Shankar sat across the wooden table from me and stirred his porridge. It was a simple enough question, but the answer was far from straightforward.

It had been six days since the discovery of Le Corbeau's corpse, four days since the doctor's finding of death by misadventure, and over a week since the course of my cure had begun. Each night Devraha Swami had poured out the potion and each night I'd drunk it, followed by a bucket-full of water and ended by retching my guts out. Each night I saw a little improvement, slept a little better, had fewer hallucinations of Bessie Drummond, of Israel Vogel, of the man at Lumding station, and of Philippe Le Corbeau.

I cradled a cup of warm Assamese tea between my hands.

'Not too bad.'

'Good,' said the monk. 'And last night? Did you get any sleep?'

'More than expected.' I tried to mask the surprise in my voice. Over the last few years, sleep, *true sleep* – induced without the aid of opiates or alcohol – had become but a distant memory, consigned as much to history as the cavalry charge or the Kaiser. But I *had* slept last night: a few hours, blissful and blessedly nightmare-free. Every now and then, though, generally when I was at a loose end, my body would spasm and my thoughts would turn to the O. The Devil on my shoulder would tell me I wanted a pipe ... I *needed* a pipe. I'd fought back the urges of course, and in the ashram those urges were manageable. I worried though, that out there, in the real world, back in Calcutta where I could find a pipe as easily as I could a pint of milk, I might not be strong enough to resist temptation.

'Sounds like you're over the worst of it.' He smiled. 'The last of the poison is out of your system. It should be downhill from here. We can probably stop your evening treatment.'

'You mean no more vomiting?'

The monk swallowed a spoonful of porridge. 'Unless you wish to continue?'

'No, you're all right.'

'Good,' he said. 'I think it's worked its magic, don't you?'

I fought the urge to cheer. I'd experienced too many false dawns, and like a dog who's learned that a smile is too often followed by a boot to the ribs, I wasn't about to believe that I was free of the O just yet.

I took a sip of tea and had the sensation of tasting it, almost for the first time, as though my senses were returning from exile. Suddenly I thought of Surrender-not.

'There's only one tea worth drinking, and that's Darjeeling.'

When it came to matters of tea, he, like all Bengalis, was an insufferable snob. It was true that the hills of Darjeeling fell in Bengal, but that was more the fortuitous result of lines drawn on a map by colonial cartographers than any skill on the part of the plains-dwelling Bengalis. Still, the idea that the first cup of tea that I should actually be able to taste in India would be from Assam and not Darjeeling would have horrified the fellow, and I looked forward to seeing the look on his face when I got round to telling him.

'So what now?' I asked.

'Now,' said Brother Shankar, 'you rest and regain your strength.'

That sounded good in theory, and it was true that I'd lost weight since arriving here – a vegetarian diet and a regime of vomiting will do that to a man – but I'd never been the type to rest. Indeed if you discounted my honeymoon and time spent in hospital, I hadn't had a proper holiday since 1912.

The monk read my expression.

'I'm afraid I must insist. We need to make sure you really are free of the drug ... and that you're strong enough to resist its influence. Remember, this is your one and only opportunity here. The swami-ji doesn't believe in second chances.'

The problem was the swami-ji didn't believe in alcohol either, and given I had no cigarettes, other than a few cheroots I'd managed to barter from one of the native inmates, I wasn't sure that I could live much longer without any of the three, nor that there would be much point to life without them.

'How long?' I asked. 'I don't mean to sound ungrateful, but I'm keen to get back to civilisation ... or Calcutta at least. I wouldn't be surprised if half the native officers in Lal Bazar had resigned and joined the Congress Party since I left. At the rate we've been losing men, it won't be long till the commissioner himself is forced to don a pair of gloves and turn out for traffic duty.'

The monk looked up at me.

'Of course, you won't have heard.'

'Heard what?'

'Gandhi's called off the general strike.'

I almost fell off my chair.

'Really?'

That little man had coordinated a year-long war of attrition against the authorities, turning the country on its head and bringing the government, if not to its knees, then at least to the negotiating table. And now, in the time I'd been cloistered away, vomiting up my guts, he'd decided to stop it all. It beggared belief.

'Why?'

Shankar's face darkened. 'There was an incident ... just over a week ago. Some place called Chauri Chaura in the United Provinces. A demonstration turned ugly and a mob attacked a police station. Burned it to the ground. The papers say something like twenty-five officers perished. The Mahatma's called a halt to the whole non-cooperation campaign and started a fast in penance for what he sees as his role in fostering the violence.'

I still couldn't believe it. After a year of mass marches, mass resignations and mass arrests, after asking his followers to endure the greatest hardships, that he would simply turn off a national campaign was hard to take in.

'Just like that? He's called off the whole thing because of an incident in some godforsaken village in UP?'

The monk remained silent.

'How d'you know all this anyway?'

'We might be far from civilisation, Captain, but the papers still reach Jatinga. It's been about the only story for the past week. The authorities have made sure of that.'

I watched as a small black beetle flew over and landed on the rim of Shankar's bowl. For a moment it teetered on the edge, poised precariously between life and freedom and a fall to its death. Its antennae fluttered and then it toppled in.

Shankar put down his spoon and gently plucked the insect out. He placed it on the bench and delicately wiped the detritus from its shell.

'So you see, Captain, I doubt your return to Calcutta is quite as urgent as you'd expected. Just as well really, because recovery requires patience. It's not simply a case of overcoming your physical addiction. The mental scars need time to heal too.'

The beetle scuttled off towards the edge of the bench, gave a ponderous shake of its wing casings, then fluttered off in that improbable manner that some flying creatures have.

'And what am I supposed to do during this period of *rehabilitation*?' I asked.

'Anything,' said the monk. 'You know the ashram routine by now. You could help out in the fields or the kitchens, or simply read. Whatever whets your whistle.'

The expression was unfortunate. I hadn't had a proper drink since the bar at Duncan's Hotel in Santahar. Fond memories.

'I've never really had the time for books,' I said.

'Well, you do now,' he replied. 'And consider it a blessing. Reading broadens the mind.'

'So does opium,' I said. 'Look where that got me.'

Shankar smiled. 'It brought you here, Captain. I doubt that happened by chance.'

'You think I'm here as part of some great celestial plan?'

'Who knows what the gods have in store?'

I shook my head. I had enough trouble believing that I was part of a Christian god's plan, let alone one concocted by Hindu deities. Granted, our chap's reputation for competence had taken a knock recently, what with the unpleasantness of the Great War and everything, but at least there was only one of Him. That ought at least to mean a streamlined decision-making process. The Hindu gods by contrast were legion, capricious and often in conflict. If they had a plan for me, it was probably the result of a dozen committee meetings where deals were struck and compromises made, till the outcome was something none had envisaged and no one was happy with. I was about to mention that to Brother Shankar, when it struck me that, given the way my life was turning out, maybe that's exactly what had happened. And all of a sudden I was in even more of a hurry to leave.

'There's nothing to stop me walking out the front door though, is there?'

Shankar sighed. 'No. You're free to go whenever you want. But I've a better idea if you'd care to hear it.'

I looked up at the smile on his face, the smile that suggested a deep, unfathomable certainty that a mere copper like me would never know.

'I'd like you to go and stay for a few days with a friend of mine, down in Jatinga.'

In the distance, I caught a glimpse of Mrs Carter crossing the courtyard. She looked over and beamed a smile. And suddenly I was filled with the glow of irrational optimism. He surely couldn't mean ...

'In fact you've already been introduced.'

Heavenly expectation welled up within me, my spirits took flight.

'It's that chap Charles Preston.'

And with that that they crashed back down to earth.

'You remember? You met him the morning we found poor Philippe's body.'

I nodded, then took out a consolatory cheroot and tapped it against the table.

'May I?'

Shankar had no objections. Indeed I felt he sensed my disappointment.

'Think of it as a halfway house. You get out of the ashram, but you're still close enough for me to keep an eye on you.'

'And Preston's your spy, is he?' I said, lighting the cigarette.

'He's helped out with others in your position in the past, if that's what you mean.'

I sucked in a chest-full of smoke, then exhaled.

'He seemed a rather nervous sort when we met him by the stream. You're sure I won't scare him?'

Shankar raised an eyebrow. 'He'd just found a dead body, Captain. I should think most men would be rather unnerved by that.'

I guessed he was right. For me though, the sight of Le Corbeau's corpse had hardly caused my pulse to flicker. It was just the latest addition to a roll call of death that went back to 1905. I wondered what that said about me.

'Fair enough,' I said.

'So you'll do it?'

'As long as it's all right with Mr Preston.'

'I'm sure he'll be fine with it. You might find him a rather eccentric egg, but I don't think you'll scare him.'

'I suppose not,' I said, 'as long as no more dead bodies turn up.'

TWENTY-ONE

February 1905

East London

I'd thanked Sebag and traipsed back down to the street in a daze. Rebecca, it seemed, had been correct. Vogel and Bessie were more than just tenant and rent collector. Their relationship was deep enough that she was willing to stand as a character reference for him. I wondered if her husband knew.

Once again, the issue of Vogel's motive was thrown into question. Far from asking Bessie for money and being refused, he'd actually requested her help in obtaining a loan from the Guardians and she'd agreed.

And he was up to date with his repayments.

And while Bessie's cash box had been found close to empty, there were, in light of what Sebag had told me, other more likely explanations for what had happened to the cash: Tom Drummond may have forced Bessie to part with the money so that he could go drinking with his mate, Finlay, or maybe the landlord, Jeremiah Caine, had taken the cash when he'd visited Bessie earlier that morning. Whatever had happened to it, I doubted Vogel had taken it. Still, that didn't mean he was innocent. Maybe Tom Drummond was right. Maybe Vogel had developed an unhealthy fascination with Bessie. I could vouch for how easily that could happen. Maybe he'd come clean and confessed his feelings, maybe they'd argued, and in a fit of rage, he'd attacked her.

But that too presented difficulties.

Even in the East End of London, people rarely came to profess undying love to a sweetheart armed with a hammer. Maybe the weapon had already been there? Maybe it was Drummond's and Vogel had just picked it up and used it in the heat of the moment? Of course Tom Drummond claimed he'd never seen it before, but his word was hardly gospel.

Even if it was Drummond's hammer, it would require Vogel to have argued with Bessie, find the hammer, hit Bessie, lock her door from the inside, scale the drainpipe back to his room, hide the bloodied weapon (without cleaning it) under his bed and then, cold as ice, go out to buy nitric acid as an alibi but take fright on the way back and make a run for it.

It just sounded wrong. For one thing, a man with the intelligence to plan his alibi and to lock Bessie's door from the inside would almost certainly have come up with a better scheme for disposing of the murder weapon than hiding it under his own bed. Indeed, simply leaving it in Bessie's room would have been a better option.

But if not Vogel, then who? The only other obvious candidate, Tom Drummond, had an alibi in his mate, Finlay, and claimed his wife was alive when the two men left the house. There was Jeremiah Caine, who'd been at the house that morning at around half past seven, but Drummond's claim to have seen his wife alive at half past eight effectively put Caine in the clear.

Then there was the attack on Bessie in Grey Eagle Street two nights earlier, and the two men struggling with each other. Did they have something to do with her death? Why were they grappling with each other? Had there been a disagreement? A falling-out between thieves? Had Vogel been one of them? Rebecca had said he'd come home that night soaking wet.

None of it made sense, at least not to me. Instead of pondering it further, I decided to get on with the task which Gooch had assigned me: that of questioning Bessie's employer about her demise.

Jeremiah Caine lived on the far side of Bishopsgate in a handsome town house off Finsbury Circus. It was less than a mile from Brick Lane, but in terms of the character and quality of its residents, it might as well have been on another continent. Centred on the tree-lined oval park that gave the area its name, Finsbury Circus had once been the preserve of well-heeled merchants and respectable gentlemen, and while Jeremiah Caine was certainly well heeled, the view as to his respectability depended on who you asked. To many in the East End, he was something of a hero, a Whitechapel lad who'd pulled himself up by his proverbials, an unashamed man of the people who wore his humble roots like a badge of honour. To the good gentlemen of the City of London, however, for whom the tie around your neck mattered more than the money in your bank account, Caine would always be an outsider, the wrong sort of chap from the wrong part of town.

Caine had moved to Finsbury Circus just as the real gentlemen had begun to move out: to the west, where the streets were wider and the air was cleaner. Where others had left, Caine had stayed, buying their properties and subdividing them into spaces for solicitors, accountants and shipping agents.

The front door was opened by a maid who looked like she should still have been at school, her uniform starched, pristine and half a size too large. She seemed surprised to see a constable standing on the step.

'Is Mr Caine at home?' I asked.

'Yes, sir.'

'Please tell him that Constable Wyndham from the Leman Street station would request a few minutes of his time.'

The maid ushered me into the hallway where I removed my helmet, then followed her along the chequerboard floor to the drawing room.

'If you'll kindly wait, sir. I'll let Mr Caine know.'

The room was large, bigger than that occupied by whole families across the way in Whitechapel. Tastefully decorated though, with a chesterfield sofa and two wingback chairs situated around the grate of an empty fireplace. Above the mantelpiece hung an oil painting of a clipper making its way through what looked like a force nine gale. Violent brushstrokes of white-topped waves crashed against its hull under a blackening sky. As drawing-room artwork went, it seemed a curious choice, but the door opened before I'd a chance to consider it further and in walked Jeremiah Caine.

He was dressed in the best Mayfair had to offer: Jermyn Street poplin and Savile Row chalk-stripe, all three pieces of which, despite their exquisite tailoring, sat uncomfortably on a body that had beaten its way up from the streets. His face too gave lie to the stitching: the thickened nose, the coarse brow, and the close-cropped hair of a hard man used to hard times. And then there were the two scars on his left cheek – the marks of battles long past – badges of honour back in the East End, but which here, in more rarefied circles, were merely indelible reminders of a past that was impossible to escape.

He crossed the room briskly. 'You wanted to see me, Constable?'

'Yes, sir. It's about your housekeeper, Mrs Elizabeth Drummond.'

'Bessie? Is she all right?'

'I'm afraid she's dead, sir.'

Caine sat down on the arm of the chesterfield and steadied himself.

'Dead?'

'Murdered. Beaten to death in her lodgings in Fashion Street.'

'When?' he asked, staring at me.

'Yesterday. We believe sometime around 9 a.m. I understand you were at the house earlier that morning?'

'That's ... that's correct.'

'May I ask what you were doing there?'

'I went to see that she was all right. She'd been off work the previous day.'

'You make a habit of checking in on your employees?'

The muscles in his face seemed to tense.

'I heard she'd been attacked. I was in the vicinity and I thought I'd make sure she was all right.'

'And was she?'

'She was making a recovery. Told me she'd be in today.'

'Did she happen to say anything about the attack?'

Caine shrugged. 'Not that I recall.'

'You didn't happen to pick up the weekly rent money while you were there, did you?'

Caine clenched a fist. 'I did. It made sense to, seeing as I was there. Have you any idea who would do such a thing?'

'We're pursuing certain avenues of investigation, sir,' I said. 'You'll appreciate I can't say more at present.'

Caine stared at the floor and shook his head. 'Well, it's good of you to inform me, Constable.' He rose once more. 'Please pass on my condolences to her husband.' He placed a hand on my shoulder, readying to shepherd me to the door.

Something inside me bridled. Bessie had worked for him for as long as I'd known her, and yet Caine could offer no more than empty words and a minute of his time. Maybe it was just my own guilt talking, but Bessie deserved better.

'If I may, sir,' I said, turning to him, 'the murder took place at one of your properties. I've a few questions, some matters you may be able to help clear up for us.'

His expression changed. 'I'm rather pressed for time, Constable. Maybe we could schedule something for tomorrow, maybe down at your station? Leman Street, is it? I've some friends there.'

Green as I was, I understood the implicit threat. I knew that quite a few of the officers in the East End were in the pockets of powerful men. Caine at least had the veneer of a respectable citizen. Many others, like the Spiller brothers, were criminals, plain and simple. The question that struck me was *why?* Why bother issuing even a veiled threat against a first-year constable such as me? All I wanted was to ask him a few questions. Maybe he was just one of those men who feel the constant need to impress the weight of their own supremacy on others. Or maybe there was something more. Either way, I didn't see any benefit in needling him.

'That's most obliging of you, sir,' I said. 'Rather than wasting your time down at the station, however, I could come back at a time more convenient? I have very few questions.'

My tone, I hoped, was conciliatory rather than self-abasing. Either way, it had an effect. Caine was magnanimous.

'Well, if it's only a few, I suppose I can spare you five minutes.'

I acknowledged his generosity. 'Very good of you, sir. Can you tell me how Mrs Drummond first came into your employment?'

Caine smiled. 'She approached me in the street one day. Bold as brass, she came over and told me that she was a tenant in one of my buildings and that Doyle, my man who collects my rents, wasn't doing a particularly good job. She suggested that I let her collect the rents for her building, that she knew all the tenants personally and would make sure no one fell behind. Once a week she'd pass the money on to Doyle. She did a good job, too. So much so that after six months she asked to take care of more of my properties. I said no, of course. Her own building was one thing, but there was no way I'd let a woman wander the streets collecting my money. Besides, what was I supposed to do with Doyle? It just so happened, though, that we had need of a new housekeeper, and I suggested to my wife that Bessie might be a suitable candidate.'

'Your wife?' I said.

His expression became sombre. 'My late wife, Helena. She passed away some weeks ago.'

I scanned the room. In here, at least, there seemed no trace of the deceased spouse. Not a portrait nor a photograph. Not even a memento on the mantelpiece.

'My condolences, sir,' I said. 'I'll not detain you much longer. Other than the rent collection at 42 Fashion Street and her house-keeping duties, did Bessie carry out any other work for you?'

Caine shook his head. 'No, that was all.'

'And did her behaviour over the last few weeks seem at all odd to you?'

'You'll forgive me, Constable, but I'm not in the habit of notic-ing the emotional state of my domestic staff, especially in the weeks after the passing of my own wife.'

'Of course not,' I said. 'My apologies. Do you know of any rea-son why anyone would want to murder Bessie?'

'Just because I employed her doesn't mean I knew the first thing about her personal affairs. If I were a betting man though, I'd wager it was one of those heathens who killed her.'

'You mean a Jew? What makes you think that?'

'Come now, Constable. Who else could it be? You say she was killed in her lodgings, and if it was her husband, you'd have arrested him by now. Everyone else in that house is a foreigner.'

'There's always the possibility that someone from outside num-ber 42 is responsible,' I said.

Caine looked at me incredulously. 'You think some stranger just walked in off the street, went up to her room and killed her, then sauntered back out again without anyone noticing? Not very likely, is it?'

I said nothing.

'Now if you don't mind, I'm afraid I really must insist ...'

'Of course, sir,' I said. 'If I may just ask one final question? Your man Doyle.'

'What about him?'

'Why didn't you send him to pick up the rent from Bessie? Why did you go yourself?'

Caine hesitated, then smiled. 'As I told you, I had business in the area. It made sense to pop in, check on Bessie and collect the rent. I just decided to kill two birds with one stone.'

'And what was this business you had up there?'

His expression hardened. 'It would take a while to explain, Constable, and as I said, I'm in a hurry. Now if you don't mind ...'

'Not at all,' I said. 'I'll see myself out.'

I closed the black door behind me, descended the steps to the street and paused. The conversation with Caine had unnerved me. The man was right. Bessie's attacker couldn't just have wandered into number 42, committed murder and walked out again. There were too many people, in the house and in the street outside, to make that likely. Therefore it had to be someone living there, or at least familiar with it. It was safe to rule out most of the residents: the Feldmans in the room next door and Mrs Rosen downstairs were too frail to have attacked a healthy young woman like Bessie. As for Rebecca's family, Mr Kravitz had a cast-iron alibi in that he was at work, and neither Rebecca nor her mother were serious suspects. That left Vogel, Tom Drummond and his mate, Archibald Finlay, and Caine himself, as the only other men who'd been in the house that morning. Drummond's testimony, of seeing Bessie alive when he returned with Finlay, effectively exonerated Caine, and Drummond and Finlay had been exonerated by the fact of Bessie's door having been locked from the inside, meaning the only possible exit route was out through the window and up the drainpipe to

Vogel's room. Thus, by a process of elimination, we'd arrived at Vogel as the prime suspect.

Behind me, Caine's door opened once more, and out stepped the young maid who'd shown me in. She was wrapped in a thin black shawl that covered her shoulders, and in her hand she carried an empty canvas bag. Seeing me at the bottom of the stairs, she stopped in surprise, then smiled.

'You didn't 'alf give me a fright, sir,' she said.

'I'm sorry,' I said. 'I didn't mean to startle you.'

She descended the stairs and made to pass me. From the bag, I surmised that she was off to run an errand of some sort. A thought occurred to me.

'Where are you off to, miss?'

'Moorgate,' she said, 'to the grocer's. It was Bessie's job to stock up, but ...' her face reddened, 'well, you know the rest.'

'I'm going that way,' I lied. 'Do you mind if I walk with you? I've a few questions about Bessie.'

'Course not,' she said, as I fell into step beside her. 'Be nice to 'ave a bit of company.'

'What's your name, miss?' I asked as we turned towards the gardens of Finsbury Circus.

'Lily. Lily Adams.'

'Did you know Bessie well, Lily?'

'Well enough,' she said, her eyes straight ahead, 'which is to say, I've known her since I started workin' for the Caineses, just before Easter last year.'

'Were you friends?'

The maid stifled a laugh. 'You wouldn't ask that question if you knew her. I know it ain't right to speak ill of the dead an' all, but Bessie weren't no friend a' mine. I doubt she 'ad that many friends. She was the 'ousekeeper an' I was the maid an' she never let me forget it, always on at me: *Lily, do this, Lily, fetch that*, like I was a skivvy.'

We waited for a cart to pass before crossing into the park. The stones of the path crunched under our feet.

'Did she get on with Mr Caine?'

There was a sharp intake of breath. 'I wouldn't know anythin' about that. In the 'ouse she only really took orders from Mrs Caine.'

There was something in the tone of her answer, the sudden stiffening of her body, that made me feel she was holding back.

'Of course,' she continued, 'that was until the mistress died.'

'And how did Bessie take the news of Mrs Caine's death?'

The girl stopped and faced me. 'Now that *was* odd. At first, like the rest of us, she just couldn't believe it. We'd seen Mrs Caine the day before an' she looked fine. Then the next morning she's dead, jus' like that, passed away in her sleep. She was only thirty-five. Well, you don't expect it of someone that age. Certainly not a lady. But while me an' Ada, that's the cook, got on with things, Bessie just wouldn't leave it. Started whisperin' that the mistress had been done in – said she must 'ave been poisoned or some such. Course Ada told her it was nonsense, that the mistress never ate anythin' that day what didn't come from Ada's kitchen.'

'What about asphyxiation?' I said.

She looked at me. 'You mean gas?'

'That's right.'

She shook her head. 'There weren't no gas in the room. The master had all the lights changed to electric years ago. Anyway,' she continued, 'the doctor said it was natural causes. For a week or so, that seemed enough for Bessie, and me an' Ada thought that was an end to it. Then, just last week, she started up again, tellin' Ada, who told me, that she was sure the mistress was done in.'

'Did she say who she thought had done her in?'

'Not in so many words, but it was obvious. Ada said they'd be talkin' about it in the scullery and Bessie'd look up at the ceilin' and lower her voice.'

'Why would she think such a thing?'

'I don't like to say. Some folks is just spiteful, ain't they? All I know is, the night she died, the master had his dinner and retired to bed. I don't think he never even went near Mrs Caine's room. An' the next mornin', I was the one what woke him with the news.'

'Was it you who found Mrs Caine's body?'

'Not really,' she said. 'That was Bessie. I'd gone in earlier, as I always did, to light the fire in the grate, but I just thought the mistress was asleep. I didn't realise she'd ... passed on.'

The wind came up and Lily tucked a strand of hair behind her ear.

'What happened after Bessie found the body?'

'Well, she came down the stairs an', steady as you like, told me to go wake the master and bring him to Mrs Caine's bedroom. The two of them, Bessie and the master, that is, then went in and closed the door.'

'You didn't go in too?'

'Bessie thought it best for me to wait outside. Said she didn't want me upset, and that was good of her, cos I'd have fair screamed the house down. Anyway, Mr Caine sent Bessie to fetch his doctor – Parsons I think his name is – who arrived within the hour. I don't know what happened after that. Bessie sent me home.'

'Why'd she do that?'

Lily shrugged. 'I 'spect she wanted to spare me the ordeal of seeing the mistress carted out.'

We were by now approaching Moorgate.

'This is me,' said the maid, pointing to a grocer's across the road.

'Thank you, Lily,' I said. 'You've been very helpful.'

She turned to me and beamed a smile. 'It's no trouble, Constable. And if you've any more questions, you know where to find me.'

TWENTY-TWO

I saw them before they saw me. Fifty yards up the road, a gaggle of men loitering outside the entrance to Leman Street station, their suits, fancy for Whitechapel but still cheap, marking them as outsiders, and their general air of disdain identifying them as gentlemen of the press.

The officers of H Division had had a rancorous relationship with the men of the Fourth Estate ever since the days of Jack the Ripper. While a certain deference was shown to our colleagues in the West End, the hacks who covered the East were more than happy to throw us under the omnibus if it meant a scoop or a titbit for whatever rag they were writing for.

The loathing that most of the coppers felt for them was tempered only by the fact that many of those rags also provided us with a good source of supplementary income for tip-offs. People likened the press to a pack of wolves, but that was unfair to wolves. They at least had a fealty to the others in the pack. Whereas when it came to journalists, it was every hack for himself.

The first to spot me was a short chap in brown pinstripe and homburg, leaning against a lamp post with a smoke hanging from his lower lip. While the others focused on the station doors, this one was looking out into the street. He slowly removed his cigarette, flicked it to the pavement and straightened. His face was lean, grey and in need of a shave. Looking towards his colleagues, and satisfied that none had yet seen me, he began walking in my direction, slowly at first, then faster as he approached.

'You wouldn't happen to be Constable Wyndham, would you?' he said, placing a hand on my arm.

The look on my face must have been answer enough, as a moment later he thrust a business card into my hand.

'Harmsworth,' he said, steering me into a side street and away from the police station, 'Albert Harmsworth. *Illustrated Gazette.*'

'How'd you know my name?' I asked.

'One of your colleagues was good enough to tell me. Tall, strapping young chap is what he said, and let me say, you fit the description.'

'What can I do for you, Mr Harmsworth?'

Harmsworth scratched his ear. 'It's more a question of what we might do for each other.' He looked round, scanning the vicinity. 'Let's not discuss it now, though. What time do you come off duty?'

'Seven o'clock.'

'Good. D'you know the Turk's Head? Down Wapping way?'

'I know it.'

The pub was a dive down by the river, a fair walk from Whitechapel and far enough to be fairly certain of not bumping into anyone familiar.

'How about we meet for a drink at eight?'

I agreed to meet him, partly due to curiosity and partly because I was young, naive and stupid enough to have my head turned by a reporter's faint praise.

Back at the station, I headed, not to Gooch's office, but to the locked stockroom where evidence was kept.

At the desk by the side of the room's steel door, I signed the ledger and requested the strongbox which had been removed from

Bessie's room and which contained the few coins and the keys to the other rooms. The constable in charge nodded, then taking a large key from a ring on his belt, unlocked the door and entered, returning minutes later with the small metal cash box and its key.

He placed them on the desk in front of him.

'Not to be removed from the vicinity, son.'

I thanked him, unlocked the box and opened it. Ignoring the cash and the keys, I picked up the small notebook that was also inside and flicked through the pages. It was Bessie's rent book, her record of who'd paid and who was late. Back in the day, I'd seen her write in it several times. I scanned the final page. The date, written in pencil and in her hand, was the previous Friday. I read down the list of names till I came to Vogel. Beside it was written the amount of three shillings and the word 'PAID'. I flipped further back. Over the previous two months Vogel hadn't once fallen behind on his rent.

Replacing the book, I locked the cash box and returned it to the duty constable, then sought out Inspector Gooch.

'So,' he said, poring over a map of east London which had appeared at some point during the morning and been pinned to the wall. Certain landmarks had been circled, including Liverpool Street station and the docks. 'What news, young Wyndham?'

'I've just come from Jeremiah Caine's house.'

'And?'

'He wasn't much help. He was unaware of Bessie's murder and didn't know of any reason why she might be attacked. He asked me to pass on his condolences, though.'

Gooch sighed. 'That was good of him. What about his visit to the house that morning?'

'Claims he was in the area and popped in to see if she was all right. Says he picked up the rent too.'

Gooch noted the hesitation in my voice.

'You don't believe him?'

'I believe he collected the rent. I just don't think he's the type of man who just pops in to check on his housekeeper's health, even if he does happen to be in the area.'

Gooch shrugged. 'All right, so he just went to pick up the rent and used the excuse of checking up on her to conceal the fact that he's a money-grabbing bastard. That's not a crime.'

'Agreed, sir, but he could have sent his man Doyle to pick up the cash. There's something else, too. Caine's wife died some weeks ago, asleep in her bed. The doctor pronounced death by natural causes but it seems Bessie suspected foul play.'

Gooch turned from the map to face me, his brow furrowing.

'And who told you that?'

'The maid. A young girl named Lily. She said it was Bessie who found Mrs Caine's body.'

'Did she say *why* Bessie might think that?'

'She'd no clue. Just that Bessie's suspicion seemed only to heighten in the past week.'

Gooch rubbed at the back of his neck.

'I take it you didn't mention any of this to Caine himself?'

'No, sir. My conversation with the maid took place after I'd spoken with Mr Caine.'

'Good, because the last thing we need now is to attract the ire of a man like Caine based solely on the below-stairs gossip of a maid. Now have you any more good news?'

I shifted.

'Not *good* news exactly, sir, but it appears that Vogel had recently taken out a loan from the Guardians of the Jewish Poor, to the tune of three pounds –'

'Well, that sounds like good news to me! The man was in need of money. There's your motive, Constable.'

'If I may, sir,' I said, 'there's a problem.'

'What problem?'

'The loan was in kind, not cash, and he was up to date with his repayments. And according to Bessie's notebook, he was also up to date with his rent.'

Gooch was thoughtful. 'That's rather inconvenient all round. I was rather hoping the motive might be financial. Especially now that the press have reared their ugly heads.'

'Sir?' I asked, unsure how Vogel's lack of a financial motive made things worse.

'Do you read the papers, son?'

'Now and again.'

'Then you must have noticed that certain of our friends in the Fourth Estate aren't exactly enamoured of the foreigners in our midst, especially when those foreigners happen to be Jews. They'll have a field day when they learn that our chief suspect in the murder of an Englishwoman is a Polish Jew, especially if we're ruling out robbery as a motive. The headlines'll scream everything from rape to ritual sacrifice.'

'But there's no evidence of either.'

Gooch shook his head. 'Doesn't matter, son. These things are written by the unscrupulous and read by the unthinking. Some rags print precious little but trash about perfidious foreigners and treacherous Jews every week. Don't believe me? Open the *Gazette* of a Monday morning. The only things guaranteed to be in there are bile about Jews and the weekend's football scores. And you know why? Because that's what sells papers. For them, this case is manna from heaven. "Immigrant Jew kills innocent English-woman" – now there's a story guaranteed to rile up the man on the Mile End omnibus and scare the bejesus out of his wife. You think they're going to hold back now?'

'Shouldn't we wait, then, before telling them about Vogel?'

'They'll find out. The same way they found out about Bessie's death in the first place and started camping outside our door.' He gestured to the station around him. 'Someone in this place will tell them.'

I imagined the newspaper headlines; the impact they would have. The East End had seen more than a few riots over the years.

'So you see, son,' said Gooch, 'it's imperative we find Vogel, and quickly.'

TWENTY-THREE

February 1922

Assam

The dirt track down from the ashram was bordered by the ever-encroaching forest. It veered sharply left and a panorama opened up ahead. I stopped mid-stride, awestruck by the view.

An amber sun was rising, changing from blood red to gold. Beneath it a tapestry of verdant hills stretched to a distant blue horizon, the valleys between them shrouded in swathes of silken morning mist. In the distance sat Jatinga, its white bungalows snaking down the hillside, their roofs piercing gaps in the forest canopy like rocks in an emerald sea. The air was fresh, perfumed by the scent of wild flowers carried on a dawn breeze.

A week earlier, I wouldn't have noticed any of it.

I set off once again, attuned to the sounds of the forest: the birdsong and the buzz of insects and the crunch of stones under foot. Earlier that morning, I'd said emotional farewells to my comrades in the European hut, reserving an embrace for Adler.

From Brother Shankar I'd received the warm admonishment, *'Stay out of trouble, and maybe wait a few days until you take a drink,'* and though it was good advice, I wasn't about to follow it, not without a fight. And so the journey to my new lodgings incorporated a short detour via the local post office, a small, whitewashed hut of a building about a mile outside of town. Beside the entrance, a brown-and-white mongrel lay dozing in the morning sun. It looked up and greeted me with a disaffected yawn, then closed its eyes once more.

Inside, I hastily scribbled a short telegram addressed to Surrender-not, my junior officer, care of his aunt's address in Dacca. I passed it to the old man behind the counter. The message was simple:

> PRESENCE REQD URGENT.
> PRESTON RESIDENCE, JATINGA.
> BRING WHISKY.

I left the post office with a sense of satisfaction. The last year had been difficult. I hadn't exactly treated Surrender-not well, especially at a time when he was facing enough troubles of his own, what with half his family considering him a traitor for working for the British. I resolved to make amends, starting with a few days' holiday for the lad, here in Jatinga, away from the dust and hustle of deltaic Bengal.

Set among neatly tended gardens, Preston's house was a handsome wooden bungalow, raised off the ground on stilts and encompassed by a wide veranda on which sat the usual assortment of cane furniture that was as much a feature of colonial life as the gin and tonics sipped upon them. I climbed the steps to the front door and knocked.

'Just a minute,' came a voice from somewhere inside, and I duly waited, until some moments later it opened and I found myself face-to-face with the man I'd last seen the morning we'd found Le Corbeau's corpse.

'Mr Preston.'

Charles Preston stood barefoot and with the buttons of his shirt undone, a mop of brown hair, still damp, plastered to the top of his head.

'Captain Wyndham. Shankar said to expect you today.' He ran a hand through his wet hair. 'I say, you seem to have caught me at rather an inopportune moment. I was just getting dressed. Come in. I hope you don't mind me finishing while you settle in.'

I followed him into a spacious sitting room and placed my case on the floor. The walls were decorated with framed charcoal etchings of the male human form in various contortions: the sort of art that some consider tasteful, and others consider an offence under section 292 of the Indian Penal Code. Against one wall rested a sofa of a rather modern design, strewn with shirts and the odd pair of trousers, and in the corner, a wooden dining table and three chairs, a fourth having been placed by a window and pressed into service as a makeshift clothes horse.

'This way,' he said, walking off into a hallway. 'This is your room.'

I caught him up at the entrance to a bedroom which, alongside the usual furniture, contained a shelf lined with cameras and photographic equipment.

'You're a photographer too?'

'It's a hobby of mine. Anyway, make yourself at home,' he said, disappearing back into the hallway. 'Hope you don't mind the mess.'

'Maid's day off?'

'What? Oh, I see what you mean. No, not really. She only comes twice a week. I share her with a couple of the other chaps who live nearby.' He wandered back into the sitting room, adjusting a flamboyant red silk tie. 'We each have her two days a week, and on the Sunday she doth rest.'

He looked me up and down and it struck me that he must have known that I was, at least until a few days ago, an opium fiend.

'Look, old man,' he continued, 'I know it's jolly uncivil of me to dash off just as you set foot in the front door, only I have a rather busy day ahead. You're more than welcome to stay and make yourself comfortable.' His face suddenly brightened. 'Or, if you prefer, you could come up to the club for a spot of breakfast. It's nothing fancy, but they do manage to rustle up a rather decent bacon and eggs.'

After a week and a half of nothing but rice, dal and vomit-potions, bacon and eggs sounded like ambrosia.

Five minutes later, we were walking along a dirt track that led to the main road into town. Over his shirt, Preston had donned a blue linen jacket. His tie, this time, seemed less offensive to the eyes than the one he'd been wearing the day we'd found Le Corbeau's body, but he made up for it with a silk handkerchief which poked ostentatiously from his breast pocket. All in all, he seemed to dress in what was a distinctly un-civil-engineering manner. He also struck up a running commentary on the residents of each house we passed.

'That's the Granby place,' he said, pointing out a rather shabby bungalow, the paint on its boards stained grey from the rains of the last monsoon. 'Made his money in rubber, they say, then lost it all to drink. As for the wife, well, you didn't hear it from me, but …'

I stopped listening. A car drove past, a large black car, like the one I'd seen at Lumding station. I shook my head. That had been almost a fortnight ago and Lumding was seventy miles away. I was no longer a man in the grip of the O. I had to stop the paranoia.

I forced myself to relax. The car rounded a corner and was gone.

'It's mainly forestry, you see,' I heard Preston say. 'Everyone thinks Assam is nothing but tea plantations, but those are a few hundred miles away. In these parts it's all about lumber and rock. Most of the white men you'll see round here are involved in some way with the former or the latter, unless of course they're employed by the government, or by God.'

'God?'

'Missionaries. Presbyterians mostly. Hundreds of them. It's getting so that you can't cast the first stone without hitting one of 'em. They come up to convert the locals to their version of the straight and righteous path. Doing a decent job of it too if you go by the number of churches that keep springing up. I wouldn't mind, but they're always harping on to the tribespeople about the iniquities of alcohol, and it's hard enough to get a decent drink in Jatinga without the locals suddenly thinking you're the Devil incarnate.'

The heart of the hill station of Jatinga, if you could call it that, consisted of a few wooden buildings clustered around a church, this one firmly C of E and, according to Preston, used exclusively by the area's white residents. Beside it stood a small school and a general store, run by a family of merchants from far-off Gujarat who'd been here as long as anyone could remember.

'Very handy they are, too,' said Preston. 'They'll manage to get you pretty much anything within two weeks, save for alcohol. They claim their caste isn't allowed to drink it, which is fine, but they could bring it in, couldn't they? I mean, they don't drink rat poison either, but they still stock it.'

'Where *can* a man get a drink round here, then?' I asked.

'Pretty much the only place is where we're going now: the Jatinga Club.' He eyed me warily. 'Hang on, has Shankar said it's OK for you to drink?'

'He provided some non-binding advice.'

Preston pondered for a moment.

'In that case, the bar opens at noon.'

The view from the terrace of the Jatinga Club was as fine as I'd seen for a long time, and I didn't just mean the plate of bacon and eggs which was placed on the table in front of me by a white-jacketed waiter. In the foreground stood the houses of Jatinga's British community, and beyond, Preston explained, further down the hillside and clustered around a temple, were the many mud-brick dwellings of Indian incomers to the area, the ubiquitous Bengalis that made their living from servicing the British, and the Gujarati and Marwari traders that made their living servicing the Bengalis. A good way further still were the bamboo and thatch huts of the local tribespeople, whose land this had been since time immemorial. In the distance the verdant Khasi hills shone green and beyond them the grey silhouettes of larger mountains stood out like bas-reliefs against the pale blue sky.

'Tea, sir?' asked the waiter, and my stomach turned at the thought. Instead I sent him off in search of a pot of coffee and turned to Preston.

'That house there, the three-storey one with the blue shutters. Who lives there?'

'Good eye,' said Preston, as though my noticing the grandest building in sight was somehow impressive. '*That* is Highfield, the house of Mr Ronald Carter, our local bigwig.'

Preston, who'd spent the last ten minutes dripping gobbets of gossip about Jatinga's British inhabitants with all the fervour of a Grimsby fishwife, now failed to elaborate. Which begged the question ...

'What's he like?'

He placed his cutlery on his plate and looked up. 'Nasty piece of work. Treats the town and all in it as his personal fief. They say he bought his wife – she's a beauty, by the way.'

'I think I've met her,' I said. 'Up at the ashram.'

'Possibly. I hear she helps out there. Anyway, *he's* old enough to be her wicked stepfather, and one way or another, most people around here are in his pocket.'

'Not you, though?'

'I,' he said, lifting an egg-stained fork and waving it towards me, 'have the good fortune to report to, and be paid by, the authorities in Calcutta. Carter has no pull there.'

'How'd he make his money?'

Preston shook his head. 'No idea.' He gestured at the vista with one hand. 'He owns pretty much everything that you can see before you, though. They say he bought the land from the local tribespeople for a song. Convinced them it was haunted.'

'Haunted?'

'Mmm,' he said, finishing a mouthful of fried egg. 'Inhabited by evil spirits. To be honest, they didn't take much convincing. I'm surprised no one else round here thought of it first. After all, the bloody place really is haunted.'

I looked at him incredulously.

'Don't believe me? How about I show you tonight?'

TWENTY-FOUR

February 1905

East London

A sharp wind was blowing in off the river. On Wapping High Street, men and women wrapped up as best they could and hurried through it, between sporadic pools of lamplight. A cold, stinging rain fell steadily from a sky heavy with the stench of soot and industrial effusion, as I, in my civvies and wet through, negotiated a path along the greasy cobblestones, dodging the wreckage of broken crates, gutter vegetables and horse shit.

From the road, the Turk's Head was nothing more than a black void of an entrance into a narrow alley. The pub itself – a two-storey ramshackle building of brick and board – faced the river; and beside it, a treacherous set of wooden stairs led down to a small wharf where lay the rotting hulks of several old boats.

I ducked under the door frame into the warmth of the interior and scanned the room. Across the flagstoned floor was a counter of dark wood, behind which stood a solitary barman. To the left, towards the river and under a bay window, sat a series of low tables, all occupied by men with nowhere better to be, and against the far wall, a dying fire crackled in the hearth. Harmsworth was seated at the table closest to the window. He'd clocked me first and had already risen to his feet.

He met me at the bar with a smile on his face and an outstretched hand, which, when I failed to shake it, he turned into a pat on the arm. Without his hat, he looked younger: early thirties, with slicked dark hair half an inch longer at the back and sides than was seemly.

'Good to see you, Constable,' he said. 'Sorry to drag you out in this weather.'

'It's no problem,' I said, and the truth was I had little else to do. 'What can I get you?'

'What're *you* drinking?'

'Stout.'

'That's fine for me.'

Harmsworth turned to the publican. 'Two pints of Imperial.' He turned back to me. 'So no trouble finding the place then?' It was a question not really in search of an answer, just small talk the likes of which two barely acquainted men were expected to indulge in prior to the broaching of more pressing matters.

'I've been here before.'

The barman placed two pints of dark stout porter on the counter and wiped away the overspill with a damp rag. Harmsworth handed me my pint, placed some coins on the bar and then headed for his table. I followed, pulled out the chair opposite and sat down. Beyond the window pane, the black Thames lapped at the wharf, the splash of its ebb and flow punctuating the murmur of conversation at the half-dozen tables.

The hack took a long sip, then wiped his lips with the back of his hand. 'Good of you to come.'

'Pleasure,' I said. 'What can I do for you, Mr Harmsworth?'

The newspaperman leaned forward and placed his hands on the table either side of his glass.

'As I said this afternoon, it's more what we could do for each other. Now, I've been told by one of your colleagues that you're a young man with his wits about him, and that you've a promising future ahead. Who knows, you might make inspector one day.'

I said nothing, happy to bask in the honeyed glow of his blandishments.

'Now, there's been many a copper who's had his career made by a few good stories in the papers ... Likewise, a bad article or two can ruin a man's reputation ...' he paused, letting the last sentence hang in the air. 'And I know how hard it is to make ends meet on a beat copper's wage ...'

'I'm not sure I follow,' I said.

Harmsworth stared at me, unsure if I really was that naive or just feigning it.

'I think,' he said, 'we can be of use to each other. Call it a partnership of sorts.'

I sipped my beer.

'I was hoping you might consider meeting every so often, just now and again, for a drink and a chat. I've a good many contacts, and I hear things which might be useful to an ambitious young copper.'

'And in return?'

Harmsworth gave me a smile that looked like it had slipped off the face of a cherub. 'In return, maybe you could see your way clear to passing me some details on cases you might be involved with. Cases which the wider public might be interested in.'

'Such as?'

'Well I don't need to tell you, this Bessie Drummond business – terrible news – but our readers would love to know the inside story. I'm told you're one of the officers who found her.'

I shook my head. 'She was found by other tenants in her house. They summoned the police. I was just one of the first officers on the scene.'

'There you go. You see? You're already putting the record straight. All I'm asking is that now and again you share some details that might be pertinent to the case.'

'All in the interest of giving your readers the truth,' I said.

Harmsworth downed a long sip and placed his glass back on the table. 'Exactly! You'd be remunerated for your trouble, of course. We always look after our friends. Cigarette?' He fished a packet of Pall Malls from his pocket.

I declined and took another sip. Gooch's words suddenly rang in my head like a death knell.

'Some rags print precious little but bile about perfidious foreigners and treacherous Jews every week ...'

'What exactly do you want to know?'

'Word is, the killer's an immigrant.'

'We've several suspects.'

Harmsworth's eyes widened. 'Really? Because what I heard was that you'd eliminated most everyone from your inquiries save this Jew.'

'If you know so much already, why d'you need me?'

'Corroboration. You're involved with the case, first-hand. It would be helpful if you could confirm the man's name.'

Something told me that Harmsworth's original source hadn't mentioned Vogel's name, either because he didn't know it or because he was holding out for more money.

'And what would you do with that information?' I asked. 'Print it as fact in tomorrow's paper that this Jew murdered an English-woman? I've told you already, we've other suspects.'

Harmsworth remained placid. 'Our readers have a right to know what goes on. If one of those foreigners has killed an English-woman, then the public should be told. All these people coming over here from God knows where. People are scared.'

I drank my beer. 'You're right,' I said. 'People *are* scared, and I'm not sure printing a half-baked story is going to reassure them.'

'That's why I want as much of the detail as I can get. You give me the chap's name and I'll see you right to the tune of a fiver. How does that sound?'

'I've got a better idea,' I said. 'How about you wait till we've caught and charged someone and then I'll give you the full story . . . for free.'

Harmsworth shook his head. 'And let some other bastard get the scoop on the Jew? It doesn't work that way, lad.'

TWENTY-FIVE

I walked back to Wapping High Street. The rain, heavier now, poured down in sheets, off rooftops and onto the pavement. My digs were a half-hour's walk away and I'd have happily paid twice the going rate for a hackney cab, but at nine at night, cabs in Wapping were as rare as honest politicians. Instead, buttoning my coat against the wind, I set off up Wapping Lane towards the Ratcliffe Highway.

I didn't know what to make of my conversation with Harmsworth. All my life I've been an outsider, certainly from the day my mother died and my father packed me off to boarding school. I've never understood what drives the powerful to oppress the weak, or what need the many have to harass those different from them. Maybe it was just easier: to blame someone else, someone different, for all the shit that happened to you. Someone who couldn't answer back and point out the obvious: that your troubles were mostly caused by people who looked like you, not people who were different. Maybe that was why I'd always been on the side of the underdog. Some called it contrarian. I just thought of it as being decent. As such, I found it repellent that Harmsworth might wish to use me as an accomplice to peddle his half-truths and distortions. At the same time, part of me felt flattered that a journalist might deem me worthy of attention, and the thought of seeing my name in the papers sent a frisson of excitement through my shoulders. Looking back, I'm not proud of it, but as I say, I was young. And stupid.

I reached my door, still playing the matter over in my head. Wiping the rain from my face, I reached into my pocket for the key to the front door. A voice called out behind me.

'Constable Wyndham.'

I turned to find a thin figure standing across the road, silhouetted by the light from a street lamp. The voice was familiar, and as he crossed the street towards me I recognised his profile, which is to say I recognised his nose.

'Archibald Finlay,' I said. 'I thought you'd be consoling your mate Tom Drummond on his loss. Don't tell me you just happened to be passing by my door.'

Finlay gave a laugh that descended into a cough. 'No, Constable. I was asked to come here to invite you to meet some gentlemen who've requested the pleasure of your company.'

'I seem to be very popular this evening,' I said, 'though I'm not sure I fancy spending any more time trudging around in this weather.'

The rain dripped off the end of Finlay's flying buttress of a hooter. 'Believe me,' he said, 'it'll be worth your while.'

'Well, since you put it like that, how can I refuse?'

We headed north, and it didn't take a genius to work out where we were going, though who we were meeting and why were more of a mystery. Twenty minutes later we were on the Bethnal Green Road, walking up towards the lights of the Bleeding Hart pub. The poor stag on the board above the door looked even more despondent than usual, and given the weather, I didn't blame it.

The wooden doors creaked as Finlay pushed them open, then swung back behind us. The Bleeding Hart was busier than the

Turk's Head had been, with standing room only and an atmosphere like Liverpool Street station at rush hour. A scrum of men crowded the bar, their heads lost in a haze of cigarette smoke.

'Quite a party,' I said. 'What are we celebrating?'

Finlay snorted. 'It's not a celebration, it's a wake. Another drubbing for the Irons.'

'You'd think they'd be used to it,' I said. As long as the sun rose in the east, the chances were that West Ham United would have some sort of crisis by Christmas. 'So who am I here to meet?'

'Not here, Mr Wyndham,' said Finlay. 'You're an important man, your meeting's in the back room. Invitation only.'

I followed as he pushed his way through the mass of bodies towards a door at the back. Beside it, on a chair that under him looked like it had been made for a child, sat a man with a face the colour of a swede and a body the size of a cavalry horse. He rose, gave Finlay a nod and turned the knob on the door, smothering it in the palm of one hand as if it were a golf ball.

The back room at the Bleeding Hart meant only one thing. The gentlemen who wanted to see me were none other than the Spillers, Yorkshire's very own Brothers Grimm.

The room was larger than I'd expected. The size of the bar outside and then some. It was also much less crowded. A few men, dockers judging by the size and the smell of them, sat around a nearby table playing cards under the light of a hurricane lamp. Finlay paid them no regard and continued on, past an empty billiard table and a counter being polished by a bored-looking barman, to a booth in the corner on which sat a fat candle.

"Ave a seat, Constable,' said Finlay, breaking into a mirthless laugh and pointing to the maroon-leathered bench on one side of the table. 'Make yourself at 'ome. The boys'll be down shortly.'

He made to leave.

'Finlay,' I said, once he was five paces away.

He stopped in his tracks and turned. 'Yeah?'

'This is a pub, right?'

'That's right. What of it?'

'Well, how about you fetch me a drink? It'll help me get comfortable.'

He shook his head as though in pity.

'Beer do you?'

'How about something more special? I'm an invited guest, after all. Why not a whisky?'

'Whisky?' Finlay snorted. 'You look like you're just out of short trousers.'

From somewhere behind me a voice rang out.

'Get the man a whisky ...'

Finlay's expression melted instantly into a melange of obedience and fear.

' ... And bring the bottle.'

'At once, Mr Spiller,' said Finlay, shuffling quickly back towards the bar.

I turned to see the figure of a man, the unmistakable silhouette of Martin Spiller accompanied by the sound of heavy, purposeful footsteps. We'd never met before, which is to say we hadn't been introduced, but I knew who he was. Everyone in Whitechapel knew who he was.

He was dressed in brown trousers, braces and an open-necked white shirt, the sleeves of which were rolled up to reveal forearms like summer hams. He carried himself with a poise that was impressive for a big man and suggested his bulk consisted of muscle rather than fat.

'Good of ye to come down 'ere, Constable Wyndham,' he said, taking a seat on the banquette opposite, 'especially on a night as filthy as this.'

The candlelight danced across his face, the flame reflecting in hard, dark eyes and throwing shadows over his short hair and thickset features.

'May I call ye Sam?'

I tasted salt on my lips.

'Be my guest.'

From the billiard table came the sudden thud of balls being dropped onto baize. I turned to see another figure, shaven-headed and even larger than the man in front of me, lean over and begin racking the balls.

'Don't mind Wesley,' said Martin. 'He likes to start the evening with a round or two of billiards. Lord knows he needs the practice.' Spiller broke out into a smile which, if its intention was to put me at my ease, fell short by a distance.

Finlay returned from the bar with a bottle and two glasses and placed them on the table. He bent over to remove the stopper.

'Leave it,' said Spiller.

Wordlessly, Finlay retreated into the shadows. Spiller, his eyes still trained on me, lifted the bottle and poured two large doses of liquid amber. The smell of naphtha filled the air. He pushed one glass towards me, then lifted his own.

'Cheers,' he said, then took a decent swig. I followed suit.

I felt the warmth of the whisky ease down my throat and settle in my stomach.

From the billiard table came the crack of cue striking ball, then the clatter of a dozen more scattering.

'D'you play?' asked Spiller. 'Billiards, that is.'

'Afraid not,' I said. 'Never had the opportunity.'

'You should take it up. It's a gentleman's sport. And from what I hear you're a bit of a gentleman yourself, aren't you?'

'I wouldn't say that.'

Spiller placed his glass back on the table. 'Come now, lad, the son of a schoolmaster, nephew of a magistrate, schooling at some posh place out in the country, and of course the clincher ... your hands: nails all neat and trimmed. Hardly the hands of a docker, are they, son?'

I was impressed, less with the deduction about my hands, and more with the fact that he'd done his homework. He obviously had access to my file at Leman Street. I saluted him with my glass, then took another sip of whisky.

'So I'm wonderin' how a fine young gentleman such as yourself ends up a beat copper in the East End o' London.'

'It's a long, tragic story,' I said. 'Actually, not that long, but I'll save you the details. Let's just say my prospects were curtailed by a chronic lack of funds.'

Spiller nodded. 'Aye, I've seen that before. Respectable family, all shiny teeth but no trousers. So why not join the army or the Church? Ain't that what your sort do if they've such ... curtailed prospects?'

'I considered the army,' I said. *'Join up and see the world* ... Except the places the army seems to go aren't really the sorts of places I want to see. Now if the army had invaded Venice or Florence, it might have been a different story. And as for the priesthood, it'll be a sad day for Christendom when the Almighty decides He needs my help managing His flock.'

Spiller gave a laugh, then downed the rest of his whisky. He reached for the bottle and refilled his glass.

'You're no doubt wondering why we asked you here.'

'You could say that.'

'Well, finish your drink and we'll get on to it.'

I did as ordered and downed the rest of my drink.

'Wesley!' Spiller called out.

The man-mountain at the billiard table took a shot, then straightened and turned towards us.

'Would you be so kind as to join us?' said Martin. 'And another glass over here,' he said, directing his gaze to the bar.

Wesley Spiller rested his cue against the wall, then came over and took a seat beside his brother as the barman placed a fresh glass on the table in front of him. Martin filled his brother's glass, refilled mine and made the introductions.

'Wesley, this is Constable Sam Wyndham, from the station in Leman Street. Sam, my brother Wesley.'

The familial resemblance was clear in the coldness of the eyes and the square set of the jaw.

'Wesley here has received some information which may be of interest to you,' said Martin.

'Tha's right,' said his brother.

'We understand you're looking for a Yid by the name of Vogel,' Martin continued.

I took a sip of whisky. 'News travels fast.'

Martin feigned disappointment. 'Now, now, Constable. Let's not be churlish. We all know that some of your colleagues are rather loose with their tongues. And remember, we're trying to help you.'

'Go on.'

'It just so happens that one of Wesley's acquaintances says he might know the whereabouts of this Vogel.'

'Where?'

Martin paused.

'I suppose I don't need to tell you what it would mean if you were to be the one to bring in Bessie Drummond's killer. I'm sure the papers would have a field day. I can see the headlines – "Hero copper catches East End killer". You'd be famous.'

'And what would you want in return?'

'Not much,' said Martin innocently. 'All we'd ask is you advance us a similar courtesy in the future. Maybe pass on the odd bit of chat you might come across here or there.'

'You want me to pass you information?'

'If you could, just now and then, as we would do for you.'

Maybe it was the drink, but despite my better judgement, I felt the seductiveness of his words. They were offering me the chance to catch Bessie's killer, or at the very least, our prime suspect in her murder, and in the face of such an opportunity, my reservations about Vogel's potential guilt were evaporating like the last drops of whisky in my glass. And all they wanted in return was a titbit here and maybe a tip-off there. But I was still wary.

'Why would you tell me this?'

'Come now, Constable. An innocent woman's been murdered. It's the duty of every patriotic Englishman to help the police bring the killer to justice.'

'I meant, why *me*? You gentlemen clearly have several friends in the force already. Why not pass the information to one of them?'

The brothers exchanged a look.

'You see, Sam,' said Martin, 'in our game you can never have too many friends. We were told you were working on the case and we thought you might be appreciative of the tip.'

'Probably be a promotion in it for you,' added Wesley.

I couldn't help but consider it. Arresting Vogel would certainly help me make an ally of Gooch of the Yard, and that couldn't hurt. He had stressed the urgency of collaring Vogel after all. With the press ready to print a story about an Englishwoman being murdered by a foreign Jew, a story that would no doubt lead to hostility, not just against the perpetrator but against all of the Jews in the East End, our chances of stopping tempers flaring, and possibly averting a bloody riot, would be immeasurably better if we could say that we'd already arrested the key suspect.

They say the road to hell is paved with good intentions, and I justified my pact with the Spillers on the grounds that arresting Vogel might stop a bloodbath. And if he was innocent, he'd be able to prove it and then we'd go after the real killer.

'Tell me,' I said.

Spiller smiled a lopsided grin that revealed surprisingly white teeth. He picked up his glass and gestured to his brother. 'I'll let Wesley explain, but first, a toast to our new understanding.'

The brothers clinked glasses then held them towards me. I raised mine and matched them. I took a sip. I'd like to say that the whisky tasted like ashes upon my tongue, but it didn't. The truth is it tasted just as smooth and as rich as before.

TWENTY-SIX

February 1922

Assam

Preston walked me to the steps of the club.

'Got a site inspection up on the Maibang road,' he said. 'It's not too far as the crow flies, but it's the Devil's own journey getting there. There was a mudslide during the monsoon. They pulled four bodies from the mess. Nasty business.'

He looked out across the valley.

'You've come at a good time, there's the annual dinner here at the club tonight. Anyone who's anyone in the area will be there. I should be back by five and we can head over at seven.'

The thought of a formal dinner sent a shiver up my spine. With my addiction, it had been over a year since I'd had the presence of mind, not to mention the patience, to sit through a meal with a group of strangers, and while I was now clean and confident I could return to work and take on the bloodiest of murderers, the thought of three hours of making polite conversation still scared the life out of me.

Preston noticed the look on my face.

'What? Don't like parties?'

I considered telling him the truth, then thought better of it.

'I've no suitable attire.'

'Don't you worry about that,' he said conspiratorially. 'I'm sure we can find something to fit you.'

Out of excuses, I mumbled assent, and as he headed off, I suddenly realised that the prospect of being dressed by Preston was almost as worrying as attending the damn dinner in the first place. If his choice of tie and the shirts strewn over his sofa were anything to go by, there was a fair chance I'd end up looking like a Japanese geisha.

Before he'd departed, Preston had left me with the key to his house and suggested a few local sights I might care to see.

'You should take a look at the waterfalls, and there are some wonderful views from the hills. A lot of Bengalis come up here from Calcutta and Dacca to take the air and admire the view. Big fans of nature, our Bengali friends. Mad about their "scenic beauty".'

That much was true. According to Surrender-not, Bengalis were a pastoral people, uniquely unsuited to urban living and who, in his view, wished for nothing more than a return to the land. And if the sheer amount of bad poetry they wrote about it was any measure, he was probably right about that.

'Otherwise, you could do a tour of the churches, not that there's much to see architecturally. They're all jaw-droppingly plain. Austere, even.'

I had assured him I'd be fine, then headed back up the stairs to the club's veranda.

I took a seat at the same table where we'd taken breakfast. In my absence, the remnants of the meal had been cleared away and a fresh white tablecloth laid down. Summoning the waiter, I ordered another coffee and a copy of the most recent newspaper they had, which turned out to be a day-old edition of the *Statesman*, and which arrived neatly folded on a steel tray.

Taking a sip of coffee, I scanned through the pages. Sure enough, as Brother Shankar had alluded, stacks of column inches were devoted to the incident at Chauri Chaura, eulogising the massacred officers and castigating Gandhi and his Congress-wallahs.

In search of light relief, I turned to the sports pages. Back home, Tottenham were giving Liverpool a run for their money, while in the second division, I was pleased, and shocked, to see West Ham up among the leaders.

I finished the coffee, set down the paper and decided to head out. Neither the church nor the waterfalls particularly interested me. I was a copper after all, drawn magnetically to the darker side of things. As far as I was concerned, the good deeds taught in God's house and the natural wonders of His work were as nothing compared to the complexities and intrigues of those He'd created in His image. And if Preston were to be believed, under its genteel, buttoned-down surface, the town of Jatinga boiled with passions and petty rivalries. For my part, I'd seen enough of India, and of human nature, not to doubt him.

The sun was high now and the air pleasant as I set off, back down the road towards the general store. Preston had described it as a treasure trove of a place, and while they may not have stocked alcohol, I doubted there was a general store in the country that didn't sell tobacco.

En route, I passed a native mali tending to the roadside verge. Barefoot, and with his head covered against the sun, he stood bent over, neatly trimming the grass with a pair of antiquated shears, with the forest looming large behind him. I was impressed by the sheer futility of his task. In a land as fecund as this, he seemed like Canute trying to hold back the tide, attempting to keep the might of nature at bay with nothing more than a pair of scissors. And yet he continued, probably because he was paid to do so by some sahib. No Indian would be foolish enough to think they could tame Mother Nature in such a way, but we British were cut from a different cloth. We preferred the order of a neat grass verge to the chaos of the natural forest, and we'd fight to maintain that order, unnatural as it was, for as long as possible.

The Bhagwan general store was a two-storey structure, built in the same colonial style as the other buildings, raised on stilts but without a veranda. Above the door, a freshly painted sign billed it as the 'Harrods of Assam', which was enterprising advertising if nothing else.

A bell went off as I entered, and a bald, light-skinned native looked up from behind a wood-and-glass counter. The store itself was an Aladdin's cave of flummery, with items stacked almost to the ceiling and shelves stocking everything from cooking utensils to car spares. To one side, a blonde woman, dressed in khaki shirt and jodhpurs, stood with her back to me, flicking through one of a number of magazines that sat on a rack. I recognised the perfume immediately.

'How can I help you, sir?' asked the man behind the counter.

'Cigarettes, please,' I said. 'Twenty Capstans.'

The man nodded, then turned to a shelf behind him.

'Well, who have we here? Captain Wyndham?'

Emily Carter closed her magazine and walked over. Her tone was amiable, or maybe that was just wishful thinking on my part, because she was a fine-looking woman, and I always tended to think the best of attractive women, which, when you thought about it, was rather an Achilles heel for a detective.

'What brings you into town?'

'Recuperation,' I said. 'Brother Shankar thought I might take the air for a few days.'

She placed the magazine on the counter. 'I'll take this too, Shalin,' she said, turning to the shopkeeper, 'and let me know when the brake drums arrive.'

'Very good, madam.'

The man made a note of the purchase in a ledger, then passed the book across the counter for Mrs Carter to verify. I noticed oil stains on her shirt cuff. She caught me staring and rubbed at the mark on her sleeve.

Feeling suddenly awkward, I found myself talking to fill the silence.

'Are you moonlighting as a mechanic, Mrs Carter?'

She pouted in mock offence. 'You don't think I could be a mechanic?'

'Most mechanics I know don't tend to wear lipstick,' I said, 'and if they did, I'd probably ask questions.'

The shopkeeper placed the cigarettes on the counter. I handed him a few coins and he disappeared into a back room.

'So where are you staying?' she asked.

'At Mr Preston's place.'

'You didn't fancy staying on at the ashram, then?' she asked playfully. 'Scared Shankar would make a Hindu convert of you?'

I shook my head. 'I don't think he tried. Anyway, I'd have thought British converts to Hinduism were even rarer than female mechanics.'

'You'd be surprised.'

The shopkeeper reappeared carrying a heavy package in both arms and dropped it on the counter.

'Your box has arrived, Mrs Carter. Would you like me to have a boy take it over?'

She assessed the size of the package on the counter. 'I say, Captain Wyndham, would you be kind enough to give me a hand with that?'

'Of course.'

'You don't mind?'

That was an understatement.

'I've nothing better to do.'

I followed her out into the sunshine and down the steps to the street.

'It's just a few hundred yards down the road,' she said. 'You really are a godsend.'

'Rather odd for a mechanic to be married to the lord of the manor,' I said as we walked.

Her expression changed subtly. 'You know my husband?'

I shook my head. 'No, but his reputation precedes him.'

'I wasn't always a mechanic. I became one during the war. I was in the army, you know. It's good for a girl to learn a trade, don't you think? After all, I'd no idea I'd one day marry Ronald.'

'You were in the WAAC?' I asked, not even attempting to mask my surprise.

'That's right, fixing engines, maintaining lorries, that sort of thing. I was even posted to France towards the end. We had a lark of a time.'

A lark of a time was hardly how I'd have characterised my wartime experience; however, despite the death and privations, I'd met more than a few people who, when it was all over, admitted that they'd never felt as alive or as free as during the war years.

After two hundred yards I felt the sweat start to trickle down my back. The box weighed a ton and I hadn't appreciated quite how weak I'd become since the start of my treatment.

'What have you got in here, anyway?'

'Take a guess, Mr Detective.'

'From the weight, I'd say the engine from a Sopwith Camel.'

'No,' she laughed, 'but a valiant try, nonetheless.'

'What then?'

'You'll see in a minute. Here we are,' she said, pointing to a pillar with the word HIGHFIELD chiselled into the stone in clean, elegant letters. We turned off the main road and I followed her up a tree-lined path towards the large whitewashed house I'd spied from the terrace of the Jatinga Club. Set apart, at a distance of about thirty yards, was an outbuilding that looked like a small barn. We walked up and Emily Carter fiddled with a padlock, then unwound the chain that held its doors closed. There was the scrape of wood on dirt as she opened a gap, just wide enough for a man and a package to fit through, and theatrically waved me in.

'What do you think?' she asked, as I lowered the box onto the dirt floor.

The walls of the barn were lined with shelves and crates and, on one side, a workbench. In the centre stood the hollowed-out bones of an old automobile.

'Very nice,' I said. 'What is it?'

'That,' she beamed, 'is Beatrice. She's a 1913 Bugatti Type 18, or what's left of her. I'm doing her up.'

'Where did you come across a Bugatti in the middle of Assam?'

'Found her in a knacker's yard in Guwahati. Apparently she was the property of the Maharajah of Cooch Behar until he wrapped it round a palm tree. Picked her up for a song and had Ronald transport her up here.'

I took a closer look at the car. Its royal-blue coachwork had rusted and was now coated in dust, its left side missing a wing. The engine and the driver's seat had long since gone the way of the dodo, but at the front, the starter handle was still there, as was the red badge on top of the grille, with 'Bugatti' picked out in white lettering. The ground around it was strewn with the greasy detritus of cannibalised car parts: shock absorbers, brake cables, engine components, a battery; all lying there like the bones of some fossilised beast.

Emily Carter took a knife from the workbench and slit open the package I'd been carrying. Lifting the flaps, she heaved out the large black box inside. On one side were printed the words 'Hudson Motor Car Co., Detroit MI, USA'. I walked over and helped her carry it to the workbench.

'Surely your husband could have just bought you a new car?'

'Probably,' she replied, 'but where would be the fun in that?'

I suddenly felt rather ridiculous. Here I was, standing in a barn, trying to catch my breath and discussing car restoration with a rather beautiful married woman whom I hardly knew.

'Well,' I said, 'I suppose I really should let you get on with things,' and half turned towards the door.

'You could stay a while and keep me company? I shan't be long, and then I can show you round the village. I just have a few odds and ends to sort out, and you did say you've nothing better to do.'

There was a coquettishness to her that, if I hadn't known better, would have made me think she'd taken a shine to me. But, of course, I did know better, or at least I should have. In my present emaciated state, I doubted any woman would have looked twice at me, let alone the young wife of the richest man in town.

'Do say you will,' she pleaded. 'It's been such a while since I've talked to anyone interesting, and you, Captain Wyndham the policeman, seem like you may have interesting tales in spades.'

'When you put it like that,' I said, 'I can hardly refuse.'

'Good,' she said. 'Maybe you should start by telling me how you came to find yourself in India.'

I wasn't sure how to answer. The truth was that I'd come here because I had nothing left in England. My wife was dead, as were my family, most of my friends and the better part of my soul. I'd come to Calcutta because it was a better option than suicide, though the decision had been marginal. But you couldn't say that to a woman you'd just met. Not if you're English.

I puffed out my cheeks. 'The usual story, I suspect. I fancied becoming a snake charmer.'

'And how'd that work out for you?'

'Not well. My snakes kept wandering off. A lack of charm on my part.'

She smiled. 'That *must* be it.'

'And you?' I asked. 'How does a girl from the Women's Auxiliary Army Corps, with time served in France and a knack for fixing engines, find herself a hundred miles east of the middle of nowhere and married to a millionaire?'

She paused before answering. 'It's a long story. I suppose you could say it starts at the Battle of Arras in 1917. I was engaged to a man, a lieutenant of the Royal Engineers. My David was killed, I'm told, when a tunnel he and his sappers were working on collapsed. They say he didn't suffer ... but that's what they always say, isn't it? I couldn't trouble you for one of those cigarettes you bought, could I?'

'Where are my manners?' I said, fishing out the packet and a book of matches.

I passed her a cigarette, took one for myself and lit both.

She took a ragged drag and exhaled. 'The war ended and I returned to England. But by then I was in my mid-twenties and ... well, let's just say that there weren't many avenues available to an unmarried woman over twenty-five, either marital or professional. If you're choosy about who you marry, and don't fancy being a governess or a lady's maid, then you're pretty much out of options.'

I supposed that was true. The fact was eligible young men with their limbs and sanity intact were thin on the ground after the war. Women of all classes were finding it difficult to find a husband, but middle-class women had it the worst. There were standards to be maintained after all, and marrying beneath your station was worse than being a spinster. At the same time, a woman could hardly continue as a mechanic once the war had ended. For one thing, the men returning from the front needed those jobs, and for another, well, what would the neighbours say?

'So what happened?'

'Well,' she said, 'you've heard the old maxim about India – that it's the last place on earth you can still find an English bachelor – so I did what all the other girls were doing. I bought a ticket for Calcutta and set sail in search of adventure.'

'And by adventure, you mean a husband?'

She eyed me: a glance, sly, askance. 'Captain Wyndham, I do believe you're mocking me.'

'Not at all, Mrs Carter. I meant no offence.'

'Good, because if all I'd wanted was any old husband, I could have been betrothed the week I arrived in Calcutta, earlier even. There was a man who proposed to me on the crossing itself. He was sweet enough. Very earnest. The sort of man who parts his hair down the middle. Did something terribly clever in insurance. Kept telling me what wonderful prospects he had, but I just couldn't picture myself as the wife of an actuary.

'Anyway, long story short, after a few weeks in Calcutta, a bunch of us girls, those of us who hadn't already hooked a man, were invited up to Darjeeling for the summer.' She looked wistful. 'That was quite a season. A party almost every night. I met Ronald at one. Well, he wouldn't take no for an answer, and six months later we were married.'

'What's your husband's line of business?'

'Lumber, mainly, but he has interests in a lot more besides ... Fingers in lots of pies.' The look on her face seemed almost contemplative. Then, with a shake of her head, she snapped out of it and began rummaging through a box on the workbench, before pulling out a component of some sort and holding it up with a look of triumph. As she did so, the sleeve of her shirt fell back, revealing a dark bruise on her forearm. Four distinct bruises to be precise.

I'd seen enough marks on women to have my suspicions as to how it was caused. I also knew there was little point in my asking her about it, and as it happened, I didn't need to. She caught me staring and quickly lowered her arm, the sleeve falling back into place. Gravity restored her dignity, but the act merely confirmed my suspicions. I said nothing, but now, as I looked at her face, I saw that the make-up on her right cheek looked heavier than on the other. It might have been nothing, but Mrs Carter didn't strike me as a woman who was anything other than a perfectionist when it came to her cosmetics.

'Come on!' she said, an almost artificial lightness in her tone. 'Let me show you around.'

TWENTY-SEVEN

February 1905

East London

Wesley piped up, his tone suddenly businesslike.

'My brother and I,' he said, 'run an employment bureau of sorts. We provide men and other services for many of the shops and businesses round here. One of our blokes is nightwatchman at a warehouse on Brick Lane, near them steam baths. You know? The ones the Yids all go to of a Friday? Called Shevviks or summat.'

I knew the building: the Russian Vapour Baths, owned by a man called Schevzik. The sign above the entrance said 'Best Massage in London' and offered relief against a number of ailments from rheumatism to gout, and situated as they were, opposite the Brick Lane synagogue, most of its patrons were Jews, washing themselves before going to their temple across the road.

'Anyway, last night,' continued Wesley, 'around one in the morning, our man Reggie sees a bunch o' them Yids, three lads, all shifty-looking, jimmying open one o' the windows. 'E says one o' the boys climbed through, then, fast-as-you-like, makes his way to the front and opens the door for the others.

'Well, at first Reggie thinks they're robbin' the place, but then he thinks, *"Who robs a bathhouse? What they going to steal? Soap?"* So he has a little chuckle to hisself at the thought of a bunch o' mad Yids lookin' for stuff to nick, thinkin' they're going to feel a mite foolish when they come out wi' nuthin' ...'

'And?' I asked.

Wesley placed his hands on the table. 'Well, that's just it,' he continued. 'They didn't come out. Not all of them anyway. Three went in, but only two came out.'

'You think they were hiding Vogel?'

'Either that or they killed him in there. But I'd guess they were hiding him. Why else would they break in at the dead of night? It's right in the middle of Brick Lane, but the only folks what go in there are Yids, and if, by some chance the police were to search it, they'd not be able to see more than two feet in front of themselves on account of all the steam. A man'd stand a good chance of slipping away.'

It made sense. With the ports and stations being watched, doing a runner, even if Vogel had a destination in mind, would be risky. It would be better to lie low, bide his time until the heat died down and then make a bolt for it. But lying low presented its own problems. In and around Whitechapel he'd need to stay out of sight. People knew him, and sooner or later, someone would report him to the police. Outside of the area, he'd stick out like a sore thumb, easily spotted as a foreigner and a Jew. The best plan was to stay local and off the streets, but that was easier said than done. He'd be recognised at the doss house or the soup kitchens, and judging by the state of his room, he seemed to have fled with nothing. As for money, he might have been up to date with his bills, but I doubted he had the cash for a few nights in a single room at a flop house let alone a guest house. As Rebecca had speculated the previous evening, maybe he *had* gone to the anarchists? They might be minded to help him hide from the police, and the bath house might not be a bad bolt-hole, at least till something better could be organised.

'We'll need to move fast,' I said. 'If he is at Schevzik's, they probably won't keep him there long.'

Wesley nodded in agreement, but it was Martin who spoke.

'We've done our civic duty, Constable. What you do with the information is up to you.'

I made to rise, but before I could, Martin reached over and put a vice-like hand on my wrist. 'Before you go though,' he said with a grin, 'at least finish your drink.'

I stepped out into the night, the doors of the Bleeding Hart swinging closed behind me, cutting off the raucous voices, the warmth and the smell of beer like a guillotine. The cold hit me, clearing my head as the adrenaline began to course through my veins, I focused on the chance to catch Vogel and dispelled all doubts about my Faustian pact with the Spiller brothers.

The question was what to do next. The sensible thing would be to run to the station in Leman Street, alert the duty officer and ask him to send word to Inspector Gooch, then to fetch Whitelaw and wait for orders. But Gooch lived out west, on the other side of town. Getting word to him and waiting for his arrival would take at least two or three hours. I wiped the rain from my watch. Under the light of the pub window, I read the time. It was already close to midnight. If the Spillers were right, and Vogel had been deposited at the Russian Baths at around one in the morning, he'd have been there almost twenty-four hours already. Who was to say that his accomplices wouldn't move again in the dead of night? It was the safe thing to do. Indeed they might have done so already, but I doubted it. People were still awake, some of them still in the streets. To move him now would risk detection. The odds would be better at 1 a.m. There was no time to wait for Gooch. Precious little to try and find Whitelaw either. That left me with few options.

The blue lamp above the door cast an unearthly glow on the sodden pavement outside the station house. I raced up the steps, threw open the doors and darted in, causing the dozing desk sergeant to start.

'Wyndham?' he said, looking up from the newspaper spread across the counter. 'What you doing here at this hour? You look like a drowned rat.'

'Tip-off,' I said, fighting to catch my breath. 'On the Bessie Drummond case.'

That woke him up.

'What sort of tip-off?'

'Possible location of a suspect.'

'You mean the Jew?'

'That's right,' I said. 'Who's the senior officer on duty?'

The sergeant puffed out his cheeks. 'That would be me. We can try and send word to that inspector of yours, or wait till morning.'

I slammed my hand on the newspaper on the counter. 'We need to move now! The gen might only be good for an hour or so. If Vogel's there, we need to catch him now, before he has a chance to run.'

'If?' said the sergeant. 'How reliable is this tip-off?'

'I don't know. It's second-hand and almost twenty-four hours old.'

I could see his scepticism growing.

'I'm not sure we want to be waking the inspector on the basis of a day-old, half-baked sighting.'

I ran a hand through my rain-soaked hair. My chance to catch Vogel felt like it was slipping away.

'We don't need Gooch to check out the tip-off. I could go with whatever men we have here.'

'There's just you and me here, lad. The others are out patrolling their beats. They'll most likely be back in an hour, so you'll have to wait.'

That was too long.

'I've a better idea,' I said, 'but I need the key to the gun cupboard.'

TWENTY-EIGHT

The lamps had been smashed.

Brick Lane was shrouded in damp, velveteen darkness and the baths a few hundred yards away were all but invisible. They occupied a three-storey building on the east side of the street, a striking sight in daylight, with an ornate iron awning shaped like an onion dome above the door, and the words *Russian Vapour Baths* picked out on a stained-glass background. But as I said, now you could barely see it, because the bulb in the street lamp beside it had been smashed.

The lane was dead, the usual midnight malingerers taking shelter from the deluge somewhere else. I stopped half a block away to take stock and fiddled nervously with the trigger on the Bulldog revolver. Dim light seeped through naked gaps between the curtains of neighbouring buildings, but the bathhouse remained still and black as the grave.

I ran for the shelter of the dome-shaped awning and there stopped to catch my breath. Above me, the rain hit the awning with a metallic thud before flowing in torrents down either side like the Red Sea being parted. The doors were in an alcove recessed into the brick facade. They had iron rings for handles and, pulling on them, I found them locked tight as the Bank of England, not that I expected anything less. The Spillers' nightwatchman had said the men had gained access through one of the windows, but that seemed impossible, seeing as the baths had no windows on the ground floor. From the front at least, Schevzik's bathhouse was little more than a door flanked by the entrances of other concerns: those of Rosenberg's pawn shop on the left and an ironmonger's on the right. The only windows forming part of the bathhouse were on the first and second floors.

For a moment, a cold fear coursed through me. Had the Spillers sent me off on a wild goose chase, or worse, lured me here for some other purpose? I took a breath to calm my nerves, reminding myself that the Spillers probably had half the officers at Leman Street in their pockets. They had no reason to dupe me.

Of course their man at the warehouse across the road might have been mistaken. But that too seemed fanciful. Seeing three men crawl through a window which wasn't there didn't seem like a mistake you made easily. Unless you were drunk.

In desperation, I turned and tried the doors once again. They trembled but remained firmly shut. I gave up, leaned against the wall to one side of the alcove, pulled out my fags and lit one. On a board on the wall opposite was a sign painted with the legend:

Keep fit & well with regular visits to the
Russian Vapour Baths
Invaluable relief for rheumatism,
gout, sciatica, neuritis, lumbago
and allied complaints

I laughed bitterly. I supposed if I caught the flu from being soaked to the skin tonight, I could always pay a visit in the morning in search of a cure. That's when I noticed something odd. The paint on the sign had been scratched away at one corner, revealing not coarse wood, but something smoother. I bent down to take a closer look, and with the nail of my index finger, scratched at the paint around the scar. It came away with some difficulty, but the effort was worth it. I looked closely and smiled. The sign had been painted, not on a wooden board, but onto the glass pane of a window. I ran my fingers along the base of the sign and located the outline of the window frame. It seemed old and worn, and sure enough, after a few tugs, it cracked and came away, opening in my hands.

I pulled it wide, crawled through, then fell off a ledge into the blackness beyond, landing face first on a cold, stone floor. For a moment I lay there, dazed, concerned that my unorthodox entrance might have alerted anyone holed up inside. I listened for the slightest sound, but heard nothing save the dripping of water.

Rubbing the bump on my head that was already beginning to form, I rose to my feet, my eyes adjusting to the insipid grey light that seeped in through the gap where the glass pane had been. In the gloom I made out two rows of wooden cots which I guessed were massage tables. Picking my way between them, I made for an open doorway at the far end.

Beyond was a small room, permeated by a damp chill, its floor slick with water and treacherous underfoot. I reached out and steadied myself against a tiled wall. Somewhere close by, water dripped: a regular splashing that suggested a worn seal or a loose tap.

Suddenly, over the noise of the water, I thought I heard a sound, so faint that I wasn't sure if I hadn't simply imagined it. A spastic, nervous energy coursed through my veins as I closed my eyes in concentration and held my breath. Seconds passed, slowly, rhythmically, measured out by the metronomic dripping of the water and the beating of my heart. I told myself my ears were playing tricks and exhaled. As I did, I heard it again, the muffled fall of what might have been footsteps on the floor above.

Quickly, feeling my way along the wall, I stumbled up to a door. Beyond lay more darkness. Again I heard the noise above, louder this time, and more frantic. I groped forward blindly, hoping to make purchase with something solid and finally touching a wall opposite.

Light was falling from somewhere up ahead.

I made for it. But the wall suddenly gave way to air. Once more I reached out, my hand closing around what felt like a banister. I turned, felt with my boot for the first stair and began to climb. Straight ahead, a thin shaft of light seeped out from under a door. Suddenly the step beneath me creaked like the opening of a coffin. The noises from the room ceased abruptly. I imagined Vogel, or whoever was in there, holding their breath, much as I had done minutes earlier, straining to hear, waiting for the sound to repeat itself. I thought fast and took a decision. When the element of surprise was lost, the next best thing was generally speed.

So I ran.

Full pelt, up the stairs, forsaking all pretence of masking my approach, reaching the landing and continuing headlong, smashing shoulder first into the door ahead. The wood gave way and the door swung back wildly on its hinges, slamming into the wall with a crash. I steadied myself and looked up. Before me, in the light of a flickering candle, stood a thin man with a knife in his hand and a look of unbridled fear on his face. In an instant I knew I'd seen him before. The night Bessie Drummond had been accosted in Grey Eagle Street. This was the man I'd chased and lost on the rail tracks at Shoreditch.

I reached into the pocket of my coat, feeling for the heft of the revolver, but found nothing. Frantically, I searched the other pocket. It too was empty. As a wave of panic surged within me, I realised I must have dropped it, probably when I'd entered the building and landed on my face. It was all rather inconvenient given the man in front of me had a blade. I was out of uniform, sopping wet and had just broken into the building. If he stabbed me, he'd have had a good chance of convincing a jury that he'd acted in self-defence, assuming of course that he was rich and an

Englishman. But from the look of his clothes and the skullcap on his head, I doubted he met either criterion. What's more the expression on his face gave me a whisper of hope. It wasn't the look of a killer but of a man in fear of his life.

'Police!' I said. 'Drop the knife.'

He stood there, frozen. Then the look of fear changed to one of alarm. He breathed heavily, his eyes frantically scanning the room for a way out.

'Put the knife down,' I said, raising my hands, palms open.

His eyes were now focused on the door behind me.

'Vogel,' I said.

The mention of his name caught his attention.

'There's no escape. Other officers are on the way. Don't make things worse for yourself.'

The hand that held the knife was shaking, and so, I hoped, was his resolve.

'I did not do this thing,' he pleaded. 'I did not kill her!'

'That's good,' I said. 'You'll get a chance to explain everything down at the station. Now drop the knife.'

He looked at his hand as though he'd forgotten he was still holding the blade, then slowly knelt down and placed it on the floor, before rising once more, this time with his hands up.

From behind me came the noise of a door opening, then voices. It seemed the cavalry had arrived just as the danger had passed but in time to claim the glory.

'That was sensible of you,' I said to him. 'Up here,' I shouted.

'I did not kill her!' Vogel repeated, this time shaking his head. 'You must believe me.'

'So why did you run?' I asked to the refrain of boots on stairs.

Vogel uttered a forlorn grunt of a laugh. 'Where I am from, families are killed, villages burned on the rumour that a Jew has murdered a Gentile.'

'This is England,' I said. 'You're innocent until proven guilty by a jury. Same as anyone else.'

He shook his head. 'I see the way your people look at us, the lies printed in the pa—'

He was cut off by the sound of men bursting in through the open doorway. I turned, expecting to see Whitelaw at the head of a detachment of officers. Instead the man standing there wasn't the sergeant and the men behind him certainly weren't the cavalry. Before I could react, two of them leapt out from behind their leader and came at me. The first, a lean chap with a scar on his forehead and a face like a skull, threw a punch at my head. I managed to parry the blow and a sharp jolt of pain ran up my forearm, just as the second man, this one shorter and thicker with the physique of a street fighter, rushed me. I was thrown back by the force of his charge and it took all my concentration just to stay on my feet, which was a pity because it meant I never saw the next blow coming – another to my face. This one made contact and a bomb went off in my head a second before the lights went out. By the time I'd gathered my wits, I found myself pinned to the wall, my arms held in place by the two men.

The leader approached, said something to Vogel and received little more than a mumble in reply. He spoke again and I found I couldn't understand what he was saying. My first thought was that the punch to the head had somehow scrambled my brain.

He turned to me and looked me up and down as though appraising an animal fit for the knacker's yard. He was young, though not as young as his lackeys. His eyes were dark, his chin covered by two-day-old stubble and his head by a flat cap which, like his clothes, had seen better days.

'Who are you?' He spat the words out like wasp stings. His accent was German, like Leo Dryden doing an impression of the Kaiser in a music-hall routine.

'A policeman,' I said, struggling uselessly against his two accomplices.

'That's what our friend here said –' he gestured to Vogel – 'but you don't look like one. Where is your uniform? Did you not bring a pistol to arrest such a dangerous man? Or even a truncheon? To me you look like a thief.'

'Israel Vogel is being sought in connection with the murder of Bessie Drummond. The only thing I'm here for is to apprehend him. Now tell your boys to let me go or –'

'Or what?'

'Or I'll arrest the lot of you.'

A broad smile stretched across his face, his lips parting to reveal uneven teeth.

'Brave words for a man who can't lower his arms.'

He looked to his accomplices.

'Bring him.'

Maintaining a tight hold, the thugs twisted my arms behind my back and began pushing me towards the door. I did my best to halt their progress, but it was no good, and moments later I was being propelled into the blackness and down the stairs. I continued to struggle, fighting my captors each step of the way.

'Relax,' said the leader, who in honour of Leo Dryden's characters, I'd christened Hermann. Hermann the German. 'If we wanted to kill you, we could throw you out of the window. We just want to ask you some questions. No harm will come to you … as long as you answer them.'

I felt the strength ebbing from my muscles, the tendons in my shoulders twisting to snapping point. 'Where are you taking me?'

'This is a bathhouse,' said Hermann, his voice echoing in the darkness. 'Some say the finest bathhouse in London. Don't you want to try the facilities?'

TWENTY-NINE

The light from a candle flame reflected off black water.

The room was freezing. It might have been the one I'd passed through on my way out of the massage room or it might have been completely different. I had no idea, such was my disorientation.

The German issued a command in what I presumed was Yiddish and suddenly one of my captors had taken a hold of my hair. My head was snapped back and I was led, splashing across the tiled floor, to a water-filled trough. Behind me came measured footsteps as Hermann walked over. He was outside of my field of vision but I could feel his breath on my neck and smell its sour tang. When he spoke his voice was calm, almost reasonable.

'What's your name?'

There was no harm in telling him.

'Wyndham. PC Wyndham.' I threw in my collar number for good measure.

'And, Constable Wyndham, how did you know Vogel was here?'

That was information I didn't feel like revealing.

'You're under arrest,' I said.

I heard him sigh. 'Please, Constable. That statement grows tiresome. You should tell me what I wish to know.'

'I don't need to tell you anything.'

There was silence for a moment, then suddenly my head was rammed forwards and down into the trough. Contact with the ice-cold water felt like a thousand volts of electric current coursing through my head, the shock causing me to gasp involuntarily. My mouth and lungs filled with water. I struggled, tapping into reserves of strength I never knew I possessed, but again it was to no avail. I barely moved, the grip of my captors holding me in place like iron shackles. An eternity of seconds passed, ten, twenty, thirty, then the same again. I felt my lungs cry out for air. Another ten seconds and it would be over. Just as I was about to pass out, the hands hauled me up. I choked, fighting for breath between fits of coughing. Somewhere out of my line of sight, I could feel the presence of Israel Vogel.

Hermann was speaking again.

'I ask you once more. How did you know of our friend's location?'

'Lucky guess.'

His accomplices didn't even wait for an instruction before forcing my head back under. This time though, I was better prepared. The freezing water had lost its bite and I hardly noticed the chill. I'd learned too that struggling was not just useless but counterproductive. Instead I saved my strength and my breath. In this manner I managed to eke out what felt like an additional minute but was probably closer to an extra ten seconds before my lungs burned once more beyond the limits of endurance. Darkness began to descend until again the rough hands hauled me out, and I thanked them by way of another chorus of coughs.

Hermann stood in front of me. He clamped a hand round my jaw, pulling my face close to him.

'I will ask you one last time: how did you know Vogel was here?'

I continued to cough the water out of my lungs.

'You really should tell me,' he continued. 'I do not think you will last another dip.'

I figured he might have been right about that. I decided I had to tell him something. It might only buy me a few more minutes, but when you're about to be drowned in a trough, every extra second of life feels precious.

'All right,' I said, 'I'll tell you, but get your goons to let go.'

He barked an order and I felt my two captors loosen their grip.

'Talk.'

The best lies are those built around a kernel of truth. The less you make up, the better the chances your lie will pass scrutiny.

'We received a tip-off.'

Rivulets of water dripped down my face.

'From who?'

'From a source. A Jew.'

The German took a step back.

'You're lying,' he said, but from his face, I knew he wasn't sure.

That was the other thing about a good lie. It's best if it's something the recipient already wants to believe. Rebecca had been right. Vogel had found sanctuary with a gang of communists or anarchists, and most of these outfits were ridiculous amateurs, playing at revolution. They'd always been easy to infiltrate, and as a result, if there was one thing these groups excelled in, it was paranoia. I guessed the German already suspected his group had a turncoat. All I did was confirm his suspicions.

'What is his name?'

'I don't know. He's not my snitch. He's in the pocket of my sergeant.'

'You've seen him, though?'

'Once. A while ago.'

'Describe him.'

'Black hair, medium height ... thin. It was dark, I didn't get a good look at him.'

Hermann reflected on the story I'd spun, but didn't look convinced.

'If he is your sergeant's snitch, then where is *he*? Why are you here, alone?'

'There's a raid scheduled here,' I said. 'I thought I'd get here first, catch Vogel single-handed. Maybe earn myself a promotion. Have you tried living on a constable's wage? It's not easy.'

That earned me a slap.

The leader turned to one his of compatriots and uttered something, not in Yiddish this time, but in another language: German. Even though I was possibly minutes from death, it still struck me as odd. Why the sudden change of language?

'You are lying,' he repeated.

A fear began to form in the pit of my stomach.

'It's true,' I said, the panic rising in my voice. 'You have a traitor, a police informer. That's how we knew about Vogel.'

'Oh, I believe that,' he said, with an almost studied nonchalance, 'but you're lying when you say you don't know his identity. This story of him being your sergeant's man, this is, how you say, a fairy tale. If that was the case, your sergeant would be here. No. You are here, the man is your informer. Now I ask you again, who is he?'

Before I could respond, I felt the hands tightening once more and again I was pushed head first into the trough. I realised I had to come up with something quickly. My lie, it seemed, had been too successful. The German had not only believed it, he was now pursuing it with malice. If I didn't give him a name, I was finished, but of course, I didn't know anyone in his gang. Then it struck me. The change of language. Maybe I didn't need a name? Maybe I just needed a sacrificial lamb.

This time, the dousing lasted only thirty or forty seconds before I was pulled out. Hermann was obviously keen for me not to drown before revealing the identity of his mole.

'This is your last chance. The next time they push you under, you will not be coming up again, so I urge you to tell me now, who is your informer?'

'It's him,' I said, gesturing with a nod over my shoulder to the man who held my left arm, the one whom Hermann hadn't addressed when he changed from Yiddish to German. I guessed he was probably Russian and possibly less trusted by Hermann because of it.

All hell broke loose. I felt my captors release me and I fell to my knees. There were shouts in some foreign language and no doubt protestations of innocence, and then they were at each other's throats. I looked around for Vogel. He'd backed into the shadows but made no attempt to run. Meanwhile the two German speakers were laying into their erstwhile comrade with fists and boots. The man was still trying to reason with them but it was difficult with his front teeth knocked out.

Suddenly there came a crash from the hall outside followed by the sound of hobnail boots and English voices.

'Police!' shouted a familiar voice.

In front of me, the fight stopped instantly. Hermann and his accomplice looked at each other, then with a final boot to the ribs of their former ally, they ran. Vogel made to follow them, but with what strength I had left, I lunged forward, tackled him around the legs and brought him to the ground, chin first.

'In here!' I shouted, and moments later, the size-twelve boots of Sergeant Whitelaw hoved into view.

'Bloody hell, Wyndham,' he said. 'Bit late in the evening for a bath, don't you think?'

THIRTY

Vogel spent the night on a thin mattress in a basement cell at Leman Street. I know because I passed most of the time seated on a chair outside it.

Events had moved rapidly after the arrival at the bathhouse of Whitelaw and his officers. Vogel had been taken into custody, as had the other man left behind, the one I'd fingered falsely as a police informer and who'd quickly been identified as one Yakov Bielski, a member of an anarchist sect led by a German émigré by the name of Rudy Roker, which spent most of its time radicalising the factory workers of the East End. I assumed that the man who'd interrogated me had been Roker himself, but I couldn't be sure because he and his German-speaking colleague had escaped, out through a back window, and into the night.

I'd spent a frantic few minutes looking for the revolver I'd dropped, finding it under a table, close to the sill of the window I'd fallen through while entering the building.

Whitelaw had urged me to head home and catch up on some sleep, but I'd declined, preferring to accompany Vogel back to the station and changing into uniform before keeping vigil outside his steel door.

I'd slept fitfully, though probably better than Vogel, and a few minutes before seven, having waited for the duty officer on guard to step out for a moment to answer a call of nature, I slipped the keys off his desk and let myself into Vogel's cell.

The sound of the key in the lock must have alerted him, and as I entered he was in the process of raising himself from the cot. He betrayed little surprise at seeing me. I guessed he'd had no prior experience of a police station, at least not a British one, otherwise he might have questioned the actions of a junior constable creeping into his cell first thing in the morning. But there was method to my actions. I'd be lucky if Inspector Gooch let me sit in when he questioned Vogel. I certainly wouldn't be afforded the opportunity to interrogate him myself, and in any case, I had some questions that I wasn't keen for either Gooch or Whitelaw to hear.

'My name's Wyndham,' I said. 'You might remember that from last night.'

Vogel didn't reply. He simply sat on the edge of his bed and stared at the floor.

'You said you didn't kill her.'

He looked up. 'That's right.'

'Then who did?'

Vogel's shrug was pitiable. 'I don't know.'

'Two nights earlier, you attacked her in Grey Eagle Street. I chased after you myself.'

He shook his head vehemently. 'I was protecting her!'

'From who?'

'I don't know.'

A forlorn look fell over his face.

'What were you doing there anyway?' I asked. 'Were you following her?'

'She asked me to.'

'Why?'

'She was meeting a man, she did not tell me who, only that she did not trust him. *He* is the one who attacked her.'

It all seemed rather far-fetched.

'You expect me to believe she had an assignation with a man whom she thought might attack her, and asked you along as protection? Why would she do that? Why not ask her husband?'

Vogel let out a bitter laugh. 'You have met her husband, yes? He cared only for her money.'

'But why ask the lodger upstairs?'

'I have told you already. She did not tell me why.'

'And you didn't ask?'

There was silence. Outside the cell I heard the duty officer's voice. He'd discovered his keys were missing.

'What was your relationship with Bessie Drummond?' I asked.

'It is not what you think,' said Vogel. 'She was intelligent girl. She help me, with English and with papers and forms. We become friends.'

I was out of time. I could hear the constable's boots running towards the cell. I gave Vogel a nod, opened the door and walked out into the path of the oncoming officer, rubbing the knuckles of my right hand.

'The prisoner wanted to know when he could expect breakfast,' I said by way of explanation. 'I just explained to him that this ain't Claridge's.'

The duty officer grinned. 'Bloody Yid bastard deserves more than just a smack in the mouth.'

Inspector Gooch arrived just before half past nine, began by congratulating me and then progressed to asking the same questions that Sergeant Whitelaw had the previous night: namely how I'd uncovered Vogel's location, and why I'd been stupid enough to try and capture him on my own. The former, I told him, was down to a tip-off from the nightwatchman across the road, and the latter I put down to the exuberance of youth. His desire to get on and interview Vogel meant he didn't enquire further.

As for the interview itself, Vogel was brought to a frostbitten interview room on the stroke of ten and left there to fester for forty minutes. When the inspector finally decided to commence proceedings, there was, as I'd feared, no room for me. Gooch handled it with Sergeant Whitelaw, while I cooled my heels in the corridor outside, hoping to feed on whatever scraps of conversation that filtered through the door. In the end, all I heard were Gooch's questions and Whitelaw's ever louder interjections. As for Vogel, other than once, when he raised his voice in a flat denial of involvement, his answers came through as nothing more than an indistinct mutter.

After an hour, the door flew open and the heavy frame of Sergeant Whitelaw lumbered out, his face red from exertion.

'Wyndham. Take him back to the cells.'

Vogel, head bowed, said nothing on the way back, not that I asked him anything. The route to the cells passed through busy corridors, and it seemed everyone in the building had turned out for a glimpse of the Jew who'd murdered an Englishwoman.

I waited till the duty officer had locked the cell door before heading back to Gooch's commandeered office. I knocked, then entered to find him seated behind his desk, Sergeant Whitelaw standing opposite with his hands behind his back. Both glanced at me though neither deigned to speak. Instead, Gooch sat sucking on a Navy Cut while Whitelaw's pallor gradually returned to its normal shade of grey.

'I take it he didn't confess.'

'Stupid bastard denied the whole thing,' said Whitelaw. 'Claims he left the building some time round nine and was out all morning buying supplies for his business. When he got back, there was a copper at the door and a crowd at the entrance. Someone told him a woman had been murdered. Says he took fright and scarpered, then took refuge with a bunch of anarchists.'

'What about the murder weapon?'

'We showed him the hammer. He says it's not his. Claims he's never seen it before.'

'D'you think he's telling the truth?'

The sergeant stared at me as if I'd gone mad. 'Of course not. He's lying through his teeth. Tom Drummond told us Vogel had a thing for Bessie; her door was locked from the inside and the only feasible exit was out her window and up the drainpipe to Vogel's room, which also just happens to be where the murder weapon was found. And Vogel, instead of giving himself up and pleading his case, makes a run for it and goes into hiding.' He counted off each detail on his fingers as though each was a nail in the coffin of the Jew's defence.

I could have added that Vogel had been the man I'd chased from Grey Eagle Street to Shoreditch a few nights prior, but I didn't. I wasn't sure why. Maybe there were just too many loose ends for me to be certain of Vogel's guilt. Or maybe it was my own guilt? For if Vogel had murdered Bessie, then he'd only managed it because I'd let him escape two nights earlier. It was something I'd find hard to live with.

'Does he have an alibi?'

It was Gooch's turn to pipe up. 'He says he passed several people in the street, and that the shop assistant whom he bought the nitric acid from might remember him, but it's a moot point. He claims he left the house round nine and didn't see anyone before that. The last person to see Bessie alive was Tom Drummond, who left her at around half eight. There's at least half an hour in which Vogel admits he was on the premises and for which he has no alibi. That's more than enough time to have committed the crime, made his way back to his room and hidden the murder weapon.'

I felt sick. The facts seemed damning, and yet there were still questions. Who was the other man in Grey Eagle Street, the one who Vogel claimed had attacked Bessie? Why had Bessie been so tight-lipped about the whole thing when we'd questioned her? And if it *had* been Vogel who'd attacked her that night, why hadn't she cried bloody murder, especially if, as Tom Drummond had claimed, Vogel had been harassing her for some time? Then there was the change in her emotional state in the weeks following the death of her mistress, Mrs Caine, something that both Rebecca Kravitz and the maid, Lily Adams, had attested to? Finally there was Vogel's demeanour. He just didn't strike me as a killer. He'd had the opportunity to stick a knife through me last night but hadn't taken it. Instead he'd dropped the blade and surrendered. We were missing something.

'What's wrong, lad?' said Whitelaw, slapping a meaty hand to my arm. 'Looking at you, anyone would think you were a fellow Jew, rather than the copper who caught the bastard.'

'So we're going to charge him?' I asked.

'That we are,' said Gooch, 'and then we are going to inform the gentlemen of the press. The sooner this whole matter is put to bed, the better it'll be for everyone.' He turned to Whitelaw. 'Including all of Whitechapel's Jews.'

I received a few congratulatory pats on the back as I walked down the corridor towards the entrance to the station. I needed some air, which is to say I needed a cigarette and a quiet place to think, and it was only on opening the double doors to the street that I realised my mistake. A scrum of journalists had gathered around the foot of the stairs. If word of Vogel's arrest had spread around the station, it stood to reason that by now at least one of my colleagues would have tipped off the papers. After all, knowledge was power, but only so long as no one else had it. If you wanted to make a few bob it was vital to provide that information to the press before the officer sitting next to you did.

The cacophony started immediately. A torrent of questions, each shouted on top of the last so that few were comprehensible and none answerable. Not that I had any answers to give. I just put on my helmet and dived head first through the throng until I surfaced the other side.

A few minutes later I stood in an alley, leaning against a wall, and was about to light a cigarette when Harmsworth of the *Gazette* sidled up like a jackal on the prowl.

'Mind if I join you?'

'Not so long as you've brought your own fags.'

'Absolutely.' He fished a crumpled packet from his overcoat, then patted his pockets in search of a book of matches. He gave up and looked at me.

'Would you mind lending me a light?'

I lobbed a matchbox over to him and received a nod of thanks for my trouble. He proceeded to light up, threw the spent match to the gutter and passed back the box.

'Seems you were busy after our drink last night, Constable.'

I answered with an exhalation of cigarette smoke.

'I knew I was right about you,' he chuckled. 'Destined for bigger things. Much bigger things ... and I can help you ... which is to say, we can help each other. Word is, Old Upright's going to charge the Jew you collared.'

'Once again it seems you know more than I do.'

'Come now, Constable, don't be modest. You're the hero who caught him. I want to tell the story from your point of view. Handsome young copper such as yourself, our lady readers'll love you.'

I shook my head. 'That's kind of you, but I don't think I want my face plastered all over the papers.'

'You sure? Many of your colleagues would give their eye teeth for such an opportunity. You'll be famous.'

It did sound tempting.

Harmsworth latched on to my hesitation like a shark smelling blood in the water.

'Think about it.' He reached into his coat, pulled out another small white business card and handed it to me.

'Do you get paid to give these out?' I asked. 'You gave me one yesterday.'

'It never hurts to have too many. And it makes sure you know where to find me – once you make your mind up.'

THIRTY-ONE

February 1922

Assam

A sari-clad woman sat on the ground, chewing a wad of something which, judging from her red-stained teeth, contained a fair amount of betel nut. Beside her, set out on a faded, patterned sheet, lay her wares, about three dozen sweet-smelling citrus fruits.

I'd spent the last hour taking in the sights of Jatinga, such as they were, an exercise which entailed accompanying Emily Carter as she traipsed up and down the hillside running errands while pointing out sights of interest, of which there were few, and titbits about the local British residents, of which there were significantly more.

On seeing the fruit seller, she stopped and began to barter.

'Oranges?' I asked. 'Do they grow up here?'

'Mandarins,' she corrected. 'And Khasi mandarins are the best of all. Try one.' She lobbed one over. 'The peel is a bit thicker, but it's worth it.'

I sat down in the shade of a tree and tore open the fruit. Pulling out a segment, I popped it in my mouth. She wasn't joking. The juice tasted like nectar.

'What do you think?' she asked, taking a seat on the ground beside me.

'I think you could make a fortune exporting these to Calcutta.'

She grinned. 'That sounds like an intriguing idea.'

'You'd need a point man there of course. Someone to look after the sales.'

'And count the money?'

'Naturally.'

'Well, if there's money involved, it would need to be someone trustworthy. Are there such men in Calcutta, Captain?'

'They're thin on the ground, but I think I could find you one. He wouldn't be cheap though, so you might have to settle for me instead.'

'That's sorted then. When do you leave?'

I shrugged. 'A few days, I think. I'm not entirely sure myself. As soon as Shankar says I can ... or Mr Preston chucks me out.'

A curious smile played on her lips. 'Charlie Preston,' she said. 'One of our more colourful gentlemen. I didn't realise you were a friend of his.'

'I'm not, which is to say I hadn't really spoken more than a few sentences to him before this morning. Brother Shankar suggested I stay at his.'

'That explains it,' she said, though I wasn't sure exactly what it explained. 'So why's he not showing you around?'

I popped another segment in my mouth. 'Said he had to go up to somewhere called Maibang. He's rather an eccentric bird. Seems to think this place is haunted.'

Emily Carter's expression changed. 'He's right about that. There is evil in this place. Not just in the village but over the whole valley.'

'Not you too?'

'What else did he tell you about it?'

'Nothing. Just that he'd show me tonight.'

'Of course. It's the new moon tonight. Did he say he'd be bringing you to the club?'

'That's right,' I said. 'Will you be there too?'

'Absolutely. When it comes to the new moon, the club is the only place to be.'

'What happens?'

She laughed under her breath. 'You'll just need to wait and see.'

I left Emily Carter at the edge of the path that led to her house and started walking back along the road towards Preston's place. I was about to go in when I had a change of heart. Instead, I carried on, down the hill towards the Indian settlement. Somewhere in the space of half a mile the world changed: from the staid gentility of an English country hamlet to the raucous exoticism of native India. It wasn't the first time I'd experienced it – the same dislocation occurred in Calcutta – but here the change was starker, as though two different countries had suddenly collided and ended up wedged to each other. One minute I was surrounded by hedgerows, picket fences and manicured lawns, and the next I was among the mud huts and the markets and the noisy exuberance of Indian village life.

The natives went about their business as they did everywhere outside of the big cities, as though almost oblivious to the presence of the white men who ruled them. Men on bicycles, jute bags dangling from the handlebars, weaved along a rutted mud road, past shops and tea stalls. Women in saris, their heads covered, walked past with bundles of firewood on their backs.

I stopped at a roadside shack from which the aroma of food emanated. Over an open fire, a man stirred a large steel vat, while beside him a woman cooked unleavened rotis on a flat metal griddle. In front of them were two rough-hewn benches, one of which was occupied by a solitary pensioner with silver stubble, who sat eating, slowly breaking off a piece of bread, then dipping it in the yellow curry on a plate made of dried leaves.

'How's the food?' I asked.

He looked up and smiled that ingratiating smile which we expected of Indians, and which we simultaneously despised them for.

'Food is good, sahib. Potato curry.'

I ordered some, and when it arrived, I took it and sat down across from him. With the roti in my hand, I scooped the curry and began to eat.

It must have been about half past five by the time Preston returned. I was, it seemed, still weak from my exertions at the ashram, and the morning's activities had left me exhausted. What's more, it was when I was at my weakest that my thoughts returned to opium. The drug might have been out of my system, but I wasn't sure it was quite out of my head. During the previous few nights, it had called out to me, and my body still ached at the memory. Each time, I'd steeled myself, drunk the herbal tea and returned to bed. Now though, outside of the stifling safety of the ashram, I wondered whether I'd be strong enough to resist the temptation should it come calling again.

I was lying on the bed when I heard the sound of a car coming to a stop, then a cursory conversation before the door slammed and the car drove off.

I hauled myself up and stumbled to the sitting room just as Preston entered. His tie was loose around his neck.

'Captain Wyndham,' he beamed, removing his jacket and flinging it onto the sofa. 'I hope you've had a pleasant day.'

'In a manner of sorts,' I said. 'I bumped into Mrs Carter. She all but insisted she show me around.'

'You sly old fox,' he said, fixing me with a mischievous grin. 'Of all the women in town, you just happen to meet the prettiest ... and the richest. So what did the lovely Emily show you?'

'Nothing much, to be honest, I think she just wanted some company as she went about running errands.'

'Now that I can believe,' he said, walking over to a sideboard and pulling the cork out of a bottle of gin. 'As well as being the richest and the prettiest, she's also one of the youngest – which makes her the one of the most bored. And you spent the day with her, did you? That'll start tongues wagging.'

I was about to protest my innocence, when he cut me off and shoved a glass in my hand.

'Oh, don't worry. Idle gossip is good for the soul. Especially up here in the back of beyond. In any case, none of it'll get back to her old man. Everyone's too scared of him.'

'Except you, of course.'

'Oh no, old boy. *Including* me. Ronald Carter might not have me in his pocket, but that doesn't mean I'm not terrified of him.'

THIRTY-TWO

February 1905

East London

With the charges laid, things took on a life of their own: the wheels of justice began to turn, the papers published their stories, and the madness descended. Each incendiary page became a red rag to a fearful public, providing all the proof and pretext needed by those just waiting for an opportunity to settle things with their fists.

And at the centre of the storm was Israel Vogel.

The press portrayed him as the incarnation of evil, in fact as several different incarnations – a modern-day Judas, David lusting after Bathsheba, even a second Jack the Ripper – accusing him of blood libel and ritual murder.

But outrage is difficult to maintain. There's only so many ways you can paint a man as a monster, and only so many days you can do it before fatigue sets in and papers go unsold. So when anger at the man began to ebb, they went for his people. And in the vanguard of those crying for blood was the *Gazette*, with front-page reconstructions, outraged letters, and even an editorial entitled 'A Judenhetze brewing in east London', which began:

Foreign Jews of no nationality whatever are becoming a pest and a menace to the poor native-born East Ender. They have a greater responsibility for the distress which prevails there probably than all other causes put together.

Inspector Gooch read it, then tossed it contemptuously onto the table.

'Funny,' he said, 'how the poor and wretched are always blamed for their own misfortune, isn't it? As though the Jews who wash up on our shores are responsible for the pogroms against them *and* the filth that our own poor live in.'

He gestured to the map of the East End on the wall. 'Show me the safest wards in the borough,' he said.

'Here,' I said, pointing to the area around Brick Lane, 'and here, round Fieldgate Street. We don't tend to get much trouble round there.'

'Exactly,' he said. 'The safest wards on that map are streets which are mainly Jewish. The truth is, the crime and the filth in this place have nothing to do with the Jews. In fact it was worse before they arrived. But people don't want to hear that. It's easier to blame someone else for your problems than to look in the mirror and notice the plank of wood in your eye. And rags like the *Gazette* are more than happy to provide the targets. Divide and conquer – that's their motto. And you know what? It works. It sells papers. The press, banging on about what these foreigners are doing to the country. Well, it's my country too, and my country is better than this. Whatever happened to fair play, giving a man a chance, and not kicking him when he's down? Aren't those supposed to be the things that make us British? Shouldn't we be proud to uphold them rather than vilifying the poor bastards seeking sanctuary among us?'

'But how do you fight the power of the press?'

Gooch fixed me with a smile.

'There are ways, son.'

Over the next three days, Vogel became famous and the crowd outside the station turned into a mob.

First came the coroner's report. Armed with the post-mortem and testimony from Tom Drummond, Dr Ludlow and Sergeant Whitelaw, it didn't take long for the coroner and his jury to record a verdict of wilful murder and issue a warrant committing Vogel for trial.

The following day, under the custody of Inspector Gooch, he was taken to Thames Police Court where formal statements from the witnesses were taken and a magistrate provided a committal for trial. Gooch informed the magistrate that, this being a case of murder, the trial would be prosecuted by the Treasury, and things were adjourned for a week and Vogel transferred to Pentonville Prison.

The days passed, and my doubts as to Vogel's guilt began to buckle under the weight of newspaper headlines, both condemning the Jew and praising us for catching him before he murdered more innocent young Englishwomen. There was also the personal factor: plaudits from senior officers, backslaps from colleagues, and a new-found admiration from the locals, especially the ladies, who'd read of my part in the arrest.

And I wasn't the only one whose misgivings were fading. The Jewish establishment hardly came rushing to Vogel's aid. Their papers, keen to distance themselves and their people from him, condemned the man almost as vociferously as the Gentile ones, writing him off as a madman. An aberration.

During that week, no rabbi or Jewish official visited him. No one did. Except for Rebecca Kravitz, who made the journey from Whitechapel to the Caledonian Road, waited hours and suffered the indignities heaped on her by prison guards and the public, all to provide Vogel with fifteen minutes of human company. I know because she told me, over the top of a samovar in the tea room in Hanbury Street.

She wore a thick grey shawl over her shoulders and a look of bitterness on her face.

He'd maintained his innocence to her, and added that he could no more kill Bessie than she could.

'We found the murder weapon in his room,' I reminded her. 'He's no alibi and he tried to run. But he'll get a fair trial.'

'Really? With the papers calling for his head and mobs in the street? You think a Jew will get a fair trial from twelve Englishmen?'

I said nothing. Indeed there was nothing to say.

She left shortly afterwards, without a goodbye and in a manner that suggested that I, as a copper, was part of the problem. It was nonsense of course. I was no more responsible for the way the press treated Vogel than I was for the sun setting in the west, but something about the conversation stung me. I'd see her again, at the trial, and later, when things became even more complicated, but that afternoon in the Russian tea room was the last time I'd ever really talk to her.

THIRTY-THREE

The hearing resumed a week later. Vogel entered a plea of not guilty and was committed for trial at the Old Bailey. As was the way of these things, a grand jury of twenty-three men assessed whether there were grounds to move to trial, and agreed that indeed there were, to be judged by a petit jury of twelve good men and true. It lasted three days, and Vogel had a translator who stood beside him, whispering in Yiddish whenever the English got too complicated.

Once more, the usual suspects gave their testimony: Tom Drummond and the other residents of number 42 Fashion Street, Sergeant Whitelaw, Inspector Gooch, some doctors and me.

The defence called only one witness, Rebecca Kravitz, who testified to Vogel's good character. But after everything that had gone before, it felt like a whisper in the face of a gale.

I was called on the Thursday, the second day of the trial. Standing in the witness box, I swore on the Bible and parroted Sergeant Whitelaw's testimony on how we came to find Bessie, then added my own beef to the broth with an account of how we'd arrested Vogel in the bathhouse. All the while the man sat impassively in the dock, and if it wasn't for the translator whispering in his ear every so often, I might have imagined he'd neither understood nor cared a jot of what was going on.

The final day was a Friday. I came in for the verdict, as did quite a few East End Jews, packing themselves in tight up in the gallery like they were in the cheap seats at the Shoreditch Empire.

When the verdict came, they sat, like the rest of us, in anticipation on the edge of their benches, even though there was no real doubt.

The foreman read out the verdict. 'Guilty.'

The Jews up in the gallery received it with sighs of the downtrodden. In the streets outside, it was met with the cheers of the mob.

It fell to the judge to pronounce Vogel's fate in stock phrases set out, if not in statute, then surely in the laws of tradition, which in England were often just as binding.

'And the sentence of this court is that you be taken from here to a place of execution, that you be there hanged by the neck till you are dead, and that you be buried within the precincts of the prison in which you shall have been last confined – and may the Lord have mercy on your soul.'

Vogel listened to the translation with the same indifference he'd shown through the rest of the proceedings. I suspect he'd known his fate from the moment I'd collared him at the bathhouse on Brick Lane. The sentence was a given that followed on as naturally as night followed day, and he seemed to me like a man who'd already made his peace with his god.

He was taken back to Pentonville, to his cell, and I returned to Whitechapel, to backslapping and to celebratory drinks down the pub. Yet I felt hollow, a gnawing in the pit of my stomach that couldn't be stemmed with food or, for that matter, alcohol.

My misgivings, which had ebbed so easily in the lead-up to the trial, had returned during it, and then hit me like a kick to the ribs when the verdict was read out. Now I sat cradling a pint, alone among a sea of friends and fellow officers, thinking of Vogel, of Bessie Drummond and the sin of perhaps failing her twice.

After my third pint, I made my excuses, not that anyone seemed to care, and left.

The night was wet, as most of them invariably are in Whitechapel in early spring, but not as cold as it had been, and the rain fell only in an insipid, half-hearted manner. In a fog, I walked north, then east, until the sign above the Bleeding Hart loomed out of the darkness, and caught my attention like the beam from a lighthouse.

I walked through the doors and into the fug of an East End Friday night. The place was rammed and roaring and stank of male sweat, stale beer and old fags. Over the mass of noise and bodies came the notes of a tune played on a piano. Somewhere, someone was singing 'My Old Dutch' in a high-pitched falsetto I guessed was meant to amuse. I dug my way through to the bar, ordered a pint, and unable to move anywhere else, stood there, drank it and ordered another.

It was my first visit to the establishment since the night the Spiller brothers had provided me with the gen to track down Vogel. I'd not seen either of them since, and even though this was their pub, I was already five pints down tonight and the Spillers weren't exactly uppermost in my mind. So it came as more of a shock than it should have when I received a tap on the shoulder and turned to see the yellow teeth and grinning face of Archibald Finlay.

'All right, Constable Wyndham? What an unexpected pleasure it is to see you 'ere if I do say so. May I ask what brings you?'

I tried to think of a suitably acerbic response, but it's a special man who can do so after five pints. Any more than three and my wit walks out the door.

'What business is it of yours?' I said, turning back to the bar.

Finlay squeezed his bony frame nose first through a non-existent space and positioned himself beside me.

'It's not, of course. Quite right you are too.' The smile suddenly dropped from his face. 'Only it's not me who's askin'. It's Mr Martin an' he's requestin' your company in the back room.'

I looked around. There must have been close to a hundred men in the pub, all of them probably in hoc to the Spillers in some way or other. And it suddenly struck me that I was now no different.

I downed the dregs of my pint and turned to Finlay.

'Let's go.'

Martin Spiller lounged across the velvet-trimmed seats of a booth in the back room like a medieval baron. He looked up and smiled.

'Constable Wyndham,' he said, rising from his seat, 'what a pleasure it is to see you again. Come and join me. You'll have a drink, yes?' He looked to Finlay. 'Archie, a bottle of whisky.'

I sat down as Finlay headed over to the bar and fetched a bottle. In the dim light I made out the powerful figure of Wesley sitting on a stool and propping up the counter with another couple of men.

Finlay returned with the whisky and filled two glasses, then turned to leave. He opened the door to the front room and there came a momentary crescendo of noise which faded once more as he closed the door behind him.

'You're quite the rising star,' said Spiller, a smile the size of the Severn gorge plastered across his face. 'Didn't I say you would be?'

I sipped the whisky and felt the medicinal stab at the back of my throat before it burned its way south.

'They're going to hang him,' I said. 'They're going to hang Vogel.'

'Aye, that they will. An' it's all thanks to you.'

The words dripped like acid sarcasm.

I looked at the big man on the other side of the table, the hands wrapped round the whisky glass as though it were a child's toy, hands that could crush the life out of a man and probably had. This man knew everything that happened in Whitechapel. Everything that happened ...

'He didn't do it, did he?'

Spiller gave a black snigger. 'He was found guilty, lad. By a judge and jury.'

And in that moment, I realised I'd been used.

'Who did kill her? Was it Tom Drummond?'

Spiller shook his head. 'Justice has been done, lad, and you're a hero. That's what matters. Now drink up. Enjoy yourself tonight, and remember, I might need a favour from you some day.'

I finished the whisky, stood up on unsteady legs, and staggered towards the door, my head soaked in alcohol. The heat and the stench of the front room hit me like a boot to the gut. I lunged between the bodies, flung myself out into the street and vomited into the gutter.

With my sleeve, I wiped the remnants of sick and saliva from my face, then tried to stand. The night air helped to clear my senses. I thought about heading home, but there would be nothing there except a cold bed and more demons. Instead I turned round and walked back into the Bleeding Hart.

THIRTY-FOUR

I stayed until they threw us out, and only partly because I had nowhere better to be. When I'd gone back in, I'd noticed Tom Drummond propping up a wall with a pint in his hand and a look of death on his face. I fought the urge to walk over and punch him in the mouth, partly because if I did, I was pretty sure half a dozen of his mates would return the favour and then some, but mainly because in my present condition, I wasn't sure I'd be able to hit him without falling over myself.

Instead I ordered another pint and shepherded it frugally, all the while watching Drummond across the room. If he saw me, he showed no sign of recognition; instead he spent the next few hours drinking himself into oblivion.

The pub was still full when the barman called last orders and didn't begin to empty until, taking the brass bell in one meaty forearm, he rang closing time. Then the exodus began and the punters went off into the night, heading for homes and hearths or the whorehouses of Stepney.

I watched Tom Drummond as he staggered out, then walked over to the counter, showed the barman my warrant card, told him I was a friend of the Spillers and made him sell me a bottle of gin, before hurrying to the door.

Outside Drummond and his friends were still on the kerbside, bidding each other adieu in the lurching, staggering, bear-hugging fashion of drunk men everywhere. From there, he headed off down the street in the direction of the Commercial Road, and I followed at a discreet distance.

It was only as he turned into Brick Lane that I picked up the pace and caught up with him.

'Drummond!' I shouted.

He stopped, looked slowly over his shoulder and grunted.

I walked up to him. 'I need to speak to you.'

'I got nothin' to say to you.' A gob of spittle formed at the corner of his lips.

I took out the bottle of gin from my coat and held it in front of his face.

'Not even over a drink?'

We sat in the kitchen of 42 Fashion Street. Drummond had fetched two chipped enamel mugs and placed them on the table. I pulled out the stopper of the gin, poured two generous measures and set the bottle down in front of him.

'So what did you want to talk about?' he asked, hoisting one of the mugs to his mouth.

'I want to talk about Bessie, and what really happened to her.'

Drummond snorted. 'That bastard, Vogel, killed her.'

I looked into his eyes. The alcohol, and maybe remorse, had made him careless, and in that moment, I knew he didn't believe that. He raised the mug to his lips again and drained it.

I lifted the bottle and poured him another.

'They're going to hang him.'

'Ain't you the one who arrested him?'

'I did. And if he's innocent and goes to the gallows, then there'll be blood on my hands. Yours too.'

Drummond took a long sip of gin, then placed the mug on the table. A tear trickled down the side of his face.

'Who killed her?' I asked softly. 'Who killed Bessie?'

Drummond shook his head. 'She was special, you know. Never met a woman like her in me life. Yeah, we fought like cat and dog, but I loved her.'

'Who was it, Drummond?'

'He'll kill me too,' he said, staring at the bottle of gin.

'Who?'

He looked up from the table, eyes red, moist with tears.

'Caine.'

I almost fell off my chair. 'Jeremiah Caine killed Bessie?'

'It must've been him. Bessie was all but dead by the time Finlay an' I got here.'

'Why would Caine kill Bessie?'

Drummond shrugged. 'Maybe she was stealin' from him. I'll tell ya' summink else: Finlay knew about it too.'

'What?'

'Finlay knew she'd been attacked. He were sent to clean up the mess. That mornin', when I was down the docks, Finlay sidles up and tells me he's got a message from the Spillers: they want to speak to Bessie. Says they told him to give her a message. I said he should tell me, an' I'd give it her.

'"*Nothin' doin*," he says, "*orders from the guvnor*," he says, to tell her in person and in private. So I brought him to the 'ouse. Like you, he had a bottle on him. Told me to have a drink and wait in the kitchen while he went up to speak to Bessie.'

He gulped down his gin and poured himself another.

'Well, he was up there a while, an' I was gettin' concerned, like. So I went up to see what was goin' on.'

Drummond took a breath, then downed his drink. 'The door were locked. An' then I sees Finlay comin' down the stairs –'

'From Vogel's room?'

'Tha's right. I knew something was wrong ... knew it the minute I saw his ugly face. He said it was all fine, an' that we should leave. I said I wanted to check on Bessie, but he said there was no time. That the Spillers wanted to see me. I told him I'd only be a minute. It was then he got ugly. Pushed me up against the wall an' told me that I'd stop wastin' time if I knew what was good for me. Pressed a pound note in me fist for me trouble.'

'What happened then?'

'We left. I went with him, up to the Bleedin' 'Art. He took me straight through to the back room. Martin was waitin' for me. Big Wes too. They told me Bessie'd been causin' trouble, stickin' her nose where it weren't wanted. That someone had dealt with her. Of course, I went mad, tried to get up and punch him, but Wes shoved me back in me seat and Martin passed a tenner across the table. Said there'd be another ten if I kept me mouth shut. They said they'd been keepin' an eye on the place, that Finlay had sorted it so that you lot would think it had been a break-in by the Yid who lived upstairs.'

I went through it in my head. 'Caine killed Bessie? But the door was locked from the inside. How did he get out of the room?'

Drummond looked at me as though I was stupid.

'He's the landlord. He's got keys to all the rooms.'

'And the weapon?'

'I expect he brought it with him, then left it there. The Spillers sent Finlay to tidy up. They must have been in on it from the start.'

A picture formed: Caine attacking Bessie, leaving her for dead, then locking the door behind him with his spare key; Caine then passing the key and that to Vogel's room to the Spillers; the Spillers ordering Finlay to tidy up, to make it look like Vogel had been the one to attack Bessie and make sure Tom Drummond kept his mouth shut.

'Why would the Spillers want to help Caine?'

Drummond looked me in the eye. 'All of his stuff that goes through the docks, some of it comes out tax-free so to speak. He's one of their biggest customers.'

I thought for a moment. 'I'm going to need a statement from you, confirming all this.'

Drummond shook his head. 'You'll get nothin' more from me. You know what the Spillers do to people who snitch? It ain't pretty.'

'A man's life is at stake.'

'And now so's mine. I've told you what happened. What you do with it is up to you.'

THIRTY-FIVE

February 1922

Assam

'This isn't Calcutta, Captain,' said Preston. 'You don't need to wear black tie to dinner. Lounge suits are perfectly acceptable.'

Sullenly, I took his word for it and borrowed his least garish tie and a brown suit. I'd have preferred something darker – navy blue perhaps, but brown was as dark as Preston went. We were, fortunately or otherwise, the same height; however, the jacket was tight around the arms and the trousers too loose at the waist, precipitating the need for a pair of braces to keep them from falling to half-mast. It felt like an ensemble fit for a scarecrow, especially the tie, which in itself could have frightened the life out of a murder of crows. For his part, Preston had donned a yellow ascot and velvet smoking jacket, with a silk handkerchief hanging from the breast pocket.

It was dark by the time we set off for the club, a moonless night, with the first breath of rain in the air. Further down the hillside, light from the myriad fires of the native village twinkled in a diaphanous shroud of mist. The gravel crunched underfoot as we climbed the forest road to the chirp of crickets and the croak of bullfrogs. Turning the final corner, the Jatinga Club rose before us, lit up like a birthday cake, its veranda encrusted with candles, an oasis of British civility in the midst of nowhere.

I caught the strains of violins as they floated over on the breeze.

'Don't tell me you've a string quartet up here.'

'Hardly,' Preston replied. 'Alas, nothing quite so genteel. What we have is a bunch of planters from the Scottish Highlands. Their fiddles are quite harmonious, but once they've had a few drinks and toasted the old country, they'll bring out the accordions and the tin whistles and things'll go downhill at a fair rate of knots.'

'Doesn't sound so bad.'

'It gets worse. Wait till they turn maudlin, unpack the bagpipes and start reciting Scotch poetry. You're just lucky you didn't turn up on Burns Night. That's when they bring out the curried haggis. Their celebrations are an affront to the senses.'

'Is there likely to be a large turnout?'

'Oh yes. It's the highlight of the season,' he said, patting me on the arm. 'Don't worry though, the lovely Mrs Carter will definitely be here.'

I made to protest but he cut me off.

'I daresay most of the locals will turn out. Thirty or forty souls, probably. Almost every ex-pat within a ten-mile radius tends to put in an appearance. You see, there's bugger all else to do round here. If it wasn't for the club and the terrible plays that Miss Campbell puts on down at the schoolhouse, I do believe half the Brits in Jatinga would have gone positively doolally by now. And as for the other half, they'd have shacked up with the natives.'

As we climbed the stairs to the veranda, a couple of men leaning on the balustrade nodded to Preston, then exchanged a look.

'A drink?' asked Preston.

'Whisky,' I said. 'I don't suppose any single malt makes its way up here?'

Preston looked at me as though I were mad. 'We're not barbarians, Captain. We might not have electricity, but we've taken care of the essentials.'

I followed him through the hallway towards the bar, past an elderly couple, she jewel-clad and wearing a tiara like a lost Romanov and he displaying a shrivelled chestful of ribbons on a scarlet dress uniform.

'Colonel and Mrs Montgomery,' Preston informed me. 'They've been here since practically the dawn of time. The old chuffer claims to have discovered this place – probably got lost from his regiment. Before him there was nothing here but trees and tribesmen.'

The saloon was large, dotted with square tables and dominated by an altar of a long bar at one end. A worshipful crowd, wreathed in an incense haze of cigarette smoke, had already gathered in front of it, and Preston, greeting some with a smile and others with a wave or a pat on the elbow, steered a path between them, arriving at the broad sweep of polished mahogany like the royal yacht *Alexandra* pulling into port.

'Munshi!' he said, attracting the attention of a native barman clad in a white jacket with the club's initials embroidered in blue on the lapels. 'Munshi, this is Captain Wyndham, of His Majesty's Inspector of Spirits. He's come all the way from Calcutta to test the quality of your single malts. You'd better give him your best as I'd hate for him to have to shut you down.'

The barman smiled the forced smile of a man compelled to do so and I wondered just how many times Preston had uttered that particular witticism.

'Yes, sahib,' he said with a nod, 'and your usual?'

'Absolutely.' Preston raised an admonishing index finger. 'And no skimping on the gin.'

The barman turned to me. 'We have a selection of malts, sahib.' He gestured to a shelf on a mirrored wall. I picked out a bottle of eighteen-year-old Glendronach.

'A double. Water on the side.'

In another room, the band struck up a reel. The barman placed a tumbler of deep amber whisky in front of me. 'Cheers,' I said, adding a few drops of water – enough to bring out the angels' tears.

I took a sip and marvelled once more at the miracle that changed simple spring water and malted grain into the nectar of the gods. If turning water into wine was an act of the divine, then turning water into whisky was most definitely an act of man, and I knew which I considered to be the more impressive feat.

The saloon was starting to feel stuffy with something of the atmosphere of a class reunion and the artificial camaraderie that went with it. Gobbets of conversation carried on the air: trade, the weather, politics, the usual subjects. A sense of optimism seemed to pervade the room. Gandhi had called off his general strike; the natives had done their damnedest and we were still standing, the whip still in our hand. The vindictive talked the language of retribution, while the doves counselled reconciliation.

It appeared Preston had been conservative in his estimate. There were already more than thirty people in the saloon, and I estimated the same number again dotted about the veranda and the other rooms.

Preston had attached himself to a group of men who, from their conversation of jurisdictional districts and boundary lines, I took to be those Brahmins of bureaucracy, the men of the Indian Civil Service. He rattled through the obligatory introductions: the usual bag of Harrys, Toms, Davids and Dicks. Forgettable men with forgettable names. As usual I fielded the questions a copper is always asked when in new company, then listened politely as the chat returned to issues of administration and regulation, of subdivisional drainage and district deforestation. As soon as seemly, I made my excuses and extricated myself on some flimsy pretext that was accepted by all before the whole sentence had departed my mouth.

'Absolutely, old man,' said Preston. He checked his watch. 'You might want to step outside in a few minutes though. That's when the fun generally starts.'

I took his advice, made a cursory tour of the reading room and the billiards room, then, through an anteroom, headed out to the veranda. Lighting a cigarette, I leaned against the balustrade and looked out over the valley below. A tinge of disappointment ran through me at not having come across Mrs Carter during my circumnavigation of the club, but before I could dwell on the matter, a car, a black Bentley with its hood up, pulled into the drive. It came to a stop at the foot of the stairs and a turbaned doorman promptly strode over to the rear door. He opened it, and suddenly, like a mirror falling to the floor, my world shattered.

THIRTY-SIX

February 1905

East London

I don't recall the journey home. I just stepped out of the door and walked, my head still spinning from Tom Drummond's revelations. Why would Caine want Bessie killed and why would the Spillers help him? Bessie was a smart woman. She knew better than to get on the wrong side of men like that.

I slept on it and woke with a pounding headache and the conviction that I needed to tell Inspector Gooch. But it was Saturday and he'd be at home somewhere in west London. So I went in to the station and told Sergeant Whitelaw instead.

I told him of my sojourn to the Bleeding Hart, of my spotting Tom Drummond there, of my heart-to-heart with him in the early hours of the morning, and his revelation that Jeremiah Caine had been the real killer, abetted by the Spiller brothers.

That was a mistake.

'You're mad,' he said, his face dark as a storm. 'Will Drummond give a statement to that effect?'

'Not yet,' I said, 'but I think I can convince him.'

'So right now you've got nothing but the late-night rantings of a drunk, and you think that's enough to pull in Jeremiah Caine and the Spillers?'

'His story rings true,' I said.

'Really?' said Whitelaw. 'Why in the name of all that's holy would Caine want to murder Bessie Drummond?'

'I think it may be connected to his wife's death.'

'You think?'

'Apparently Bessie was suspicious.'

'*Apparently*,' Whitelaw mimicked. 'So you can't even be sure of that.' He looked at me in despair. 'Tell you what. Off you go, confirm your motive and find some hard evidence. Then we'll worry about taking it to Gooch.'

In terms of corroborating the motive, maybe there was one person who could help me. I walked out of Leman Street and headed for Aldgate station, then took the Underground railway to King's Cross and thence a hackney cab up the Caledonian Road.

The warders were easily impressed. A flash of a warrant card and a newspaper cutting with my name on it were enough to secure five minutes with the condemned man in an empty room.

Led by a guard, Israel Vogel shambled in and was placed on a chair across the table from me. I nodded my thanks and his jailer retreated and took up station at the door. Vogel seemed surprised to see me. The last time we'd spoken directly was the morning after I'd arrested him, back in the cell at Leman Street.

He looked at me expectantly.

'How are they treating you?'

'Good,' he said. 'Since the trial, the guards are nice to me.'

I could understand that. Whatever his crimes, there was little point in tormenting a man who had only a few weeks left to live.

'Do you come with news?'

'Of a sort, but not exactly good news.'

'I did not do this. I did not kill Bessie.'

'I believe you,' I said.

'Then what can you do? You can free me? You tell them it was not me?'

'It's not that simple. They won't believe me without evidence. And I don't have any yet.'

Vogel slammed a hand on the table in frustration. The guard moved forward, making to restrain him, until I waved him back.

'Even with evidence they will not believe you,' said Vogel. 'They will say the Jew is guilty. The Jew is always guilty.'

'This isn't Russia,' I said. 'There are laws here. You have a right of appeal to the Home Secretary.'

But Vogel didn't seem to hear. He was looking up at the barred window.

'Sometimes I wish I was born a bird. They are free. No barriers. No walls. They go where they please and no one stops them.' He sighed, then looked at me. 'Why you did come here?'

'I need to ask you some questions. I need to know what Bessie told you: that night you went with her to Grey Eagle Street. Did she say who she was meeting? Or why?'

Vogel threw his arms in the air. 'She tell me nothing! All she say was *follow me in case there is trouble.*'

'What about before that? Did she say anything to you? Anything that was bothering her?'

Vogel closed his eyes and leaned back in his chair.

'She is complaining about her husband: he is no good, he is all the time taking money from her ...'

'Did you ever see her with Jeremiah Caine?'

Vogel frowned. 'The landlord?'

'That's right.'

He shook his head slowly. 'I do not think so.' Then, suddenly, he sat upright. 'There is one thing though. You know Bessie was his housekeeper? She tell me something about death of her mistress.'

'Go on.'

'Bessie is the one who finds woman's body in the morning. For one, two weeks later she is having bad dreams, waking up in night. She say her mistress have dark marks on her –' he pointed to his chest – 'like she is being burned. From then Bessie is different. Maybe scared, even.'

'Think,' I said. 'Did she say anything else?'

Vogel shrugged.

I tried a different tack. 'The man you fought with, that night in Grey Eagle Street. Could that have been Caine?'

Vogel looked up at the ceiling in search of inspiration. 'No. It was dark. I not see him clearly but it was not him. Hard face, nose like crow's beak. Thin, not like most dock men.'

So it hadn't been Caine, but it might have been Finlay. Then again, it might have been one of a hundred other men in the area.

'Did she ever mention Martin or Wesley Spiller?'

'Time's up,' said a rough voice behind him. I looked up to see the guard already walking over.

Vogel leaned across the table and grabbed my arm. 'You will help me?'

'I'm going to try,' I said.

I spent the journey back to Whitechapel trying to piece together what Vogel and Drummond had told me: Drummond thought Bessie had been attacked by Caine and that the Spillers had sent Finlay to clean up the mess; and Vogel's description of the man he'd fought in Grey Eagle Street sounded a lot like Finlay too. Maybe Caine had asked the Spillers to do his dirty work, and when Finlay had failed, he'd decided to deal with matters himself.

Had Bessie discovered something about Caine's wife's death? The maid, Lily, had also mentioned that something in Bessie had changed after that. Was it something Caine would be willing to kill her for? Was she trying to blackmail him?

A picture formed in my head. Bessie finds the body of Mrs Caine, dead in her bed. She realises something about the death that others miss. She tries to blackmail Caine with the information. He agrees to pay her, tells her to meet him, or his representative, in Grey Eagle Street. Instead he contacts the Spillers and orders them to kill her. Archibald Finlay is dispatched to Grey Eagle Street to execute the task, but when he attempts to kill Bessie, Vogel intervenes, holding him off until, alerted to the scene by Bessie's screams, Whitelaw and I arrive.

Having failed once, Caine realises that Bessie might tell all to the police. It would be impossible to lure her into the open again, so he goes to Fashion Street, under the pretext of collecting the rent, to kill her in her own lodgings and the Spillers send Finlay to tidy up and frame Vogel.

It was already dark by the time I reached Aldgate. Still, I was in good spirits. I had a motive and I had a theory. One that made sense of the circumstances. What I didn't have was any proof or a sworn statement from Drummond.

I got off the train and headed straight to Fashion Street. The door to number 42 was opened by Mrs Rosen, the woman who occupied a room on the ground floor.

'I need to see Tom Drummond,' I said. It was unclear whether she understood, so for good measure, I repeated the name once more with vigour.

She nodded, led me through to the kitchen and asked me to wait.

When the door reopened, it wasn't Drummond, but Rebecca Kravitz who entered.

'I'm looking for Tom.'

'He's not here,' she said. 'He went out this morning and hasn't come back yet.'

That was frustrating.

'When you see him, please tell him I need to speak to him, urgently.'

'Has this anything to do with Israel?'

'I can't say. But I have been to see him.'

Her eyes brightened. 'You spoke to him? How is he?'

'He's bearing up. Better than you'd expect.'

'I can't understand how they could convict an innocent man,' she said. 'Would they have convicted an Englishman on such flimsy evidence?'

It was a good question, and one I couldn't answer.

'His case is with the Home Secretary now,' I said. 'He'll decide whether there's any reason to overturn the verdict or grounds for a commutation of the sentence.'

'And will they find such grounds?'

I doubted it. Not unless I managed to find some proof of his innocence or scrape a statement from Drummond.

'It's possible,' I said. 'Don't give up hope.'

THIRTY-SEVEN

I came back the following morning and woke half the street with my banging on the door. Again it was Mrs Rosen who answered, and again it fell to Rebecca Kravitz to inform me that Drummond hadn't come home the previous night.

For the first time, a seed of doubt lodged in my mind. Had he done a runner? Was he holed up somewhere like Vogel had been, or was he just lying drunk in a gutter? For now I hoped it was the latter, and anyway, from what I knew of the man, it seemed the likeliest possibility. I thanked Miss Kravitz and asked her to send a message to me at Leman Street, as soon as Drummond turned up.

My next stop was west, this time in search of the records into the death of Helena Caine. Under English law, any death which is sudden, violent or unnatural must be reported to a coroner. Mrs Caine was a reasonably young woman, in good health, and had died in her bed, possibly with marks on her chest. If that didn't qualify as sudden and unnatural, I didn't know what did.

She had died at their house in Finsbury Circus which, though less than ten minutes' walk away, fell not in the Borough of Stepney, one of the poorest places in the country, but in the square mile of the City of London, which was one of the richest..

Even though I was off duty, I'd made sure to wear my uniform. It helped me talk my way into the coroner's offices despite it being a Sunday. I asked to see the report into Mrs Caine's death, and after a ten-minute wait, it duly arrived, brought along with a cup of tea by a rather sweet old lady.

I thanked her and opened the file. Inside were a number of documents including the doctor's report, witness statements, the coroner's final report and a copy of Mrs Caine's death certificate.

I started with the coroner's report, which pronounced a natural death as a result of a sudden cardiac arrest. I moved on to the doctor's report. Sure enough, it stated the same cause of death, albeit couched in the cold, clinical language of medical men. There was no mention of any marks on Mrs Caine's chest, nor of anything else untoward. I sighed in frustration. If there was any suspicion that Helena Caine had died of anything other than natural causes, it hadn't made it to the coroner's report.

With little else to do, I flipped through the witness statements pinned to the back of the report. Not only did the City of London have a separate coroner's office, it also had its own police too, distinct from the Metropolitan Police, and the statements had been taken by some City of London copper whose name I didn't recognise.

The first was a statement from Jeremiah Caine which told me precisely nothing. He'd been woken by the maid, Lily, and had rushed to find his wife dead in her bed. The next was a short statement taken from Lily herself, again adding nothing new. A final page, however, appeared to have been ripped out, and done so in a hurry. I knew because a small torn fragment remained tacked to the pin at the top.

A shiver ran down my spine.

Why had that page been removed and by whom?

I'd probably never find the answers to those questions, but there was possibly one way of discovering what had been on that page.

I left the coroner's office and headed for Bishopsgate, close to the boundary between the City and Whitechapel. The City might have its own separate police force, but a copper was a copper, no matter which particular crest adorned his helmet. Some of the City boys drank in pubs on our side of the divide, mainly because the beer was cheaper. I'd made friends with a couple, and now I hoped the offer of a pint or two might persuade them to help with my inquiries, because while witness statements are appended to the coroner's report, there was a good chance that a carbon copy would be kept as a record in the station from which the constable had been dispatched.

It was a gamble of course. Finsbury Circus was almost equidistant between the police station at Bishopsgate and another at Wood Street. It was just as possible that the statement had been taken by an officer from the Wood Street station, but seeing as I had no mates there, Bishopsgate seemed the sensible place to start.

I walked in and asked for a constable called Gleeson.

'He's out on his beat,' said a desk sergeant. 'Should be back in half an hour or so.'

'Please tell him Wyndham from Leman Street station came looking for him. And tell him there's a pint waiting for him in the Ten Bells when he comes off shift. I'll be there for the next hour.'

The Ten Bells public house was an odd place. On Commercial Road, it sat on the edge of the two worlds of the City and the East End, and uniquely was frequented by the denizens of each in equal measure, with top hats and pinstripes vying for service at the bar with flat caps and sack coats. On a Sunday afternoon though, the place was quiet and I was a pint and a half down when Gleeson, all six foot three of him, walked in.

Spotting me, he came over. 'Wyndham,' he said. 'I hear you're hobnobbing with the top brass these days. To what do I owe the pleasure?'

'Trying to keep my feet on the ground,' I said. 'And what better to remind me of my humble past than having a drink with the lowest in the ranks? So do you want a pint or not?'

He laughed, then slapped me on the back and I felt my teeth rattle.

His drink arrived and we shared a toast.

'Now,' he said, wiping his mouth after a long draught, 'what can I do for you?'

I feigned hurt. 'I can't invite a mate for a drink without having some ulterior design?'

'It's the middle of a Sunday, Wyndham, and we're both in uniform. Pull the other one, mate.'

'Well, if you're going to be like that, there *is* one thing you could help me with.'

Gleeson eyed me suspiciously. 'Go on, spit it out.'

'I need to see a copy of some witness statements. Details relating to the death of a woman called Helena Caine of Finsbury Circus. She died on the sixth of January.'

At the mention of the name, Gleeson's expression hardened.

'You mean Jeremiah Caine's wife?'

'That's right.'

'What d'you want to see those for?'

'It might have a bearing on something that happened across in our patch,' I said vaguely. 'You could bring them here. I only need a quick look.'

'OK,' he said finally, 'I'll see what I can do, but I expect another drink, even if I don't find anything.'

'Fine,' I said. 'Drink up. The next one'll be waiting for you when you get back.'

He returned forty minutes later, a bleak look on his rugged features. He sat down on the stool beside me and sighed. I ordered him his drink.

'Thanks for trying,' I said.

Suddenly he grinned, reached into his tunic and pulled out a sheaf of papers and slapped them triumphantly on the bar. Each was inscribed with the same handwriting as in the coroner's file, but the text on these pages was the curious blue of a carbon copy.

'This what you're looking for?'

I grabbed up the papers and turned immediately to the final page. There, at the top, were the words I hoped to find:

WITNESS STATEMENT OF MRS ELIZABETH
DRUMMOND
OF 42 FASHION STREET, WHITECHAPEL

I read on, drinking in the words, and stopped at a paragraph two-thirds of the way down:

It was I who found her. I went to wake the mistress at the usual time but she didn't answer. I went to her bedside and tried to rouse her, but she was clearly dead. Her skin was cold, with what looked like burn marks on her chest.

Neither the doctor's report nor the coroner's report had mentioned anything about burn marks.

I turned to Gleeson, thanked him and returned the papers to him.

'Keep these papers safe somewhere. Don't return them to the file.'

I gestured to the barman.

'Get this man a whisky. It's on me.'

'Very kind of you, mate,' said Gleeson. 'You not having one?'

'I have to leave,' I said, rising from the bar stool. 'I need to go see a doctor.'

THIRTY-EIGHT

Dr Ludlow's rooms were round the corner from Fashion Street and they were closed, the door secured with a heavy padlock and the windows barred and shuttered to prevent ingress by any souls who might desire to unlawfully liberate any of the medicines within.

I banged on the door nevertheless, not because I felt there may be someone inside but because it seemed like a good way of relieving my frustrations. Suddenly a window opened on the floor above and a middle-aged man with short grey hair and half a mouth of teeth stuck his head out.

''E's not in, mate! Don't you think the ruddy great lock on the door's a bit of a giveaway? Call yourself a copper?'

'Know where I can find him?'

''E lives up Bethnal Green way, but you won't find him there, not at this time, not of a Sunday. Your best bet's the church. 'E goes to the big one with the spire in Spitalfields. Y'know the one I mean?'

'Christ Church?'

'Tha's the one.'

'Of course.' I sighed. The church sat almost next door to the pub from which I'd just rushed.

Fifteen minutes later, I was outside the white stone facade of Christ Church Spitalfields, just in time for the doors to open and the congregation to spill out. I waited at the gates, checking each face till I saw Ludlow, accompanied by a woman and child.

'Dr Ludlow,' I said, as he walked down the path, 'I need your help.'

Ludlow packed his wife and daughter into a hackney carriage, then turned to me.

'Burn marks you say?'

'That's right. On the chest. They were definitely there at the time of death but it's possible they might have disappeared by the time a doctor got round to examining the body.'

Ludlow gave a chuckle. 'That's hardly likely if they were actual burns.'

'All I can tell you,' I said, 'is that the woman in question was in good health and found dead in her bed. The housekeeper who found her described what seemed to be burn marks on her chest. There was no mention of anything similar in the medical report or the coroner's report.'

'Maybe the marks were something else?' The doctor shrugged. 'Maybe a rash or some such thing? To the housekeeper's untrained eye it might have looked like a burn, but the doctor would have known better and left it out of his report.'

That, I supposed, was possible, but it didn't explain why Bessie's witness statement had been removed from the file. My gut told me that what Bessie had noticed were actual burn marks, and that someone had impressed upon the doctor, and possibly the coroner, to issue a verdict of natural causes.

'Let's say they were burn marks. What could they be, and how could they come to be found on a dead woman's chest?'

The doctor looked at me gravely. 'There could be more than one explanation. Do you suspect foul play?'

'I'm afraid so.'

'In that case, I suppose the most likely hypothesis is that the contusions were what we call Joule burns. They're caused by electricity.'

And suddenly the pieces clicked into place.

Caine had murdered his wife, electrocuted her in her bed, then bribed the doctor to write a whitewash of a report and procure a coroner's verdict of death by natural causes. But Bessie Drummond had been the one who'd found her mistress's body. She'd seen the Joule burns and, though she might not at first have known what they meant, she was a smart woman. It wouldn't have taken her long to speak to a doctor, just as I had done, and find out their true significance. From there the rest flowed like water down a hillside. I guessed she confronted Caine, tried to blackmail him and he'd killed her, called in a favour from the Spiller brothers and had her witness statement removed from the coroner's file. I daresay he could have had the copy at Bishopsgate police station removed too – he was a man with many friends after all – but I supposed he'd simply not realised there'd be a carbon.

I finally had it all. And I would take it to Gooch first thing in the morning.

THIRTY-NINE

There's a reason why the young and idealistic become the old and cynical. It's called experience.

They fished Drummond's body out of the Thames at Wapping Steps at some point that night. I found out the next morning when I arrived at Leman Street at eight. Gooch wouldn't arrive before nine, but Sergeant Whitelaw was already there.

'He was seen drinking on Saturday down Limehouse way. The theory is he got drunk, fell in and drowned. He wouldn't be the first fool to do so and I daresay he won't be the last.'

I stared at the sergeant, and I thought he avoided my gaze.

'The Spillers had him killed,' I said. 'To stop him talking to me. I wonder how they knew?'

Suddenly he was on his feet, and standing an inch from my face, his own deathly serious and contorted like the Devil.

'Now you listen to me, son. You be careful what you say. The Spillers might have seen you walk out the Bleeding Hart together, or they might have found out one of a dozen other ways, or Drummond could have just topped himself cos he was a drunk and a waster. You go shootin' your mouth off and you're liable to find yourself in the kind of trouble that neither me nor Gooch nor anyone else'll be able to get you out of.'

We stood there, squared up and toe-to-toe. My fists clenched, I was itching to throw a punch. But that would have been stupid. I'd have been kicked off the force for a start and then I'd be of precious little help to Vogel or anyone.

I stepped back and exhaled.

'We can still save Vogel,' I said. 'You asked why the Spillers might be involved. You said find a motive and evidence. Well, I've found them. We need to arrest Jeremiah Caine.'

Whitelaw stared, wide-eyed. 'Do you know what you're saying? Jeremiah Caine isn't just some Johnny-off-the-street. You better have a rock-solid case before you accuse him of *anything*, let alone murder. Because if you don't, he'll finish you.'

'I've got a case,' I said. 'There's a witness statement from Bessie, saying she saw what looked like burn marks on Helena Caine's body.'

Whitelaw shook his head in disbelief.

'That's it? That's your case? A housekeeper sees marks on a body. Did the doctor see them? What did the coroner's report say?'

'Nothing,' I admitted. 'Caine must have paid them off. But taken with what Vogel and Drummond told me, it all adds up!'

'Vogel's a convicted murderer and Tom Drummond's dead. Now unless you managed to get him to sign a statement before he jumped in the Thames, you've got precisely nothing.' He ran a hand through his hair. 'Listen to me, son. That's not a case, that's the end of your career, and Gooch'll tell you the exact same thing.'

He was right about that.

The inspector sat me in his office and explained the facts of life.

'We should pass the details on to the Home Office,' I said. 'Tell them there may be doubt as to Vogel's guilt.'

Sitting on the edge of his desk, Gooch shook his head. 'This isn't grounds for doubt,' he said, 'it's just speculation.'

'Shouldn't we at least bring Caine in for questioning?'

'And say what? A junior constable has got it into his head that you murdered your wife and then had your housekeeper killed because she found out and was trying to blackmail you?'

'Why not?' I said. 'That's what happened.'

Gooch looked at me as though I was trying his patience.

'Leaving aside that you've absolutely no proof to justify that assertion, you know what he'll do? He'll deny it all, then see to it that none of us ever work a case again. He's a powerful man, and powerful men have powerful friends.'

'So we just let him go? Is that justice?'

'It's life, Constable . . .'

He stood up and walked towards the window. 'I think this whole case has affected you more than you realise. I think you feel responsible for sending a man to his death, even though he's been found guilty by a jury. I think this whole Caine business is just your attempt to salve your own conscience. But you shouldn't feel guilty. You did your job and you did it well.'

I tried to protest. 'You told me in this very office that we needed to live up to the best in ourselves. Now, when we have the chance to play fair by Vogel, you're just going to let him hang?'

Quoting his own words back to him triggered something. 'Look, son. You fight the battles you can win. And those you can't . . . well . . . if you're convinced you're right, you just have to think of another way. If you can't tackle something head on, try and hit it from a different angle. You're a smart lad. You'll think of something.'

I left his office with his words ringing in my head like a bell. I made for the locker room and changed into my civvies, then headed out the back of the station and into the first boozer I could find in search of enough drink to drown my conscience. It wasn't enough, however, and an hour later, I found myself out on the streets once more.

The rain was coming down again, a constant drizzle falling from a gunmetal sky as though the heavens were weeping, mourning for Bessie, and Vogel, and God knew what else. In the premature, preternatural half-light, I traipsed through the roads, blood up and senses dulled by the four pints I'd downed in the pub.

My destination: Caine's town house off Finsbury Circus. I turned into the darkening street, its genteel stillness in sharp contrast to the noise and dirt and bustle of Whitechapel.

No lights shone in the front windows. Indeed there was no sign of life at all. Nevertheless I climbed the steps to the door and pulled on the wrought-iron knocker that hung beneath a blackened lion's mouth.

The maid, Lily, answered, her initial surprise at the sight of me soon tempered with a smile.

'Constable,' she said, 'what brings you 'ere?'

'I need to speak to Caine. I've some more questions.'

Her nose wrinkled, possibly in disappointment, though probably at the scent of alcohol on my breath.

''Fraid 'e's not home yet. An' you're not in uniform.'

'Call it a social visit. When are you expecting him?'

''Ard to say, really. Though 'e's usually back by six. D'you want 'a come in an' wait?'

I was about to decline, but then thought better of it.

'All right.'

Lily led me through to the drawing room where Caine had received me on my last visit.

'Will that be all?'

'Actually, Lily,' I said, 'before you go, could you tell me a little about Mrs Caine?'

Her brow furrowed. She seemed in two minds, unclear whether talking to me about her late mistress would be breaking confidences.

'Please,' I said. 'It'd be a real help.'

'What d'you want to know?'

'Was she unwell before she died?'

Lily shook her head. 'Not that I remember. She seemed in good 'elf right until the night before she passed.'

'Could you show me the room in which she passed away?'

She hesitated.

'It would only take a minute.'

She wavered. 'Awright, but quickly. I don't want to get into no trouble.'

I followed her back into the hallway and up a flight of stairs to Helena Caine's room. Lily turned the handle and stood aside for me to enter.

The room was cold, the air tinged with the musty chill that suggested no one had entered it for many days. Against the far wall was the bed, large and soft-looking, and to either side a table, on one of which stood an electric lamp: a brass stick with a blue-and-green stained-glass shade.

I walked over to the lamp and took a closer look. A thin black plaited wire ran from the base to a box on the floor. I reached under the shade for the small brass dial and turned it.

Nothing happened.

I tried again, turning the knob first one way, then the other. Again nothing. I looked under the shade.

'There's no bulb in here,' I said, more to myself than to Lily.

The maid looked confused. 'Don't matter. No one's bin in 'ere since the mistress passed away.'

I looked around. On a dresser beside the window sat a few silver-framed photographs. One showed a countryside setting, a handsome woman in her late twenties, posing with a large dog.

'Is that Mrs Caine?'

'Tha's right,' said Lily. 'Long time ago by the looks of it. I ain't seen that dog round 'ere.'

'Did she and Mr Caine get on?'

Her face fell.

'I don't ...'

From downstairs came the sound of a door opening, and Lily froze.

'Hell! That'll be the master. 'E can't find you 'ere.'

She grabbed me by the arm and rushed towards the door.

We were halfway down the stairs when Caine appeared. If he was shocked to see me there, he didn't show it. I supposed it took more than the unexpected sight of a policeman on his stairs to disconcert a man who'd come up the hard way.

'You're that copper, aren't you? The one who was here about Bessie's death.'

'That's right,' I said.

'Care to tell me what you're doing in my house?'

'I came to ask you a few questions.'

He gave a thin smile. 'Really? Except you don't seem to be in uniform.'

'I thought it might be better to keep it off the record for now.'

'I'm intrigued,' he said, his eyes widening. 'You'd better come into the drawing room, then, instead of prowling round my house.'

Lily went to speak, but Caine cut her off with a glance and a raised hand.

'We'll talk later, Lily.'

I followed Caine into the drawing room.

'Don't be too hard on her,' I said. 'I practically ordered her to –'

Caine spun round, a look of venomous contempt writ large on his face.

'What are you doing here, Constable?'

'I know what you did,' I said. 'I know you killed your wife. I know Bessie found out, and smart girl though she was, I expect she tried to blackmail you. You asked the Spillers to take care of her, luring her to a meeting in Grey Eagle Street, and when that failed, you went round to Fashion Street and killed her yourself, then got the Spillers to pay off Tom Drummond and tidy up your mess. And now, just as Drummond was going to come clean, he ends up face down in the Thames. Another of your victims.'

Caine was silent for a moment. Then he growled a laugh.

'You smell like you've been drinking, Constable. Though being drunk is hardly an excuse for what you've done, coming round here and casting all sorts of aspersions without any proof.'

'I've got a copy of Bessie's witness statement,' I said.

There was a flicker in those hard eyes.

'I don't know what you're talking about.'

'I know you electrocuted your wife. Do you deny it?'

'Unless you're here to charge me with something, I don't need to deny it.'

'An innocent man is going to hang for your actions.'

'Careful, sonny,' he said. 'Now I'm going to give you one chance to save your career. Walk out of here now and we can forget this unfortunate incident ever occurred.'

'And if I don't?'

'It'll be the end of you.'

I shook my head. 'What are you going to do? Report me?'

Caine laughed under his breath. 'Believe me, that would just be the start of it.'

'Is that a threat?' I asked.

'That's right,' said Caine. 'And something you should know about me, son. I always follow through on my threats.'

FORTY

I left Caine's house with the faint appreciation that I might have signed my own death warrant. Not that I cared. At that moment my own life felt worthless. Guilt welled up like bile in my throat. The body count was rising. Helena Caine, Bessie and now Tom Drummond. In a few weeks, Israel Vogel would be added to their number.

I reached into my coat pocket and nervously pulled out my Capstans. A square of white card fell out and onto the ground. I bent down, retrieved it and turned it over. It was one of the business cards Albert Harmsworth of the *Gazette* had given me. With a bitter laugh, I crushed the damn thing, shoved it back into my pocket and extracted my matchbook.

I lit a cigarette, smoked it down to the fag end, and it was only as I stubbed the butt into the pockmarked yellow mortar of a brick wall that it struck me. I fished out Harmsworth's crumpled card and flattened it out. *Albert Harmsworth*, it read, *Crime Desk, Illustrated Gazette*. At the bottom a telephone number and a Fleet Street address.

'You'll think of something,' Gooch had said.

With a look to the heavens, I smiled, pulled my coat tight around me and headed back to Leman Street station.

*

Harmsworth answered on the sixth ring.

'I've got a story for you.'

The rain fell like bullets and I sought sanctuary under the oversized portico of St Paul's. I watched as Harmsworth, his overcoat slick and buttoned to the collar, struggled up the hill from Ludgate Circus. As he walked up the great steps, the bells of the clock tower chimed the quarter-hour.

'I could have come out to Whitechapel,' he said as we shook hands.

'No need,' I said. 'I fancied a change of scene.'

'You fancy a pint?'

'No.'

Instead I accompanied him to a coffee house on Paternoster Row.

'I must say, I was surprised when you telephoned,' he said, hanging our sopping coats on an overloaded and precariously balanced stand beside the door. 'Last time we met, I got the impression you weren't exactly keen to talk to the press.'

'Things are different now.'

I took a seat at an empty table while Harmsworth ordered the coffee. The place was warm and stuffy and busy for the hour – how many people went to a coffee shop once the pubs had reopened for the night? I guessed the numbers had been swelled by passers-by seeking shelter from the elements outside. By the window, a grey-faced, grey-uniformed nanny sat with a steaming cup in her hand, her thoughts several thousand miles distant, while her charge drew patterns in the condensation.

'So,' said Harmsworth, taking a seat, 'what's so bloody important that you couldn't mention it over the telephone?'

'First,' I said, 'we need to establish some ground rules.'

A pretty waitress brought the coffees as I told him my conditions. In no way was my name or position to be mentioned, either directly or even obliquely. After today, he was not to contact me again, at least not for a year till whatever furore had passed.

'Naturally,' he said, breezily waving away my concerns. 'You'll have full anonymity. I always protect my sources.'

'And there's one more condition, but we'll get to that later.'

'Fair enough,' he said. 'Now what is it you want to tell me?'

I sat there, sipped my coffee and spelled it out for him: everything I'd pieced together, from Caine's murder of his wife, through the murder of Bessie and the framing of Israel Vogel to Tom Drummond's drowning only twenty-four hours ago.

By the time I'd finished, Harmsworth was sweating like a condemned man, beads of perspiration glistening on his top lip.

'We can't print any of this. Caine'll sue. He'll take us to the cleaners.'

'He might,' I said, 'but you're insured. And anyway, isn't that a decision for your bosses to make?'

Harmsworth shook his head. 'They wouldn't print it anyway. You want them to splash a story across the front page saying the Jew we've been pillorying is innocent and the real killer is a respectable English businessman? The paper would be a laughing stock.'

'If they're smart, they'll print it,' I said. 'For a start, Caine's not a respectable anything. He's an East End hatchet man with more than average smarts who's bought and bullied his way to where he is. He's a man above his station, no more a member of the establishment than you or me. I think there'd be quite a few among the great and the good who wouldn't mind seeing the likes of Caine taken down a peg or two. As for the Jews, don't tell me Lord Rothermere or Northcliffe, or whoever it is that owns your paper, really believes a few thousand immigrants in the East End are a threat to the nation?'

Harmsworth shifted uncomfortably in his seat.

'He just wants to sell papers,' I said. 'And this story will sell: corruption, the death sentence hanging over an innocent man – trust me, people will lap it up. Admit the *Gazette* was duped. Start one of your moral crusades, for Christ's sake. It's what you're good at. Your public will love it. Caine might try to sue you, but you can crucify him in the court of public opinion. You might even become famous.'

He looked at me and I could see the cogs turning.

'Why are *you* so keen to see Caine take the rap?'

What to tell him? That I felt personally responsible for Bessie's death? That this was guilt, or the last vestiges of love, or some wretched combination of the two? Was trying to save Vogel my attempt at atoning for my sins ... for my weakness?

Probably.

'Because Caine's guilty,' I said.

'Let me talk to my editor.'

FORTY-ONE

Two days later, when the presses at the *Gazette* started turning, Caine's name was all over the front page. At 7 a.m., I bought a copy from the vendor outside Whitechapel station. It turned out to be a prescient purchase. They were sold out by nine.

The days ticked by and the stories multiplied. One paper after another began to follow the *Gazette*'s lead, like sheep taking courage from the beast immediately in front. I marvelled at the irony. The same rags that had a week before been attacking not just Vogel but all the Jews of Whitechapel were now turning their fire on Caine. Maybe it was a quest for justice, or maybe just a quest for more sales. After all, there's only so long you can scream about the sky falling in on people's heads before your readers look up and realise that it's still there.

Caine, of course, threatened to sue, not only the *Gazette* but the others as well. That too was an irony. You could, it seemed, be sued for telling the truth about one rich man, but spread a thousand falsehoods about the poor and you still got off scot-free.

But the tide was turning. Vogel was becoming, if not a celebrity, then at least a cause célèbre. There were questions in Parliament and talk of appeals to the Home Secretary. So I was in bullish mood as I left the station one night. I stopped and picked up a copy of the *Gazette* from the grey-haired old geezer with the stoop and three-day-old stubble who sold them on the corner of Hooper Street. Sure enough it contained details of a new inquiry which had been launched into the circumstances of the death of Helena Caine. It seemed that, one by one, Caine's friends in high places were deserting, and the word in the station was that a warrant for Caine's arrest was imminent.

So it was rather upsetting, then, that two feet from my front door, I should be waylaid by a gent asking for light, and that as I reached into my coat, I should feel the bomb-blast thump of a cosh against the back of my head and my own lights should go out.

I came to with a searing pain in my temples which was complemented by a burning in the tendons of my shoulders. My senses gradually returned and I found myself tied to a chair, my arms lashed firmly behind me. I tried to free myself, but any movement resulted in a jolt of pain as my arms wrenched from their sockets.

I stopped struggling and forced myself to breathe. To get a grip. To figure out my circumstances. Wherever I was, it was cold, pitch-black, wet and silent. There was a tang of the Thames in the air, that dull, sewage-laced aroma which permeated the areas closest to the river.

I shouted for help, my voice echoing in the stillness. It suggested a large space. A hall or, more likely, a warehouse. There were plenty of them by the dockside, and if the docks were where I'd been brought, it stood to reason who'd ordered my abduction.

I shouted once again. This time my vociferation was met with a fist to the back of the head.

A voice behind me called out, 'Keep it down, sonny, if you know what's good for you.'

The voice sounded familiar, but with my brain still scrambled, I couldn't quite place it.

A moment later a light came on and Martin Spiller was standing above me.

'Sam,' he said. 'It pains me to see you like this, lad. I thought we had an understanding.'

'Why am I here?'

'You were warned not to ask any more questions about the Bessie Drummond business, remember? Just take the credit for catching Vogel and let nature take its course.'

'He's innocent.'

'Not according to the courts.'

'You've seen the papers. He was framed. Stitched up by Jeremiah Caine.'

Spiller grimaced. 'That's the problem, you see. Mr Caine is a business associate of ours, and he says you're the one who's been spreading these lies to the press. Claims you've been blackening his name. Of course, Wesley and I vouched for you. Told him you were a friend. That you'd never do something like that, but he doesn't seem to be convinced. Asked us to bring you in for a friendly chat.'

'We've had our chat,' I said. 'Can I go now?'

Spiller feigned surprise. 'You misunderstand. Not a chat wi' me. A chat wi' him.'

There was a scrape of metal on the hard floor, the sound of someone rising from a chair, and then Jeremiah Caine appeared and stood next to Spiller. He was dressed in a long black overcoat with a fur-trimmed collar.

'Constable Wyndham.' His voice was firm, but level. 'Do you realise the trouble you've caused?'

I laughed under my breath. 'I'm beginning to.'

My words were met with a punch to the face, and suddenly I tasted blood in my mouth.

'It's a shame it's come to this,' he said. 'Mr Spiller tells me you're a bright lad. You could have gone far.'

'Why'd you do it?' I asked. 'Why'd you kill her?'

'Who? Bessie or my wife?'

I spat out a mouthful of blood. 'Your wife. I know why you killed Bessie.'

Caine smiled thinly. 'You remember Henry the Eighth? Same reason. Helena was Roman Catholic. She wouldn't give me a divorce.'

'So you electrocuted her? You couldn't have just poisoned her, like every other disgruntled husband in London? A spoonful of arsenic in her tea?'

'You'll never stand out if you do what everyone else does. Besides, it seemed appropriate,' he said. 'Modern, even. Who'd have thought the bloody housemaid would figure it out?'

For a moment he seemed genuinely perplexed.

'Bessie was always a bright girl,' I said. 'But you could have just paid her to keep quiet.'

Caine stared at me in disgust. 'And let myself be blackmailed by some charwoman? I don't think so.'

In the distance a ship's horn blew. Spiller turned to Caine.

'You need to go,' he said. 'I'll take care of this.'

'You're sure?' asked Caine.

'Unless you want to get your hands dirty again.'

Caine nodded. He made to leave, but then thought better of it. He stopped, turned, and walked back to me.

'It'd be rude to leave without saying goodbye, Constable Wyndham.'

With that he launched another fist at my face, and had it not been for the ropes around my limbs, this one would have knocked me off my chair and possibly into the following week.

By the time I regained my wits, Caine had left the room and Martin Spiller stood in front of me once more.

'I've got to hand it to you, Wyndham. Going to the press was a bloody clever move. I doubt Caine ever thought he'd be brought down by a bunch of newspapers.'

I considered making some quip about the pen being mightier than the sword, but it wasn't funny enough to justify the risk of another punch to the face.

'He'll hang for his crimes,' I said. 'Now that the investigation's been opened, it's only a matter of time.'

Spiller shook his head. 'Alas no, my young friend. I'm afraid not. You see, Caine's still got one or two friends left. They've tipped him off that the warrant for his arrest'll be issued soon. Told him to get out of the country, and that's just what he's doing right now. Hopping on a steamer and sailing off into the sunset.'

'Not exactly a happy ending,' I said.

'Happier than yours though.' With that he called out, 'Finlay!'

There were footsteps and then the cadaverous frame of Archibald Finlay appeared. A blade glinted in his hand.

"Allo, Constable Wyndham. I must say, I never expected for things to end like this. Can't say I'm upset though. You're an arrogant little shit. Slittin' your throat'll be a pleasure.'

I needed to think quickly. I turned to Spiller and clutched at my last straw.

'Wait,' I said. 'Hear me out. D'you really want to kill a copper? That's the sort of thing that'll make life difficult for you and your business associates.'

Spiller rubbed the side of his face. 'I don't see as how I've much choice. After what you've done, letting you go would be bad for business.'

'It doesn't have to be,' I said. 'Especially if Caine's fled the country. I'm not interested in going after anyone else. The only thing that mattered to me was catching Bessie's killer. Think about it. Killing me would be a wasted opportunity.'

Spiller smiled. I could see him running the numbers in his head. 'I'll need to discuss it with my brother.'

With that he walked out, with Finlay a few steps behind.

He never came back that night. No one did. It took me several hours to loosen my bonds, but eventually I managed it, and crawled out of the warehouse in time to see the sun coming up.

The day after, a warrant was issued for Caine's arrest in connection with the death of his wife Helena. By then of course, Caine was en route to the West Indies. Word was put out, and a few days later, the navy carried out an interdiction on the high seas. They failed to find him. Several of the crew said they'd seen him jump as the destroyer pulled alongside. Others would later claim he'd never been aboard.

I remembered the painting I'd seen in his drawing room the day I'd first met him – the clipper caught in a gale on the high seas. Had it inspired him to take his own life or fake his own death? Either way, I could take no satisfaction from the news. Even if he was dead, I felt cheated. I wanted to have been there. To have seen his face in those final moments. To see the fear, the realisation in his eyes. And if he was alive ... well, that didn't bear thinking about.

The coroner would issue a verdict of death by misadventure. It was the same day they hanged Israel Vogel.

FORTY-TWO

February 1922

Assam

The car door opened and out stepped the blessed vision of Emily Carter, draped in green silk and with the wealth of nations glittering around her neck. Any pleasure I might have taken from seeing her was, though, replaced by shock a moment later. The other door opened and I was confronted with the figure of a man dressed in a tailored dinner jacket, wing-collared shirt and black tie. This time there was no doubt. His hair may now have been iron-grey and the prizefighter's physique may have gone, but the features on the cold, hard face were still the same.

This was the man I'd seen at Lumding station; the man who'd killed his wife, ordered the execution of Bessie Drummond; the man who'd sent Israel Vogel to the gallows and who by all rights was supposed to be dead: Jeremiah Caine.

A snap of fear, cold and violent, ran down my spine. I watched as he walked round the car, took Emily Carter's hand and led her towards the steps. Without once glancing at each other, they processed up the stairs like royalty, stopping to acknowledge the flattery of courtiers en route. And then they were at the door and disappearing into the club. I felt a hand on my elbow.

'There's your adversary,' said Preston. 'Mr Ronald Carter, lord of Jatinga. She's too good for him of course, but, as they say, money talks.'

Before I could react, there came a crashing thud, then another two in quick succession. Something hurtled to the ground, hitting the veranda a few feet from where I stood. It was a bird, stunned and broken. Within moments another smashed into the terrace. In shock, I turned to Preston.

'It's starting,' he said.

I looked out across the valley. Everywhere, birds were falling out of the sky, throwing themselves to the ground like hailstones. The veranda suddenly thronged with bodies as the people inside, English members and Indian staff, stepped out to witness the scene. Behind me a waiter uttered a prayer under his breath.

I was suddenly overcome by a sense of deep foreboding. The sight of so many innocent creatures crashing to earth was as sinister an occurrence as I'd witnessed, at least since the war, and coming as it did, just as the man I'd known as Jeremiah Caine arrived, suggested something gravely portentous, as though the birds were reacting to the arrival of the Devil himself.

'What the hell's happening?'

'The curse,' said Preston. 'I told you there was something malevolent here. Every February, on the night of the new moon, something possesses the birds passing over Jatinga. It makes them hurtle to earth and kill themselves.'

And suddenly I remembered my scripture: the story of Legion, the demons cast out by Jesus into a herd of swine.

And all the devils besought him, saying, Send us into the swine, that we may enter into them. And forthwith Jesus gave them leave. And the unclean spirits went out, and entered into the swine: and the herd ran violently down a steep place into the sea, and were choked in the sea.

Like every schoolboy in England, I'd been taught the story, but I'd never believed in its literal truth. Not until now.

The slaughter went on, and those, like Preston, who'd seen it before began to retreat inside. I stayed, rooted to the spot, my head a maelstrom of emotions. A door opened behind me and a pool of yellow light spilled onto the veranda. I caught the scent of a familiar perfume, and then Emily Carter was beside me, placing a silk-gloved hand softly on the balustrade.

For a moment I was speechless.

'Enjoying the view, Captain?'

I said nothing.

'They're starlings,' she said. 'Suicide birds.'

I watched as in the valley below a group of tribesmen set about those birds still alive with clubs and sticks.

'Why do they do it?'

'Fear,' she said. 'The same reason men the world over attack anything they don't understand.'

'I meant the birds. Why do they come here to die?'

She smiled. 'Everyone has to die somewhere, I suppose. And personally, I can't think of a better place. Can you, Captain?'

We talked for some minutes, till behind us the door opened and out stepped a waiter who announced dinner.

Emily Carter took a sip from her glass.

'Brace yourself, Captain,' she said. 'This is where the fun starts.'

I wanted to stop her, to warn her, to say something at least, but I didn't. I just stood there as she handed the empty glass to the waiter and disappeared inside.

Preston appeared in the doorway.

'My word, Wyndham, I thought you'd look happier. Come inside, man. Dinner's on the way.'

I followed him blindly, still trying to come to terms with everything. My first thought was to confront Ronald Carter, to expose him as Jeremiah Caine. To arrest him and haul him back to Calcutta so that he could be ... what exactly?

The truth was Caine hadn't been charged with anything in India. Any chance of bringing him to justice had probably died the day Tom Drummond was fished out of the Thames, and I could no more arrest him now than I could flap my arms and fly. I could still expose him, as I had done seventeen years earlier, but things were different now. This was his town: the people in *his* pocket. Who would believe the word of a recovering opium fiend over that of the richest man in the region? And even if they did, why would they care?

Then I remembered Emily Carter's bruises. She would care, even if I had to sit her down and force her to listen to every word of the ugly truth: that she wasn't the first woman to be married to the man, and that I wasn't about to let her share her predecessor's fate.

Yet the hard fact remained. I felt the bile rising. There and then I reached a resolution: if I couldn't get justice, I'd still get vengeance – for Bessie, and Vogel, for Helena Caine and even Tom Drummond. As for how I'd get it, well, I had absolutely no idea.

The saloon passed in a blur and suddenly we were in the dining room: a large space laid out as if for a wedding, with a rectangular top table on a stage overlooking a number of circular ones, each with places for six or eight, and all filling up fast. In a daze, I followed Preston as he made a beeline for one near the back where his administrative pals were already seated. On the stage, Ronald Carter, the man who'd once been Jeremiah Caine, was taking his place at the centre of the top table.

It suddenly struck me that, in one of those bizarre twists of fate, until our chance encounter at Lumding station two weeks ago, we'd both believed the other to be dead: he drowned at sea, and I at the hands of the Spiller brothers. When seen like that, it seemed almost predestined that we should both end up here tonight.

I took a seat at Preston's table, angling my chair so that my back was to the stage. A roar of conversation emanated from the neighbouring tables and swept over me like a monsoon torrent. Ours by contrast seemed remarkably silent. Maybe ours was the table of waifs and strays: odd people who didn't fit in, thrown together at the last moment. That was fine by me. In my present state of mind, I could as much partake in small-talk as I could speak Japanese. Finally though, I forced myself to concentrate. Across from me sat a priest, a big chap, with grey mutton-chop sideburns and a radish-hued face that suggested a constitution pickled in alcohol. He was dressed in a coal-black suit and matching shirt, from the neck of which poked the pure-white ticket stub of a dog collar. The man sat there like a storm cloud waiting to break, his eyes firmly trained on the top table. Beside him, and to Preston's left, sat Dr Deakin, the man who'd carried out the post-mortem on Le Corbeau. The doctor, too, seemed in restrained spirits, his hand wrapped around a tumbler of whisky which he occasionally and shakily raised to his lips.

He caught me staring and gave me a nondescript nod of recognition. I had a sudden urge to ask him about the Belgian: to see if he was certain there had been no water in the poor chap's lungs, but judging by his demeanour, now hardly seemed the appropriate juncture. 'What did you make of it?' asked a voice to my right. I turned to the man seated there. He was young, flame-haired and soberly dressed in a dark suit, with a green silk cravat around his neck the only nod towards any sort of flamboyance. Beside him sat a little mouse of a woman, whom, from the wedding ring on her finger, I took to be his wife.

'Excuse me?'

'The birds,' he said. 'Dashed peculiar, no?'

It wasn't exactly the term I'd have chosen. Peculiar was a word you used when the weather was unseasonal, or your manservant was late with your breakfast; not when ten thousand birds just fell from the sky.

'Indeed,' I said.

The man introduced himself. 'Alan Dewar,' he said, then introduced his wife, 'Celia', for good measure. 'The locals believe it's a curse.'

'I've heard.'

'It wouldn't surprise me. There's nothing good about this place.'

'You're not a local?'

Dewar shook his head. 'No fear. We live up near Langting, best part of a day's drive from here.'

I wondered why he and his wife would make such a journey, as neither seemed to be particularly enjoying themselves. I considered asking, but thought better of it, mainly because I'd no wish to divulge my own reasons for being here, which I might have to do, should they reciprocate the question.

Dewar picked up a spoon from the table and held it like a schoolteacher making a point with a stick of chalk. 'Still, this is the twentieth century. We're supposed to be past the days of superstition. There's a rational, scientific explanation for even the strangest of occurrences.'

Normally I'd have been inclined to agree, but in my present state I didn't know what to believe. Nevertheless, a scientific answer would be very welcome.

'It has to do with ley lines and the earth's natural energy,' said Dewar. The priest sitting across from me became suddenly animated.

'Nonsense!' he roared. 'Ley lines indeed. Do not debase the Lord's work with such claptrap!'

'Science isn't claptrap, Reverend,' retorted Dewar. 'It'll free the world from the sin and guilt and religious dogma you and your ilk pour down the throats of the savages you set out to convert. I –'

There came a clinking of metal on glass. From the top table. A man seated at the end had risen to his feet and, tapping his glass with a fork, was appealing for silence. A gradual hush fell over the audience below in the cheap seats.

'It is my very great pleasure,' he said, 'to welcome you all to the New Moon dinner.' His tone was that of a minor official calling a meeting of a parish council to order. There was a smattering of applause and a raucous cheer at a faraway table from a fat man already the worse for drink.

'It has been quite a year …' he continued, 'despite the most trying of circumstances …' I turned in my seat and focused on Emily Carter. She seemed to have stopped paying attention and was staring, glass-eyed, into the middle distance. I doubted she had any inkling as to the real identity of the man sitting next to her, though judging by her bruises, she already knew the *type* of man he was.

The master of ceremonies moved on to a eulogy of Ronald Carter, the sponsor of this and, it seemed, pretty much every other dinner hosted at the Jatinga Club, which bordered on hagiography. At the mention of her husband's name, Emily Carter snapped out of her reverie. There was a round of applause, and onstage, Ronald Carter basked in the adulation. Emily clapped too, scanning the room. And then her gaze settled on me. There was something in her look. Something hard, almost unnatural. The better part of me hoped she might be sickened by the adoration directed at her husband.

Jeremiah Caine, the man who now went by the name Ronald Carter, rose to his feet and acknowledged the applause like the Sun King amid his courtiers.

With a gesture, he appealed for silence.

'Thank you,' he said, then turned to the audience. 'Friends. Thank you all for coming out on this most special of nights in our calendar. I know many of you have travelled far and long to be here, and while most of you are veterans of past dinners, we also have some newcomers, here for the first time. To those I would issue a special welcome. As you will have seen a few minutes ago, Jatinga is a very special place, and while not all its wonders are as spectacular as the annual Night of the Birds, one can justly say that this place is unique, and that we who have chosen to make it our home and those who may just be visiting are indeed fortunate.'

'Tell that to the dead Belgian,' muttered Preston under his breath.

'Whether or not you believe that the birds carry away the sins of this valley, there can be no doubt that we, the British community of Jatinga, have been blessed. Sheltered from both the elements and the winds of communal strife raging across this country, our land is fertile, our trade routes secure and our merchants and traders have grown rich ... and fat.' He gestured to a corpulent figure at one of the tables, eliciting a ripple of laughter. 'So let us give thanks for the bounty of *our* land, and enjoy the fruits of *our* labour.'

He raised his glass and lifted it skyward as the assembled guests rose to their feet.

'Ladies and gentlemen,' he said. 'To Jatinga.'

A ragged echo rippled across the room as the guests repeated the toast, then drank. I watched as Emily Carter took a long sip, almost emptying her champagne flute. She turned to her husband and whispered something, and for a moment I lost both from sight as a phalanx of white-jacketed waiters spread across the room, silver platters held aloft. Then the waiters cleared and I found Jeremiah Caine staring directly at me, and in that split second, I saw the mask drop.

FORTY-THREE

I kept my back to the stage and made innocent conversation with Preston, Pastor Philips and the others. Meanwhile the cogs kept spinning. Caine had recognised me. That much was certain.

Surrender-not would have called it *kismet*, told me it was my destiny to meet Caine tonight, after so long, in this place where the birds fell from the sky.

The question was, what to do. Caine was probably sitting at the top table wondering much the same thing. He'd tried to have me killed once before. Would he try again?

The sensible thing would be to stand up, walk out the door and not look back till I was a hundred miles away. But sensible had never really been my preferred modus operandi, not if it made me look weak. I wasn't about to let Caine run me out of town, even if it was the sensible move.

There was another option of course, one that spoke to the blood raging through my veins.

Kill him before he killed me.

But slaying a man had never come easy. Even when done in the line of duty, sanctioned by king and country and absolved by its churchmen, I'd never taken satisfaction from it. This would be murder, and cold-blooded at that.

It should have felt worse, but it didn't.

I could rationalise it as self-defence, but really, it was thirst for revenge. Killing Caine would lance the boil, cauterising the wound that had wept and festered within me for seventeen long years. The minutes bled by, and as I sat there and made small talk about rubber and teak, and tea and trade routes, my mind raced with plans of how I might murder him.

The conversation around the table died, till Preston resurrected it, ironically with more talk of death.

'So,' he said, turning to Dr Deakin, 'that boy we fished out of the stream. Did you ever discover what happened to him?'

The doctor shot him a look I couldn't quite read.

'Nothing to discover,' he said. 'He slipped, fell, and died from the blow to the head.'

Pastor Philips stared at the doctor. 'Who's this?'

Deakin reached for his whisky, raised it to his mouth and emptied his glass. 'Just someone from the ashram,' said Preston. 'A Belgian lad. Poor bugger got lost and fell into a stream. My men and I found him while out surveying.'

The priest gave a snort of derision. 'Just happened to slip and fall, eh? How unfortunate.'

The doctor grimaced and looked like he was about to reply when the conversation was cut short with the arrival of dessert and with the tinkling of cutlery on glass once more. I looked over to see the master of ceremonies back on his feet.

'Ladies and gentlemen, your attention please.'

This time it took a second, more protracted striking of knife on champagne flute for the assembled guests to come to order.

'Ladies and gentlemen,' he continued, 'we have a very special treat for you tonight. All the way from his cave in the Himalayas, we have secured at great expense, for your delectation, the one and only, the celebrated Hindu mystic, Fakir Ramaswamy.'

An alcohol-fuelled roar of applause erupted from the guests and a bearded, stick-thin Hindu holy man, dressed in little more than a loincloth and a scowl took to the stage. He was received by the audience with a mixture of false applause and mockery, like some fairground freak-show exhibit. His hair, coarse, jet black, reached down past his shoulders and together with his beard and deep, kohl-encrusted eyes gave him the look of an Indian Rasputin. I'd seen fellows like him before, and guessed he was as much a mystic as I was. Nevertheless, men like him were incredibly popular at a certain type of social soiree, and who was I to judge how a man made his living?

The fakir waited for the shouts to die down.

'Good evening,' he said. 'And velcome.'

Squalls of muffled laughter emanated from the crowd.

'And a jally good welcome to you, too!' shouted some wag at the back.

More laughter.

The Indian ignored it.

'I vill need two chairs ... and one table,' he said, a bony finger held up in confirmation, and soon two men from the audience were hauling a couple of chairs and a folding bridge table onto the stage. The fakir thanked them with a shake of his head and the clasping of his hands in *pranam*. One of the men reciprocated the gesture. Once more came laughter from the crowd. Once more the Indian ignored it.

'And now one volunteer?'

The guests broke out in nervous murmur. It was one thing to mock an Indian; quite another to be part of his act. Slowly, nervously, a few hands went up. Then someone in the crowd shouted, 'Carter!'

That galvanised the flock. The man calling himself Ronald Carter was the chieftain here. It stood to rights that he should be the one to be volunteered. The air was rent with cries of *Carter, Carter, Carter.*

Carter.

The man I knew as Jeremiah Caine acknowledged his tribe with a gracious wave of his hand. Rising, he strode to the centre of the stage and towered over the fakir. The Indian directed him to a chair, then took his place opposite, the bridge table between them.

Silencing the crowd with a look, he turned back to Caine. 'Your name is Mr Carter?'

'Correct.'

'Mr Carter, you seem most popular with the gentlemen and ladies present here tonight.'

Caine gave a nod. *Noblesse* bloody *oblige.*

'Tonight, Mr Carter,' the fakir continued, 'I shall tell you what the future has in store, but first, I am needing some informations.'

Caine nodded once more.

'You are living here in Jatinga?'

Another nod.

'How long now you are living here?'

A rub of the chin. 'A long time. More than a decade.'

'That is good. It is long enough time.'

Caine's smile faded. 'Long enough for what?'

'Long enough to become a part of this place. Your soul is tied to it, sahib.'

At the tables, nervous laughter. Caine scratched his ear.

'And now, sahib, will you tell me your date, time and place of birth?'

Caine scowled, patience worn thin. 'Let's just get on with it, shall we?'

The fakir stared at him. 'Very well, sahib, but without such details, there is no guarantee of accurate prediction.'

'I'll take my chances.'

'Please I may see your right hand?'

Caine placed it on the green baize and the fakir took it with both hands, turned it, and made a show of examining it.

'I see you have led interesting life, sahib. There has been much success, much money I think?' He flashed a smile at Caine, and then at the audience. 'He is a very rich man, no?'

'You certainly know your stuff, Gunga Din!' came the wisdom of an inebriate.

The fakir returned to examining Caine's palm.

'I see no children.'

Caine gave an austere nod.

'And two wives?'

Caine's face darkened like nightfall.

'Afraid not, old boy. Just the one.'

The fakir stared back at him.

'Maybe I've one more to come?'

A laugh went up – a collective release of tension – from the fakir, from the audience, from Caine himself. Only *I* didn't laugh, and neither did Emily Carter. I caught sight of her, sitting with a rictus smile painted on her pretty face.

'Let us turn to the future,' said the fakir. 'I . . .' The man paused. A look of grim fascination spread across his thin features.

'Yes?' said Caine.

'I see . . . death.'

He stood up as though a thousand volts had just passed through him, his chair toppling over behind him, then rushed from the stage. The audience sat stunned, then exploded in a chorus of boos while the MC went after the fakir. It was Caine who restored decorum, waving the crowd into silence.

'No expense spared bringing him here? Believe me, he'll be going back third class.'

As if on cue, the phalanx of white-coated waiters descended, replacing dessert bowls with china tea and coffee cups. Some of the assembled took the opportunity to stretch their legs, to go for a smoke or a chat with friends at other tables.

I watched Emily Carter rise and make for the nearest exit. Her husband, engrossed in conversation, ignored her. I rose and followed her as she headed for the veranda.

She stood with her back to me, staring out over the hills. Her bare shoulders rose and fell with heavy breath.

'Emily?'

She turned quickly, eyes wide. Behind her, the night sky had cleared. The clouds that had blanketed the valley were gone, as were the birds, swept clean from the sky.

'Captain Wyndham. You startled me.'

'I'm sorry.'

She shook her head. 'Please don't apologise. It's been rather a traumatic evening. First the birds, then that two-rupee palm reader and his talk of death.'

'I wouldn't worry,' I said. 'It's all a lot of rot. These fortune tellers have a flair for the melodramatic. You'd be just as upset if he'd said your husband was going off with a new love to start afresh in Tahiti.'

She tucked a loose strand of blonde hair behind her ear. 'I suppose you're right.'

I chose my next words carefully.

'And anyway, the little man never said whose death he foresaw.'

Her expression changed. 'Excuse me?'

I shrugged. 'He just saw death. He didn't say it was your husband's. There's always the chance that he saw the death of someone else.'

Her skin tightened, forehead creased in confusion. 'I'm sorry. I'm not sure I follow.'

'Maybe your husband has a hand in someone else's death?'

She took a step back, and suddenly there was anger in her eyes.

'Are you suggesting my husband might kill someone?'

There was disdain in her tone. Disdain, but not outrage or incredulity.

She knows, I thought, *or she at least suspects*. I took a gamble.

'You pointed me out to your husband earlier.'

'That's right,' she said. 'What of it?'

'Why?'

'Because he'd asked.'

'And why would he do that?'

'Jatinga's the sort of place where the curtains twitch, Captain. Someone must have reported to him that I'd been seen showing a strange man around town. When he got home today, he asked me who I'd been with.'

It was exactly what Preston told me would *not* happen. That the good people of Jatinga would be too scared to be the bearer of bad tidings to their Ronald Carter.

'Did you tell him my name?'

' ... Yes ...'

'And what did he say?'

She sighed. 'Look, Captain Wyndham. I don't know what this is about, but –'

'*What did he say?*'

'He asked what you did.'

'And you told him I was a policeman?'

'Yes.'

'How did he react?'

'He went silent. Stalked out of the room. Didn't say anything else until he asked me to point you out at dinner.'

'That's because we've met before,' I said. 'Except he wasn't called Carter back then. His name was Caine, Jeremiah Caine.'

Emily Carter took another step back, but there was nowhere to retreat to.

She shook her head vehemently. 'What?' she said.

'He fled the country,' I said, 'England, that is. After killing his wife.'

I expected tears. I expected the fury of a woman shocked at such allegations levelled at her husband. Instead all I received was a flat denial.

'You must have the wrong man, Captain.'

'I don't think so,' I said, 'and judging by your bruises, I have a feeling he's still more than happy to deal out violence to a woman.'

Instinctively she moved a hand towards her face.

'He *has* been hurting you, hasn't he?'

Her features contorted, the flawless suddenly polluted, made imperfect by my words. Her eyes glistened. 'What gives you the right to ask a question like that of a woman you've only just met?' She spat out the words like weapons.

Of course I had no right, other than that of a man who knew what her husband was capable of.

'You need to leave him, Emily,' I said. 'You need to get out of that house as soon as possible.'

The door behind us opened, the yellow light obscured by the solid silhouettes of a couple of men. They strode out, fat cigars wedged between fatter knuckles.

'I should get back inside,' she said, making towards the door.

She stopped at the entrance, and turned.

'This woman you claim he was married to. How did she die?'

'She was electrocuted.'

She gave a bitter laugh. 'Well, that's one thing to be grateful for, I suppose,' she said. 'There's no electricity here.'

FORTY-FOUR

I didn't stay much longer. I'd no wish to spend another moment in the presence of Jeremiah Caine and his coterie, at least not unless it was beside his grave or in the confines of a prison cell. I made my excuses to Preston, told him I needed fresh air, and he voiced no objections. Indeed he voiced nothing, seeing as his attention was fixed firmly on the gentleman friend he was propping up the bar with. Still, I was fairly sure my words registered.

I took the road back down the hillside. The air was thick – a fog of damp grass and woodsmoke – and the forest echoed with tribal shouts and flickered with the flames of a dozen torches. Halfway down I crossed paths with a party of ebony tribesmen, semi-clothed and fully armed with blades and bamboo lathis. I looked on as they scoured the undergrowth for injured birds. Finding one, they staved its head in, then picked it up and deposited it in a large hessian sack which one of their number carried slung over his back.

As I passed, their chatter died, replaced with cursory nods and sullen, suspicious glances quite different to the inquisitive looks one generally received from lower orders of natives in places where a white face wasn't common.

Preston's bungalow was deathly still, its silence broken only by the ticking of the clock in the hallway. I lit a candle and stumbled through the sitting room in search of the drinks cabinet, found it, and in the absence of any whisky, poured myself a large measure of gin.

I sat down on the sofa beside a pile of Preston's shirts and sipped. Killing Caine wouldn't be straightforward, but out here, without a warrant or backup, it was still easier than arresting him. The first task was to get my hands on a weapon – a revolver preferably, but any firearm would do. Even if I decided to kill the man some other way, a gun was good insurance should he choose to come after me. The problem was, I'd no idea where to find one. I doubted Preston kept one. He just didn't seem the type. As for the ashram, there was more chance of discovering a sirloin steak within its walls than there was of finding a firearm. There was the possibility that the general store might stock a rifle or two, something for warding off wild animals, but Preston had told me that the owners were from Gujarat, and most Gujaratis, like their most famous son, Gandhi, had an issue when it came to the taking of life – any life. Some of them, those who followed the Jain religion, even wandered about with masks over their mouths, lest they accidentally inhale and kill an insect. There was no reasoning with such people.

Draining the glass of its last drops, I rose, made my way to my room and stripped out of Preston's suit and shirt, before wandering through to the bathroom. On my return I blew out the candle, got inside the mosquito net, lay back on the bed and worked out a plan.

First thing in the morning, I'd head down to the post office and telegraph police headquarters in Calcutta, asking for any information, including outstanding arrest warrants, on both Ronald Carter and Jeremiah Caine. I assumed there'd be none, but it never hurt to check, especially if it saved me doing something more zealous.

Nevertheless I wouldn't waste time waiting for their response. Instead I'd use it judiciously, searching for a gun. The image of Le Corbeau's dead body floated into my consciousness. The puckered scar, the lifeless corpse, the marks on his trousers. A shiver crossed my shoulders. He'd been of my height and build. In the dark we'd have looked similar. Had someone thought he was me? It was my second night at the ashram. The night after I'd first met Emily Carter, Caine's wife; two days after Caine had seen me in Lumding station. My mind raced. Had Caine already sent someone to kill me? Had Le Corbeau been murdered by mistake?

Suddenly I felt the familiar pang within. The call of the O, fuelling my paranoia, clouding my judgement. In a panic, I concocted the flimsiest of plans. I told myself I needed to find a weapon and fast. If not a gun, then a blade would do. I'd send Caine a note, telling him to meet me in the clearing in the forest near the ashram where Le Corbeau had been found, to discuss the price of my silence.

He might suspect a trap, but he was a man used to buying loyalty and my request for cash was, I hoped, something he'd readily believe. I'd tell him to come alone, remind him that I knew how he'd killed Bessie Drummond and wouldn't take kindly to any attempt by him to try something similar with me. When he turned up though, I'd kill him in cold blood.

It wasn't much of a plan, but then I wasn't much of a murderer.

It was dark outside and sleep was hard to find. It had started with the adrenaline rush from seeing Caine, but then, as I lay in bed, something else took over: that primal urge that had been my driving force for almost the last two years. My body ached, the sort of pain that could only be salved by a hit of O. I fought it, which is to say I lay there with a pillow over my face, but that voice at the back of my head, the one that always whispered such sweet poison, refused to be silent.

Just one pipe ... Just to help with the sleep ...'

It was tempting.

Extremely tempting.

And then I told myself that all of this had started with just one pipe. Just one to help with the sleep.

I must have dozed off at some point because the next thing I knew, I was waking to the sound of someone fiddling with the front door. My first thought was that it was Preston, coming home after consuming a skin-full and having trouble getting his key in the lock. The next moment, there was a crash and I heard the front door smash back on its hinges. Instinctively I lifted the mosquito net, rolled out of bed and onto the floor. There were voices in the hallway beyond. Indian voices in a foreign tongue. I cursed myself for having been so stupid. Caine had been sharper than I'd expected. I should have done the smart thing, left the dinner and been halfway to Lumding by now. Instead I was standing here in my underclothes and his killers were on the other side of the door. I stood up and frantically searched for a weapon, but there was nothing. The seconds slowed. I heard the men making their way through the house. Any moment now, they'd reach my room. I looked around in a panic, searching for something, anything I could use to defend myself.

Then I saw it – a rectangular tin box on Preston's camera shelf. I grabbed it, pulled open the lid and poured the powdery contents into a heap on the floor. Reaching for my trousers, I pulled out my matches and made ready.

Suddenly the door to my room burst open. I made out the shapes of two stocky men. Something in the hand of the first man glinted in the half-light. I struck my match and it flickered to life. Closing my eyes, I dropped it into the mound I'd heaped on the floor. It was flash-powder: a mixture of magnesium and potassium chlorate, used for lighting a room when a photograph was taken. There was an explosion of brilliant white light which registered on my retinas even though my eyelids were shut tight. Quickly I opened them to find my two guests groping about, temporarily blinded by the flash. I wasted no time smashing the first man in the face and felt a sharp, satisfying pain run up the length of my arm as my fist connected with his nose. He yelled out, dropping his knife. I followed up with a punch to his gut, then a knee to his head as he doubled over.

Behind him, his accomplice, still blinded, began to back out of the room. Picking up the knife, I stepped into the hallway after him. The man stumbled, knocking over a chair on his way to the front door, and I roared a volley of curses at him to make sure he didn't have any second thoughts about helping his friend.

Barring the front door, I returned to my room. At least my first problem had been sorted. I *had* a weapon. The man on the floor was still out cold. I lit a candle and bent down to take a closer look. He was a native, with the slightly oriental features that the locals of the region possessed. Pouring a glass of water from the jug on the desk, I took a sip, then threw the rest onto his face. He came to with a start, raised a hand to his head, and then saw me standing above him. A look of panic spread across his bloodied face.

'Stay where you are,' I said, brandishing the knife and ending any scope for debate.

I felt an anger building within me at the thought that this man had the temerity to try and kill me, and I considered punching him again just to make myself feel better. I resisted the urge, however. I needed to question him. And him lying on the floor while I stood punching him while dressed in nothing but my underwear wasn't exactly standard interrogatory procedure.

'Get up. Slowly. And keep your hands above your head.'

I gestured him to a chair by the desk.

'Sit. And keep your hands where I can see them.'

The man eyed me warily but did as ordered.

Keeping the knife trained on him, I put on my trousers.

'What's your name?'

The man said nothing.

'Who sent you?'

Again the only response was the ticking of the clock in the hallway. Not that it mattered. It was patently obvious who'd dispatched him.

It was impressive how quickly Caine had been able to martial his forces. But maybe I could turn this to my advantage. Maybe there was a way of extracting justice for all those whom Caine had killed without having to get him to sign a confession, or me having to murder him. And the most satisfying part was that Caine had given me the ammunition himself.

I tried again, this time taking a different tack.

'You can read English?'

The man nodded slowly.

'Good,' I said. From my pocket, I fished out my wallet and extracted my warrant card. 'You know what this says?' The man stared at the blue, dog-eared document. 'Well, I'll tell you. It says I'm an officer of the Imperial Police, and attacking an officer is a serious offence. People have been hanged for less.'

Fear registered in the man's eyes; a blacker, deeper fear than before.

'Now I'll ask you again. What's your name and who sent you?'

'My name is Deori. Bogoram Deori. I work for Mr Carter.'

'And he sent you to kill me?'

He said nothing, but slowly nodded.

'And has Mr Carter asked you to kill anyone else?'

Deori shook his head in confusion. 'Sahib?'

'A week ago – did you kill a man and leave his body in a stream up near the ashram?'

'No, sahib. I swear it.'

I used to have a good instinct for telling when a man was lying, but with my descent into opium addiction and the improvement of my own ability to lie, it seemed I'd lost the knack for telling the difference between truth and fiction. I stared hard at him, hoping the scrutiny might cause him to crack, but I saw nothing.

I shook my head and changed tack.

'Can you write in English?'

The man seemed unsure of what I was driving at.

'Yes.'

'Good,' I said. I walked over to the bed and pulled the case off a pillow and threw it to him. 'Clean yourself up. I can't have blood all over your confession.'

While Bogoram Deori washed his face and hands with water from the jug and dried them on the pillowcase, I searched the desk drawer, retrieving pen and paper.

'Here,' I said, passing them to him. 'Get writing.'

I dictated his statement, outlining that on the orders of his employer, Mr Ronald Carter, he and an accomplice had come here with the express intention of killing me, then got him to sign and date it.

'This letter will stop them hanging me?'

'Not quite,' I said, 'but we're not finished yet.'

On a fresh sheet of paper, I got him to write out the same confession, but this time I added a line to the effect that, despite having been ordered to commit murder, Deori could not bring himself to carry out his instructions. That he'd come to me and confessed all. Once more, he signed and dated the sheet. I held one in each hand and brandished them at him.

'This first letter sends you to the gallows. The other sends you home as a free man. Which one I submit will depend upon your cooperation. Understand?'

Deori nodded.

'Right then, here's what we're going to do.'

FORTY-FIVE

'We need transport.'

Deori shrugged. 'Only few sahibs have car here.'

We were standing outside his hut in the native settlement further down the valley. The sky was still black and I judged it must be sometime between two and three in the morning.

As I'd anticipated, Deori's accomplice, a man called Boja, had retreated back to the village to lick his wounds, and we'd found him holed up in a neighbouring hut. Unlike Deori, Boja could neither read nor write, so I wrote out similar statements and, colouring his thumb with ink from Preston's fountain pen, I'd got him to place his thumbprint at the bottom. Now I needed to get those documents to the nearest police post and lodge what was called an FIR, a first information report, the basic document declaring that a crime had been committed and which set the wheels of justice in motion. The problem was, the nearest thana was in Haflong, almost five miles away.

'But,' said Deori, 'the Gujarati who owns general store, he has a lorry.'

'Of course he does,' I said. It stood to reason that the owner of the finest emporium in Assam would need a vehicle to transport his merchandise up here.

'Let's go wake him.'

*

The windows above the Bhagwan general store were curtained and dark. Nevertheless I strode up the front steps, banged loudly and kept knocking until those inside must have thought the door would give way. Eventually the glimmer of candlelight flickered through the muslin screen behind a barred window, followed by a tentative voice.

'Yes?'

'Police,' I said. 'Open up ... please.'

There came the scraping of bolts. The door opened a crack and half a face peered out. I placed my warrant card in front of it.

'Police,' I said. 'I need your help.'

Twenty minutes later, and after furnishing him with a ten-rupee note and written reassurance that the Imperial Police Force would cover the cost of his fuel and any additional expenses to the tune of a further twenty rupees, I was seated next to Mr Shalin Bhagwan in the cab of his lorry, while Bogoram Deori sat in the back among a number of crates. We'd left his accomplice, Boja, behind, as there seemed little benefit in dragging him along too.

A smile on his round face, Bhagwan whistled a tune as he drove. His initial fear at seeing me had quickly transformed into something different, the moment he'd sensed an opportunity to make a profit. Not only had he negotiated a rather tidy sum for what was in effect a ten-mile round trip, he'd then decided to take advantage of the unforeseen opportunity and loaded his lorry with goods that he needed to take to Haflong in any case.

The journey along the rutted and winding hill pass took almost an hour and the sky was beginning to lighten with the first hint of dawn as we passed the sign welcoming us to Haflong.

Bhagwan dropped us outside the police thana and promised to be back within half an hour. 'I will drop off some items with my brother-in-law, Vimal, and come straight back. His shop is close by, not five minutes distant.'

There was, I realised, no point in arguing with him. Even if I'd told him to wait there, he'd have insisted we stop off at his brother-in-law's on the journey back. This way at least, I hoped we'd save some time.

The police station was quiet. A lone constable dozed behind a grilled counter, the dancing flame from a hurricane lamp throwing shadows over the blue walls. I rapped on the grille and he woke with a start and dabbed at the dribble on his chin.

I brought out my warrant card and placed it on the counter. 'Good morning,' I said, smiling. I pointed to Deori. 'This gentleman was sent to kill me and now we're here to lodge an FIR.'

The sun was visible between the hills by the time Mr Bhagwan returned from his brother-in-law's. It had taken him considerably longer than thirty minutes, but that wasn't a problem given that it took almost an hour for me to fill out the paperwork and convince the constable, whose name was Singh, that I was deadly serious about arresting Mr Ronald Carter and, if he valued his career, that he should be too.

I felt some sympathy for him. Carter was a rich and powerful sahib and he was just the nightshift at Haflong police station. In normal circumstances, he'd no more think of arresting Carter than he would consider getting into bed with a python. It took a call to provincial headquarters in Guwahati before he finally provided me with the correct forms.

'Right,' I said, filling out the last of them. 'Let's go and arrest him.'
'Sir?'

'We need to go and arrest Mr Carter,' I said. 'Now.'

The constable shook his head in that peculiar Indian fashion. 'That is not possible, sir. Decision to arrest Carter sahib needs to be taken by District Superintendent Turner.'

'And where do I find District Superintendent Turner?'

'He is in Silchar, sir. Seventy miles from here.'

'Call Silchar station,' I said. 'Tell them to get an urgent message to Turner. Tell them Captain Sam Wyndham of CID in Calcutta requests his assistance in Jatinga. How long will it take him to drive to Jatinga from Silchar, by the way?'

'Three hours at least.'

'And what time is it now?'

The man checked his watch. 'Quarter to five.'

'Tell them I'll meet him at the Jatinga Club at half past nine.'

The constable nodded, then put through the call.

I headed out into the dawn with Deori in tow, lit a cigarette, tossed one to him and considered the irony of having a smoke with a man who'd been sent to murder me.

The constable stepped out of the station.

'Call is made, Captain sahib. You want me to lock up the thana? The day constable will not arrive before eight o'clock.'

'Do that,' I said, 'and be prepared to spend the next hour in the back of a lorry.'

FORTY-SIX

Bhagwan's truck creaked to a halt near the path up to the Carter residence. It was 6 a.m. All the way back I'd wrangled with the question of what to do in the hours until District Superintendent Turner from Silchar turned up at the Jatinga Club so that I could officially arrest Jeremiah Caine. As the lorry had rumbled back up the road to Jatinga, my fears began to surface: Caine would have discovered his plot to kill me had failed and was even now making a run for it; worse, he was planning another attempt and he'd carry it out while I sat twiddling my thumbs waiting for Turner to show up.

Now, as I sat outside his house, I convinced myself there was no point in waiting. I'd set the wheels in motion, and it was enough that I was a detective and that I had a uniformed constable with me. Besides, there was a good chance that in his present guise as Ronald Carter, Caine's malign influence reached as far as Silchar. For all I knew, Superintendent Turner or his colleagues might be in his pay, just as I suspected several officers back in Whitechapel had been seventeen years earlier. I thought it best, therefore, to present Turner, when he arrived, with a fait accompli. And there was no time like the present.

We'd deposited Deori back at his village with instructions that neither he nor his comrade, Boja, were to show their faces up in the white town for the next twenty-four hours. What's more, having given his statement and now my key witness, I impressed upon him that should he try to abscond, I would find him and the consequences would be as severe as the sky falling on his head.

After reassuring the shopkeeper, Bhagwan, that my letter authorising the payment of an additional twenty rupees to cover his fuel, wear and tear, and shoe-leather costs would be honoured by the authorities at Lal Bazar, I descended from the cab. In reality there was no guarantee that they would, but Bhagwan struck me as a persistent chap, the sort who'd probably relish the epistolary struggle with a minor functionary in the accounts department of police headquarters, even if it took a year or two to get his money.

With Constable Singh in tow and to the sound of early-morning birdsong, I began to climb the tree-lined path towards Highfield, past the open doors of the outbuilding where Emily Carter kept her wreck of a Bugatti. The house, whitewashed and pristine, stood upon a rise some yards further on, an air of somnolence hanging over it like a silken sheet. The cane chairs sat deserted on the veranda, the front door was locked tight, and above, the windows of the upper storey remained shuttered. That was fine with me. Indeed, I took an almost perverse pleasure in the thought that I'd be rousing Caine from his bed, just as he'd done to me hours earlier.

I climbed the front steps, then stopped and turned to Singh.

'How old are you, son?'

The question seemed to throw him. 'Eighteen, sir.'

Roughly the same age I'd been when I'd confronted Caine for the first time.

I ordered him to knock on the door. It was a petty act, but I assumed it would be even more galling for Caine if the young Indian constable made the physical arrest.

He rapped loudly. 'Police! Open the door!' he shouted, then maintained a steady hammering until the first stirrings of life were heard from inside.

The door finally opened and a petite maidservant in a black-and-white uniform stood in front of us with a quizzical look on her face.

The constable uttered something to her in the local language, and though the words were foreign, there was no mistaking the edge of authority in his voice. The maid stood aside to let us enter.

'Where is he?' I asked. 'Where's Ronald Carter?'

'Master sahib is still asleep.'

'It's time to wake him. Take us to his room.'

For a moment she seemed unsure. Waking the master of the house at the behest of two strangers wasn't something that came naturally to her, even less so the act of escorting them up to his bedchamber. I nodded to the constable and he growled at her again. That seemed to provide the required encouragement and she ushered us across the polished mahogany floor and up the wide staircase in the centre of the hallway.

She stopped at a door near the top of the stairs and knocked gently.

'Master sahib?'

We waited for a response that didn't come.

She knocked again. 'Master sahib?'

I lost patience.

'I'll do it myself.'

I rapped hard on the door, loud enough, I thought, to wake the dead. It certainly stirred others in the house. A door across the landing opened and a face peered out. It was Dr Deakin, the man who'd been seated at our table at dinner the previous night, and who'd written the report on Le Corbeau's cause of death.

Ignoring him, I knocked again, then tried the door handle.

Locked.

'Where's the key?' I asked the maid.

She shook her head. 'With Master sahib.'

I knelt down and tried to look through the keyhole, but found my view obstructed. The key was in the lock on the other side of the door.

'Ronald Carter,' I shouted, 'open up! You're under arrest.'

A familiar voice rang out from the stairwell. 'What the devil's going on?'

I turned to see Emily Carter, a white silk dressing gown wrapped around her, descending from the floor above like an avenging angel. For a woman just roused from sleep, she cut a surprisingly resolute figure.

'Captain Wyndham? What are you doing?'

'I'm here to arrest Mr Ronald Carter,' I said, 'also known as Mr Jeremiah Caine, on a charge of attempted murder.'

'That's ridiculous,' she said. She rubbed a hand across her temples. As she did, the sleeve of her gown slid back, revealing the blue-black bruise I'd seen before. The one on her face, though, was neatly powdered.

Along the corridor, another door opened. This time it was Charles Preston who stepped out. He was in his underwear and looked incredulous.

'Wyndham?'

I tried to hide my surprise at seeing him and instead turned back to Emily Carter.

'I need you to open this door.'

'I can't. Ronald's got the key. Are you sure he's inside?'

'The maid thinks he is. I take it this *is* his bedroom?'

'That's right.'

'The key's in the lock on the other side. I'm afraid if he refuses to open up, I have to assume he's attempting to escape. I'm going to have to force it open.'

Before she could respond, I gave Singh the order to break it down. The constable took a few paces back, then rushed at the door, hitting it with his shoulder. There was a thud, and the crack of wood. He took a step back, then attacked the door again. This time it gave way. Singh fell forward, carried over the threshold by his own momentum.

I rushed in, expecting to see Caine making a bolt for it through a window. Instead the room was in darkness, windows shuttered. The air was unnaturally warm, and thin shafts of light fell through the slats of the shutters. In the centre of the room, covered in the fine gauze of a mosquito net, stood a large brass bed, its headboard an intricate sculpture of metalwork. Cautiously, I walked up to it, keenly aware of the eyes of Mrs Carter and several others at my back. Through the netting, the outline of a figure was visible.

I lifted the gauze and saw Caine lying there, face down, his head turned to one side.

'Carter,' I called out.

There was no reply.

I fumbled with the mosquito net, pulling out a section from beneath the mattress and reached inside. Caine's pyjamas were damp to the touch, as were the thin sheets. I grabbed his hand. It was cold, and lifeless. Frantically I felt for a pulse, but found nothing. His hand dropped heavily back onto the bed as I let it go. I turned to find Emily Carter and Charlie Preston a few steps away.

I shook my head.

'Get Dr Deakin.'

FORTY-SEVEN

Jeremiah Caine was dead.

I didn't need a doctor to tell me so, but it was always nice to have professional confirmation. It turned out that after the previous night's dinner, Caine, now calling himself Ronald Carter, had invited some of the guests back to his house for more drinks and to spend the night. Among those who'd availed of his hospitality was the good doctor Deakin, who now entered Carter's bedchamber in borrowed nightshirt and slippers and pronounced what everyone in the room already knew: that at some point during the night, the Grim Reaper had called for their host.

As the maid opened the shuttered windows and let in a cooling breeze, a flood of conflicting emotions welled up within me. There was no satisfaction at the thought that Caine was dead. Indeed I felt cheated. Caine had escaped justice, lived out a comfortable life, albeit in deepest, darkest Assam, and just as he was about to be brought down, he'd escaped once again, some might say to face a higher justice, but I couldn't be sure. Hell was fine, if it existed, but I'd still have preferred for Caine to first face a more material reckoning: one that involved a prison cell with iron bars.

A sense of shock pervaded the room, as other guests, woken by the commotion, came out of their rooms. Charlie Preston crossed himself.

'That fakir was right,' he said. 'He foresaw Carter's death. It was the curse.'

The last thing I needed was a bunch of hysterical house guests going on about curses and evil spirits. I gestured to Constable Singh.

'Get these people back to their own rooms. Let them get changed, but no one's to leave the house. Understood?'

'Yes, sir,' he said, then began to herd the guests out of Caine's bedchamber.

That left Dr Deakin, Mrs Carter and me.

'Any thoughts as to time of death?'

The doctor puffed out his cheeks. 'It's hard to say precisely. I should think several hours ago at least. Possibly sometime around two or three in the morning.'

A shiver ran up my spine. Could it be that Caine had died at the precise moment that his henchmen had come to kill me? I didn't believe in karma, but the events of the last ten hours, starting with the arrival of Caine just as the starlings started killing themselves, had severely shaken my lack of faith.

'What about cause of death?'

The doctor shrugged. 'Hard to tell. I'd need to take a better look. Help me take the netting down.'

'Don't trouble yourself,' said Mrs Carter. 'I'll have the maid do it.'

The girl lowered the mosquito net and the doctor set to work, first examining Caine's corpse from all sides, then turning him over onto his back. As he did so, the coils of the mattress creaked. A coil-sprung mattress was unusual in India. In this part of the world most mattresses were just large sacks filled with wadded cotton. Only the very rich had such mattresses, even in Calcutta.

As for the net, it consisted of four triangular sheets of muslin, stitched together with a stiff cord to form a pyramid, the top of which was tied to a hook on the ceiling and the base of the sides tucked in between mattress and bed frame.

As the doctor worked, I turned to Emily Carter. She seemed in a daze, her hair loose over one shoulder, and her eyes moist.

'What time did he retire for the night?'

'I ... I couldn't say for sure. Around 1 a.m. maybe? I think that's when the party broke up.'

'How did he seem?'

She stared back at me as though she hadn't heard the question, or as though she was caught in a nightmare and none of this was actually happening. I didn't blame her. Last night I'd told her that her husband wasn't whom he claimed to be, that he was a killer, and now he himself was dead in his own bed.

'Mrs Carter.'

Her eyes focused. She snapped back from wherever it was she'd been.

'How did your husband seem when he retired for the night?'

She pondered. 'Agitated, not quite himself. Probably worried by what the fakir had said.'

Or maybe, I thought, he was just nervous about his plan to have me murdered.

'But how?' she continued. 'How could he have known?'

'What?'

She looked up, her face drained of colour save for the area beneath one eye that had been heavily made up to conceal other offences.

'The fakir. How could he know that Ronald was going to die?'

'That's odd.' Deakin had unbuttoned Caine's nightshirt and was staring down.

I walked over and stood beside him. Caine's chest was a mass of silver hair on greying flesh.

'Look,' he said, pointing at a patch of discoloured flesh. 'And here – another one.'

With two fingers he touched one of the patches below where Caine's heart had once beaten. The skin was raw, the flesh different from the area around it.

'What are they?' I asked. 'Bruises?'

'I don't think so,' said the doctor.

'Then what?'

'I'm not sure. It's almost as though the skin here has been burned.'

'What?'

'I don't quite understand it. I've never seen anything like it before.'

Suddenly I recalled the words from Bessie's witness statement that had been torn from a coroner's report years before.

'Her skin was cold, with what looked like burn marks on her chest.'

'If I didn't know better,' continued the doctor, 'I'd say the marks are consistent with –'

'Electrocution,' I said, finishing his sentence.

FORTY-EIGHT

'Impossible,' said the doctor. 'There's no electricity within several hundred miles. The marks must have been caused by something else. They're probably older injuries.'

I left him to finish his work, deposited Emily Carter into the care of her maid, put Constable Singh in charge of the other members and guests of the house, and with my head spinning, left for the Jatinga Club in time for breakfast before District Superintendent Turner showed up.

I wasn't sure what I was going to tell him. I'd dragged him across seventy miles of harsh terrain to arrest a man I'd accused of attempted murder and who was now lying dead in his own bedchamber with strange marks on his chest that suggested he might have been electrocuted in a locked room a few hundred miles away from the nearest source of electricity. It was a state of affairs so bizarre that even suggesting it would make me sound mad.

Yet I'd have to tell him something.

It was past eight by the time I wearily climbed the stairs to the club's veranda and took a seat at the same table I'd had the morning before and stared out at the view. It was unchanged since the previous day and yet also utterly different. Where yesterday this had

been a picturesque valley dotted with handsome colonial bungalows, today it was a malevolent place where birds came to die in
their thousands and at whose heart stood a mansion that a murderer had made his lair, and where now he himself lay cold, his
death foretold by a Hindu mystic.

A waiter approached and I ordered black coffee and a plate of
eggs, then set to work on a story for Superintendent Turner. Half
an hour later, I was on a second cup when the waiter reappeared.

'There's a gentleman here to see you, sahib.'

I checked my watch. I hadn't expected Turner to arrive before
nine. It seemed he'd made excellent time.

'Show him over.'

The waiter shuffled nervously. 'I'm afraid that is not being possible, sahib. He is one Indian gentleman.'

My first thought was that my visitor must be my erstwhile
attacker and now new-found friend, Bogoram Deori. I assumed
he'd something more to tell me and had tracked me down to the
club. Of course Indians weren't allowed within its premises unless
they worked there, and so the man had been kept waiting at the
entrance.

Placing my napkin on the table, I stood up and followed the
waiter towards the front entrance. There, to my surprise, I found
not Deori, but a bespectacled young chap dressed in a white cotton
kurta and matching dhoti. I couldn't help but smile.

'Bloody hell,' I said. 'You're a sight for sore eyes!'

'I brought the whisky,' said Surrender-not. 'Now what's the
emergency?'

I let out a laugh, as much at his attire as at his words.

'You're looking well,' I said, beaming as I walked down the
stairs. It was only the second time I'd seen him in native dress.
'What's with the outfit? Don't tell me you're joining Gandhi's
resistance.'

'Not quite,' he said, 'but I *have* been thinking. Given that I *am* Indian, I should at least try to dress as one ... when I'm off duty of course. Besides,' he said, pointing to the building behind me, 'even if I dressed in a Savile Row suit, they still wouldn't let me in there.'

I might have hugged him if I didn't think he'd be mortified by the gesture. Instead I settled for a handshake and a clap on the back.

'You've lost weight,' he said, smiling.

'I've spent a fair part of the last fortnight eating nothing but rice and dal and vomiting.'

'I'm glad,' he said. 'You were beginning to get fat.'

'Laugh while you can,' I said. 'Remember, you've got the body of a Bengali *babu*. In a few years your mother'll marry you off to some girl who'll feed you till your belly is as big as your mouth.'

'And I'll be proud of it too!'

'How was the treatment?' he asked as we walked down the road towards the tea stall where I'd tried the potato curry the day before. 'Are you free from ... addiction?'

'Haven't touched an ounce in two weeks.'

He turned and stared at me. 'And no cravings?'

'Nothing I haven't been able to handle.'

'I am very glad to hear that.'

'And you? How was Dacca?'

'Fine. Dacca is like Calcutta in a coma: recognisably Bengali, but nothing much ever really happens.'

'You got bored?'

'Yes,' he said. 'It was wonderful.'

The stall was open, the woman once more squatting on the ground, tending to her stove. This morning it was luchi she cooked, lighter and greasier than the rotis of the day before, and a staple of Bengali breakfasts. Surrender-not ordered two teas, and a stack of luchis and potato curry for himself.

'So what have you been up to?' he asked, scooping up a mouthful of curry. 'Is recuperation agreeing with you?'

'It's complicated,' I said, checking my watch.

'Have you somewhere to be?'

'I need to get back up to the club for nine.'

'Are you meeting a lady?'

'I wish,' I said. 'If you must know, I'm meeting the district superintendent. Someone who tried to kill me died last night.'

He looked up from his meal, a scrap of luchi all but dangling from his lip.

'It's a long story,' I sighed.

'Well, you better start telling me now because I want to hear it before this DS arrives and it's already a quarter to nine.'

'Very well,' I said, 'but you won't thank me for it.'

I took a breath and started on the tale of the murders of Helena Caine and Bessie Drummond in 1905 and all the subsequent events that culminated with birds falling from the sky and the mysterious death a few hours ago of the man I once knew as Jeremiah Caine.

FORTY-NINE

'I have noticed,' said Surrender-not as we walked back up the hill towards the club, 'that wherever you go, people tend to die.'

'That's nonsense.'

'What about that railway sub-inspector out near Bandel last year? You ask him for a railway timetable and twenty minutes later he's dead.'

'He was hit by a train,' I said. 'I don't see how that was my fault.'

'I didn't say it was your fault. Just that people seem to die around you. Remember my paternal grandmother? She died two days after she met you.'

'She was eighty-nine years old.'

'And now this fellow, Carter or Caine or whatever his name is. He sees you after seventeen years, and five minutes later he too is dead. You have to admit, it's curious. I'm thinking I should introduce you to my uncle Pankaj. I've never liked him.'

A dust-covered Vauxhall was parked outside the club, its driver, a native, stood close by, idling in the shade of a tree. With a nod of the head, Surrender-not gestured to the veranda.

'That must be your superintendent.'

A tall Englishman with a moustache like a walrus and a khaki uniform with enough silver on his epaulettes to start a small bank stood with his arms folded, having a conversation with one of the club's waiters.

'Come on,' I said. 'Let's go and meet the chap.'

'You know I'm not allowed up there,' said Surrender-not.

'You *are* in your capacity as a police officer, and a crime may have been committed.'

'*Has* a crime been committed?' he said nervously, trying to keep up as I strode towards the stairs.

'Lord, I hope not,' I said.

'Superintendent Turner?'

The man turned. 'You must be Wyndham.'

The look on his face suggested that my presence here was as pleasing to him as a dose of the clap.

'That's correct, sir. Captain Wyndham of Calcutta CID, and this is Sergeant Banerjee.'

Turner scrutinised Surrender-not with much the same displeasure as he had me, which was refreshingly egalitarian.

'Why's he dressed like a bloody coolie?'

'He just got here,' I said. 'He's been on holiday.'

'If he's on holiday, then he's no business walking into this club. Tell him to wait outside.'

'Sir, if I may –'

'Now look here, Wyndham. What's all this nonsense about you filing an FIR against Ronald Carter? The man's a respected businessman. Now I don't know what you're doing out here, but I suggest you leave as soon as possible. I don't care if you're Calcutta CID or the aide-de-bloody-camp to the viceroy, you can't simply turn up here and start causing trouble.'

'His real name's Caine, sir, not Carter,' I said, 'but I'll withdraw the FIR.'

He raised a wary eyebrow.

'Well, good, but I don't know what the devil you think you're playing at, dragging me –'

'I'm withdrawing it because he's dead.'

The colour drained from Turner's face.

'What?'

'He died, sometime during the night.'

'And you know this, how?'

'Because I was the one who found him. I went to arrest him two hours ago. The maidservant knocked on his bedroom door. When she couldn't rouse him, I broke the door down. He was dead in his bed.'

The superintendent turned away and gazed out over the valley.

'Natural causes?' he asked, his back still towards me.

'I ... It's not clear.'

Turner spun round. 'What do you mean, *not clear*?'

'There was a doctor in the house. He performed a cursory examination. He found some odd marks on Carter's chest.'

'Odd, how?'

'Burn marks.' I could have elaborated, but I doubted that would help. The man wasn't exactly enamoured of me dragging him out here in the first place, and telling him that the marks were consistent with electrocution in a place devoid of electricity would merely confirm his suspicions that I might have a screw loose.

'I left the doctor to carry out a more detailed observation.'

Turner rubbed a meaty hand across the back of his neck and sighed.

'I'll arrange for the body to be taken to our facilities in Haflong for a post-mortem. Carter was an important man in these parts. People will ask questions, especially when it gets out that his body was found by a policeman from out of town who'd come to arrest him. Those questions will end up at my door and I can't afford for there to be any room for doubt. I want to know how he died, and if there was foul play I want to know who's responsible.'

I stared at him incredulously. 'You want me to investigate?'

'No,' he said. 'That would hardly be appropriate. Your sergeant there –' he nodded towards Surrender-not who stood at the bottom of the steps – 'I take it he's not wrapped up in any of this?'

'He's not.'

'And is he CID too?'

'Yes, but –'

'Then he's more qualified to handle this than any man at my disposal.' He turned to Banerjee. 'You. Sergeant. Get up here.'

Surrender-not flicked his cigarette to the ground and made haste up the stairs.

'Right,' said Turner, 'Sergeant …?'

'Banerjee, sir.'

'Has your captain filled you in about the tragic circumstances?'

'He's told me that a man died last night.'

'That man just happened to be rather important. I'm charging you with investigating the circumstances around his death.'

Surrender-not stared, eyes like saucers. 'Me, sir?'

'That's right. Captain Wyndham tells me you're a CID man.'

'That's correct, sir.'

'Well, then. There's nothing more to be said. If there's even a hint that Carter's death isn't from natural causes, I want to know about it. And I'll want to know who's responsible.'

'Is there a hotel in town?' asked Surrender-not.

Turner shook his head.

'Then you won't mind me using this place for lodgings.'

Five minutes later, Turner was gone, his Vauxhall throwing up a cloud of dust as it sped away. Surrender-not and I stood watching from the veranda of the Jatinga Club.

'Well done,' I said. 'Fifteen minutes ago, that man wouldn't even let you up the steps of this club. Now he's got you staying here and running a possible murder investigation.'

'Is it too early to open that bottle of whisky?'

'Probably,' I said, 'but I don't really understand Assam time. The sun comes up in the middle of the night, so who knows?'

'Odd, don't you think?' said Surrender-not. 'Putting an Indian in charge. Still, it's worth it, if only to be able to sit and have a cup of tea in an Englishman's club.'

FIFTY

'So, *boss*,' I said. 'Where'd you want to start?'

'A bath and a nap would be nice,' said Surrender-not. 'I was up half the night on the train to Lumding.'

'How about you settle for a tour of the scene of the crime and a look at the dead man before Turner has him shipped off to Haflong?'

'You mean *potential* crime. I thought we were hoping he died of natural causes.'

'Indeed,' I said. 'That would be best for all concerned.'

'I suppose the scene of the potential crime would be traditional.'

'Right you are. Scene of the potential crime it is.'

We walked out and back towards Highfield.

'This fakir chap,' said Surrender-not, 'the one that read this man Carter's palm last night. Is he a genuine prognosticator?'

'What do you mean by *genuine*?'

'Is he real or is he a fraud?'

'Aren't they all frauds?'

'Maybe in England,' said Surrender-not. 'Not in India.'

'Don't be ridiculous. How could he possibly know the man's fate by simply looking at his palm?'

'And yet he did, didn't he? He said your friend Carter would die, and that's exactly what happened.'

'His real name was Caine, not Carter,' I said, becoming irritated with the way the conversation was going, 'and he wasn't my friend.'

'Apologies,' said the sergeant. 'The fact is, though, he predicted the death of this man. Your *sworn* enemy.'

'I'm glad you're enjoying yourself,' I said. 'Carry on like that and I'll have you on traffic duty when we get home. I'm sure you'll find that just as amusing.'

The shutters had been opened at Highfield. Constable Singh had tried to confine the guests to their rooms but, in the way of a brown man giving orders to white folk, had been ignored. He had let them out but drawn the line at them leaving the confines of the house, which some of them had interpreted to include its generous grounds.

Charlie Preston was out taking a stroll. As Surrender-not and I approached, he halted, then made a beeline for us, a thin smile on his face.

'I say, Wyndham, what the jolly hell's going on? Why are we being kept here like prisoners?'

'You're not prisoners,' I said, 'you're helping with inquiries. What were you doing here last night, anyway? I thought you said Carter was no friend of yours.'

'Yes, well,' he stammered, 'when the man asks you to his house, you don't say no.'

'Well, I'm also someone you don't say no to. So make sure you get back inside and wait there till my friend Sergeant Banerjee here decides whether or not he wants to interview you.'

Preston looked Surrender-not up and down.

'If he's a policeman, why's he dressed like that? Shouldn't he be in uniform or something?'

'My uniform's in Calcutta,' said the sergeant. 'I can have it sent for, but it would mean keeping you prisoner for longer.'

Dr Deakin had finished his further examination of Jeremiah Caine, covered the body with a white sheet and retired to his room. With the sun now high, the bedchamber was flooded with light and dust motes danced in the eddies from the draught as we entered.

I'd sent the maid off to fetch Deakin while Surrender-not circled the bed as though it were a beast that needed a wide berth.

'You're not going to look at the body?'

'I'll wait for the doctor.'

'It's a dead body,' I said. 'It won't bite you.'

'Probably not. Still, better to be safe than sorry.' He walked around the room, taking in the scene from all angles like a little brown Sherlock Holmes. 'Interesting bed.'

'What?'

'The bed.'

'What about it?'

'Well, it's brass.'

'So?'

'I haven't seen one of these since my time at Cambridge.'

He had a point. Most beds in this part of the world, at least those used by Europeans, were wooden and of the four-poster variety, not necessarily from notions of grandeur, but because it was easier to hang a mosquito net over a bed with four posts than over one with none.

'Look at this house,' I said. 'Caine was hardly short of a few bob. I'm guessing he liked spending it on shiny things.'

There was a perfunctory knock at the door and Deakin entered the room.

'You called for me, W—'

He stopped mid-sentence as his eyes fell on Surrender-not.

'Who's this?'

'This is Sergeant Banerjee, of Calcutta CID,' I said. 'The district superintendent has charged him with investigating the circumstances of the death of the man you knew as Ronald Carter.'

'But there's nothing to investigate,' blustered Deakin. 'From what I can tell, the man died of natural causes. A heart attack probably.'

'But, Doctor,' I said, 'it was you who pointed out the scorch marks on his chest.'

Deakin ran a hand through his thinning white hair. 'Yes, but I told you, that must have been a previous injury.'

'Show me the marks, Doctor,' said Surrender-not, his tone firm. The doctor stiffened almost imperceptibly.

I couldn't help but smile. In the four years I'd known him, Surrender-not had matured. The boy who wouldn't say boo to a goose if it was British, now spoke to Englishmen with the authority that befitted his status as a police officer. I supposed that at least some of that change had come through sharing lodgings with me, the mystique of the ruling class fading in light of the mundane; but much of it was also down to the events that had transpired over the last eighteen months. Gandhi's general strike had led to a polarisation of attitudes. Suddenly people – British as well as Indians – were forced to choose which side they were on, and even those like Surrender-not and me, who favoured the middle ground of mutual respect, were finding it difficult to resist hardening our behaviour.

The doctor slowly pulled back the sheet, revealing Caine's grey, lifeless face, then his torso, shorn now of his night clothes, before stopping a respectful distance from his navel. Surrender-not inched forward, his face an image of distaste. The marks were, if anything, clearer than when I'd seen them before: dark, almost charred welts against the yellowing white flesh of Caine's corpse.

'You have seen marks like this before, Doctor?' he asked, his eyes fixed on Caine's chest.

'No ... yes ... which is to say, I've seen something similar.'

'And the cause of those similar marks?'

'Electrical burns,' said the doctor, 'but obviously that's not possible here.'

'You think these marks may have been caused earlier? I mean prior to the man's death?'

'I don't know what to think,' said the doctor. 'Besides, where would the man come into contact with electricity?'

The sergeant lapsed into a contemplative silence.

'What about a lightning strike?' he asked finally.

The doctor dismissed the notion with a laugh. 'Impossible. I don't remember a lightning storm last night,' he said. 'Besides, the man was in bed in the middle of the room and the walls are two inches thick. If, by some miracle, a bolt of lightning were to strike, it would have to come through the windows. That would bring it into contact first with the wooden shutters, none of which show any scorch marks. Even if there was such a storm, which there wasn't, the chances of Ronald Carter being killed by a lightning strike are a million to one.'

'And yet the man is dead, with these marks on his chest.'

The doctor raised his arms in a gesture of helplessness that suggested it was hardly fair for him to be held accountable for facts that defied a logical explanation.

Surrender-not returned to his examination of the torso.

'Please, Doctor, lower the sheet.'

Deakin did so and the sergeant continued his observations. Slowly, methodically he inspected the corpse, stopping at Caine's left arm.

'Do you know whether the deceased was left-handed?'

Deakin's brow furrowed. 'I believe he was, but I don't see what –'

'Captain Wyndham, would you mind asking Mrs Carter whether her husband was indeed left-handed?'

'Yes, sir,' I said, thoroughly bemused by his antics.

'And, Captain,' he called from behind me, 'please ask her for a list of everyone who was in the house last night.'

I left the room, sought out the maid and followed her downstairs. 'Memsahib is in the library,' she said.

'Mrs Carter?' I said, as the maid showed me in. 'I'm sorry to disturb you, but I need to ask you a question.'

Emily Carter stood beside a set of French windows. She turned, and I noticed her make-up was smeared. The track marks of a tear ran down her right cheek, peeling a path through the powder which concealed her bruise. Suddenly the question seemed superfluous.

'I'm sorry,' I repeated. 'I can come back later.'

Something sparked in those blue eyes, now moist and red.

'No, no,' she said. 'Please, come in.'

'You're sure?' I asked, more out of politeness than any genuine desire to give her a chance to rethink.

'You wanted to ask me something?'

'My colleague has asked for a list of everyone who was in the house last night.'

She thought for a moment.

'Other than Ronald and myself, there was Dr Deakin, Pastor Philips from the Baptist church in Haflong, Mr and Mrs Dewar – he runs one of Ronald's companies upcountry somewhere – and your friend Charlie Preston. Oh, and the maid, Ranjana, and Thakur, our houseboy, of course.'

'We'll need to speak to you all in turn. Would you let them know, please?'

'So it's true, then?' she said. 'Ranjana mentioned an investigation had been launched. But she said you were in charge.'

The maid had seen me and Surrender-not arrive together and naturally assumed that the Englishman would be in command.

'Normally I would be, but the district superintendent decided that mightn't be appropriate, given the events of the last few hours.'

'But why is an investigation even required?' she asked. 'You saw for yourself. You found him dead in his bed.'

'Superintendent Turner thought it best to err on the side of caution. After all, your husband was an important man. He had friends in high places, and no doubt some enemies too.'

'Of course,' she said. 'Is there anything else?'

'Just one more question for now,' I said. 'Was your husband left-handed?'

She looked up. 'It's rather an odd question. Why d'you want to know?'

'I can't say. I've just been tasked with finding out.'

She nodded. 'The fingers of his left hand were always stained black or blue with ink. He'd smear it as he dragged his hand across the page as he wrote ...'

She caught me staring at the bruise on her face and gave a gallows laugh. 'On occasion, some of it would end up on my face.'

I felt the heat break out on my neck.

'When did he do that to you?'

'Three days ago. He was drunk and ... well, it was hardly the first time.'

I looked at her face. Gone was the well-heeled lady of the manor and in her place sat a girl, and I realised that those tears which stained her cheek might not be of grief, but of relief. I had a sudden desire to sweep her up in my arms and hold her, but Englishmen didn't do that. Instead I opted for words of reassurance, stunning in their emptiness.

'He's gone now, he can't hurt you any more.' And even as I finished uttering the sentence, I knew it was a lie. Her face would heal, the bruises would disappear, but the mental scars ... well, sometimes they never fade. 'I'm sorry,' I said, and turned to go.

I left Emily Carter to come to terms with her loss and liberation and returned to give Surrender-not the good news.

'Definitely left-handed. Mrs Carter confirms it.'

The sergeant gave a nod, then turned to Deakin.

'Thank you, Doctor. You are excused.'

The doctor's face reddened to a scowl, not that Surrender-not noticed, having already turned back to me. Receiving no purchase from Surrender-not, Deakin turned his scowl towards me, was met with the same disregard and then stalked out of the room in high dudgeon.

'So? What's your theory?'

Surrender-not shook his head. 'I haven't got a theory.'

'Then why the fuss about him being left-handed?'

He walked up to Caine's corpse and pointed at the man's left arm. 'Take a look.'

I noticed the ink stains on the man's fingers.

'And now, further up,' said Surrender-not.

Then I saw them: a number of pinpricks of dried blood on the inside of the elbow, where the forearm met the bicep. I looked up at a grinning Surrender-not.

'Drugs?' I said. 'Caine was injecting himself with something?'

'Not injecting ... he was *being* injected.'

'Of course,' I said. 'If he was left-handed, it would have been easier for him to inject himself in his right arm.'

'And our friend the doctor never mentioned the marks in his examination of the body.'

'You think Deakin might be involved?' I said. 'That he might have administered some sort of overdose? But why? Let's not forget it was the doctor who first suggested that Caine's death might be something more than just natural causes. He was the one who drew attention to the marks on Caine's chest. If he was responsible, why mention anything untoward?'

Surrender-not shrugged. 'I don't know. But death by lethal overdose feels a lot more plausible than death by electrocution in a town without electricity.'

'Did you question him about it?'

'Not yet,' he said. 'Even if the cause were an overdose, we wouldn't be able to prove it out here, not before the results of the post-mortem in Haflong, and I wouldn't want to tip our hand to Deakin while the body's still under this roof.'

'Turner's men should be here soon. We should pass on a note to the pathologist telling him to look for signs of overdose or poisoning. In the meantime, do you want to start questioning the others?'

'That can wait,' he said, smiling. 'First there is someone else we need to speak to.'

FIFTY-ONE

The sun was high in a sky that, when you gazed at it, seemed as deep as an ocean.

On the ground, a solitary chicken pecked at the dust outside the Maa Kali guest house, a single-storey building in the Indian settlement that rested precariously on its brick stilts and on one side overlooked a sheer drop of several hundred feet to the valley below.

A simple enquiry at the Jatinga Club had elicited the information that the fakir had been put up for the night at the guest house.

I leaned against a tree, smoking a cigarette, and watched the chicken while Surrender-not ventured inside, hurrying back soon afterwards with a face that suggested there was strenuous activity in store.

'He's gone,' he said. 'Left less than an hour ago. The owner thinks he was heading for the main road from where he could hitch a lift to Lumding. If we hurry, we can still catch him.'

The road to Lumding intersected the path down from Jatinga at the foot of the valley, beside a concrete shed half submerged by the flora. There was no traffic, and no sign of the fakir.

In Surrender-not's eyes, the first flicker of doubt was beginning to supplant grim determination.

'He must have already found a lift.'

'You're sure he's making for the Lumding road?'

'That's what they said at the guest house,' said the sergeant, doubling back and rechecking the area around the shed as though he might have somehow missed the fakir hiding in plain sight.

I walked a few yards and peered along the road disappearing into the forest. Something caught my eye. High up in a tree, a scrap of saffron amid the field of green.

'We should wait here,' continued Surrender-not, 'he might come back.'

'We could do,' I said. 'Or we could try and do some investigating.'

I pointed out the orange cloth among the leaves of the tree and Surrender-not immediately caught its significance. Any other colour and I'd have assumed it was just a rag that had been blown there, but saffron was the colour of the Hindus, and to them certain trees held a special place. All across India, the same small flag could be seen amid the branches of certain sacred trees, and at the foot of those trees often stood –

'A shrine!'

'What better for a fakir to pass the time than in a spot of prayer?' I said.

Surrender-not laughed as we set off down the track towards the tree.

'How's that for a piece of detective work for a man recovering from opium addiction?'

'Not bad,' he replied. 'Especially for a Christian.'

We smelled the incense first. The sweet scent of sandalwood floating in the air. The fakir sat cross-legged on the ground; before him the great tree with the saffron pennant in its branches, almost a hundred feet tall, its thick grey trunk gnarled with age, and at its foot a small red shrine containing an idol.

The man rocked gently as he recited a mantra, his intonation a bass humming that reverberated across the forest around him and seemed to cause the very trees to vibrate.

Something must have alerted him to our presence, as he stopped when we were still twenty feet away. Bringing his hands together in *pranam*, he touched his forehead three times, then stood and turned towards us, betraying no sign of surprise.

'You are Ramaswamy?' asked Surrender-not in an almost respectful tone.

He looked even more like Rasputin than he had the previous night.

The man smiled, white teeth standing like gravestones in the forest of his beard.

'*Hā baba. Kee chow?*'

'You were at the Jatinga Club last night?'

'Yes.'

'You read the palm of a man called Carter,' I said.

His face darkened. 'I read a man's palm, that is correct. I do not remember his name.'

'You said you saw death in his palm. What did you mean by that?'

The man looked at me as though the question made no sense.

'I meant exactly that. I saw death.'

'How did you see it, this death?' asked Surrender-not.

The fakir laughed. 'How can I explain it to you, *baba*? How do you explain water or a rock to someone who has no concept of these things? I see it because simply it is there.'

'Whose death did you see?'

'That I cannot say. It may have been the gentleman himself or it may have been someone else. All that can be said is that the man's actions result in death, and as you are here, searching for me, I should think that such a death has already occurred.'

His words were measured and clear and devoid of the panto-mime accent and mannerisms which characterised his performance at the club.

'The man whose palm you read died last night,' said Surrender-not. 'The circumstances are suspicious. Is there anything you can tell us which might be helpful?'

'You are police?' asked the man.

'That's correct.' Surrender-not pulled out his warrant card and showed it to him.

The fakir peered at it. 'Sur-en-dra-nath Banerjee,' he intoned. 'Sar-gent? *Baah! Khoob bhalo.* How was he killed?'

I interjected. 'We don't know for sure that he *was* killed. He might have died of natural causes.'

The fakir shook his head. 'No. The death I foresaw was not peaceful.'

'He may have been poisoned,' said Surrender-not, 'or ...'

'Or?' asked the fakir.

Surrender-not turned to me as though seeking advice.

'Don't look at me,' I said. 'It's your case. Tell him if you want to.'

'His body shows signs of electrocution ... but that would be impossible.'

'Why impossible?'

'Because for one thing,' I said, 'there's no electricity within a hundred miles of Jatinga, and for another, the only door to his room was locked from the inside, and the window was shuttered.'

The fakir ignored me and fixed his gaze on Surrender-not.

'I do not expect the sahib to understand, but you, *baba*, you should know better. Your name, after all, is Surendranath.'

Surrender-not stared back, his brow knitted in consternation. 'What does my name have to do with this?'

'Sura – Indra – nath,' said the fakir. 'You are named after Lord Indra, king of the gods.'

Surrender-not looked none the wiser.

The fakir let out a laugh. 'You have been living in the world of the sahibs too long, *baba*. Remember the story from the Rig Veda; remember how Indra slew the demon Vritra. Surely you must know the weapon of the god whom you are named for?'

A sudden clarity seemed to hit Surrender-not like a slap in the face. He staggered backwards.

'What is it?' I asked.

'The *vajra*?' he said.

'The what?'

Surrender-not swallowed hard. 'The god Indra,' he said. 'The *vajra* is the weapon he uses to strike down demons and evil-doers ...'

'What about it?'

'It is a thunderbolt, and it is unstoppable.'

He turned back to the fakir. 'You're saying this man was struck down by the gods? But how is that possible?'

'You do not believe it is possible? The gods work in their own ways. In this place birds fall from the sky to their deaths. If that is possible, why should not this man be slain by a thunderbolt from Lord Indra?'

FIFTY-TWO

'You don't believe any of that rot?' I asked as we puffed back up the hill.

Surrender-not, however, seemed less than sure.

'You said Caine was an evil man, that he killed his first wife by electrocution, and now he is found with the same marks in circumstances where it is impossible for those burns to have been created by the hand of man. Yet you discard the possibility of divine retribution?'

'I admit there would be a poetic justice to it, but divine retribution?'

I'd lived through enough horror in the trenches to know that retribution, if it came at all, was generally dictated by the hand of vengeful men rather than that of a just god.

'Besides, what I believe is irrelevant,' I said. 'What matters is what we can prove. If you want to tell District Superintendent Turner that Caine's death was caused by a thunderbolt from Lord Indra, then good luck to you.'

Surrender-not lapsed into a laboured silence, conserving his breath, and, I felt, to contemplate what he knew to be true: that even in India, where the deities could teach those on Mount Olympus a thing or two about capriciousness, there was no way a detective sergeant could ascribe a death to electrocution by a god.

*

Back at the house, Surrender-not established his base of operations in the library. It was an elegantly appointed affair with book-lined shelves covering almost every inch of the walls, comfortable sofas situated around a fireplace, and through a set of French windows, the veranda and a view over the valley below.

I helped him rearrange the furniture into a setting which we considered less convivial and more inquisitorial, placing two high-backed chairs opposite the low sofa next to the fireplace, which itself was somewhat of a novelty to both of us after years spent in the torpid heat of the Bengal plains.

'We should light the fire.'

Surrender-not fixed me with a stare. 'Are you feeling the cold? You might be coming down with the flu or something.'

'I'm fine,' I said. 'I want our guests to feel the heat. Let them sweat a bit. Heat helps to loosen men's tongues.'

Twenty minutes later, and with a fire blossoming in the grate, Constable Singh ushered the beatific figure of Mrs Emily Carter into the room. The bruises on her face had once more been expertly camouflaged with cosmetics, to the extent that one who hadn't seen them would think they'd never existed. But her eyes were raw and red. The grief of a widow was a strange thing. She wasn't the first woman I'd seen cry over the death of the man who'd beaten her. Surrender-not directed her to the sofa, then took his place on the chair beside mine. As he sat, Emily Carter shot me a look which suggested she found the notion of being questioned by an Indian rather curious.

Surrender-not introduced himself, then for no reason other than nerves, also introduced me.

'The captain and I are already acquainted,' she said.

Banerjee's head bobbed vigorously.

'As you may be cognisant, I have been entrusted by Superintendent Turner, the district chief of police, to examine the circumstances surrounding the unexpected passing of your lately deceased husband. You will therefore appreciate, no doubt, the requirement for myself and Captain Wyndham to ask of you several questions of an interrogatory nature, all of which will be most relevant and pertinent to the smooth and efficacious progress of this inquiry.'

Emily Carter stared at him as though she suspected he'd recently swallowed a thesaurus.

'Please, ask your questions.'

From the pocket of his kurta, Surrender-not pulled a little note-book and pencil. 'Please start by telling us, in your own words, the events around the discovery of your husband's body this morning.'

Emily Carter tugged distractedly at the cuff of her sleeve. 'The first I knew anything was wrong was when I heard Captain Wynd-ham shouting at the front door. That must have been around six o'clock. I believe the maid let him in and took him up to Ronald's room.' She looked to me. 'I heard the captain calling for my hus-band to open the door. That's when I decided to see what was going on. I left my bedroom and came to find the captain kneeling and shouting through the keyhole. I asked him what he was doing, and he told me he was here to arrest Ronald.'

'And what followed?'

'The captain asked for the key to Ronald's room. I told him I didn't have one, and he proceeded to break down the door ... or maybe he asked the Indian constable to do it ... I'm afraid I don't remember exactly who did what.'

'And then?'

'The door was forced, and I remember Captain Wyndham rush-ing into the room. He said he thought Ronald might be trying to flee, but we found him in his bed ...' Her voice trailed off. 'I think someone called for Dr Deakin – he'd stayed over last night. I think it was he who pronounced Ronald dead.'

'Thank you,' said the sergeant. 'If I may, please could you tell me the happenings of the previous evening from the time you departed the Jatinga Club?'

Mrs Carter eyed him curiously. 'Is that relevant?'

'Please indulge him,' I said. 'The sergeant can be quite persistent in his pursuit of information.'

'It must have been sometime around eleven. The proceedings were winding up a little earlier than usual. That fortune teller had put rather a downer on things, and no one seemed much in the mood to stay on.'

'Your husband included?' asked Surrender-not.

'Absolutely. He didn't seem himself.'

Surrender-not looked up from his notebook. 'In what way?'

'He seemed distracted. I suppose nobody likes to hear they're going to die.'

'And yet he still invited a group of guests to his home for drinks?'

Mrs Carter nodded. 'That was all arranged in advance, almost a little tradition. The Dewars live too far upcountry to make the journey home at that hour, and the doctor is an old friend. He lives about five miles away but often stays over after events at the club. Pastor Philips was a rather more recent addition. We only came to know him in the last year, and like the Dewars, he lives out towards Maibang, but Ronald invited him to the dinner and was insistent he stay the night.'

Surrender-not scribbled the details. 'So they were all good friends of your husband?'

A faltering smile crept onto Mrs Carter's lips, but she said nothing.

'What about Charles Preston?' I asked.

Mrs Carter's brow furrowed. 'Now that *was* odd,' she conceded. 'Ronald never had much time for the likes of Preston. I honestly couldn't tell you why he invited him last night. Maybe Mr Preston could enlighten you.'

I already had rather a good notion of why Charlie Preston had been invited: namely to keep him away from his bungalow when Caine's *goondahs* turned up to kill me.

'So what happened once you returned to Highfield?' asked the sergeant.

'The usual,' she replied. 'We all sat around, in here as it happens, having a few drinks, most of the men outside by the French windows with their cigars, no doubt talking commerce, Celia Dewar and I on the sofa. Pastor Philips, I remember, was very keen to discuss preparations for Easter.'

'And your husband?' asked Banerjee. 'How did he seem?'

'Fine, I think. He was rather subdued at first. Maybe it was that fakir's prophecy, or possibly some business matter playing on his mind. He left the room at one point, called out of the room by Thakur, our houseboy, to deal with something.'

'At what time would that have been?'

Emily Carter shrugged. 'I can't be sure. Probably before midnight.'

'And do you know what it was regarding?'

'As I say, I assumed it was a business matter, at least that's what Ronald said when he returned.'

'How long was he away for?'

'Fifteen, maybe twenty minutes I should think.'

'And no one else left the room?'

'Not at that point.' She hesitated. 'Though now I think of it, I believe Deakin may have popped out for a few moments.'

'The doctor?' said Banerjee.

'That's right.'

'And how did your husband seem once he returned?'

'I really can't tell you,' said Mrs Carter. 'As I said, I was here on the sofa with Celia. Ronald was over there –' she pointed to the

French windows – 'with the men. That was pretty much it till Mrs Dewar decided to retire for the night. After that, the party broke up and everyone drifted off to bed.'

'And what time would that have been?' asked Surrender-not.

'One-ish, I think.'

'Your husband included?'

'I believe so. He had a drink while Ranjana and Thakur showed the guests to their rooms, then said he was heading up himself.'

'And you?' I asked.

'Me?' she said. 'I waited for Thakur to come back down after seeing to my husband, told him to tidy up and gave him instructions to pass to the cook for breakfast – she normally arrives at half past six – then went upstairs myself. Ranjana came up too, to help me out of my dress.'

'And then?'

'Then I retired to bed, and the next thing I remember is waking to you and your constable banging on the front door.'

'What about during the night? Did you hear anything untoward?'

She closed her eyes in concentration. 'Something did wake me. I assumed it was a thunderstorm. The weather up here is like that back home, it changes every ten minutes. I couldn't tell you exactly when, but it was a few hours before you arrived.'

Surrender-not ruminated for a moment. Then pivoted.

'How was your relationship with your husband?'

Emily Carter looked to me.

'Tell him the truth,' I said. 'You've nothing to hide.'

Emily Carter fidgeted with the ring around her finger.

'My husband … was not a kind man. He was prone to fits of temper, which he often took out on others, sometimes violently.'

Surrender-not listened intently. When he spoke, his voice was gentle.

'Did he strike you?'

'Occasionally.'

'Were you ever in fear of your life?'

Once more Emily Carter looked to me. Her eyes glistened.

'I ...'

I gave her a nod of encouragement and received a look of bitterness in return.

'I don't wish to discuss this with a ...'

'A what?' asked Surrender-not. 'A policeman? Or do you mean an Indian? You find it distasteful?'

Emily Carter checked herself.

'Careful, Sergeant,' I cautioned.

Surrender-not repeated his question. 'Were you ever in fear of your life, Mrs Carter?'

This time she answered him.

'There were times when I thought he might kill me. On one occasion ... Ranjana was so concerned she tried to intervene. Ronald gave her a hiding for that.'

Surrender-not swallowed back his distaste.

'So on more than one occasion, you felt your husband might kill you? Did you never think to take steps to prevent him?'

She stared at him incredulously, then turned in distress to me. 'Sam. Please tell him to stop. I've just lost my husband.'

I felt a sudden rush of blood. This was a woman in need. A woman who'd come to my aid when I was little more than a broken wreck. She was a victim here. She deserved respect and Surrender-not was treating her no better than he would a native washerwoman.

'You'll stop this line of questioning *now*, Sergeant.'

Surrender-not looked over, a startled expression on his face, but he knew better than to protest. Instead he changed tack.

'Did you ever mention your husband's ... violence to anyone else?'

'Of course not, but certain people knew. Dr Deakin for one. He tended to me when Ronald once fractured my arm. I told him it was an accident, of course, but he saw the other bruises. I'm sure he knew the truth.'

'Dr Deakin was physician to both you and your husband?'

'That's right.'

'And was your husband in good health?'

'Generally speaking,' she said, 'for a man of his age. He suffered the occasional bout of arthritis, but nothing major.'

'Was he taking any medication?'

'Yes, but Dr Deakin would be better able to tell you exactly what.'

'Specifically, was he taking any medication intravenously?'

A shadow of doubt passed over Emily Carter's face. 'I'm sorry?'

'He means, was he injecting any medication, or other substances?' I said.

Mrs Carter scratched her earlobe, then stared as though struck by a revelation. 'Dr Deakin had recently begun prescribing a dose of injections. Again you'd have to ask him exactly what they were. I think it was one every five days.'

Surrender-not and I exchanged a glance.

'And was it the doctor who administered these injections?'

'Yes.'

'When did he administer the last one?'

She hesitated. 'Three, maybe four days ago.'

'So he didn't inject your husband last night?'

'I don't think so. Why would he?'

'That,' said Surrender-not, 'is a very good question.'

'What the hell was that about?' I asked as Constable Singh ushered Mrs Carter out of the room.

'What?'

'Your recreation of the Spanish Inquisition just now.'

'She had a motive to kill her husband,' said the sergeant calmly.

'For Christ's sake, so do I and half the people in this village, I'd wager. She's a woman in shock. You can't just accuse her of murder.'

'I didn't accuse her of anything. I merely asked her a few questions and she reacted badly because she felt it beneath her to be questioned in such a fashion by an Indian.'

'Nonsense,' I said, but I had no words to follow it up. Instead I rose and headed towards the French windows, hoping to draw a line under the conversation.

I stared out at the vista beyond. Clouds had materialised as if from nowhere, shrouding the valley in their tendrils as the first drops of rain tapped against the windowpanes.

I mulled over the exchange and came to the conclusion that I was right to admonish him. Admittedly, my feelings about Emily Carter were rather complex. She was the angelic figure who'd found me wandering that night at the ashram, shepherded me back and nursed me. She was also the person I'd become acquainted with yesterday morning, the beautiful, intelligent woman who could strip a truck engine or fix up a Bugatti. Reconciling that woman with the one bruised and abused by her husband was difficult, but whatever she was, I couldn't see her as a killer. And even if I was wrong on that score, she could hardly have murdered him. She had no access to the room and no means with which to commit the deed.

'I think Mrs Carter has been through a lot,' I said.

'Enough to make her contemplate killing her husband?' said Surrender-not behind me.

'Don't be ridiculous.'

'You don't think she's capable?'

'Of what? Persuading the gods to electrocute her husband?'

'Maybe not.'

'Then what?'

'Persuading Dr Deakin to murder him instead.'

The rain began to fall more heavily, like daggers upon the battered earth. I watched as Thakur, the houseboy, ran back towards the house from the barn, his shirt collar turned up against the squall.

'Do you remember a thunderstorm last night?' asked Surrender-not.

'I can't say I do,' I said, 'but then I spent the best part of the night driving to and from Haflong. It's quite possible there was a thunderstorm here while I was gone. Does it matter?'

'If there was a thunderstorm,' he said, 'there would have been lightning. And if there was lightning, there is a chance that ...'

'What? That the god Indra chucked a bolt through Carter's shuttered window and knocked him off? Don't start that again. If you want my opinion, I think you'd be better off preparing your questions about injections for the good doctor Deakin.'

'Oh, don't worry I will,' he said, then called out to Constable Singh.

'Tell the doctor I'll see him now.'

FIFTY-THREE

I took a sip of sweet, tepid tea from a fine bone china cup.

It was very much in keeping with our surroundings, but less so with the interrogation that was going on. On the sofa where Emily Carter had sat now rested Dr Timaeus Deakin, his face pink, his collar moist and his tea untouched on the table beside him.

Leaning over the chair next to me, his hands on its back, stood Surrender-not, building up a nice little head of steam.

'So you claim to have been a friend of Mr Carter's for over fifteen years, is that correct?'

'That's right. Over fifteen years now,' said the doctor, mopping at his brow with a handkerchief.

'And yet, as his friend, you failed to mention to the officer who tasked you with examining his body anything about the puncture marks on his left arm.'

'I've told you already,' protested the doctor, 'I didn't mention it because it wasn't relevant. Captain Wyndham asked me to look for anything suspicious. The puncture marks weren't suspicious because I already knew what had caused them. As I've said, Carter suffered from rheumatoid arthritis, which in recent weeks had grown worse, causing him significant distress. I prescribed a course of morphine injections which helped relieve his pain, and I administered the injections myself.'

As a detective, Surrender-not had long ago mastered the art of looking sceptical, even when confronted with what might realistically be regarded as the truth. In this case, his face suggested he didn't believe a word of it.

'And did you administer one of these injections last night?'

Deakin shook his head. 'No. I could hardly give the man a dose of morphine before the do at the club. He was the most important man there. All eyes would be on him.'

'And when you came back here after dinner?'

'In front of the likes of Pastor Philips and that fool Preston? Absolutely not. I administered one injection every five days. The next wasn't due till tomorrow.'

'Is your medical bag here, Doctor?' I asked.

The doctor looked up in surprise. 'What?'

'Did you bring it with you last night?'

'I did. I knew I'd be staying up here last night and thought I'd take advantage and make a few house calls this morning while I was in Jatinga.'

'And would you have a syringe in your bag?'

'I'd assume so.'

'And morphine?'

The doctor shifted uncomfortably. 'Absolutely not. I'd only carry medication I knew I needed today.'

'Ronald Carter left the room for a period of approximately fifteen to twenty minutes last night. Is that correct?'

'Yes.'

'And, we understand you were also absent from the room for part of that period.'

The doctor looked like someone had just branded him with a red-hot poker.

'What?'

'Did you or did you not leave the room, during that time?'

His expression changed from one of fear to indignation.

'I might have visited the WC, but that was it. Are you seriously suggesting that I followed Ronald out of the room, surreptitiously injected him with something and then returned here?'

Surrender-not said nothing.

Deakin's hands trembled in his lap. 'Utter nonsense. I can't even remember when I visited the lavatory, but I can tell you, I certainly didn't see Ronald en route and I most definitely didn't inject him with anything. For God's sake, man, it was I who first pointed out the odd marks on his chest. Why would I do such a thing if I had anything to hide?'

'And yet you later informed us that Mr Carter had died of natural causes,' said Surrender-not.

'Because that's what it had to be!' he said, running a hand over his balding head. 'The door was locked from the inside and the man was dead in his bed. The marks on his chest were odd, but there was no way he could have been electrocuted, so what else could it have been but natural causes?!'

'An injected overdose or a poison,' said Surrender-not calmly.

The doctor's face turned an interesting shade of puce and for a moment I feared he might do himself an injury, which would have been most inconvenient, not only for the purposes of our investigation, but for the wider community as I doubted there were any other doctors in a ten-mile radius. He turned to me in exasperation. 'Captain, I demand you end this charade. I've shown this jumped-up little *darkie* more patience than he deserves. I refuse to answer any more of his accusations.'

'In this matter,' I said, 'the sergeant doesn't answer to me. He reports directly to District Superintendent Turner. I'm afraid my hands are tied.'

The doctor stood up, rattling the teacup on its saucer. 'I don't care if he reports to the viceroy in Delhi or to God Himself, I refuse to go along with this farce.'

He glared at the sergeant, and Surrender-not stared right back.

'Thank you, Doctor,' he said finally. 'You have been most helpful. That will be all for now.'

'He's right, you know,' I said, as the maid cleared away the cups. 'There's no evidence to suggest that Deakin was involved in Caine's death.'

Surrender-not had dismissed the good doctor and, after a cursory search of his medicine bag, told him he could set off on his rounds, as long as he returned to the house thereafter.

'For the purposes of this inquiry,' said Surrender-not, 'please refer to the deceased as Ronald Carter. Calling him Caine only adds to the confusion. And Dr Deakin did have the means and the opportunity to poison the man.'

'Really? The *means* possibly, but the opportunity? Even if he did follow Caine, I mean Carter, from the room, do you honestly think he could inject the man with some substance without him realising? And then Carter comes back here and happily continues entertaining his guests? It doesn't make any sense.'

'Doesn't it? What if he told Carter he was giving him another dose of morphine but instead injected him with an overdose or some slow-acting poison?'

'But why would he? He was Carter's friend.'

Surrender-not smiled. 'I'll leave it to you to figure that out. If there's one thing I've learned, it's that often it takes an Englishman to work out the frankly bizarre reasons why one Englishman might seek to kill another.'

I looked at him and felt a sudden shiver pass through me. 'Be careful, my friend. A few hours ago you said you hoped this was merely a case of death by natural causes, and now you're concocting murder theories involving slow-acting poisons. I hope you're not thinking of turning this into a witch-hunt.'

Surrender-not met my eye. 'Where there are witches, should we not hunt them?'

FIFTY-FOUR

A gong sounded on the stroke of midday summoning the Carters' guests to lunch.

There was a knock on the door and the maid, Ranjana, entered and invited me to join the luncheon party in the dining room. No such offer was extended to Surrender-not, possibly because the idea of taking lunch at high table with an Indian who was questioning them while dressed like he'd just arrived from pilgrimage might have caused a certain anxiety and indigestion among the assembled Britishers.

And so, in solidarity with my colleague, I declined and requested sandwiches for the both of us. The maid nodded demurely, then disappeared down the corridor. Taking advantage of the hiatus, I stepped through the French windows onto the veranda for a cigarette.

As I stood there, I noticed the boy, Thakur, emerge from the side of the house, and make his way down the hill towards the outbuilding and the main road. In his arms, he carried a large box and from the way he shuffled down the slope, I presumed it was also heavy.

I stubbed out the butt of my cigarette, made a mental note to ask him what he was carrying, and headed back inside, just as the maid returned bearing a fresh round of tea and two platefuls of cucumber sandwiches which, in true British fashion, had been liberated from their crusts. They tasted of absolutely nothing and it was almost a relief when we'd finished them and were able to call in the next suspect.

Still wearing his dress shirt and smoking jacket from the night before, Charles Preston ambled into the room, took in the view from the windows and then sat himself down on the sofa. To my surprise, he appeared to give me a wink.

'I must say, Wyndham, when you turned up on my doorstep yesterday morning, I'd no idea you were going to cause such a hullabaloo. D'you mind if I –?' He extracted a silver cigarette case from his breast pocket and tapped it.

'I'm not in charge here,' I said. 'My colleague Sergeant Banerjee is. I'm sure he won't mind you having a cigarette, though.'

Surrender-not nodded his assent.

Preston opened the case, took out a gold-filtered smoke and popped it in his mouth before pulling out a silver lighter and holding the flame to the cigarette. 'So,' he said, taking a drag and exhaling, 'you think someone knocked him off then?'

'We're examining all the circumstances surrounding his death,' said Surrender-not.

'Mmm,' said Preston, cigarette between his lips, 'I admit it is all rather odd, the old man dying like that immediately after that palm reader said as much. Even more so the fact that he popped his clogs just before the captain here turns up to arrest him. Rumour is, you think old Ronald Carter was not whom he claimed to be. Is that true?'

'If you don't mind,' Surrender-not interjected, 'I think it best if we ask the questions.'

Preston stared at the sergeant and tried to suppress a smile. 'Oh absolutely, Mr Mahatma. Please, carry on.'

Surrender-not winced.

'Captain Wyndham tells me you weren't a particularly close friend of Mr Carter's. Is that accurate?'

Preston exhaled another cloud of blue-grey smoke. 'Not really. I wouldn't have described myself as *any* sort of a friend of Ronald Carter's, close or otherwise.'

'And yet he saw fit to invite you back to his home last night?'

Preston winked again. 'Trust me, dear boy, I was as shocked as you are.'

'But you came along, anyway?'

'I was curious. I always get a frisson of excitement around powerful, dangerous men, and let's be honest, who doesn't? I mean, whether you liked him or not, and most people did not, Ronald Carter was the big chief. The most important man in a fifty-mile radius. He was like the sun: the centre of our orbits and impossible to resist. I doubt anyone would have said no to him.'

'So why did he invite you?'

Preston shrugged. 'No idea. It's not as though he had much to say to me once we got here. Nor to anyone else for that matter. Trappist monks probably throw better parties. But as I said, I doubt many of those here last night would have considered Carter a friend, Dr Deakin maybe, but not the others. Certainly not Pastor Philips or Alan Dewar.'

'Why would that be?'

'Didn't I tell you yesterday that Carter had people in his pocket? Well, Dewar and the pastor were two such prizes. Ronald Carter was a collector, you see, but where other men collect stamps, he collected people. He liked having a hold over them. He *loved* humiliating them. It gave him a sense of power.' Preston gave a weary shake of his head. 'It's sad, really. The richest man in the region – you'd think that would be enough for him, but it wasn't. There was a spitefulness to him, a constant need to be acknowledged as better than everyone else. He was like some feudal baron craving fealty from his subjects. The truth, though, is all he really got was fearful subservience.'

'What hold did he have on Dewar?' asked Surrender-not.

'Now that *is* an interesting one,' said Preston. 'Dewar's father started a logging business in the hills around Maibang about thirty years ago. Proper hardwood for export, not the cheap rubbish you get round here. Built it up from nothing to a point where he was sending several barge-loads to Calcutta each week in the dry season. Upon the old man's passing, Dewar inherited the whole shooting match. Did pretty well too, at first. But then the war came and the bottom fell out of the market. That's when Ronald Carter started sniffing around. Carter'd already bought up one or two other timber companies that had gone to the wall. Picked them up for a song, so the story goes, then started undercutting the market, which with his deep pockets he could afford to do. Dewar ended up getting himself into debt with the banks. He was hoping to turn things around last year, but then came that landslide at the end of the monsoon. It closed the Maibang road for weeks and meant Dewar couldn't transport his logs up to the barges at Tezpur without an eighty-mile detour each way. It killed whatever chance he had of saving the business, and just as the banks were threatening to foreclose, along comes Ronald Carter who agrees to take on the bank's debt and provide a bit more; only Carter's money comes on rather tougher terms. Carter wanted shares in the business and suddenly Dewar's Timber and Logging becomes RC Timber and Logging, and Alan Dewar ends up working for Ronald Carter who treats him like a serf, belittling the man in front of his own wife. The irony is that it was one of Carter's construction companies that was supposed to be reinforcing the earthworks at Maibang when the landslide occurred.'

'What of Pastor Philips?' asked Surrender-not. 'What hold did Ronald Carter have over him?'

'That I don't know, but whatever it is, you can bet it's powerful. You just need to look at Philips's face to see he was no fan of Carter.'

'And Dr Deakin?'

Preston rubbed at the stubble on his cheek. 'That's a strange one. The doctor may have been the only man in the district who actually appreciated Carter's company. Maybe it has something to do with that Hippo-whatsit oath they take, or maybe Carter had done him some favour in the past, but Deakin, I think, was genuinely fond of the old bugger.'

Surrender-not and I exchanged a glance.

'Tell me about last night,' said the sergeant.

'What do you want to know?'

'After dinner at the club, you returned here at Mr Carter's invitation for drinks?'

Preston nodded. 'That's right. In this very room, as it happens.'

'And at one point, Ronald Carter was called from the room by his houseboy, ostensibly to deal with some business matter. Is that correct?'

'Yes.'

'At what time would that have been?'

Preston shrugged. 'I'd say around midnight, probably, give or take ...'

Surrender-not made a note in his little book. 'And he was gone for ...?'

'Twenty minutes or so.'

'During that time, did anyone else leave the room?'

Preston shook his head. 'Not that I recall ... but then I'd taken a bit of a stroll on the lawns for a while.'

'By yourself?'

'No. Alan Dewar was with me. The pastor had started talking about God, and, well, I'm afraid I was a bit squiffy and may have made one or two off-colour remarks. Dewar suggested we might take a walk and clear our heads.'

'And this was definitely while Ronald Carter was out of the room?'

'Yes. You see, we got back just as his lordship returned.'

'What about Dr Deakin?'

'What about him?'

'Last night, while Carter was out of the room, did Deakin leave the room at all?'

Preston leaned forward. 'You know what. Now you come to mention it, I do believe he might have done. I remember looking back up at the house at one point and seeing only Pastor Philips standing outside. I'd assumed Deakin had gone inside to join the ladies, but it's possible he'd left the room. What? You don't think old Deakin had something to do with Carter's death?'

Surrender-not said nothing.

Preston gave a dismissive laugh. 'That's ridiculous. The only way Deakin could have killed him would be by boring him to death. No, if you want my opinion, if anyone was likely to have bumped Carter off, it would be Dewar. He's not one to let bygones be bygones. Indeed he's more likely to go out of his way to punch a bygone in the face, if you know what I mean. The man's got a hell of a temper. Yes, I could definitely see Dewar killing old Carter. A pillow to the face or a couple of hands to the throat, that would do it. And I tell you what –'

'Thank you, Mr Preston,' said Surrender-not. 'I'd suggest you keep such speculation to yourself.'

'Absolutely! Though if you do end up arresting him, please let me know first. I'd like to buy the chap a drink.'

FIFTY-FIVE

Alan Dewar looked about forty but dressed like a man half that age. His wife, Celia, in Alice band and floral frock, looked younger still, and with the porcelain skin and flame-coloured hair of a Celt, seemed rather unsuited to any climate south of the Arctic Circle.

After hearing Charlie Preston's testimony, Surrender-not had greeted them with all the cordiality of a firing squad, ushering them with a nod towards the sofa, where they now sat, their hands entwined in a touching show of marital solidarity.

'As you know,' commenced Surrender-not, 'your host, Mr Ronald Carter, passed away during the night under circumstances which have been deemed suspicious. My name is Sergeant Banerjee and I have been charged by the district superintendent with investigating the affair. In that regard, I would like to ask you a few questions.'

The Dewars nodded.

'Perhaps you could start by telling me of your relationship to Mr Carter, and how you came to be guests here at Highfield last night.'

Dewar ran his tongue over his lips. 'We knew each other through business. I run a logging firm up near Langting,' he said. 'Carter was a shareholder.'

Surrender-not nodded and made an entry in his notebook. 'Please tell me, in your own words, how you came to be at the dinner last night and what occurred after you arrived here from the Jatinga Club.'

Dewar squeezed his wife's hand. 'Carter invited us to that bloody stupid dinner. I'd rather not have come, to be honest. It's a long way from Langting to here, but Carter was insistent. He said he had a remarkable evening in store for us. If I'd known he meant all those birds flying into the ground and a snake-charmer fellow predicting his death, I'd have stayed at home. Celia here was most upset by the whole thing and wanted to go straight to bed when we got back here, but Emily Carter was having none of it. I expect she wanted some company of her own age as opposed to being stuck with fossils like Deakin and Pastor Philips.

'Anyway, the party here afterwards turned out to be a bit of a damp squib. Old man Carter always liked to be the centre of conversation – he'd react badly if he wasn't, start putting other people down, that sort of thing – but last night he was actually rather quiet. He seemed nervous, almost as if he believed that fakir's prophecy.'

'What did you talk about?' asked Surrender-not.

'The fakir, obviously, but then the usual matters: politics, the situation on the plantations now that the general strike's over ...'

'Did Mr Carter leave the room at any time?'

Alan Dewar rubbed his chin. 'He did, as a matter of fact. That houseboy of his came out to the veranda where we were having a smoke and told him there was a message for him or something. He was gone for a good long while.'

'And did anyone else leave the room during that time?'

Dewar puffed out his cheeks. 'I couldn't tell you. I took a walk down the gardens for a while. Wanted some fresh air.'

'That would be with Mr Preston?' asked the sergeant.

'That's right. In fact, he needed the air more than I did.'

'Any idea how long Carter was out of the room?'

Dewar smiled. 'I'm afraid I didn't time him. I say, you don't mind if we help ourselves to a drink, do you? The sun's past the yardarm, or at least it would be if you could see it.'

Surrender-not looked to me. I had no objections. In fact I quite fancied a drink myself.

'Help yourself,' he said.

Dewar got up, walked over and lifted the lid of a drinks cabinet made up to look like a sepia-toned globe.

'Celia?' he asked.

His wife demurred.

'Suit yourself,' he said, picking out a bottle of expensive-looking single malt and a tumbler. 'Captain Wyndham? Something for yourself, or are you on duty?'

'Not officially,' I said, rising from my seat and walking over to the now open hemisphere of the drinks cabinet. I helped myself to a whisky and returned to my seat accompanied by a glare from Surrender-not. It gave me a certain satisfaction.

'Were you close friends of Mr Carter?' asked Surrender-not.

Dewar took a long sip from his cut-glass tumbler. 'Let's just say he enjoyed our company.'

'I suppose that's one way of putting it,' I said. 'From what we've been told, it was your logging company he most enjoyed. We understand that he effectively forced you into bankruptcy, then came along and offered to clear your debts in exchange for shares.'

'It's true,' said Dewar, shifting in discomfort. 'Carter had lately become a significant shareholder in the business.'

'A significant shareholder? Come now, Mr Dewar. Carter became the majority shareholder, didn't he? It became his company and you were reduced to working for him. You were at his beck and call. That's why you *had* to come last night, despite having no wish to. What I don't understand is *why* he would want you to come in the first place.'

Dewar bristled. 'Because that's just the way he was. He liked making other people dance to his tune.'

'That sounds like a decent reason to want rid of him,' said Banerjee.

Before he could react, Celia Dewar put a hand on her husband's wrist.

'Captain,' she said, 'you've heard the expression, *keep your friends close and your enemies closer*? Well, Ronald Carter had precious few of the former and a great many of the latter. If you were invited into his presence, you could be sure it was because he wanted something from you or wanted to remind you that he'd already taken something from you and that there was nothing you could do about it. He was the sort of man who took delight in seeing others kowtow to him – not sycophants, he tended to grow tired of them, but rather men whom he knew didn't like him but who had little alternative but to do his bidding. My husband had no fondness for Ronald Carter, but the same could be said for others in the room.'

'Such as?'

Celia Dewar smiled. 'Maybe you should ask Pastor Philips about the land around his church, and the sad demise of members of his flock.'

FIFTY-SIX

Pastor Philips had the physique of a Russian bear and a crumpled, weather-beaten face which, at that precise moment, looked like it was about to burst.

'That's a damned lie, ye wee heathen runt!'

Emily Carter had described him as a gentle giant, but from where I stood, there didn't seem anything gentle about him. He towered over Surrender-not, his cheeks red and spitting fury, like he was contemplating strangling the sergeant with his bare hands, which didn't seem particularly Christian.

Banerjee stared the pastor in the eye. 'Sit down, sir.'

There was a steel in his voice, something I hadn't heard before, and it served to fuel a feeling within me that something in him had changed during his time away in Dacca.

For a moment they both stood facing each other like rutting stags before the pastor seemed to remember that he was a man of God and sat back down on the sofa.

'I ask you again,' said Banerjee, 'is it true that you were paid by Ronald Carter to convince the widows of two members of your congregation to drop their charges of manslaughter against him?'

That, at least, is what Alan Dewar, generously assisted by his wife, had gone on to tell us.

'It wasn't like that at all,' fumed Philips.

'Then maybe you could correct our misapprehension,' said Surrender-not.

The pastor sat back, wringing his hands together like he was squeezing the moisture out of a sponge.

'It happened about eighteen months ago. Most of the tribesmen in the valley are employed by one or other of Carter's concerns. These two were employed by his construction company, part of a gang who were building up the earthworks at Diyung to protect a stretch of the Maibang–Barabond road. It was the tail end of monsoon season, and by rights they shouldn't have had any business being up there until the weather cleared, but Ronald Carter insisted on it. They were reinforcing the earthworks when a landslide occurred. Three men were dug out of the mud alive. Deakin was the doctor who saved them. Four others weren't so lucky. Two of them were just boys – thirteen and fourteen.

'The dead were all members of my congregation. In these parts, it's often the case that matters like this are dealt with by payment of … let's call it reparations, rather than recourse to the courts. Carter asked me to intercede on behalf of his companies and I did so. I didn't like it, but you have to remember that Carter was king of the valley. There was no way some illiterate villagers could have won a case against him.'

Surrender-not did a poor job of hiding his disgust, and this time it was his turn to battle to keep his anger in check.

'And Carter paid you for your services?' he spat.

Philips balled his fists. The blood drained from his knuckles.

'He made a donation to the church fund.'

'And was that donation by chance larger than the amount paid to the grieving families of the deceased?'

'The size of it is irrelevant.'

'Why did you accept Carter's invitation last night?' continued Surrender-not. 'Was it to try to obtain some more *donations* for your church?'

'I didn't want to come,' he snarled. 'There's something unholy about this place.' He turned to me for support. 'You saw it last night too, Wyndham. The birds falling like hailstones from the sky as though possessed, then Carter's death ... I came because ...' For a moment he was lost in his own thoughts, then seemed to snap out of it. 'Look, Wyndham,' he said, 'I don't know what sort of game you're playing here, but I'll not be spoken to like that by the likes of a jumped-up subaltern. You better tell your man to mind his place or he'll be sorry. I know a man's dead, but that's got nothing to do with me, and it certainly doesn't give this *babu* here the right to insult me.'

I gave Surrender-not a look of warning, then turned to the pastor.

'I'm certain the sergeant meant no offence,' I said, 'and I'm sure he'll amend the tone of his questions from here on.'

Surrender-not of course did nothing of the sort.

'Why did you come, Mr Philips?' he said. 'Was it to plead your case before Carter in the hope of squeezing more cash out of him?'

When Philips spoke, his voice was a whisper. 'Carter insisted I come. I tried to discuss the matter of money with him, told him that the tribals needed their church – it's a focus of their community – but he said he'd deal with the matter in the morning.'

'Except by this morning, he was dead,' said Surrender-not.

Philips looked up. 'Maybe it was divine retribution?'

'Maybe it was,' said the sergeant, 'but if so, by which god?'

Philips failed to see any humour in the comment.

'There *is* only one true God,' he said.

After that, Surrender-not had very little left to ask the pastor, and two minutes later, I hustled Philips, still fuming, from the room.

'You better keep that wee shite in check, Wyndham,' he growled. 'Just who does he think he is, turning up here dressed like that, interrogating his betters? Bloody uppity Bengali – you should remind him that he's not in Calcutta now. He might get away with that sort of insolence back there, but we don't take too kindly to it up here in the hills.'

I tried pouring oil on troubled waters.

'I'll speak to him.'

'Make sure you do.'

'I've one last question,' I said. 'Did you perchance hear a thunderstorm last night?'

The pastor stared at me quizzically.

'Forget thunder and lightning, I don't think it rained at all last night.'

Surrender-not was by the French windows, staring out at the rain.

'What the hell are you playing at?' I asked. 'First Dr Deakin, then the Dewars, now Philips. Are you deliberately trying to aggravate people?'

He turned slowly to face me as I walked back to where he was standing.

'A man is dead,' he said.

'I know that, but that man was an evil bastard and there's no evidence that he died of anything other than natural causes. What's more, there's nothing to suggest that *any* of these people had a hand in his death. For Christ's sake, Surrender-not, what's got into you?'

He gave me a look unlike any I'd seen from him before.

'Please don't call me that.'

'What?'

'You know what. We've known each other for almost three years. I have saved your life and stood by you in times when no sahib did. You call yourself my friend, yet you don't even make the effort to call me by my real name?'

'You know,' I stammered, 'that I have trouble with the pronunciation. And everyone in the department calls you Surrendernot ...'

The sergeant shook his head. 'Only sahib officers call me that. The Indian officers and the constables do not.'

'What are you saying?'

'I'm saying that as my friend, you should call me by my name, not some mockery of it.'

'You insult a pastor because you're upset about my pronunciation of your name?'

'*I* insulted the pastor?'

He took a step back.

'I addressed him with no derogatory epithets. He on the other hand called me a heathen runt, a jumped-up subaltern. You have nothing to say about *that*? *He* took a bribe to settle a case involving two dead Indians, but *I* am the one who is being insulting?'

'That's not what I –'

'Dr Deakin called me a *darkie* and Mr Preston mocked me as *Mahatma*. You didn't find those insulting? Or do you believe that an Englishman can say whatever he likes to an Indian, but when an Indian has the temerity to question an Englishman, then that is an insult to the sahib?'

'What's brought all this on?' I asked limply.

With one arm, the sergeant gestured out of the window. 'Look around you, Sam. This past year, while you were in an opium haze, the country out there burned. It has changed. Even the common man is waking up to the insults of British rule. If the best of you cannot treat an Indian with dignity, then what hope is there?'

I stared at him, standing there in his white cotton dhoti and leather sandals, and, in a moment of painful clarity, realised he was right. But realisation of wrongdoing is a million miles from admission of guilt, and I certainly wasn't honest enough to admit anything of the sort to him.

Something in his features changed: a flicker of the eyes and then a softening of his expression.

'I'm sorry. I should not have said that about your ... addiction. It was wrong of me.'

There it was: the olive branch, extended once again by the Indian; because it was in his nature, because he was a man of conscience, and because in India an Englishman could never be the one to apologise.

'Forget it ... Surendranath,' I said.

Despite himself, he smiled.

'Did I get it right?'

'No,' he said. 'You murdered it, but I appreciate the effort. Maybe you should just call me Suren for short?'

'I could do. Or I could stick at it. There's probably still some time for me to practise before you throw all of us sahibs out of India.'

FIFTY-SEVEN

The rain had stopped and glowing embers of a red sun dipped below the cloud line to the west. Surrender-not, Surendranath rather, was seated on the sofa where his suspects had sat earlier, poring over the jottings in his notebook like a student before an exam.

I too had been thinking: reflecting on our conversation. In hindsight, I should have realised something was wrong when he'd turned up dressed like Rabindranath Tagore. In the three years I'd known him, he'd only once worn the traditional dhoti, and then only for a function on an especially auspicious day during the festival of the goddess Durga. Now suddenly he'd arrived here dressed from head to foot in homespun like the perfect Congress-wallah. Something in him had changed since he'd waved me off from Howrah station a few short weeks ago, or more likely the change had started earlier and I'd been too caught up in my own drug-addled affairs to notice. Maybe he'd been considering it all through the last year of the general strike. The Congress Party had called for Indian officers in the police and the civil service to resign their posts, and a good many had done so, but not Surendranath, and it had driven a stake through his relationship with his family. Now though, with the strike ended, maybe there was space for cooler heads and warmer relations to prevail. I supposed he'd spent much of his time away in Dacca in contemplation of such things.

'I blame myself,' I said.

The sergeant looked up.

'For what?'

'For your new-found nationalist zeal. I should never have told you to take some time to think about your future.'

'True. That was a mistake. As you say, nothing good ever comes from giving a Bengali time to think.'

I walked over and eased myself into the chair opposite.

'So, what do you think? Did one of our fine group of guests bump him off, or did he die of natural causes?'

Banerjee put a hand to his chin like a bespectacled, dhoti-clad version of Rodin's *Thinker*.

'Where to begin?' he sighed. 'A man, guilty of murdering others, dies in a locked room, with burn marks on his body, hours after his death is foretold to him by a fakir and after he has given orders for the killing of another man. Is his death murder, or from natural causes? If murder, then how, and by whom? If from natural causes, then what a remarkable set of coincidences that his death should time almost exactly with the moment he'd sent men to kill another?'

'How could he have been murdered?' I asked. 'The door was locked from the inside, with the key still in the lock. I saw it there. Inside the room, the windows were shuttered, and Carter found in his bed with no evidence of a struggle. That would suggest that he went to bed alive and that no one had access to the room after he'd locked the door.'

'All of the guests who stayed here last night had reason to dislike their host,' said Banerjee, 'Philips, Dewar, Preston ...'

'Not Deakin.'

'Are you sure? Maybe the doctor had a change of heart. Maybe he was disgusted at Carter's violence towards his wife. Maybe she persuaded him to do it. Or maybe it was that landslide last monsoon that cost the lives of Philips's parishioners and Dewar his business. Deakin was the first doctor on the scene. He helped pull the bodies from the mud, including those two children. It may have affected him. He would know the work was being carried out on Carter's orders, in which case it might have changed his opinion of his old friend. Maybe the three of them planned to kill him together? They'd all been invited to stay, and assuming Carter had sent invitations at least a few days in advance, they'd have had time to concoct a plan.'

'Which would be what, exactly?'

The sergeant shrugged. 'To get Carter inebriated, then for the doctor to inject him with something, or maybe just slip something into his drink. Of course, when Carter also invites Mr Preston and is called away by the servant, they're forced to improvise. Dewar takes Preston for a walk on the lawns while the doctor slips out of the room, possibly with the intention of telling Carter he needs to administer another morphine injection.'

'What about the burn marks on his body?'

'Maybe he somehow received them beforehand?'

'That's quite a story,' I said, 'and that's all it is: a story. There's no evidence to corroborate any of that.'

'There are still the results of the post-mortem to come,' Banerjee replied. 'If he *was* poisoned, then I'd hope we'd see some evidence in the report.'

'You'd need to do more than hope, my friend. Let's say you're right, and Dewar, Philips and Deakin did indeed kill him –'

'Mrs Carter too, possibly.'

I ignored the comment.

'If there's nothing in the post-mortem report suggesting a poisoning, they'll go scot-free, even if they admit the whole thing to you as they skip out of the door.'

The sergeant nodded grimly.

'D'you want to call it a night?' I asked. 'We've interviewed all of the guests.'

'There's still the servants,' said Surendranath.

Thakur was a lanky chap with a bad case of acne and the ungainly limbs of a fledgling stork. He shuffled into the room in blue trousers that were an inch too short and a threadbare woollen jumper that had probably provided nourishment to a fair few moths through the summer months. Under a thicket of black hair he had dark, intelligent eyes and wore a guarded expression.

The boy introduced himself, and Surrender-not offered him a smile and a pat on the shoulder as he showed him to the sofa, then took a seat beside him.

'You speak good English.'

'Thank you, sir,' said the boy. 'I learn in church. Every Sunday, memsahib make me go. She is teaching me herself also.'

'How did you come to be working for Mr and Mrs Carter?'

'My uncle works for Master sahib as driver. When Master sahib tell him he needs one boy to do odd jobs – fetching, carrying, this sort of thing – my uncle suggest me.'

'How long have you been working here?'

'Two years, almost.'

'And you live in the house?'

The boy nodded. 'My village is two days' journey from here. I return home every six months for one week.'

'To see your parents?' asked Banerjee.

'That is correct, and my wife.'

'How old are you?'

'Sixteen. I will be seventeen in two months.'

Surrender-not considered this for a moment, then returned to his questions.

'Tell me what happened when your master and memsahib returned from the club last night.'

Thakur paused, running a hand across the fluff on his chin.

'Master sahib and guests are coming home late in evening, long time after all birds is falling. Memsahib is taking guests to drawing room, but Master sahib, he is calling me to one side and telling me to fetch one man, Bogoram Deori, from tribal village.'

'Did he tell you why?'

The boy shook his head. 'No, sir. He tell me only bring him to the house. It is very late and I am also scared to go to Deori village, but Master sahib tell me, so I must go. I go to village and find Deori and bring him to master's study, then I go to call Master sahib.'

'Did you accompany Mr Carter back to his study?' I asked.

'Master sahib talk to Deori in private. I wait outside door. Ten minutes later, door opens and Master sahib tell me, show Deori out.'

'What happened after that?' asked Surrender-not.

'I take Deori to back door, then return and wait for guests to finish party.'

'Did you see Dr Deakin or any of the other guests outside of the room at that time?'

Thakur thought for a moment. 'I see the doctor.'

'Where?'

'In the hall, talking to Master sahib. Then both are returning to the party.'

Surrender-not and I exchanged a glance.

'Then what happened?'

'I wait in the hall. When guests go to bed, I help Ranjana to take glasses and plates to kitchen. After this I go up to my room.'

'And did you hear anything during the night?' asked Surrender-not. 'Thunder perhaps?'

The boy sat forward, his eyes widening. 'I definitely am hearing something. Not storm, though. I hear some person on stairs to the top floor, where my room is situated. It is strange because all other bedrooms are on floor below. Only I am in the top floor I think maybe one guest became lost looking for lavatory.'

'What about Ranjana?' asked Banerjee. 'Doesn't she also have a room in the attic?'

Thakur shook his head. 'No, sir. Her room is next to memsahib's quarters on first floor, along corridor from Master sahib's room.'

'The first floor?' I asked.

'That is correct, sir. She needs to tend to memsahib.'

They say that even the greatest tapestry can be unravelled from one loose thread. What goes for tapestries holds for lies too. For thirty seconds I was lost among my own thoughts. By the time I tuned back into the conversation, Surrender-not was asking about thunderstorms again.

'It is possible,' replied Thakur. 'We are often having lightning here. I don't recall last night –'

'Forgive me,' I said, interrupting, then turned to the houseboy. 'The footsteps you heard on the stairs. What time was that?'

The boy's face crumpled. 'I do not know, sahib. I have no clock.'

'But was it soon after you went to bed or later?'

'Later, sahib. Much later.'

'One last question,' I said. 'Apart from your room, what else is up on the top floor?'

'Not very much. There is one empty room, one room which memsahib uses for storage, and also door to the roof.'

The sergeant had no more questions and sought to dismiss the lad. I stood there and nodded dumbly as he asked if I concurred. Now was the time to tell him about my loose thread, but something held me back. I told myself it was nothing, just a misunderstanding that I could soon clear up, and there was no point in needlessly muddying waters that were already murky.

But looking back, it's possible that was the point at which I began my own deception. I wasn't a spiritual man, but even I would admit that there was something other-worldly about Jatinga. From the ashram of Devraha Swami to the suicide birds and the unexplained death of Jeremiah Caine, it was like nowhere I'd been before. Charlie Preston believed there was a curse on the valley, that the place was evil. But what if the opposite were true? What if this was a place where wrongs were righted and trespasses, if not forgiven, then, at least, accounted for? I thought of the fakir and the god Indra with his lightning bolt. Maybe I held back from telling Surrender-not my concerns because, like the fakir, I'd had a premonition of the truth? Or, what was worse, maybe I'd had a premonition of my own shameful reaction to it.

FIFTY-EIGHT

'You're not staying?' asked Suren as Thakur left the room. 'The maid's the only person we've left to interview.'

'I need twenty minutes to meditate.'

'Meditate?'

'It's part of the post-opium regime. I have to meditate for twenty minutes.'

'And you need to do that now?'

'Same time every day. That's what the monks said.'

I headed for the door. The monks had said nothing of the kind, but at that moment, I needed a chance to think more than I needed to hear the maid's testimony.

'I'm sure you can handle it by yourself,' I said. 'Or are you scared of talking to maids now?'

'No,' he bridled, 'well, not much.'

'Then it's settled. You question her. I'm going to find a spot quiet enough for contemplation.'

'Sam,' he said, as I reached the door, 'you're sure nothing's wrong?'

'Absolutely,' I said, and with that I opened the door and stepped out as, behind me, Suren pressed the button on the wall, summoning the maid.

*

Back in the hallway, I waited a few moments before chasing after Thakur.

'Yes, sahib?'

'I want to see the rooms on the top floor.'

'Very good, sahib. Please wait.'

A few moments later, he returned holding a hurricane lamp, then beckoned me to follow him up the stairs.

There wasn't much to see. I dispensed with his own room after a cursory glance, then tried the door to the roof. It was bolted shut and a dirty mass of cobwebs covered the frame, suggesting it hadn't been opened in a while.

The two other rooms were all but empty.

'I thought you said that the memsahib used one of these rooms as a workshop?' I asked the boy.

'Yes. This is the room, sahib,' he said, pointing through the open door of one the empty bedrooms. 'But this morning, she is asking me to clear all the things from here into the outhouse.'

'The boxes you've been carrying to the barn? Did they come from this room?'

'That is correct, sahib. Memsahib wanted room cleaned. I think with Master sahib death, she no more will be working with these car things.'

'Thank you,' I said, taking the lamp from him. 'That will be all.'

He gave a curt bow and I closed the door behind him, then looked around. The room seemed to have the same dimensions as Carter's bedroom below, though, as befitting of an attic room, the ceiling was much lower and the walls sloped inwards. Unlike Carter's room, however, this one was almost bare, lacking a bed or carpet or many of the usual sticks of furniture commonly found in a bedroom.

Instead, against the far wall, beneath a window, sat a workbench similar in form and dimension to the one I'd seen in the outbuilding, but whereas that had been strewn with mechanical components, this one was clear, and, I found as I ran a finger along it, clean, as though someone had recently taken a cloth to it.

Against another wall sat an almirah and a chest of drawers. I walked over and, by the light of the hurricane lamp, opened the doors of the wardrobe and peered inside to find it empty. I moved on to the chest of drawers, pulling out each drawer in turn and once more finding nothing at all.

I stood up and scanned the room, looking for signs of anything untoward, but there was nothing here save a cadaverous emptiness. Whatever might have been in here was long gone, and the place had been scrubbed as clean as an operating theatre. Someone had come up to the second floor during the night. Thakur had heard them. Maybe Emily Carter had too, but she'd dismissed it as thunder.

In that moment, I felt a strange mix of emotions: a hollow disappointment at having found nothing, but also, I realised, a twinge of relief. I turned towards the door and decided it was time to stop looking.

I walked across the centre of the room. If I'd been five inches to either side, that might have been the end of it. Instead I strode down the middle and caught my shoe on the edge of one of the boards that made up the bare floor, tripped and fell to the ground. The hurricane lamp fell too, its glass bowl shattering and its flame extinguished. I pulled myself onto my knees and, blind in the darkness, sat there until my eyes adjusted to the gloom. Around me lay strewn the myriad glass shards of the lamp's globe. I reached over and righted the broken object. The wick was still in place and, extracting my matchbook, I tore off a match and struck it. Reaching in between the jagged edges, I relit the lamp, placed it on the floor, then stood up and, with my foot, studied the uneven floorboard which had almost caused me to break my neck. I gave it a tap with the toe of my shoe. The board wobbled ever so slightly, and suddenly I realised the thing was loose.

I knelt down, and with the aid of one of the larger shards of glass, managed to prise the board up from the floor. Placing it to one side, I brought close the hurricane lamp and peered down into the void, hoping to find something hidden. Instead there was nothing, just an empty space and a large metal bolt, held in place by an iron nut.

I pulled out the lamp and placed it beside me on a bed of broken glass. My mind raced. Something felt wrong. I knew I'd been lied to. I just didn't know why. I tried piecing together fragments until a picture formed in my head: a man, alone in a locked room, dead in his bed. But the pieces didn't fit. I was missing something, I felt it in my gut. And behind that feeling lay fear, a cold, amorphous dread at the back of my mind that I already knew what had happened.

FIFTY-NINE

Through the door of the library I saw Surendranath silhouetted against the candlelight. I wondered what, if anything, I should tell him and decided that for now, at least, it was best to keep my thoughts to myself. He noticed me watching, then came to meet me.

'How was your meditation?'

'What?'

'Your meditation.'

'Not particularly enlightening.'

He examined me and a look of concern came over his soft features.

'What happened to your hand?'

I looked down and for the first time realised that I was bleeding. A steady trickle of crimson ran from the palm of my left hand, down the length of my index finger.

'I had a slight accident with a hurricane lamp.'

I felt in my pocket for a handkerchief, all the time avoiding his gaze.

'Did you get anything from the maid?' I asked.

'Nothing useful. Just what we already knew: that Carter left the room for twenty minutes and when he came back he was accompanied by Dr Deakin; that the party ended around one-ish and the guests retired for the night. Carter went to his own room and the maid saw no obvious signs of distress.'

'So we're no clearer on your theory? You should get down to the telegraph office,' I said. 'Send the message to Turner reiterating that we need the post-mortem to look for signs of poisoning or overdose.'

'Good idea,' he said. 'Shall we go now?'

'You go on,' I said. 'I want to have a word with your suspects. Make sure they all understand the consequences of leaving before you say they can. I'll see you back at the club in an hour. Dinner's on me.'

I walked with him to the front door then made my way back along the hall to the library and watched until his white-clad form disappeared down the hill. The sound of voices could be heard from the larger drawing room and I assumed that Mrs Carter's guests had congregated there, forced to spend another night at Highfield on the orders of a little Indian sergeant in a dhoti. Not that I thought any of them were guilty. Far from it, though it would have made things easier if they were. That at least would mean I wouldn't need to lie to Suren, because by now I feared that was exactly what I would need to do.

Once more I summoned Thakur.

'Where's your memsahib?' I asked.

'Memsahib is with guests in large drawing room.'

I followed him to the door, took a breath, knocked and entered. The guests were assembled on sofas set around a fire burning in the grate. All except Alan Dewar, who was seated on a stool behind a rather magnificent grand piano. Their expressions ran the gamut from expectant to aggrieved, but pointedly omitted anything remotely friendly. In their midst sat Emily Carter, a vision in black, with a handkerchief clasped tightly between her fingers and the consoling arm of Celia Dewar on her shoulder.

She greeted me with a tearful smile but said nothing, and it was Alan Dewar, preceding his remarks with a few portentous bass notes of Beethoven, who spoke first.

'There you are, Wyndham. We thought maybe that coolie of yours had sent you off on an errand somewhere.'

I ignored the provocation and instead turned to Emily Carter.

'May I speak to you for a few minutes? In private.'

She dabbed at her cheek with the handkerchief.

'We were about to sit down to dinner, Captain. You could join us?'

From their expressions her guests seemed to welcome my company as much as they would a case of malaria. Not that I blamed them. Breaking bread with a copper who'd spent most of the day interrogating them wasn't exactly conducive to stimulating dinner conversation. Maybe that's why I found the offer tempting. Nevertheless, I declined.

'I really would appreciate five minutes of your time,' I said.

With sullen acceptance, Emily Carter made her apologies and followed me out of the room, her guests reacting as though she were St Perpetua being led off to martyrdom and I was the bull that gored her to death.

I led her into the library where Surendranath and I had spent so much of the day. The fire had died in the grate and she shivered, rubbing her arms against the chill.

'Have a seat,' I said, turning my back to her and walking towards the French windows.

'What is it you wanted to ask me?'

For a moment I stared out of the windows. A fine mist had descended, obscuring the valley below to such an extent that it was hard to identify much more than the outlines of a few houses and trees.

I turned to face her.

'Is there something ... anything ... you've not told me?'

'What do you mean?'

'Anything to do with your husband's death.'

She hesitated, and once more dabbed with the handkerchief at the corners of her eyes, the very model of the grieving widow. And, it struck me, maybe she was? She wouldn't be the first woman who'd cried at the death of her tormentor.

'You didn't perhaps drop a hint to the doctor, or one of the other men, about what your husband was doing to you? Something that might make them take matters into their own hands?'

Emily paused. Her face reddened, and when she answered, she sounded indignant.

'Are you asking me if I persuaded one of them to murder my husband?'

'I –'

'How could you even think such a thing? You think I'm that weak and feeble that I'd throw myself on the mercy of the likes of Dr Deakin or Pastor Philips, or your friend Preston? Or do you think I manipulated them? Used my feminine charms?'

I shook my head. 'I'm sorry. I didn't mean it like that. I only –'

'And for the record, Captain: no, I did not ask any of them to murder Ronald. My husband died in his bed,' she said firmly. 'Neither I nor anyone else had anything to do with it. Now if there's nothing else, I really should get back to my guests.'

I watched as she left the room and disappeared into the darkness of the hallway beyond. I walked over to the sofa and all but dropped onto it and held my head in my hands.

Was I going mad? Without a shred of proof, I'd accused a grieving widow of instigating the murder of her husband. And why? Because of a gut feeling? I hadn't had an ounce of opium in two weeks but it still felt as though I'd fallen through the ground into another reality. The whole thing was ridiculous, and yet I couldn't shake the suspicion that something was out of place.

All I had, though, were the marks on Carter's corpse, the same ones found on the body of his first wife, some footsteps heard by Thakur on the second floor in the middle of the night and a sense that things were still being hidden from me.

SIXTY

There was a world of difference in the atmosphere at the Jatinga Club that night. For a start there were no birds falling to their deaths, though that, it seemed, had caused the members of the club rather less consternation than the sight of a dhoti-clad native eating supper within the wooden walls of their hallowed institution.

After my ill-advised overtures to Emily Carter, I'd left High-field with the onset of a headache and wandered back to the club to meet Surendranath. He was tucked behind a table in an unobtrusive corner close to the kitchens, yet to the other diners he couldn't have been more conspicuous had he stripped down to a loincloth, painted himself in the colours of the nationalist tricolour and sung 'Vande Mataram', the song of free India, at the top of his voice.

Not for the first time, I was forced to contemplate the nature of my compatriots. We liked to think of ourselves as a noble race, the architects of the greatest empire the world had ever known, but our behaviour was still rooted in the narrow-minded mentality of that wet little island whence we came. The truth was we wasted an inordinate amount of time and energy on our petty hierarchies and hypocrisies. We were moved to outrage at the thought that a man with a different shade of skin might have the temerity to eat in the same room as us, all the while blithely dismissing the fact that this was his country and we were the foreigners in it.

I walked between a sea of eyes and took the seat opposite. Surendranath sat with a lime juice and a ragged menu, poring over the latter with the same solemnity with which he'd reviewed his case notes earlier.

'What looks good?' I asked him, as a black-coated waiter, the only other native in the room, scampered over and placed a napkin on my lap.

'Nothing, as far as I can tell.' He tossed the menu onto the table. 'God, I miss Calcutta. I don't mind eating English food, but this doesn't even sound like *good* English food.'

He gestured with a nod towards the door beside him. 'And the dishes coming out of that kitchen give new meaning to the word *bland*.'

I picked up the menu.

'You want me to order for you?'

'Why not?' He smiled. 'That way, all blame will lie with you, the senior officer.'

'As it should. Did you send that telegram?'

Suren nodded. 'What's more, I got a reply. It seems Carter was a very special man around here. They've already commenced the post-mortem. We should have the results by tomorrow morning.'

'Well, that's cause for celebration.'

I pointed to his glass of lime juice. 'Are you going to join me in a proper drink, or will you be sticking with that Gandhi-water all night?'

'I think a proper drink is in order,' he said. 'We have not yet had a chance to celebrate your victory over the opium.'

'Good,' I said, and beckoned to the waiter.

'Two whiskies. And make 'em large,' I said. 'On second thoughts, just bring us the bottle.'

Suren stared at me, wide-eyed.

'What?' I said. 'We're celebrating.'

An hour later, suitably assisted by a rather decent bottle of Highland Park, we'd exhausted discussion on a range of matters diverse yet dear to us, encompassing my time at the ashram and his days in Dacca, his thoughts on my rather rocky, and some might say non-existent, relationship with a woman called Annie Grant, and my advice with regard to his estranged family. The conversation returned, finally and despite my best efforts, to the subject of Ronald Carter's death.

'This case,' said Suren, picking over the gelatinous entrails of an insipid caramel custard, 'I just don't know what to make of it. A man dies, asleep and abed, and I can't for the life of me see how it can be anything other than poison or a natural death. Yet, despite being a hundred miles from the nearest light bulb, he is covered in burn marks suggesting electric shock.'

'I'm sorry to have dropped you in it,' I said. 'Look on the bright side. It'll all be over tomorrow once the post-mortem results arrive. If there's any sign of overdose or poison, we'll arrest Deakin and Dewar and that awful Scottish preacher, what's-his-name.'

'Philips,' said Suren.

'That's right, Philips. We'll arrest them all. If on the other hand, there's nothing to suggest foul play, we shake their hands, let them go off on their merry way, and then catch the next train to Calcutta and some ridiculously fiery cuisine more in keeping with your tastes. What do you say?'

Suren looked up from his plate. 'I must say, I've never known you to be so calm about a potential crime going unpunished before. Maybe the ashram cured you of more than your opium addiction?'

'The man I wanted to arrest is dead,' I said, 'and as far as I'm concerned, that's a pretty good outcome. Rest assured though, as soon as we reach Howrah station, I'll be back to my insufferable best.'

The sergeant nodded, but something told me he wasn't quite convinced.

Surendranath walked with me out onto the veranda where we shared a smoke. There was a smile of smug satisfaction plastered upon his face and I guessed he was enjoying making a small bit of history as the first non-white guest of the Jatinga Club. That was fair enough by me and I certainly didn't begrudge him it.

Finally I left him and headed for my billet at Charlie Preston's place. It was not quite 10 p.m., but it had been twenty hours since I'd been awoken by the noise of a man intent on murdering me, and I was now physically, mentally and post-prandially exhausted.

The road down the hill was deserted, its surface glistening under a coat of new-fallen dew. The mist was thicker than before and I groped my way through a darkness alive with the calls of crickets and bullfrogs.

Preston's place was much as I'd left it: the splintered jamb of the front door and the smashed pot by the entrance. I considered rigging up some makeshift means of securing the door, but after a minute's thought gave up on the notion. For one thing, I reckoned the chances of being attacked two nights in succession were low, and for another, I was too tired to actually think of anything that might help keep the door closed.

Leaving it ajar, I headed through to the pitch-dark bedroom, removed my shirt and shoes and, forgetting that the mosquito net was still up, threw myself towards the bed, only to find myself with a faceful of muslin mesh. There came a sharp snap, as one of the cords securing the net to the wall gave way and the whole thing collapsed around me.

It took the best part of thirty seconds to extricate myself from the damn thing, and having done so, I lit a candle, then started on the process of resurrecting it, reattaching the cords at each corner to hooks on the wall. It was a tedious process, best left to servants, and I couldn't recall the last time I'd had to hoist one. But as they say: needs must, and all that. It should have occurred to me then and there, but fatigue had hijacked my synapses, and I'm ashamed to say, I passed out bereft of any inkling of how close I was to the truth.

SIXTY-ONE

I awoke to a splitting headache and the sound of someone banging on the remnants of the front door. Lifting the side of the mosquito net, I crawled out, got to my feet and looked for my shirt.

From outside came the dulcet tones of my colleague, Surendranath.

'Sam! Are you there?'

'Hang on,' I grunted. My temples pounded at the sound of my own voice and my mouth tasted like Blackpool Sands.

Stumbling into the hallway, I made it to the front room, opened the door and blinked against harsh daylight and the brilliant white kurta top, trousers and cream chador which comprised Suren's ensemble for the day.

I pointed to the broken lintel. 'You could have just come in,' I said. 'You can see the door's buggered.'

'I didn't want to presume,' he said. 'This might have been the wrong house.'

'I see,' I said, standing aside and ushering him in, 'and banging on a broken door while shouting my name at the top of your voice is perfectly sensible behaviour in that context, is it? Anyway, what time is it?'

'Eight,' said Suren. 'Five past eight, actually.'

'What time are you expecting news of the post-mortem?'

'By noon at the latest.'

'Wonderful,' I said. 'It was good of you to wake me in time.'

'I thought we might take another look at the evidence.'

'Fair enough,' I said. 'Make yourself at home while I get dressed. I'd offer you tea, but there's no one here to make it.'

Suren shook his head. 'This is why we should never travel without servants.'

'Don't start all that again,' I said, and headed off in search of a basin of water, a clean shirt and a tube of aspirin.

Twenty minutes later, having failed to find either shirt or aspirin, and wearing one of Preston's polo tops, I emerged back into the front room with my hair combed to what I hoped was an acceptable standard. Suren was seated on the sofa, his nose buried in one of Preston's trashy novels.

He looked up.

'Come on,' I said. 'We're going to finish this today, but first I need breakfast.'

The shack at the outskirts to the Indian part of town was busier today, with three patrons instead of the usual old man. The curry was different too – cauliflower rather than potato – and Suren ordered two plates, which we ate with rotis while I tried not to say or do anything which might worsen my headache. Which made me think. 'How come you don't have a hangover this morning?'

'Because I have the best antidote to a hangover.'

'And what might that be?'

'*Youth.* You, on the other hand, are getting old.'

An hour later, we were trudging back up the hill to Highfield. As we approached, the boy, Thakur, emerged from the house and headed down to the outbuilding.

'What's in there?' asked Suren.

'An old car,' I said. 'Emily Carter's been fixing it up.'

'She knows about cars?'

'She was a mechanic during the war. It's odd though ...'

'What is?'

'Remember yesterday, the boy told us Emily Carter had a room upstairs which she used for storage?'

'Vaguely.'

'Well, I went up there. The room was empty. Thakur spent half of yesterday emptying it out and bringing the contents down here. Said the memsahib had told him to.'

'You think we should take a look?'

'Can't hurt.'

Thakur reached the outbuilding ahead of us. Somewhere in the forest beyond, a bird called out. The door to the barn was ajar and from inside spilled the soft yellow light of a hurricane lamp.

I knocked on the wood of the door and entered with Surendranath half a pace behind. Thakur, his back to us, was tinkering with a box on the ground by the far wall. He spun round, his eyes wide as though fearful of finding a dacoit in front of him, or maybe a ghost. I raised a placating hand and smiled.

'Can I help you, sahib?' he asked.

'I just wanted to show my friend here the car. They're a passion of his,' I lied.

'Absolutely,' chimed Surendranath. 'Can't get enough of them.'

I glanced around the barn. It was pretty much as it had been the day Emily Carter had shown me round, except now the shell of the Bugatti had been covered over with a dusty tarpaulin and there were several more boxes and crates dotted around the periphery. The one that the boy was hovering beside looked familiar.

'Would you mind removing the sheet?' said Suren.

The boy nodded, and eager to please, quickly made his way to the car and removed the cover. The sergeant made a show of running his hand along the coachwork as I edged myself closer to the box on the floor. Soon I was in no doubt. It was identical to the one I'd carried here from the general store a few mornings earlier.

Surendranath seemed unimpressed by what was left of the Bugatti.

'This was a fast car?'

'It was at one time,' I said.

I turned to the boy. 'What's in the crates? The ones you brought down from the house.'

He shrugged. 'I do not know, sahib. Heavy though,' he said with a grin.

I walked over and lifted the flap. Inside was the large, black rubberised car battery with the seal of the Hudson Motor Company on one side.

'What is it?' asked Suren.

'Come and take a look.'

'Is that a –?'

'That's right,' I said. 'A car battery. Just the thing a new car would need.'

He gave me a hard stare. 'It's also a source of electricity.'

Suddenly I realised he was right. Here was electricity in a place that had none. Still, it meant nothing.

I shook my head. 'You can't electrocute someone with a car battery. The voltage is too low. The only way you could kill someone with it would be to drop it on their head from a great height.'

Suren turned to Thakur and pointed to the boxes and the equipment scattered on the workbench in the corner. 'Do you mind if I take a look?'

'Please.' He smiled.

I watched as the sergeant walked over to the bench, picked up a few small parts – spark plugs and other greased engine components – and examined them in the light of the hurricane lamp. He then moved on to the boxes. The first was filled with a plethora of springs, lumps of machined metal and bolts, but the second was different. It contained disassembled circuit boards, copper wires and exotic components. He pulled out the items, one at a time, and placed them on the workbench. Most of the pieces meant nothing to me – I was no mechanic after all – but then he fished out one particular object which I did recognise, and abruptly I felt as though the air had been knocked out of me. It was a hollow square of metal, two sides of which were covered in a mass of copper wire. The coil on one side was wound more tightly than on the other. They'd been a common sight in the trenches during the war.

A growing sense of panic began to engulf me as Suren continued to rummage through the remaining crates. He seemed to sense my unease.

'Is everything all right?' he asked, looking up.

'Fine,' I lied. 'It's just the after-effects of my detoxification regime.'

And then, at the bottom of another crate I saw something else that I recognised. Involuntarily, I held my breath as Suren pulled it out.

It was a device, encased in metal and about the size of a typewriter without the keys, affixed to a wooden base with wires protruding from it. A small metal plate read General Electric Company.

'Any idea what this might be?'

I knew what it was. Two years in military intelligence during the war hadn't taught me much about car engines, but it had furnished me with a working knowledge of electrical devices. This was what we used to call a motor generator, or sometimes an oscillator.

I turned from the device to Surendranath. The flame from the hurricane lamp flickered, throwing dancing shadows across his face.

'Search me.'

'So what now?' he asked, returning the components to their crates.

'Maybe we take one more look at Carter's room?'

'You think we might have missed something?'

I did. But I wasn't about to tell him that just yet. Instead I shrugged and turned to the houseboy.

'We need to see Carter sahib's bedroom once again.'

'Of course, sahib.'

A torrent of thoughts rushed through my mind as we walked up the hill to the house. A picture was building, so fantastical that it hardly seemed possible. Nevertheless, I felt a deep unease. Jeremiah Caine's first wife had been electrocuted. Bessie Drummond had been murdered in a room made to look as though it had been locked from the inside. If Caine, now calling himself Ronald Carter, had died the way I was beginning to suspect he might have, then this was more than poetic justice – the parallels bordered on the supernatural.

I shook my head and told myself to get a grip. I was getting ahead of myself. As yet I still had nothing tangible, and part of me hoped I never would.

Carter's room was much as it had been when we'd seen it the day before, only this time of course it was devoid of a corpse and the sheets had been pulled from the bed. It already smelled of dust and mothballs and I never ceased to be surprised at how quickly the traces of a person's presence could disappear. A man could sleep in a room for ten years, and within days of his departure, every trace of him could be gone.

'What are we looking for?' asked Suren.

I wasn't sure what to tell him. I wanted the truth, I *needed* the truth, but a voice in my head told me to be wary of sharing my suspicions too quickly with my colleague.

'Anything odd, I suppose,' I said, examining the bed, pressing down on the mattress, 'anything that seems out of place.'

The sergeant looked about him, then threw up his hands.

'I can't see anything untoward.'

That was good. The trouble was, neither could I. There seemed to be nothing that might corroborate the theory that was taking shape in my mind.

I made for the window. The pane was closed, as were the wooden shutters beyond, just as they had been when I'd first entered the room that morning to find Carter dead in his bed. There was no lock on the window itself but the shutters were held closed by a small metal latch on one of the doors, the pin of which fitted into a hook on the other. Was it possible that someone could have exited the room via the window, closing the shutters behind them on their way out?

I opened the window, reached out to the shutters and released the metal latch. I pushed them open and they hit the walls on either side with a thud. Lifting myself up, I clambered onto the sill and peered out, much as I had done from Bessie Drummond's window all those years earlier. As I crawled forward, I realised that that single act had set off a chain of events which had culminated in an innocent man being sent to the gallows.

'What are you doing?' asked Suren.

'Checking to see if someone could have left by the window.'

'And?'

The ledge beneath was thin and fragile, and I doubted it would take the weight of a fully grown man. I looked up and down. The floor above and the roof beyond were out of reach. There was no drainpipe or other means of scaling the distance. Similarly the drop to the veranda below was almost two storeys and the fall would be enough to break bones. What's more, given the narrowness of the window ledge, I realised it would have been impossible to have closed the shutters from the outside and still have room to stand, especially with a crate-full of equipment.

I edged back inside, dropped to the floor and turned to Suren.

'I doubt you could leave the room via the window. The drop is too great and there's no way up to the roof or the floor above. I can't see how anyone could have been in here, killed Carter and got out.'

'You thought one of the guests might have come in through the window, injected Carter with an overdose, then left the same way?'

'Possibly.'

That hadn't been what I'd been thinking, but if that's what Suren surmised I had, it was fine with me. As for my theory: the one that had been forming in my head since last night, which had seemed almost feasible when Surrender-not had uncovered those components in the boxes in the outbuilding, that theory now lay in tatters. Smashed on the rock-hard fact that there was no way in or out of Carter's bedroom, save through a door locked from the inside.

'So where does that leave us?' he asked.

It was a good question.

I shrugged. Maybe Deakin, Dewar and Philips *were* responsible for Carter's death. Or maybe there was something bigger at work. A supernatural something that had struck a lightning bolt through Carter's chest and maybe caused Le Corbeau to slip and fall to his death. Or maybe it was all just coincidence and bad luck. 'I suppose your poisoning theory is now the only game in town.'

'But we can't prove it.'

I glanced at my watch. 'It's almost eleven. Maybe we should get to the telegraph office?'

SIXTY-TWO

The forest fell still, the preternatural quiet broken only by the crunch of gravel beneath our feet. Suren and I walked in silence towards the telegraph office, our reserve belying a rising tension. Not that there was much left to discuss. For his part, I knew the results of the post-mortem would decide whether he had a case against Carter's erstwhile friends, or if he'd have to chalk it down to natural causes, however odd, and let them walk free.

The office was little changed from my previous visit. The paint still peeled from the wooden boards that fronted the hut and the same pye-dog lay dozing in the morning sun as it had done two days earlier. To all intents, time had stood still here, yet in those forty-eight hours, circumstances had changed beyond recognition.

The hinges yielded a shriek of protest as Suren pulled open the door and paused.

'After you, sir,' he said with a smile.

I eyed him suspiciously, unable to recall the last time he'd called me *sir*.

'Enough of your lip, Sergeant,' I said, stopping beside him. 'Anyway, this is your case. It's only fitting that you read the telegram first. I'll wait out here.'

'You're sure?'

'Absolutely.'

He was about enter, then halted and turned towards me.

'Do you think they're innocent?'

I shrugged. 'I really don't know.'

'Do you *want* them to be innocent?'

With one hand I rubbed the stubble on my cheek.

'Now *that* is a good question.'

Suren entered the hut, and I strolled over to a thick tree stump out in the sunshine, close to where the dog lay napping, and sat down. From my seat, I looked out across the forest clearing towards the road into town. There, less than a mile away, three men sat, unaware that the whole course of their lives hung in the balance, dependent upon a few words transmitted telegraphically from twenty miles distant, printed on a slip of paper that was even now being read by the sergeant.

I thought about Suren's final question and realised that for me their guilt, or otherwise, presented a certain conundrum. I had no love for the man who'd called himself Ronald Carter, and I was hardly unhappy at the fact of his demise. But if Messrs Deakin, Dewar and Philips hadn't killed him, that meant the bastard had died peacefully in his sleep and evaded justice of any kind for his crimes. As far as I was concerned, it would be a far better state of affairs if they actually *had* murdered him, even if it left me with the dilemma of having to arrest them for committing the act.

There came once more the creak of unoiled hinges and I turned to see Surendranath walk out, his expression funereal.

I stood up.

'Well?'

He handed me the slip of blue paper. I read it, then folded it into a square and placed it in my pocket.

Surendranath gave a sigh.

'Come on,' I said, patting him on the shoulder. 'Let's go and deliver the news.'

We fell into stride beside each other, and walked silently back along the road to Jatinga.

Once more I knocked on the door of Highfield in a manner more civilised than I'd done the previous day. Once more it was the maid, Ranjana, who opened it. Surendranath asked her to call her memsahib and then assemble the other guests in the library.

Some minutes later Suren and I entered the room, to be met with ashen-faced stares from the Carters' guests. The furniture had been returned to its original positions after our sessions of interrogation the day before, and now the sofas sat facing each other in front of the fireplace and separated by a mahogany coffee table.

The Dewars occupied one sofa, while Emily Carter, flanked by Deakin, took the other. Pastor Philips took up station by the French windows while Charlie Preston, after giving the polo shirt I was wearing a rather curious look, propped himself up against the globe of the drinks cabinet.

Suren gave a cough, artificial and intended to silence, then walked to the centre of the room like the prophet Daniel visiting the lions. Six sets of eyes tracked his movements and six faces stared at him, some in expectation, others with expressions and no doubt sentiments less benign.

'Ladies and gentlemen,' he said gravely. I braced myself. 'We have received the results of the post-mortem performed on Mr Ronald Carter. It states that the cause of death ... could not be ascertained. In light of this, there are no grounds to delay you here any further. You are all free to –'

His final words were lost amid the curses and sighs of relief. Only Emily Carter remained emotionless.

One by one they rose, and in groups of two and three left the room, some studiously giving me the cold shoulder, others making a point of proffering a few choice words which I duly took on the chin.

The exception was Charlie Preston, who managed to see the funny side.

'I must say, old man, this has been a right wheeze. I hope you'll come and visit us again soon. And keep the polo shirt,' he said. 'Think of it as a gift.'

I turned to Surendranath and handed him the telegram.

'Here,' I said. 'A souvenir of your first case in charge.'

He unfolded it and read it again:

CAUSE OF DEATH UNCLEAR.
CAUSE OF SCORCH MARKS ON TORSO
UNCLEAR.
NO TRACE OF MORPHINE OR OTHER TOXIC
SUBSTANCES DETECTED.

'I honestly thought they'd killed him,' he said. 'I still can't believe it's a coincidence that Carter drops dead hours after the fakir foretold it.'

'Maybe it is, or maybe they just used some toxin which the doctors couldn't detect,' I said. 'Look around. We're in the middle of a subtropical forest. Who knows what exotic poisons the tribes round here distil from the trees?'

I thought of the herbal remedy I'd been fed for ten days up at the ashram. Who was to say there weren't other such potions out there, ones that were less benevolent?

'Or,' I continued, 'maybe it truly was the work of the gods. Vengeance for his past sins.'

Suren glanced over. 'You don't really believe that, do you?'

'No,' I said. 'But I'd like to.'

'Can we go home now?'

'Don't tell me you're not enjoying yourself, Sergeant.'

He shook his head. 'This place is too cold and too hilly for Bengalis.'

'You think this is bad?' I said. 'You should try Scotland. But very well. Go and pack and I'll meet you up at the club in half an hour.'

He gave me a knowing look. 'Let me guess, you're going to say your goodbyes to Mrs Carter.'

Five minutes later, I accompanied him to the front door where the scene resembled checkout time at the Ritz. The Dewars and Deakin were milling around, awaiting the arrival of horse-drawn transport, while Thakur struggled down the stairs with their valises. Suren, in a gesture of magnanimity, wished them a safe journey, then set out on his own one back to the Jatinga Club.

I made stilted conversation with them. According to Alan Dewar, Preston had already left, heading for his bungalow, and Pastor Philips was still in his room, presumably packing or saying his prayers.

Of Emily Carter though, there was no sign, and as to her whereabouts, her guests in the hallway were no wiser than I. Bidding them goodbye, I headed for the stairs and up to the first floor. There, I knocked on each door in turn, hoping that one would be opened by the lady of the house and not the Baptist preacher.

There was no response from either of the first two rooms, but then I reached the third door and everything changed.

I knocked, perhaps a tad more vigorously than was necessary or proper, but none of that would have mattered had the door been firmly shut. It wasn't, and instead, the force of my knock caused it to swing open to reveal Ranjana, standing on the bed, fiddling with a mosquito net. I assumed this had been one of the rooms occupied by the Carters' guests, and now that they'd left, the maid was taking the chance to tidy. She swung round in surprise, lost her footing and for a moment it seemed she might topple to the floor. At the last second though, she grabbed hold of the mosquito net and steadied herself.

'I didn't mean to startle you,' I said. 'I was looking for your memsahib.'

She looked at me with those expressionless eyes that servants reserve for their social betters whom they consider to be wasting their time, and made to step down from the bed.

'I find her for you, sahib.'

'No hurry,' I said apologetically. 'Please, finish what you were doing.'

The girl nodded, then returned to unfastening the mosquito net from the large hook that hung from the centre of the ceiling. She untied it, and as the diaphanous sheet fell to the floor, I had an epiphany.

The mosquito net.

With a certain grace and a disregard for British standards of decorum, she silently descended from the bed and began to gather up the net, pleating its yard of muslin neatly before storing it in a chest at the foot of the bed, all the while trying her best to ignore the British detective who was staring intently at her every action.

She turned for the door.

'One moment, sahib. I fetch memsahib.'

'Wait,' I said, and caught her by the shoulder. 'I need to see the net that was hanging over your master's bed the night he died.'

She looked at me as though I was mad, but she knew better than to question a sahib. With a nod, she led me down the corridor to Ronald Carter's room, turned the handle and entered.

Ranjana opened the almirah, knelt down and rummaged in its base then re-emerged with the mosquito net in her hands. Just from looking at it I could tell this net was different from the one in the other room. It looked stiffer, less delicate and wasn't folded nearly as neatly as the other had been. And then I saw a glint of metal.

'Place it on the bed,' I said.

Wordlessly, she obeyed, and then I ordered her out of the room. I examined the thing, then looked up at the hook on the ceiling from where it had hung the night Carter had died. Then I wrapped it in a bedsheet, picked it up and headed out of the room, suddenly knowing exactly where Emily Carter would be.

SIXTY-THREE

'I thought I might find you here.'

Emily Carter spun round, a hand held to her mouth in shock.

'Captain Wyndham. You frightened me.'

I somehow doubted that.

She glanced curiously at the bundle in my hand as a nervous smile played on her lips.

'What are you doing?' I asked.

She ran a hand over the workbench.

'I suppose you could call it spring-cleaning.' As if to emphasise the point, she took the box containing the Hudson car battery and placed it in a wooden crate beside her. 'I've decided to get rid of the car. I'm not sure I've the heart to work on it now that Ronald's gone.'

'It's probably for the best,' I said. 'From the look of it, I don't think you'd ever have got that thing working again.' I glanced at the crate. 'I mean, fitting a battery to a 1913 Bugatti would suggest you don't know the first thing about the car.'

I walked over to the tarpaulin that covered the Bugatti, pulled it off and knelt in front of the radiator.

'See this?' I said, pointing to the handle that jutted out from between the front fenders. 'You know what this is, don't you?'

Emily Carter bridled, tossing back her mane of blonde hair.

'You mean the crank handle?'

I stood up. 'Very good,' I said with an intended insincerity. 'That Bugatti never needed a battery because the starting mechanism was this crank handle. It was mechanical, not electrical.'

Her eyes darkened, though her face remained impressively impassive.

'But you already knew that,' I continued, 'as would any mechanic worth their salt, especially one who'd served in the WAAC as you did.'

Emily Carter said nothing.

'You didn't need the battery for the car, did you? You needed it as a source of electricity to murder your husband.'

She shook her head. 'Maybe it's my turn to educate you, Captain. It's impossible to electrocute someone with a car battery. The voltage is too low.'

'That's true,' I said, walking over to one of the crates, 'and that may be why I thought little of it at first. Then yesterday I saw your houseboy hauling this box of things here from the house. That made me curious and this morning my colleague and I came over and had a look inside. Of course there were car parts, but that was just camouflage for the components you really wanted.'

I reached into the crate and pulled out the hollow metal block with the wires coiled around it, then brandished it in front of her.

'This is a transformer, isn't it? And if you wire it the right way, you can use it to increase the voltage in a circuit. And that –' I pointed to the device on the workbench with the small metal plate which read General Electric Company – 'if I'm not mistaken is an oscillator, otherwise known as a motor generator, and I'm guessing you know what it does?'

This time she dropped all pretence.

'It converts direct current to alternating current.'

I nodded. 'And AC is better for triggering a heart attack than DC. Don't ask me why.'

'So you think I went into my husband's room with a car battery, a transformer and an oscillator, wired it up to his chest, without him waking, electrocuted him, then cleared away the whole contraption without anyone noticing and miraculously locked the door from the inside?'

I looked at her, I have to say, with a hint of admiration.

'I admit, I had been thinking along those lines. I just couldn't figure out how you got back out of the room. But now? Now what I think is that *you* are one of the smartest people I've ever met.'

'I'm flattered,' she said, her voice deadpan, 'but I still don't see how you think *I* managed to kill Ronald.'

'In that case, let me explain. A number of things made me suspicious. When my colleague, Sergeant Banerjee, was questioning you, you said that the first you knew something was amiss was when you were awoken by the noise of me trying to gain entry to the house. That you came from your room to find me banging on your husband's bedroom door.'

'That's right,' she said. 'I did.'

'Except your bedroom is on the first floor. The same floor as your husband's and the rooms of all your guests. But when I first saw you yesterday morning, I was standing outside your husband's door and you came, not along the corridor, but *down* from the *second* floor. At first I couldn't explain why you would lie to us.'

Emily Carter looked to the ground and shook her head.

'Then the boy, Thakur, told me you sometimes used a room up there as a workshop, and that the room was directly above your husband's bedroom. Why would you need a workshop on the second floor of the house when you already had this whole barn to work in? I decided to take a look. But when I went up there last night, the room was empty, because you'd already asked Thakur to clean it out and bring all the equipment back down here.'

Emily Carter gave a dismissive shrug and brushed a pile of dust from the workbench onto the floor. 'I still don't know what you're driving at, Captain, and unless you've got anything tangible to add, I'd be grateful if you left. I have a husband to bury and a lot of work to –'

'I think you connected up your electrical devices – the battery, the transformer and the motor generator – in the room on the second floor. I think you raised the floorboards in the centre of the room and connected it to the bolt that holds the hook which descends into your husband's bedroom, and then you connected it to this.'

I opened the bundle, took out the mosquito net and tossed it at her feet. The reflection from one of the insulated wires glinted in the light.

'It's ingenious,' I said. 'You ran copper wire through the stitching of the sides of the mosquito net, connected it up to the bolt on the ceiling and then completed the circuit by touching the ends of the wires to the bed frame and the springs in the mattress. You waited for your husband and your guests to fall asleep, then, in the dead of night, made your way upstairs to the room above, connected up your battery to the transformer and the oscillator, and linked them to the bolt holding the hook to which the mosquito net and its wires were connected. The voltage would have been enough to cause his heart to pack up. I'm guessing the burn marks on your husband's body were where the mattress springs came closest to his flesh.'

She said nothing.

'I've got to hand it to you,' I said. 'In all my years, I can't recall coming across a more innovative method of murder. Electrocuting a man in a place where there's no electricity. It verges on the artistic, and, given the circumstances in which he disposed of his previous spouse, it's almost poetic. However did you think of it?'

'I knew who he was,' she said simply. 'Helena Gibb was my aunt.'

'His first wife?'

Emily nodded. 'She was my father's sister. He died in 1900, leaving my mother with three young children to raise. It was Aunt Helena who provided for us, for our upkeep, our education. And then she died. I was twelve. The first time I met Jeremiah Caine was at Aunt Helena's funeral. It was only months later that the papers reported she'd been murdered, electrocuted in her bed. By then of course, he'd fled and supposedly been drowned at sea.

'Anyway, Helena's death meant the end for us. Without her support – her money – my mother fell apart. I had to leave school to care for her and my sisters ... I had to ... do things no woman, let alone a girl, should be forced to do ... but I did them, to save the others.'

She wiped a tear from her cheek and it felt like a stab at my chest.

'That might have been it for me,' she continued, 'a fallen woman.' She smiled bitterly. 'And I can tell you, a middle-class woman has further to fall and little chance of redemption. But then the war came along, and the WAAC, and that was my ticket out of that life. I joined up, learned a trade, and the rest you already know ... sort of. I came out here after the war, met Caine, who was now calling himself Carter. I recognised him at once. He'd no idea who I was, of course. The last time he'd seen me, I was twelve years old and veiled in funereal black.

'That's when I decided to repay him for what he'd done to my family.'

It was quite a story, yet I wasn't wholly convinced. 'You couldn't find another way of killing him? You had to marry him first? That seems rather convoluted.'

She shook her head, as though I were being obtuse. 'You fought in the war, Captain. After four years of death and destruction, would it have been enough to merely accept the German surrender and all go home? No, we needed some form of vengeance, of reparations, something to make the pain and the suffering worthwhile. It was the same for me with Jeremiah Caine. I wanted, I *needed*, some measure of restitution too. I wanted to kill him, but I wanted his money too.'

'So you married him.'

'It wasn't difficult to persuade him. He practically begged me to become Mrs Carter.'

'And the bruises?' I asked. 'Were they part of the illusion? Self-inflicted injuries to arouse my pity?'

'They were real enough,' she protested. 'His abuse started immediately after our wedding night when he realised I wasn't exactly virginal.' She gave a laugh. 'Ironic, isn't it? That he should be so offended by my lack of purity, when his murder of my aunt was the very cause of it. Of course he threatened to divorce me, but he never went through with it. I suppose the loss of face he'd have to suffer in front of all these people up here whom he lorded it over would have been too great.

'But that's not to say I wouldn't have met the same fate as Aunt Helena. I remember being thankful there was no electricity up here. He'd have to come up with another way to get rid of me. It got me thinking . . .' She looked ruefully at the transformer and the oscillator on the workbench. 'Then, one day, Ranjana was complaining about the metal bedstead in his room, and it just came to me in a moment of divine inspiration. It took a while to assemble all the pieces, but finally, the battery arrived and you helped bring it up here. Then, the other night, when the birds were dying and that fakir mentioned Ronald's death, it felt like fate was telling me it was time to act.' She looked up at me. 'The thing I haven't worked out is whether the fakir knew I was going to murder Ronald that night, or whether I did it *because* he mentioned it. You won't believe me but I felt as though something took control of me and almost guided my hand.'

I stared at her, the violent bruise clearly visible on her face, and suddenly I thought of Bessie the night we'd found her in Grey Eagle Street. I thought of all the people who'd died because of the malevolent spell cast by Jeremiah Caine: of Helena, of Israel Vogel and Tom Drummond, and maybe even poor Philippe Le Corbeau, though we would never know for sure, and in that moment, any remaining doubt I had disappeared. I walked over to the work-bench, picked up the transformer and began to pull apart the wire coils.

Emily Carter stared at me. 'What are you doing?'

I pointed to the oscillator. 'You need to get rid of that. Throw it off a mountain somewhere, and burn that mosquito net. Better still, I'll do it.'

She stood there in shock. 'You're not going to arrest me?'

'Your husband didn't just kill his first wife. He also murdered someone I once cared about. She was clever and beautiful like you, and I let her down. He deserved the death sentence for his crimes. Maybe you were just destined to be the executioner.'

She kissed me gently on the cheek.

I pulled the last of the wires from the transformer, threw them under the seat of the gutted Bugatti and covered the whole thing once more with the tarpaulin.

Then, picking up the mosquito net, I shoved it back in its make-shift sack and left the barn.

SIXTY-FOUR

On the way out, I picked up a can of turpentine and trudged back up the hill, then round to the rear of the house. At the foot of the garden stood a secluded spot, screened from sight by a row of babul trees. There, I threw down the sack with the mosquito net, unscrewed the cap on the turpentine and doused the whole damn lot.

I reached into my pocket and fished out cigarettes and a book of matches. I opened the crumpled packet, withdrew the last cigarette, and with oddly shaking fingers, popped it into my mouth. Crushing the packet, I tossed it onto the pile and stared at the book of matches: a gaudy thing of red and gold that reminded me of one of Preston's ties and which I must have picked up in Chinatown weeks earlier. From its face, a fat Buddha looked out and beamed contentedly. I opened it. From the forest of twenty red-topped cardboard matches that had once stood like a platoon of soldiers, only two remained, the rest reduced to nothing but jagged stubs. I tore out the penultimate and struck it against the thin strip of emery on the reverse and watched it spark to life. Cupping it against the wind, I held it to the tip of my cigarette, inhaled, then blew out a cloud of smoke. I looked at the weak flame, slowly burning its way down to the end of the short cardboard wick, and uttered a prayer. For a moment I stood there transfixed.

I didn't hear him approach.

'Are you going to do it?'

I spun round to see Suren standing there. His expression was one of almost serene calm. The flame flickered and died between my fingers.

He walked over, stood beside me and peered down at the sack. A corner of the mosquito net poked out one side.

'Did you think I wouldn't work it out?'

'I almost didn't myself,' I said, staring straight ahead. 'I only managed it because of a wartime fondness for electrical components. How did *you* figure it out?'

'I had the advantage of watching your odd behaviour.'

'Nonsense,' I said. 'My behaviour's been odd all year.'

'True,' he smiled, 'but not like this. I may not have known what the components were, but once I saw the battery, and your reaction to it, I knew something was wrong.'

'You want me to explain it?'

He shook his head. 'Not really. I suppose it was the wife who killed him.'

'Yup.'

'Stands to reason,' he said, still staring at the pile. 'I might have trouble talking to pretty women, but you can never say no to them.'

I turned to face him. 'It's not like that.'

'Isn't it?' There was disappointment in his eyes. 'We should arrest her. Anything less would be a perversion of justice.'

I felt the bile rising in my throat. 'Justice? You think that murdering bastard deserved justice? Did you think that maybe his death *was* justice? Maybe Emily Carter was the instrument of that justice. Maybe she was Lord Indra's thunderbolt or the tool of an avenging Jehovah. Either way, there'll be precious little justice in seeing her hanged.'

Surendranath gave a bitter laugh. 'Since I was a boy, I have been told by Englishmen about the virtues of English justice: *"It is honest and fair and has no truck with sentiment or partiality."'* He recounted the words in the voice of an English schoolmaster. 'And yet, when it comes down to it, your standards of justice are as arbitrary as anyone else's. How then do you dare to presume to tell Indians what is right and wrong in our own country?'

'Now isn't the time for a political debate,' I said. 'And as you may have noticed, I'm hardly a poster boy for the British Empire. All I know is, Emily Carter doesn't deserve to go to the gallows for the death of her tormentor.'

Surendranath stared at the trees. Long seconds ticked by, and still he said nothing.

'Well?' I asked eventually.

He turned and looked me in the eye.

'Burn it.'

The flames took hold remarkably quickly, their orange tongues dancing hypnotically, and for the longest moment, Surendranath and I stood there, watching as the netting turned to ashes.

'Are you going to report this to Turner?' I asked.

'Report what? That you burned a mosquito net in a garden?'

The smoke suddenly grew black and acrid. I coughed as the rubber insulation around the copper wire which Emily Carter had sewn into the stitching of the net began to char and burn. Suren held a handkerchief to his mouth. Soon there was nothing left but a pile of black ash and thin filigrees of copper wire.

As I turned to leave, Suren took hold of my arm.

'Remember what happened here today, Sam,' he said. 'There may come a time when I ask *you* to look the other way too. For justice, or for me.'

AUTHOR'S NOTE

London, July 2019

Death in the East was not the novel I set out to write. True, I had
wanted to write my take on the classic locked-room mystery,
however, initially I had no intention of setting any of it outside
of India.

In the end though, circumstances meant that I had little choice.
Like many people, I've been saddened by the condition in which
Britain, and much of the world, finds itself. From the United States
to Europe and Asia, the rise of populism has seen the growth of
anger, extremism, fear of the other, and the erosion of tolerance
and decency.

In the UK, much of this anger has been directed at immigrants:
on those coming to our shores either as refugees or simply in search
of a better life for their families.

But this country characterised by fear and intolerance, is not the
Britain I know and love, and it is not the Britain which offered
sanctuary to the Jews of Eastern Europe between 1880 and 1914, or
the Asians fleeing persecution in Uganda in the 1970s. Nor is it the
Britain which invited the Windrush generation from the Carib-
bean, or those from the Indian subcontinent like my father and
mother, to come here in the 1950s and 60s to help rebuild a

shattered post-war nation and fill our need for cleaners, bus drivers, carers, nurses, doctors, teachers, engineers and so many other roles.

But every step forward, it seems, is met by a backlash: a fear of things changing for the worse. But each time intolerance has raised its head, from Mosely's Blackshirts to Enoch Powell's rivers of blood and the National Front of the 1970s, the good, decent majority of this country has taken a stand against it. I have hope that the same will happen this time.

And I wanted this to be a book about hope. About remembering who we are as a nation, so that we may try to live up to those standards of tolerance and decency and fair play that I believe still run through us.

P.S. Birds really do commit suicide in Jatinga.

ACKNOWLEDGEMENTS

It's hard to believe that this is the fourth Wyndham and Banerjee novel to see the light of day, and as usual there are so many people who deserve credit for sculpting the finished article.

In particular, I owe thanks to Rabbi Rashi Simon for the insight into the Jewish community of the East End, and to Ariella and Carl Tishler for being my first readers and educating me on Jewish culture. Any errors are mine, and not theirs.

Thanks also to my uncle, Dr Gautam Banerjee, for his invaluable advice on the physics of electrocution. I hope we came up with a means of murder that might have made Agatha Christie proud.

A special thank you too, to all the booksellers, especially the staff at Waterstones, for being such great supporters of Wyndham and Banerjee. I wouldn't have a career were it not for your love for the books.

I'm indebted once more to the team at Harvill Secker: to my editors, Sara Adams and Jade Chandler; to Anna Redman, Sophie Painter, Dan Mogford and Katherine Fry. I'm also grateful to Jane Kirby, Monique Corless, Lucy Barry, Penny Liechti and all the foreign rights team for helping Sam and Surrender-not travel across continents. Thanks too, to Liz Foley, Rachel Cugnoni, Richard Cable, Bethan Jones, Noor Sufi, Beth Coates, Tom Drake-Lee and the wider team at Vintage for all their support, and to my agent, the very talented and ridiculously handsome Sam Copeland, and the team at Rogers, Coleridge and White for all their hard work.

Thanks of course, to all those good friends who let me borrow their names without worrying too much about what I'd do to them: to Martin and Wesley Spiller, Shalin Bhagwan and Vimal Bhana; and to the Red Hot Chilli Writers, Vaseem Khan, Ayisha Malik, Alex Caan, A. A. Dhand and Imran Mahmood: thanks for all the *bakwaas*.

Thank you also to Ruby Chamberlain for looking after the terrible two, and finally of course, thank you to my darling wife, Sonal, for putting up with me. Twelve hundred years and counting . . .

Abir Mukherjee is the bestselling author of the Wyndham & Banerjee series of crime novels set in Raj-era India. His debut, *A Rising Man*, won the CWA Endeavour Dagger for best historical crime novel of 2017, was shortlisted for the MWA Edgar for best novel, was a Sunday Times Crime Book of the Month, and Waterstones Thriller of the Month. His second novel, *A Necessary Evil*, won the Wilbur Smith Award for Adventure Writing, was shortlisted for the CWA Gold Dagger for best crime novel of 2018, and was featured on ITV as a Zoe Ball Book Club pick. His third novel, *Smoke and Ashes*, was also chosen as a Waterstones Thriller of the Month and named by the *Sunday Times* as one of the 100 Best Crime & Thriller Novels since 1945. It was shortlisted for the CWA Historical Dagger, the HWA Gold Crown and longlisted for the CWA Gold Dagger. Abir grew up in Scotland and lives in London with his wife and two sons.